Cover, interior book design, and eBook design
by Blue Harvest Creative
www.blueharvestcreative.com

Cover illustration by
Christina Zakhozhay

Editing provided by
Bailey Karfelt

The Angel Of Elydria
Copyright © 2013, 2014, 2016 A.R. Meyering

Published by
Innisfree Press

ISBN-13: 978-0692283745
ISBN-10: 0692283749

Visit the author at:
www.armeyering.com &
www.bhcauthors.com

Visit the author's website
by scanning the QR code.

OTHER BOOKS BY A.R. MEYERING

THE DAWN MIRROR CHRONICLES

BOOK 2
EDEN UNDONE

BOOK 2.5
THE HUNTER'S BOND

BOOK 3
NELVIRNA SLEEPS
RELEASING 2017

OTHER NOVELS
UNREAL CITY

MULTI-AUTHOR COLLECTIONS
IN CREEPS THE NIGHT
FEATURING THE STORY "THE DANDELION CHILD"

To my cousin,
for her words on the dock and
for all her words since.

She knew it was always there. She could feel it hovering, breathing, and beckoning to her at the crossroads where a dream would take the wrong turn into a nightmare.

A.R. MEYERING

THE ANGEL OF ELYDRIA

BOOK ONE OF THE DAWN MIRROR CHRONICLES

INNISFREE
Press

Valencia, California

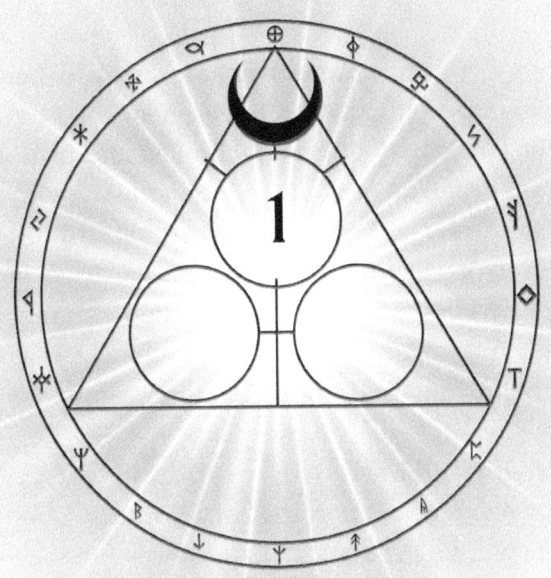

THE LAST MORNING

Through the haze of sleep, Penny knew that this particular dream was dangerous, though it began as any other dream might.

Penny wandered through a forest, searching for an eerie voice that called her name. She found herself at a lone apple tree that didn't belong in the sea of pines.

Dig...I've got to dig, *her dream-logic ordered.* The entrance is buried here. Someone once showed me how to get there, it was...

Penny dropped to her knees in front of the fruit tree.

The atmosphere changed. Her awareness became too clear—so much so that it seemed to sting her eyes. She was awake inside of her dream, but lacked any form of control. The vividness intensified to the point of agony and Penny tried to scream. Nothing came out. A violent gust of wind knocked her off her knees and onto the ground.

All at once an immovable pressure crushed her. Talons gripped her body as a great white heron swooped in front of her eyes. The bird's beak appeared crooked and malformed.

The heron drove its beak deep into her body with a mercilessness that paralyzed her, its knife-like bill drilling into her abdomen. Horror electrified Penny and she tried in vain to wriggle free. A burst of revulsion assaulted Penny when she realized that the massive bird was searching for something within her body. She was still unable to scream but somehow felt no pain.

The bird grew still and with a swift yank withdrew from the wound, revealing an enormous black spider clamped in its beak. Eight spindly legs twitched and twisted in the air, probing for something to hang onto.

A deep, resonating voice split through Penny's panic. "I have removed it. Now you will be hidden no more."

This time Penny screamed and the clear, sharp sound drew her back into reality. She tumbled onto the hardwood floor amidst a shower of various fluffy pillows. Her eyes snapped open and Penny found herself face-to-face with the grin of a teddy-bear.

Penny sighed as she untangled herself from her homemade quilt and sat up. Grumbling, she ran her fingers through her tousled black hair and started to rearrange her bed, listening to the footsteps pounding up the hallway.

Penny's door flung open as her inquisitive mother popped in. "What's all the noise about?" Paulina asked, failing to sound nonchalant. Her long black hair was pulled back, hidden under the usual bandana. Her gray eyes flitted over Penny with concern.

"It was nothing—just had a weird dream, that's all," Penny told her with a yawn and her mother gasped with intrigue. Penny ignored her and moved to the closet to arrange the day's ensemble.

"A dream? Was it unusual?"

Penny scoffed a little under her breath and suppressed the urge to roll her eyes as she inspected a skirt from her bedroom floor, then tossed it aside. "It *was* pretty vivid actually, but—"

Penny was interrupted by an excited giggle from her mother. "Hold that thought—I'll go get the dream dictionary. It could be a sign! We've got to interpret it while the imagery is still fresh in your mind. Sit tight!" Her mother tramped back downstairs, muttering to herself.

Penny shook her head as she pulled a jacket and striped shirt from her closet and slunk to the bathroom. As she got dressed and brushed her teeth, her mother returned to lob question after question about her dream through the bathroom door. Penny slapped water onto her pale, heart-shaped face and smoothed her hair as she answered. Her wide blue eyes and youthful features suggested she was younger than her actual age of twenty.

"A spider, huh? It says you have a good chance of finding money or getting a letter from an old friend," Paulina muttered, her excitement palpable even through the closed door.

Penny tried to focus on her mother's words as she did her best to tame her short, wiry black hair. This was a familiar ritual with her mother. *At least she isn't trying to cast a spell to keep me safe from inauspicious omens today,* Penny thought before she opened the bathroom door.

"Lookin' good, kid," Paulina said in a chipper voice, looking over Penny's skinny, boyish frame swimming within her jacket. "Need me to drive you over to the college today?"

"No thanks, Maddie's picking me up," Penny said as she descended the stairs. It was a cozy house with just enough room to move around in. Penny much preferred it to the dingy apartment on the other side of town that they had occupied before. There was something charming about the sleepy little neighborhood where they'd settled.

"Oh well, I need to get to the shop anyway," Paulina sighed. "Remember, you've got to be there too right after class because my plane leaves around five and heaven knows I'm going to need extra time. I *know* I've forgotten something. I always forget something."

Penny stopped on her way to the kitchen. *Of course—Mom's going to see Grandma this weekend.* Penny shook her head, which still seemed to be filled with cotton, and scanned the counter to see if there were any muffins left. The kitchen smelled of exotic spices and sunlight poured in through the windowpanes, dappling the many aromatic herbs and flowers that her mother grew to sell in their store.

Penny grinned when she found a wealth of fresh muffins on the counter and plucked up her favorite—banana nut. She turned to leave, stopping when she noticed her mother collapsing into the chair beside the kitchen table, rubbing her temple.

"Is something wrong?" Penny asked, drawing closer. It wasn't at all like Paulina to react this way about seeing Penny's grandmother; she more often than not spoke of the woman with a kind of forced optimism.

"Oh, it's nothing. I've just had a little bit of a headache since I woke up…I think it might be a migraine coming on…" her mother mumbled.

Penny stood by her for a moment, bewildered. "A migraine?" she inquired, surprised. "You never get migraines."

Paulina shrugged. "Never too late to start, I guess—anyway, you'd better get outside. Madeline will be here any second and you don't want to keep her waiting."

"Well, don't work too hard. See you later." Penny waved to her mother, swept up her book bag that lay by the door, and slipped outside.

Penny grimaced upward as she took a bite out of her muffin. Gloomy blankets of deep gray clouds covered the Oregon sky and the humidity was palpable in the autumn air. She hummed as she took a seat on the curb in front of her house and stared at the whispering woods growing alongside the houses on Hillshire Lane. Her mind flashed to the image of a twitching mess of legs being extricated from her body cavity and a sick feeling washed over her.

As she sat waiting, Penny thought she sensed a peculiar heaviness pressing down from somewhere high in the sky, as if a huge balloon, filling with air, was threatening to pop. The wind whistled by and brought a flurry of burnt orange leaves with it. The nippy breeze succeeded in undoing any progress that Penny had made in arranging her hair.

Something feels really off today. Maybe all that prophetic dream junk she always talks about might actually mean something for once, Penny mused.

Heavy moisture clung to her cheek. The clouds were swollen with rainwater, and the only sound was the rattling of dead leaves blowing across the gravel. Penny shook her head again and smirked at herself.

Yeah, right. If anyone hangs around Mom enough they'll start looking for cosmic messages in alphabet soup. It was just a stupid dream; I shouldn't let it get to me. I've gotta cheer up—it's Friday, after all.

It was those insignificant moments she spent, sitting alone on the curb, which Penny would always think back on after the end of her life on Earth; the simple act of staring into the pines with her peace yet unbroken, while the wind raced onward to wherever it was destined to die.

THE QUIET OF morning was disturbed as a car glided around the corner and the chorus of an 80s rock song rang out through the neighborhood. Penny stood and waved to the driver as the car rolled up alongside her and stopped. She yanked open the door and jumped into the passenger seat, then lowered the volume with a brisk turn of the knob before looking over at Madeline.

"Glad to see you're cheerful as usual," Madeline said with equal parts mirth and annoyance, her pink star-shaped earrings swinging as she drove off. Madeline's wispy blonde hair hung around her shoulders and her blue eyes scanned the road, buried under vibrant pink eye shadow. She was a striking beauty and this often proved to be a source of insecurity for Penny.

"So, I think I'll be getting a solid B for today's essay. How'd yours turn out?" Penny asked, though she already had an idea what the answer might be.

Madeline gave a derisive laugh and turned the music back up. "I didn't even do it—practice ran late. Besides, Arlington is crazy if he thinks any normal person can handle this workload. Why do teachers always seem to think that we only have *one* class to keep up with?" she scoffed.

"He *is* kind of ridiculous, I'll admit, but all the same...you probably shouldn't just blow it off," Penny replied, her words transforming into a massive yawn.

Madeline shot her a look. "Let me guess. You stayed up all night again, didn't you? Please, *please* tell me you're not reading that girl-power detective series for the fourth time," she moaned.

"Fifth," Penny mumbled under her breath.

"Wow. You *still* haven't changed since the sixth grade," she teased.

Penny ignored her comment. For the rest of the drive, she listened and nodded as Madeline told her about all the praise her dance instructor had given her last night.

Twin Rivers Community College was a small, out-of-the-way school hidden among the overgrowth of trees that crowded the Oregon town. The buildings were dilapidated, weatherworn, and charmless.

Madeline parked and they made their way toward the campus, the biting chill on the wind carrying invisible droplets of rainwater. Halfway across the parking lot, Penny noticed Madeline stumbling and raised her eyebrows. Her friend's face had taken on a peaky color and her usual spunky nature seemed strained.

"You okay?" Penny asked.

"Yeah… I just started feeling a little messed up—bad head-ache. It's this drab weather," she said in a shaky voice and smiled, trying to recapture her usual level of energy.

Penny's brow furrowed. "My mom had a headache, too. I'll bet something's going around. Don't come near me, I can't get sick this close to midterms." She drew away from Madeline.

"I just hope I can make it through Arlington's class without falling asleep. As if it wasn't miserable enough already," Madeline sighed. They wove through the thin crowd of students shuffling their way to class, and drops of cold rain began to splash down.

"Argh! Let's hurry!" Penny exclaimed, using her book bag as an umbrella. They sped over the misty grounds until they reached the overhang outside their classroom and scurried indoors, dripping all the way over to their seats.

It was a cramped, square classroom with twenty or so desks crammed into it. A young man in the front row stared in a stupor at the words their professor scribbled onto the blackboard with chalk. A group of girls in the seats behind Penny shrieked with laughter at something on the screen of a cell phone they were passing around. Professor Arlington set the chalk down with a curt click and swiveled around to face the class. He was a willowy young man with soft, mousy brown hair that hung in an elegant curtain to his chin. A pair of round glasses were always sliding down his nose; Madeline sometimes kept a tally when she was particularly bored. Since he was skinny and rather tall, he had something of a stretched look about him. He clapped his hands together and peered around at the class with a half-smile.

"All right, everybody. I trust you've all been working long and hard on your papers, yes? Did anyone have a particularly exciting thesis they'd like to share?" he asked in his usual brisk tone, his hopeful smile fading when nobody so much as blinked an eye in response. Penny could almost feel Madeline's annoyance radiating off her.

Penny felt a little sorry for their professor—she had taken a liking to him and his optimistic efforts to teach literature to a group of people that had little to no interest in the subject. While Madeline classified him as 'intolerable', Penny harbored a quiet admiration for his enthusiasm. Yet with the unrelenting work-load he assigned, she could understand why he was scorned by the majority of the students. Professor Arlington sighed before moving to collect the papers from the six or seven people who'd bothered to complete the assignment. Penny held her paper up as he walked by and Professor Arlington added it to the stack, and then halted, swiveling his head back to look at her. Penny felt a bit peeved at his apparent surprise; she was one of the few students who could be relied upon to complete every assign-ment. His pace slowed significantly, and Penny worried she'd fall asleep before he made it back to his desk.

At the front of the classroom, Professor Arlington turned and looked around the room. Penny watched him in a sleepy daze. Madeline's head was down on her desk and the rest of the class had already assumed their usual coma-like positions in anticipation of his lecture. The professor's eyes skimmed across Penny and he rubbed his forehead, his expression strained.

"Class…is dismissed," he said in a quiet voice.

Startled, Penny sat up and blinked in astonishment. He had never dismissed, let alone cancelled, a class before. Half of the class straightened up but stayed silent, now rapt with atten-tion. Professor Arlington appeared even more uncomfortable when no one stirred.

"Did I misspeak? Class is dismissed!" he repeated with sharper enunciation, his face growing chalky.

"But—sir," a girl from the back spoke up. "We just got here—"

"I am quite aware of that, Miss Winslow. Please, all of you, leave."

In a state of befuddlement, the students started to pack up. Penny rose from her seat, took her book in hand and strode from the classroom with Madeline close beside.

"What was that all about?" Penny asked, still surprised. "Do you think he's mad no one did the essay?"

"Maybe he got sick, I don't know," Madeline said with disinterest.

"He didn't look sick, he looked upset," Penny insisted, reaching for her bag to prepare for another sprint through the drizzle. She stopped short. "Oh no — I left my bag!"

"Then go get it," Madeline said, exasperated. "I'm cold and my head hurts. Let's hurry up and get out of here."

Uneasy about intruding on her professor after he'd ordered them to leave, Penny plucked up her courage, doubled back, and cracked open the door. When she peeked inside, her heart all but stopped beating.

Through the crack in the door, Penny could see Professor Arlington standing at the back of the room, surrounded by thousands of tiny points of white-gold light that looked like bubbles floating in a glass of champagne. In shock she watched him move his hand along the empty space in front of him, drawing strange, silvery writing. The letters hung in midair, bleeding like ink from a fountain pen. They hovered for a moment, then pulsed with a bright flare and faded.

He waved his hand again and produced more silvery writing from thin air. The lettering looked to Penny like arcane runes, shimmering as bright as tinsel. Professor Arlington wore a tormented expression, as if enduring an inordinate amount of pain. The lights in the room flickered from a surge of energy that seemed to radiate from the center of the room. Trembling, Penny backed away and let the door slam, trying to remember how to breathe.

That—that wasn't real, I'm hallucinating, it's not possible… Penny's mind raced even faster than her heartbeat, and she felt an alarming rush of lightheadedness. She swiveled around and charged away from the classroom at full speed to where Madeline stood waiting for her. Penny splashed through the mud to her, adrenaline pumping through her veins.

"M-Maddie!" Penny choked out, her voice sounding foreign to her own ears. Madeline looked over, her expression telling Penny that she was in a sour mood. "I—I—"

"What happened?" Madeline asked, looking impatient..

"In there—he was—it was—I can't even explain," Penny said in a fluster, cursing herself for being unable to articulate what she had seen.

Madeline let out a long sigh. "Honestly, Penelope..." she hissed as she trudged past.

Realizing Madeline was heading to the classroom, Penny yelped out loud, unable to stop herself. "Maddie, no! Don't go in there, please!" she shouted and chased after her, her voice sounding high and unnatural. She ignored the sidelong glances she was getting from bystanders. "It's dangerous—please!" Her anxiety doubled.

Madeline flashed Penny an irate glare and marched into the classroom. Penny froze and felt the blood drain from her face as the door shut behind Madeline. Just as she forced her legs to unstick themselves and move forward to rescue her friend, Madeline exited the classroom.

With a nonchalant stride that Penny hadn't expected, Madeline joined her, Penny's bag in hand. Dumbfounded, Penny's lips parted in disbelief as Madeline shoved Penny's bag at her and kept walking. With a little groan, she jolted after Madeline.

"Did—did you see it?" Penny asked in an unsure tone. "Did you see the...?" she trailed off, unable to find a word for what she had witnessed.

Madeline's brows arched in irritation. "Listen Penny, you don't have to pretend any more. I should've just gone with you. I know how anxious you can get...with your fainting spells and all."

Penny's frustration overwhelmed her. "I'm not making anything up! I saw something—something impossible in there! You've got to believe me, Maddie," she sputtered, her nerves jangling.

"What? What was so mind-blowing, hmm?" Madeline inquired, no longer concealing the annoyance in her voice.

Penny's expression darkened; if she tried to explain herself, she would sound insane. "It was—I don't know—why are you so mad all of a sudden?" She crossed her arms over her chest.

"I have a pounding headache, I'm soaked through, we drove out here for no reason because apparently Arlington is blossoming into a drama-queen, and you're trying to play some weird game that I'm really not in the mood for," Madeline shot back.

"You saw *nothing* out of the ordinary?" Penny demanded, growing defensive.

"Nope! Everything was perfectly fine. He even wished me a pleasant afternoon. Must be my lucky day." Madeline came to an abrupt halt as they stepped into the wet parking lot. "Now, do you want me to take you home or are you walking over to the shop?" she asked in a business-like tone.

Penny stared down at her worn gray low-tops and exhaled. "The shop…"

"Well, have fun at work. Bye." She waved a half-hearted goodbye to Penny and stalked away. Penny ran her fingers through her damp hair and shut her eyes, disturbed by the possibility that what she had seen could have been the product of an unsound mind.

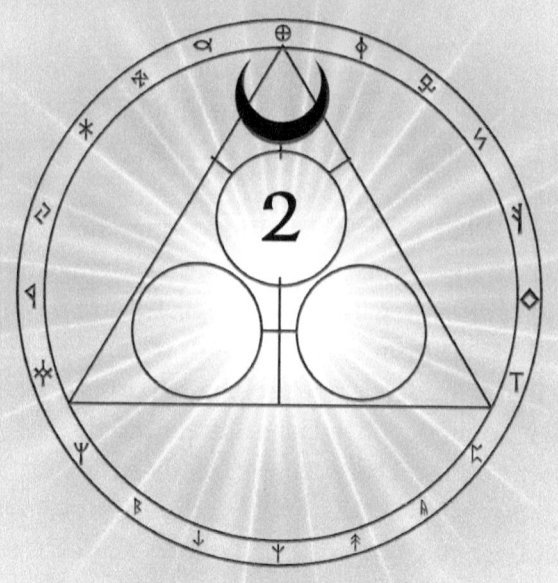

SIMON SHAW

Penny maneuvered down the rain-slick pavement, still involved in a fierce argument with herself. The storefronts she passed were foggy with perspiration from the rain, which had eased to a light drizzle. A handful of people walked the streets of the small Oregon town with their heads down and their hoods up.

Penny settled into a state of numb disbelief and reached the decision that what she had witnessed at the college was a hallucination. It was a bitter pill to swallow.

Sleep deprivation. It must be sleep deprivation. She nodded her head as if trying to convince someone else. She passed the aged community theater that from time to time hosted near intolerable productions of plays like *The Importance of Being Earnest* or *Annie*. The marquee's feeble lights tried their hardest to pierce the gloom, but it went unnoticed by the trickle of street traffic. On the other side of the theater stood a hole-in-the-wall coffee shop that Penny frequented when she had time or money to spare. The sputtering neon sign fixed to the front blazed the word 'Open' beside a litany of peeling adverts. She squinted at the sign, struck with inspiration.

A strong dose of caffeine. That's just what I need. Penny pushed aside the shop door and was greeted by a welcome wave of warmth. She stood in line, ordered a double cappuccino, and settled at a table with a brimming cup of hot, frothy milk and coffee.

As soon as the warm beverage touched her lips she started to calm down. The rain came and went in sheets, and she busied herself watching the preoccupied pedestrians shuffle by in their trench coats and boots. Penny was just beginning to hope that she might be able to fully recover from the shock of her bizarre hallucination when a peculiar man strutted into the coffee shop.

A sleek, black magician's costume clung to his frame, complete with top hat and bow tie. He stopped just inside the doorway, rainwater flowing off his hat and onto the floor of the shop, creating a mess. He peered around as if searching for something, earning annoyed looks from the employees. He was an inch or two below average height, and stroked a thin brown mustache and goatee.

Ah. Of course. A magician, Penny thought with a frown. *I'm going to try not to read too much into that.*

A small burst of adrenaline jolted through Penny's already shaken system when the magician's gaze fell on her. *Oh please, no. Not me. I don't want to be the lucky volunteer from the audience. Don't look at me.*

The man in the top hat strolled up to her table, his shiny black shoes clicking on the floor. Penny went rigid as a soft smile flowed onto the man's lips, causing his skinny mustache to curl upwards. His hands slid into his pocket and with one fluid motion he pulled out a deck of playing cards.

"Excuse me Miss, would you be so kind as to examine these cards for me and confirm that this is, in fact, a normal deck of playing cards?" He bent over and handed her the cards, looking around at the customers in the shop in an attempt to capture their attention. A few people drew nearer in vague curiosity.

Penny glanced through the flurry of hearts, diamonds, clubs, and spades. The gaze of unfamiliar eyes upon her began to make her sweat, and she grew clammy as he gestured with a strained smile for her to answer.

"Uh...yeah. Um, they're real," Penny stuttered, hating the attention.

The man swiped the cards from her palm and spread them out in a neat fan.

"Now—pick a card, any card," he grinned, and Penny felt her cheeks burn. She pinched the top of a glossy card from somewhere near the middle of the deck, then peeked down to see the Ace of Hearts resting in her palm. She looked into the magician's face, awaiting further instructions. The man appeared to be only a few years older than she was, with hair a dark shade of sienna and warm brown eyes. The smile which he glinted at Penny had something of an irresistible, devil-may-care quality to it.

The magician put a hand over his eyes. "Now show it to the crowd without letting me see, and place the card on top of the deck."

Penny did as she was told, and watched as he set the deck down in front of her. From somewhere within his cloak and cape, the man in the top hat produced a silver wand with a crystal set onto one end. It gleamed in the dull lights of the coffee shop as he swung it around his head while mumbling nonsensical spell words under his breath. Penny bit her tongue from laughing at his serious expression. The man struck the cards with the tip of his wand and flipped the deck over.

Every card in the deck had become the Ace of Hearts. Some scattered applause echoed around the shop and the magician grinned with satisfaction.

"Thank you, ladies and gentlemen! If you liked that, then you will be sure to enjoy the show at the Gonzago Theater, right next door! Tonight and tomorrow only, folks!"

Penny assumed he would leave then, and was astonished when he sank into the chair in front of her with a smug smile.

"Impressed?" he asked as he pocketed the deck.

"Um," she shrugged, her mind racing to think of a suitable compliment. "Y-you're a regular David Blaine?"

The magician's expression dampened. An awkward silence descended over the table for a moment. It was this familiar sense of discomfort that always seemed to occur when Penny encountered new people. She couldn't think of a single thing to say to the man, so she stewed in her awkwardness while staring at her knees.

"Aren't you going to ask my name?" the man broke the silence and Penny looked up with a frown.

"Erm, what's your name?"

"Glad you asked!" he chorused, regaining his sense of boundless energy. "I am Simon Shaw, master magician and illusionist *extraordinaire*." The pose he struck after he finished this well-rehearsed introduction was too much for Penny. She laughed behind her hand, and the man called Simon frowned again. She stifled the laugh with a cough.

"Sorry," Penny offered with an apologetic grin. "I didn't mean to—you just sort of took me by surprise." Simon's expression softened somewhat, but he remained quiet. "Um…is there something I can do for you?"

"Oh, it's nothing really. I just can't stand to see a beautiful girl sitting alone on a day like this." He shot her what seemed to be his trademark smile, and it was Penny's turn to frown.

This is just the sort of person my mother always warned me about…

"Sorry, I'm late for work. Gotta go," she lied, rising from the table and heading for the door.

Simon inhaled through his teeth and scrambled up behind her. Ignoring his pursuit, she walked away from the shop and turned onto Willow Street in the direction of her mother's shop.

"W-Wait! Come back!" he shouted after her, but she kept moving and pretended she'd heard nothing.

"Hold on, Penelope! Please, I need to talk to you."

Penny stopped dead. Her heart picked up what now seemed to be the popular tempo of the day. She swiveled around to see Simon staring at her. Quiet words flew from her mouth before she could cage them. "I don't remember telling you my name," she said, more to herself than to Simon, but he heard anyway. His expression became serious.

"I—just let me explain, don't run," he began, and Penny took several cautious steps backward. His eyes were wide and every muscle in his body seemed taut as he advanced on Penny, his hand extended.

Instinct took over her body. Penny sprinted down the slippery sidewalk, alarm sirens wailing in her head. With all the courage she could muster she shouted back at him over the slap of her wet shoes on the pavement, "*Leave me alone!*" In the distance a sign with the words "Willow Street Wonders" swung in the wind.

Her mother waited inside that shop; behind those walls was safety. Penny reached the door and groped for the handle, wrenching it open and bursting inside the shop as if she were riding a fierce gust of wind.

Paulina was reading behind the counter and looked up with a start, her glasses slipping off her nose and onto the glass display case. Penny scrambled behind the counter, panting. Paulina looked at her, her mouth agape. "Penny! What in the world is the matter with you? What are you doing here so early?" she asked with surprise.

Penny took several sharp breaths and fought to speak. "There's a man coming! A magician or something—" she sputtered. "D-don't let him in!"

Her mother's brow furrowed and she looked at Penny with concern, and then rose to peer out the front window. "There's nobody out there, kid."

Penny scurried over to the window and pressed her face against the glass. The street was deserted. She backed away, befuddled.

"Two magicians came by earlier doing tricks and left some flyers. Was that who you saw? I think they're just promoting their show," Paulina continued in a tone that tried to comfort.

Penny exhaled and hung her head. It was the second time that day she'd come off as deranged. She kept her face as straight as she could, but she was beginning to feel sick, panicked, and vexed all at once. "Sorry. I could've sworn…it's just that he… never mind," she mumbled as she leaned against the counter.

Her mother gave her a reassuring smile and waved it off. "No big deal. You can never be too careful, eh?" Paulina said, handing Penny an apron, which she fastened with shivering hands. Her mother removed her own apron and bustled into the backroom through a sparkling, beaded-curtain.

"You seem better. That migraine's all gone?" Penny inquired, her heartbeat returning to normal.

"It is, actually. Seems to have cleared up completely," Paulina called back. Penny leaned up against the wall of the shop and inhaled. The fragrant air in the shop always had a calming effect.

The walls of Willow Street Wonders were piled high with herbal oils, scented candles, and dried sage wound into bundles. A huge trough of what Penny assumed was every type of incense known to mankind stood by the door. Bottled rosewater and glass containers of wild herbs lined the walls, glittering in the gloom. Paulina always kept the lights turned low in their shop, saying that it created a mystical ambience. Penny suspected she did this so the customers couldn't see what a sorry state most of the books were in.

Over their eight years of business, Penny had become a bit fed up by her mother's blind devotion to supernatural nonsense, but she had to admit there was a certain romance surrounding a life spent in the dusty, dreamlike world her mother had built for them, brick by crumbling brick. After a few moments of noisy rummaging in the back, Paulina returned holding her handbag and several books underneath her arm. She took an exhausted breath and displayed her most confident smile for Penny.

"Might as well get to the airport early, just in case," she said.

"Isn't it a bit *too* early, though?" Penny couldn't keep the anxiety out of her voice, wondering if the magician might come poking around again.

Her mother nodded, as spirited as ever, before she turned serious. "Now, you know the drill. I sent the tarot readers home early, so don't worry about them. And *please* do not forget to lock up properly."

Penny nodded, trying hard to keep from rolling her eyes. Her paranoia would never allow her to forget such things.

Paulina grinned wryly and put her hand on her hip. "Got a message for Grandma?"

Penny scoffed. "Oh, I've got a message for her all right, but I don't think she wants to hear it." Her mother gave her a reprimanding look. Penny scowled right back at her. "The woman *hates* me, why would I have a message for her?"

"She doesn't *hate* you," Paulina admonished with a frown. "She just—"

"I think you've forgotten how she refers to me as 'the shame of the family.' The reason 'your life is in shambles' was how she put it." Penny put on a shrill voice and wagged her finger, "*Where* does *that girl get the nerve to exist? Honestly! In my day we never dared to be born if—*"

"That's enough." Paulina's voice held a hint of danger, but Penny still bore a defiant smile. "There's food for you in the fridge, and *please* will you get to bed at a reasonable hour? Also, you might want to take one of the aquamarines with you before you go if you think that creep is still out there; they'll protect your aura from negative energy. Oh, and if you're feeling *particularly* troubled, go ahead and borrow one of the silver rune pendants we got in last week—those'll keep you safe for sure," Paulina insisted.

Penny snorted and nodded. "Thanks, Mom, I'll see you Monday. Be safe, and have fun with the dragon lady." She jumped up as Paulina was about to leave. "Oh, and don't forget your glasses!" She plucked her mother's glasses from the display counter and handed them to her. Paulina pulled her into a tight hug, pressed the car keys into Penny's hand, then bustled out the door and was gone.

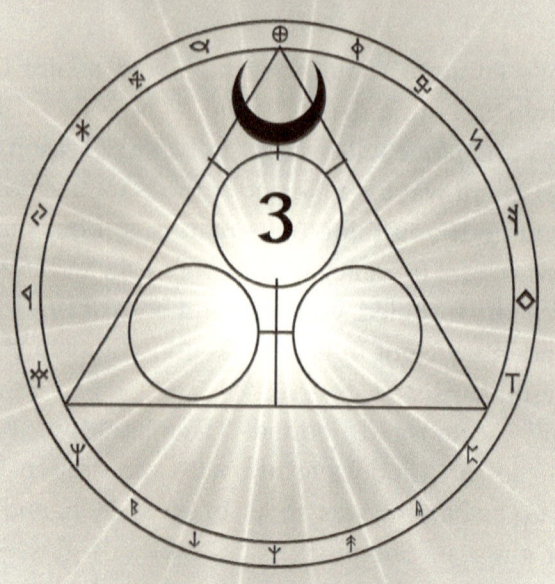

GALES AND GLOOM

Penny spent the rest of her shift at Willow Street Wonders convincing herself that everything was all right.

The rainstorm banished any hope of customers dropping by. Early afternoon melted into twilight and Penny remained at her post, lost in silent introspection. She sat on the stool behind the counter as figurines of old, forgotten gods and heroes watched her with unseeing eyes. Beside them were curtains of talismans and amulets, and jeweled dragonflies perched among darks rows of incense and dried herbs. Penny tapped at the crystal ball on the counter beside her, amusing herself with the warped vision of the arabesque shop.

Prickles of worry that Simon Shaw might return nagged at her, but after a few hours of unrelenting rain, Penny started to believe that she was safe.

It hardly seems real now...Maybe I did imagine it, she thought and tried to whistle, but the sound died on her lips. The cloud-covered sun had long since sunk behind the mountains and shadow had swallowed up the world. The only source of light was a lamp with a stained-glass shade.

Uncomfortable, Penny shifted and grabbed a magazine from underneath the counter. The cover showed a doctored image of a flying saucer looming above some nameless desert city. Penny flipped the magazine open with reservations. When seven-thirty came around at last, she'd had enough.

Not even the zealots are going to come around in this weather, she thought as she rose and undid her shop apron. Finishing her closing duties, Penny made sure to triple-check everything before clicking off the light and locking up.

Moving through Willow Street Wonders in the dark had always been eerie, and the noise from the raging storm did not ease the oppressive sensation that made her skin rise with goose bumps. Penny walked along the walls in the darkness with her hand extended and felt her fingertips graze cold metal. From the weak glow of the streetlamps she could see fragments of silver tinkling against each other. Penny removed one of the pendants from its identical siblings. It was one of the silver rune pendants her mother had mentioned; they'd received a small shipment of them from somewhere in Europe last week. Penny examined the silver disc with the runic carvings on it. With the reassurance of knowing no one could witness her lapse in rationality, she hung the black cord around her neck.

It is supposed to be a very powerful talisman. I'll just borrow it for the night.

Penny drove home with her brain on auto-pilot and sloshed to her front door through the torrents of rain. She scowled as she stepped through the doorway. Her mother hadn't left the heater on.

Penny tossed her bag in the corner and then raced upstairs to the shower. Feeling warmer, she scared up a meal and collapsed on the sofa, wrapping herself in a cocoon of fluffy blankets to guard against the frigid air in the house.

The night drifted away and Penny found herself curled up in bed with *Murder at Woodrow Manor,* flipping through the pages and relishing the most dramatic twists of the story. Beside her bed were a stack of novels of the same genre that she had already devoured.

Seven-and-a-half chapters later Penny was fast asleep, one hand still clinging to the book. Somewhere past midnight, she woke with a start as a tortured wail split the night.

Penny sat bolt upright in bed, frozen in terror. Her chest began to rise and fall in shallow breaths. The room had been plunged into thick darkness and objects that were mere inches away had become invisible. Though she guessed the sound might have been from a waking dream, Penny had never felt more paralyzed with fear in her life.

It had been a wretched chimera of screams; the voice of a dying animal, the wail of a baby, a Styrofoam shriek, metal grinding against itself—and yet none of those things. It was alive—but no human could have produced that cry. The small hairs on Penny's arms prickled as she strained to listen for something more. Another realization swept over her.

I fell asleep as I was reading. I left the lights on—I know I did.

Nauseating horror enveloped her. Reeling, she jumped out of bed and threw herself against her bedroom door that stood ajar. The bang of the door snapping shut echoed throughout the house and she fumbled to lock it with trembling hands. She backed away, half expecting something to begin pounding on it from the other side.

What should I do, what should I do? Penny thought in a panic, standing in the center of the room and hugging herself. *Should I wait to see if it happens again? What if it does? What if it doesn't? What was it?!*

"I've been having weird dreams lately. It was just a dream... just a dream..." her voice sounded meager in the overbearing darkness, like a tiny boat lost at sea. "The power's out because of the rain. There's nothing wrong...I'm okay." She took a deep, shuddering breath and began to recover.

The scream tore through the night again, this time a gut-tural bellow that oozed with agony and rage. It was so loud it seemed to resonate within her chest, and Penny cringed downward with a frantic yelp. It had come from just outside the house.

Whimpering as her body rocked with tremors, Penny crawled over to the window. She crouched just below it, domi-nated by fear for several long, uneventful moments until her curiosity beseeched her to look outside. With the utmost cau-tion she lifted her eyes above the ledge of her windowsill and peeked out through the gap in her curtains.

Through the thick sheets of rain and sloshing murkiness of the woods beyond the glass, Penny scanned the scene for anything out of the ordinary. Dreading the worst, she was surprised to find that there was nothing but the pines thrash-ing in the wind.

Am I seriously going crazy here?

Penny gripped her hair, wondering where she had left her cell phone. Calling for help was starting to seem like a better idea by the second. Before Penny could move to find it, out of the trees lurched an abomination so hideous it convinced her that her blood could freeze. The arms were disproportionately long and pale as an exhumed corpse. Ugly splotches of gray-ish-pink mottled the waxy flesh. With a speed Penny did not anticipate from something that looked so decayed, it burst into the street with a gut-wrenching leap.

Penny felt her consciousness slipping when she saw its face and grasped the wall for support. It looked as though it had once been human, but the eyes were huge and filmy white, and the lower jaw had been reduced to a few splinters of twisted bone. A serpentine, venom-black tongue lolled and surged from its throat. From its elbows, spine, and rib-cage sprouted thorny bones that pierced through the skin and shredded the remnants of something that might've once been clothing. Its mangled face contorted in unfocused wrath. With a sharp glance upward, as if it had spotted her peering at it from the window, it lunged forward, crawling on its belly with a swiftness that made Penny's stomach pinch.

Penny whimpered, unhinged by terror, and skittered across the floor in frantic desperation, knocking over the stack of books beside her bed. Between great, gasping breaths, Penny tried to focus, her eyes scanning the dark shapes of her room for a weapon of some sort and finding nothing. A deafening crash downstairs elicited from her a scream and a peal of dread. Penny nearly wept from the fresh wave of despair that smothered her. *Oh God. Now it knows where I am.*

Unable to think, Penny backed against the wall as blood-curdling howls roared downstairs. Things once treasured could be heard shattering to bits on the ground.

I can't believe this…I'm going to die here. Ripped to pieces. This is really it. This is how it happens. Penny's mind raced as a cold stillness took over her body and she clung to every minute detail in her diminishing time. She hugged her shoulders, cringing from the crashing noises intensifying by the moment. Footsteps pounded on the stairs and down the hall. It was over.

A crippling shock jolted through her body as the bedroom door was thrown open and a face came out of the darkness.

A familiar face. A friendly face.

"P-P-Professor Arlington?!" Penny gasped, not daring to believe her eyes.

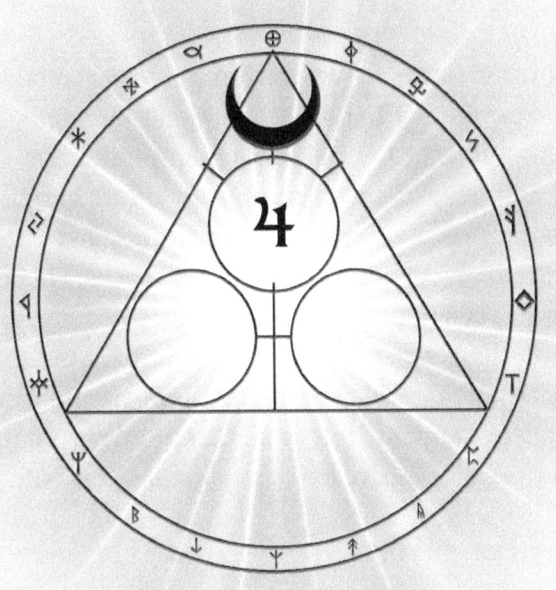

BUTTERFLIES IN THE
SITTING ROOM

Penny's breath caught in her lungs as she gaped at her literature professor. Not wasting a moment he grabbed Penny's hand and dragged her into the hall.

"Are you hurt?" He looked her over, his voice strong but coursing with panic.

"No! B-but, Professor! There's— there's a m-mon—"

"Don't worry. I dealt with it accordingly." Their eyes locked in an intense gaze, but the room was too dark for Penny to make out his expression. He pushed his glasses up, seized Penny by her upper arm and led her down the stairs. The fright that had lessened at his appearance flared up again.

"Where are we going?" Penny cried.

"Somewhere safe," Professor Arlington answered.

After coming downstairs, Penny choked, inhaling an acrid, oily, burning smell. The furniture lay in pieces all over the floor. Fragments of broken glass caught the feeble light, and at the edge of the room a smoldering heap of greasy ashes piled around scorched bones. It was now apparent what had become of the monster. Penny halted to goggle at the sight, but Professor Arlington jerked her along without missing a step. The front door had been knocked completely off its hinges. Realizing that the professor was planning on leading her outside, she ripped her arm away and retreated a few paces. He blinked at her, seeming taken aback by her reaction.

"I'm not going out there!" she warbled. Outside, the rain was a veritable cascade and Penny was barefoot and still dressed in her pajamas. Professor Arlington's brow furrowed and he grabbed her again, this time latching on with a stronger grip.

"OW! Hey!"

Professor Arlington forced a resisting Penny over the slippery door and into the rain. Penny dug her heels into the mud in an attempt to free her arm.

"Let me go or I'll scream!" she threatened, trying not to think of what cruel trap would await her if she played into the hands of her captor. There was no stopping the dreadful images that came to mind.

"I would strongly advise against that," Professor Arlington yelled over the rain. He pulled a key ring out from his pocket and dragged her toward a car that was parked some ways down the street. "It's dangerous here. If my conjecture is accurate, more of those creatures are on their way this very instant."

Penny weighed her options and found herself being tossed into the passenger seat of the professor's car and shut inside.

Penny had always imagined that if she was ever to be kidnapped by someone, she would throw a righteous fit against her assailant. She was surprised to find she instead felt numb. Shock had debilitated her. Professor Arlington got in the driver's side and wiped the lenses of his glasses on his sleeve. Everything around her seemed to be happening miles away as the car shuddered into life. Her ruined house sped out of view and was swallowed by the night.

Before long the questions in her mind burned too hot to be contained. "How did you know where I live, Professor?" Penny asked in a quivering voice, staring forward. He didn't answer right away, and Penny peered at him from the corner of her eye.

"I followed you from school. First to that shop, then to your house." His eyes stayed focused on the road.

Penny's chest tightened. "*What?*"

"I had to!" he defended. "Please believe me, Miss Fairfax, I mean you no harm. The only reason I followed you was to understand why you're radiating such an intensely high volume of magic."

Penny's lip trembled in stunned silence. *I…I must have heard that wrong.* She shook her head, eyeing him. "Okay, you need to tell me *exactly* what's going on here!"

He bit his bottom lip. "When we get there. I need to concentrate—I'm actually, ah, a rather poor driver," he admitted.

"Where are we going, anyway?" Penny asked, disregarding his words.

"My house." Again he sounded discomfited.

"*Excuse me?*" Penny spouted. "What if I don't *want* to go to your house?"

His expression became muddled. "Apologies, but you haven't got a choice," he said, firm yet with a sympathetic tone. "Now please hush up. These weather conditions are less than optimal, if you hadn't noticed."

Penny felt her stomach twist and crossed her arms over her chest, resolving to spend the rest of the drive in a hostile silence which she hoped would conceal her fright. She considered her chances of trying to leap from the moving car, but decided against it. He'd only catch her again, even if she was lucky enough to survive.

The car sped like a bullet through the torrents of rainwater spilling from the sky and every so often a pair of headlights flashed by. Professor Arlington hadn't been exaggerating when he told Penny he was a terrible driver. At every stoplight he punched the brakes so hard Penny was forced to clutch the side of the car door to remain balanced. Twice Penny grabbed the wheel to avoid a collision.

"How in God's name did you get your driver's license?" Penny exclaimed after he came close to smashing into a car waiting at the stoplight in front of them.

"Might I remind you what I *just* said about questions, Miss Fairfax?"

"Um. It's a green light..." Penny pointed at the illuminated intersection before them and the car shot to life with a violent jerk.

At last Professor Arlington pulled onto a gravel road devoid of streetlights and into the driveway of a weather-rotted, Victorian style house that seemed to have been concealed on purpose. No lights shone from inside.

"Is your wife asleep in there?" Penny kept her voice monotone, hoping there would be someone else inside. Professor Arlington opened door and stepped out into the rain.

"I'm not married," he said before shutting it again with a bang.

Penny told herself she wouldn't budge from her seat, but Professor Arlington extricated her and yanked her up the slippery porch steps and into the house. She wrenched her arm free of his gentle-but-firm grip and was corralled into the center of a cramped foyer.

"Let me go!" she spat as he clicked the light on and locked the door behind him. The professor ushered Penny into a sitting room off the foyer. His house looked just as Penny had imagined it would: crowded with beat-up antique furniture, and shelves upon shelves of books. His home was even smaller than hers, and there seemed to be a fair amount of clutter dashed haphazardly about. Penny was led to a purple armchair and asked to sit. She spied a pile of some of the most recent homework he'd assigned lying on a table by the kitchen door. Professor Arlington wiped his glasses dry on a small rag he'd taken from the counter and glanced hesitantly over at Penny. She glared right back.

"Erm, do you want anything? Tea, perhaps? A towel?" he inquired. Penny narrowed her eyes. He cleared his throat and looked down at his shoes. "I'll take that as a no, then."

"Care to tell me what's going on here?" Penny snarled. Her wet pajamas clung to her like an uncomfortable second skin, but she fought back shivers as she mustered up the most fearsome gaze she could.

Professor Arlington's expression sharpened. He looked over at her, scrutinizing, and sat down in a chair opposite hers. "Don't you think you're the one who should be giving *me* an explanation?" he asked with grave seriousness in his voice.

"*Me?*" she exclaimed. "*You* actually have the nerve to expect answers from *me?*"

"I've no time for this." He leaned forward with eyes blazing, and for the first time in her life Penny heard him raise his voice. "Tell me at once. How are you producing all that magic?"

Penny shrunk back into her chair.

"I have never encountered any one person in this world who can radiate that much raw magic—much less in a day's time! Yesterday you were the picture of normalcy. In fact, regularly you produce almost no magic at all—and now this. So, yes. I believe that justifies an explanation."

Drugs. This man is on drugs. I've got to get out of here. She drew her knees to her chest and took short little breaths, silently planning her escape route. Professor Arlington's expression changed from angry to alarmed.

"You—you didn't know?" he croaked. She shook her head and he scratched at his. "No, that's not feasible. How could you not *know?* Don't you feel it? I can't have been the only person who was put off by all that energy."

Penny shrugged, at a loss for what to tell him but needing to distract the crazy man while she planned. "I...guess...my mom and Maddie—they both had headaches, and Mom's headache went away after I left, but that was nothing. This is *insane,* I mean…" she mumbled.

"Let me try to explain. When you came into class this morning, it was as if…as if a speaker had been turned up to an unbearably loud volume. A speaker that had once been silent. You really have no idea how this change occurred?" he asked her, leaning forward, his hands on his knees. There was an intense passion and excitement in the way he spoke, as if he had been anticipating this moment for years.

"Do you have any idea how crazy you sound?" Penny shot back, still hugging her knees.

"Stuff and nonsense! I'm not delusional, I'm merely—confused—" he said with impatience, waving off her question. "Now the question is—"

"Ok, psycho. Prove it, then. Prove *magic* is real," Penny challenged, seeking to end this charade at once.

Professor Arlington flashed an irate glare as if to say that there was no time for such games, but gave a conceding sigh. With a lazy flick of his wrist, a spiral of the same silvery rune writing Penny had seen him produce earlier that day bloomed out of his index finger. The shimmery runes shot through the air, transforming into a flurry of fire-blue, incandescent butterflies. Ghostly wings fluttered around in the air as Penny leapt to her feet, breathless.

"How in the—" she cried. Her heart was racing again, but this time out of excitement.

"Is that proof enough for you?" Professor Arlington questioned, watching her dumbfounded look with mild amusement.

"What are they? What are *you?*" Penny breathed, tiptoeing underneath luminous wings in wonderment.

Professor Arlington snapped his fingers and more silvery runes shot from his hands like tiny arrows and pierced into each of the jewel-bright butterflies. With a collection of pops, their short-lived flight was quelled. They dissipated into a shower of blue stars and faded from existence. Penny's look of astonishment fell along with them, and she turned to face Professor Arlington, who was trying to repress a smug smile.

"Was that the same sort of thing you were doing this afternoon?" she asked, regaining her composure and taking her seat again.

"Of course. I'm pulling the magic from around us and shaping it to my will," Professor Arlington explained, looking distracted. "The life-forms of Earth naturally produce an energy called magic, and I can manipulate it to work enchantments."

Penny stared at him with glassy eyes, dumbstruck. She processed what he had just said, uncertain of what to think. "What are you? Some kind of space alien?" she speculated.

Professor Arlington choked and covered his mouth with his hand. Penny's cheeks grew hot and she scowled in humiliation as he burst out laughing. "D-don't laugh! The way you worded it—anyone would make that mistake!"

He caught his breath after a few more chortles, and cleared his throat. "I apologize again, Miss Fairfax," he said, his voice trembling with another laugh. "But to answer your question, no. I'm human. But I wasn't born in this world."

Penny snorted. With each question he answered, two more popped up in its place. "Oooh-kay…so, there are other *worlds*, apparently. And what do you mean by 'an energy called magic'? How do we…um, produce magic?" She crossed her arms, trying to wade through the tangled mess of information.

"Yes, there certainly are other worlds—well, there's at least one other. The world I was born in. Nelvirna." He scratched the side of his head. "And magic…I mean—well, it's rather complicated. I'm not entirely sure I *thoroughly* understand it myself. Let me think." His face pinched as he tried to collect his thoughts. "It's difficult to describe a sense that others cannot experience. Imagine trying to explain color to a man who's been blind his whole life."

"Every living thing on Earth processes a specific form of energy that we called 'magic' in my home. It comes from the

Earth itself—raw and unrefined—and it is transformed unconsciously into usable, potential energy. I can sense where it is, similar to how you would feel heat, and expend it however I please. It sort of just *hangs* around in the air and is especially concentrated around human beings and animals. Some naturally process a great deal, while others produce only a small amount. It's what you might think of as an *aura*, I suppose," he explained, gesturing to the air around Penny. She nodded to show she followed.

"Well, anyway, I just *pull* the magic out of those auras and use it to perform various types of enchantments. This morning the field of magic fixed around you was...*staggeringly* immense. It was more than—well, thousands of people's auras combined. In fact, it was so powerful that it was flowing directly toward me, possibly because I was the only thing around that had the ability expend it. I've been spending your magic in different enchantments all day long as I've tracked you—but even now it's still difficult to bear."

Penny digested this in silence for a moment. "Do you think that's the reason why that...*thing* attacked me?" She fought back a shiver at the memory of the wretched being that had crawled out of the forest.

"I don't know, to be perfectly honest. In my entire life I've never seen anything remotely like that creature." His look was almost pleading. "Do you have even the faintest clue about why this is happening? Any reason *at all*?"

Penny racked her brain for a moment and shook her head. "I'm sorry. I don't have a clue."

The professor laughed soberly and rubbed his temple. He looked crestfallen as he repositioned his glasses yet again, studying the carpet beneath his feet. "To hear this, Miss Fairfax..." he paused and sighed. "It's disappointing, I must admit."

Penny looked at him with mild concern. "Why? What exactly were you expecting?"

Professor Arlington looked into her eyes and for the first time since she'd known the man, she saw real pain behind them. He seemed to sense Penny's surprise and cast his eyes away. His mouth opened and he hesitated.

"I—"

Penny's eyes fell to the window behind Professor Arlington's chair, where the face of a stranger, dead-eyed and chalk white, stared right back at her.

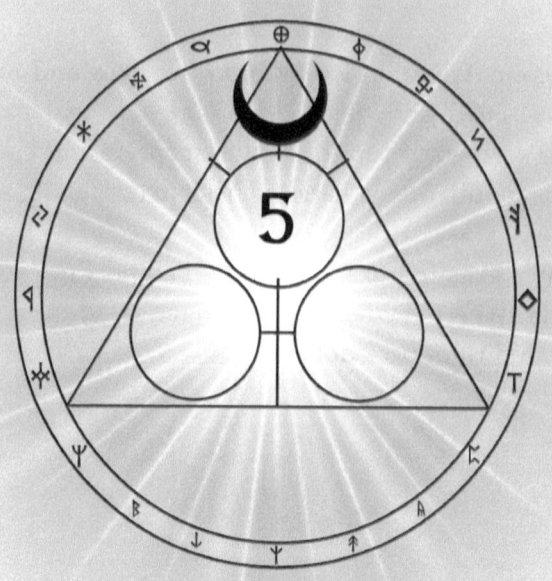

THE GOLDEN THREAD

Penny leapt from her chair and let out a strangled yell. Professor Arlington scrambled up, looking about for what startled her. Seeing the man staring in at them from outside, he froze. Penny cowered behind her professor, clutching the back of his shirt. The man outside was too still. He didn't blink, nor did his eyes move.

"Do you know that man?" Professor Arlington whispered.

Penny made a small noise to show she didn't. Without warning the skin on the man's face started to stretch. His teeth sprouted into tusks. Both eyes rolled back into his head, leaving two gaping sockets as the skull grew long and malformed. He put his hand up to the window as if reaching out for help, and bones burst through his fingers, becoming razor-edged claws.

Penny fainted. Professor Arlington was shaking her gently as a blast of freezing cold air as the window shattered brought her back to reality with a shock. The demonic creature leapt into the room with that awful inhuman wail. Penny was so frightened she could not manage to utter a sound. Her legs were still limp as Professor Arlington pulled her to her feet and dragged her down the hall. The creature bounded behind them, snarling and gnashing its jaws. Professor Arlington turned back to face it, and with a sweeping motion of his hand, an arcane circle wreathed in gold light burst forth through his fingers, blocking off the entire hallway. The beast threw itself against the disc barrier and it began to crack like glass.

Noises of devastation sounded in the kitchen, followed by a furious pounding on the front door. Penny had a mere second to share a terrified glance with her teacher, whose hand she held with a vice-like grip. More abominations were coming.

"Hurry! This way!" Professor Arlington said, making a mad dash for the basement door. Behind them, the arcane circle shattered and the beast thundered forward, jaws open wide, ready to sink its tusks into their flesh. The door slammed behind them just in time. An ominous thud sounded, followed by an enraged shriek.

"They're everywhere…they're all around the house. What do we *do*?" Penny panicked as Professor Arlington created a stream of silver runes, enchanting the door. Penny felt an intense rush of lightheadedness and wobbled in place.

Out of the trembling quiet, another crash resonated. The two of them stared at the door with fierce intensity. The basement was cramped and windowless, and the only light came from the faint glow of the arcane enchantment on the door. Penny could hardly see Professor Arlington as he turned around to face her, but she could tell from his silence and stony demeanor that something was very wrong.

"There must be…at least five of them…maybe more," Professor Arlington sputtered.

"That will keep them out, though. It'll keep them out, right?" Penny gasped and drew closer to him.

"Not for very long." His voice was weak and Penny's chest deflated when she saw the hopelessness on his face.

"You can fight them, though. You got that other one! These ones should be nothing, *right?*" Horror surged through her like a runaway train. Another deafening crash came, and they scurried farther away from the door, which rumbled and shook with the force of the creatures behind it.

"Miss Fairfax, I—" Professor Arlington breathed, "—I was never trained in combative enchantments. I...cannot act quickly enough to destroy this many."

"What is that supposed to mean?" Penny blanched. "You can't be serious! You—"

With an ear-splitting crack, the door and the enchantment that barred it began to splinter. Penny watched in transfixed terror as a long, scythe-like bone pierced through the wood. Gripping Professor Arlington's arm, she willed him to react, but he hung his head in despair.

"What are you doing?! Don't just stand there! At least *try* to fight them!" Penny begged him. Paralyzed, the professor watched as huge chunks of wood splintered away from the door.

Her fear and frustration reaching a boiling point, Penny stamped her foot and cried out in rage, *"DO SOMETHING!"* She pushed him as hard as she could and he stumbled. Tears stung at her eyes, and Penny felt her knees give out as she saw something dark and snakelike forcing its way through the network of splinters that was once a door.

"Please," Penny implored with a sob, fighting to stay on her feet, "Please don't let me die here."

As if Professor Arlington had been jolted by electricity, his expression contorted into one of wounded anguish. Her words had stung, but they seemed to have gotten through to him. With a sharp gasp, he slapped a hand to his forehead. "Of course, why didn't I think of—come here." He grabbed Penny around the shoulders and she clung to him as the door exploded into bits.

The last image Penny saw before shutting her eyes was Professor Arlington's hand reaching outward into the darkness of the basement in a dire grasp for nothing at all.

Expecting to feel needle-sharp fangs rip through her body, Penny screamed, but the burst of pain never came. Without warning it was as if she had been sucked into a powerful vacuum and was hurtling through space at several hundred miles per hour. Her eyes were pulled open by the sheer force of the pressure and she saw everything around her empty away into a void, like she had been riding atop a rocket that launched straight into a curtain of impenetrable darkness. The air was stolen from her lungs. A catastrophic nothingness stretched out around the both of them. Professor Arlington still clutched her and she clamped down on the folds of his shirt, sure that if she let go she would be torn apart by the powerful force that sucked them through the void. The deep pit of emptiness continued on for minute after excruciating minute.

Let it stop, let it stop, oh please, let it stop. Kill me, I don't care, just let it end.

Her prayers were answered as the terrible sensation came to an abrupt halt with the feeling of being ejected from the end of a long tube. They were tossed through the air and Professor Arlington was thrown from her grip before she landed hard on her shoulder, her head bouncing onto a hard surface. All her senses were swept from her body. Then there was only deep, visionless sleep.

CONSCIOUSNESS CAME BACK to Penny in shallow levels. She was aware that she was rocking back and forth, her legs dangling and her head rolling from side to side. With a groan, Penny forced her eyes open and found herself staring up at the strained face of Professor Arlington.

Realizing that he was carrying her, Penny kicked up her legs and cried out in protest. Her sudden reaction startled him into dropping his hold, and she tumbled onto a dirt road. Still gasping, Penny scrambled to her feet and steadied herself. She looked around and the intense dread returned. An unfamiliar, rustic setting stretched out behind them, and before them stood a high-walled town cluttered with buildings, steeples, and roofs ornamented with stone carvings.

"*Where are we?*" Penny turned on Professor Arlington, spitting with rage and fear. He held out his hands and she backed away, trembling in her pajamas in the center of the dirt path, looking like a bedraggled mouse that had escaped disappearing into a sewer drain.

"Miss Fairfax, try to stay calm," he pleaded and crept toward her.

"Explain this. *All of this,*" Penny snarled, balling up her fists.

"I suppose I—I should...." he tried, his face ashen. Penny felt a heightened wave of panic pass over her. "Perhaps you had better prepare yourself. This might come as something of a shock, Miss Fairfax," he warned and Penny's body stiffened.

"What do you mean?" she urged. "Tell me where we are *now*." Her fingers flexed.

Professor Arlington let out a dejected sigh and his shoulders dropped. "You're not going to accept this straight away, I'm sure. But if you want the simple facts of our situation, it *appears* that in my struggle to escape from the basement..." He hesitated for a long moment and winced as he looked at Penny. "...that I may have *unintentionally* brought us to—to another world."

Penny stared at him in disbelief and shook her head. "You — you've got a really bad sense of humor," she said.

"Please, I know it's hard to come to terms with. I responded the same way when I first came to Earth." Professor Arlington reached out to touch the side of her arm. "We can make the best of things if we only just—"

"Don't you *dare* touch me, you creep!" she screamed, slapping his hand away and dashing toward the cobbled road of the town. Wherever she was, there had to be someone sympathetic to her plight. She could borrow a cell phone to call her mother, or the police. Someone would help her reach safety.

Professor Arlington's footsteps scraped behind her as he tried to catch up and Penny quickened her pace. Bursting through the gate and onto the street, Penny staggered to a stop and gaped.

The gables and towers of the town spiraled up toward the sky looked as if they belonged in another time-period. The people that bustled by on their busy ways wore frock coats, silken gowns and tall hats, gold-rimmed spectacles, goggles with lenses the color of wine bottles, frilled bonnets, stockings with boots, and all manner of strange clothing. Gas-lamps lined the tightly-wound streets. Fair ladies sported feathered hats with tiny fake birds that almost looked and sounded alive. All around them the alluring scent of baking goods wafted, coming from a warm bakery with an ornate crafted crystal window. Further down the street, huge piles of alien, jewel-like fruits were stacked high, while a man with a bowler hat and wild mutton-chops shouted at the passing crowd in a language Penny couldn't even begin to identify. Penny choked back a yelp as a small collection of fuzzy brown bird-like creatures with huge orange eyes hopped past in a little flock. A child in a lacey headdress and pinafore chased after the flock.

"Miss Fairfax! Please wait!" Professor Arlington's voice called from close behind her. Penny turned away and bumped into someone. She turned to apologize, and felt the blood drain out of her face as she looked into the eyes of a creature she had no name for. It had needle sharp teeth glittering under a snake-like nose and two round golden eyes that looked just like a toad's. Though its face was monstrous, the creature stood upright and wore a smart suit. It spoke to her in a foreign tongue, using a polite but scolding tone.

Penny did an instant about-face and shot past Professor Arlington, biting her tongue hard enough to stop from screaming aloud in hysteria. Through the narrow, crowded street she went, colliding with townsperson and signpost alike. The afternoon sun had stained the town an orange-red, only adding to the surreal nature of what she was seeing.

She hurtled around the corner of the street, anxious to put as much distance between herself and the creature she'd bumped into as possible. Weaving through a line of carts in an alleyway selling what she hoped were just a collection of bizarre souvenirs, she burst onto another main street covered in flags and iron archways. Penny stumbled back until she felt a wall behind her, and pressed herself up against it, gawking at what lay before her.

Penny no longer needed convincing that this was a different world. Only a few feet away, an eight-foot-tall, black-scaled dragon wearing a cravat and a long coat purchased a fine cut of a meat from a bald butcher with a robust mustache. Penny stared shamelessly in its direction.

Black scales. Huge talons, a pair of wings. That...that's a dragon. I'm actually looking at a dragon right now, she thought as a whine escaped. Another one of the short, toad-like creatures played a flute in the center of the street, busking for spare change. Penny slid down the wall, transfixed and horrified all at once, when a voice beside her made her look up.

A man and another creature that made Penny's heart surge were addressing her with concern. The thing beside the gentleman had the head of a lion and the horns of a ram, though it wore an elegant cloak and monocle, stood upright and spoke politely to her, as if asking what the matter was. It reached a comforting paw in her direction, trying to help her up. The words were pure gibberish to Penny, and the sheer confusion, panic, and frustration of the moment brought tears to her eyes.

No, she scolded herself, averting her eyes to look only at the cobblestones. *Don't cry. Don't let this break you. I know there's a...a cat man standing right there, but just stay calm. Take a deep breath. Find Professor Arlington.*

Not knowing what else to do, Penny rose on shaky legs and bowed to the strange pair. They blinked at her in astonishment as she pushed between them, racing back the way she had come, searching the crowd for Professor Arlington. She called out, her heart leaping every time her gaze fell upon one of the unfamiliar creatures that populated the town. Winding down another alleyway, her heart sank once more.

I don't recognize this...I...I'm lost. Penny bit her bottom lip, anxiety raging out of control inside of her. She looked about for something that would help her and spotted a clock tower rising above the other roofs.

I'll be able to get a good look from there, she realized and ran in its direction. Her feet were bruised and raw by the time she located it. Panting, she circled the tower until she found a set of stairs. Not bothering to ascertain whether she was allowed inside, Penny climbed them, emerging onto a wooden platform that overlooked the town. She leaned against the railing, trying to catch her breath and make sense of the landscape. Beyond the city walls lay idyllic farmland, and only small collections of twinkling lights could be seen below the dusty purple sky. In the distance was a great cluster of trees that seemed to stretch on forever. South of the town was a valley nestled among green hills that extended until they transformed into a small mountain range shrouded in a veils of mist. Tiny villages were visible in the forms of quivering star points, but even in the farthest regions, Penny found no hint of anything familiar. She squinted at the horizon and thought she could just see the shining surface of what appeared to be a river, but it might have been a trick of the light.

She turned her gaze then to the town itself and searched for any sign of Professor Arlington. After an hour of studying the area, darkness blanketed the town and ended her search. In the sky among the waking stars, two moons gleamed in the sky above Penny, and she could do little else but stare up at them in dizzy horror.

Her chest feeling as if it had been emptied, Penny let herself sink to the ground. She took several deep breaths and ran her hand through her tangled hair, her cut and dirty feet aching as the cold air numbed her limbs.

Then something very peculiar caught her eye in the gloom. A thin thread of golden light floated in the air beside her. She tapped it, discovering it felt like a strand of silk. With a shock, Penny realized it sprouted from her chest and led over to the staircase. She touched the spot where the thin golden thread fed into her collar bone and gave it an experimental tug. She felt nothing.

How long has this been here?

A noise sounded from below the platform, echoing softly at first, but growing louder with each passing moment.

Footsteps.

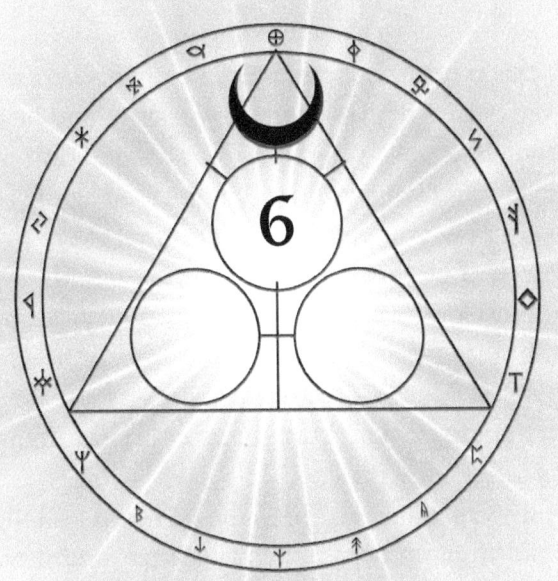

UNDER ELYDRIAN SKIES

Penny stood back up with a gasp as the footsteps grew closer. The golden thread trembled and Professor Arlington's head poked into view. He climbed onto the platform, looking irritated and holding the delicate thread in his free hand. Penny felt relief flood through her.

"*There* you are," he drawled. "I see you're still in one piece."

"How did you find me?" she asked, astonished.

"Simple." Professor Arlington gingerly tugged at the golden string and it melted away into thin air. "A tracking spell."

Ah, magic spells. Of course. Penny thought with sarcasm. She faced him with a frown. "Thank you," she said with humility. "F-for coming to find me, I mean. I'm sorry I ran off like that, it's just..."

"It's quite a shock to the system, I understand completely. Still, I could've done without roaming all over the town trying to find you," he said, and Penny grinned a little. He exhaled and walked over to where she stood.

"This...this is really happening, isn't it? This isn't a dream." Penny looked at him with a solemn expression and he nodded. His hand twitched upward as if he was considering putting a comforting hand on her shoulder, but decided against it.

"Look—I know you've no reason to trust me at this point, but...it really will be for the best if we stay together. It's true we hardly know one another, but I guarantee you that somehow I'm going to get you home. I can't help but feel responsible for this."

"Wait a minute...If you brought us here so easily, can't we just... go back?" Penny frowned.

"If only it were that easy," he sighed. "Before last night, I've only managed to jump between worlds once, and it was completely by mistake—in a moment of panic. I spent the better part of these last four years trying to figure out anything I could about trans-world travel, but it's amounted to nothing more than mere speculation. I can't tell you how frustrating it is to know that I *have* this ability, but am unable to use it. But where there's a *can*, there's a *how*—so there's got to be somebody or something that has an explanation," Professor Arlington mused.

"Well, as long as we're mixed up in this, we might as well make the best of it, hmm?" He leaned his head to the side and tried to smile. "So, um— I'll look out for you until I find a way of getting us back. What I mean is—you can trust me, I suppose," he added, sounding afraid of what he was promising.

Penny was taken aback and blinked several times, unsure of what to say. "Th-thanks," she mumbled.

An awkward silence ensued, and then Professor Arlington gestured for her to follow him down stairs.

Stepping back out into the street, Professor Arlington spoke again. "If I'm going to be completely honest, I need you. I'm unable to perform any sort of enchantment or spell of any kind without you around—I use your magic, remember? The people in this world don't give off the same type of aura I was talking about earlier—"

"Then how did you cast the tracking spell?" asked Penny with a raised brow.

"I had to wander around until I could feel your magic," he admitted. "Anyway, I believe our first order of business is to get some proper clothing, a meal, and shelter."

"And how do you intend to pay for all that? Were you thinking of bartering your sweater vest? I'm not sure if Argyle is *in* right now, though," Penny scoffed, gesturing to a nearby man in a purple frock-coat.

Hector shrugged. "I...summoned some money earlier, when you were still asleep," he told her.

Penny processed this, her eyes narrowing. "Summoned? Like, you—conjured it out of thin air?"

"No, not exactly. It's impossible to make something out of nothing—surely you must know that. Just because I call it *magic* does not imply that it can break the rules of science," Professor Arlington said, choosing each word with heightened caution. "I simply used a spell to summon up a bit of money from the collective source of private funds of the populace and banks of this nearby region."

Incredulous, Penny laughed. "Oh, so this is just a round-about way of saying that you *stole* it!" she cried.

"I know it sounds immoral!"

" —*is* immoral," Penny corrected.

"But just think of it as—as a mandatory donation to those who are in need," he argued, looking a bit troubled himself before breaking down with a sigh. "It was only a little from each person. I doubt they'll even notice anything is missing."

"I can't believe you." Penny shook her head.

"All right, then, we'll do it your way. I'll send the money back and we'll have to do our best to find a job in a world we don't belong in, so we can find our way home *eventually*. How does that sound?"

Penny contemplated this and fell silent. "Ok, I see your point."

"Keep in mind; I've done this all before. I was wrenched from my home world, Nelvirna, to Earth with only the clothes on my back and I somehow managed to integrate my way into your immeasurably peculiar society," he told her with some assurance.

"You could do with a little more integrating, if you ask me..." Penny grumbled, and he either didn't hear or chose to ignore her. "Hey, wait...If you're from a different world, how did you learn English so fluently in just four years?" she asked and he stood up straighter.

"That, Miss Fairfax, is an excellent question. Thank you for reminding me," he said in a manner that made her feel like she was back in the classroom. Without any explanation, the professor knelt down and began drawing a strange pattern onto the stone with a bit of chalk he pulled from his pocket. He marked strange lettering and symbols into a circle, then took a minute to inspect it.

"Oh no, that's not quite right, let me see..." he mumbled to himself as Penny stared down at him. After rubbing out a circular cipher and replacing it with a series of zigzag lines, he stood up and nodded. "There we are." He grabbed Penny by her shoulders and pulled her into the center of the circle.

"Um, Professor—"

"Be prepared—you may feel a little lightheaded," he warned.

"Whoa, what? Wait a second—" she protested, but Professor Arlington clapped his hands together and a bright flash of aquamarine light erupted from the ground Penny stood upon. Stars streamed past her eyes and an overwhelming sensation that was akin to being inside a high-powered washing machine swept over her. The lights faded away and she lost her balance, falling to the ground, the bright after-image effect burning her eyes.

"All done! How are you feeling?" she heard Professor Arlington ask, but his voice sounded odd.

"What in the world was that about?" Penny wheezed as he helped her to her feet.

He beamed, kneading his hands together with excitement. "Hah! It worked! You just spoke to me in my native tongue. I can't believe I remembered how to do it properly."

"You—wait, how? What did you do?" she demanded.

"I just put a very useful enchantment on you, which also serves as an answer to your previous question. You see, where I'm from, scholars are required to know all the languages in our world, so we developed a universal communication spell—it's actually quite fascinating. Basically, the magic takes the *intention* of what the speaker is trying to say, and makes it possible for the listener to understand by having the words come out in the language you need to use—all without you having to learn a thing! You'll be able to tell the difference between what's being said and gain control over which language you speak after a while, but as for now, just let it come naturally."

"So, you're saying I can speak every language *ever* now?" Penny gasped, her heart pounding with excitement.

"That's a very rudimentary way of looking at it. But, yes. What's even better is that the spell will be effective for the next five years or so."

"That's incredible...thanks, Professor!"

"Um, feel free call me Hector from now on. No need for formalities anymore, I suppose," he said with a shrug.

Hector? Penny realized with a bit of surprise that she'd never heard his given name before. It felt strange to be on a first-name basis with the man she'd only known as her stern professor.

Professor Arlington smudged away the ring of symbols and they set off for a line of shops. Penny stayed close to him as they traversed through the bustling streets. The town seemed to have gotten livelier after dark. Alongside the gas lamps were luminous balls of different colored lights trapped inside glass orbs, hanging outside shops windows and dropping from eaves. Penny drew closer and observed that the inside of the orbs were tiny clusters of crystal giving off brilliant light. Professor Arlington looked back and waited for her to catch up, then led the way up the road, threading through the stream of citizens in their outlandish clothing. Their attention was stolen by a man with an ornate mask performing a complicated juggling act in the square. Penny stared wide-eyed into a shop window filled with sparkling accessories in the shapes of different beasts and dragons that moved and fluttered around the display.

They wandered around the nighttime marketplace between the glowing lamps of pale blue and misty green until they spotted a shop with an assortment of different clothing displayed in the warmly lit windows. With a sinking sense of disappointment, Penny saw that she could not read the shop's display sign.

"Hey! Your spell is already broken! The sign's still in their language," Penny said as she pushed the door open and heard the tiny silver bell overhead tinkle.

"The spell only functions with spoken communication," Hector explained.

The problem was forgotten as Penny found herself confronted with several specimens of opulent and striking clothing. Delighted, she browsed through what might have passed off as costumes from a fantastical film and set about admiring flowing silk gowns and parasols until Hector reminded her that they were impractical. The shopkeeper, a curvy woman with ginger-blonde hair and a pair of spectacles, rushed over after seeing Penny's excitement and ushered her around the shop, prattling on. Penny spotted a sophisticated blue traveling jacket with intricate gold embroidery in the back of the store.

"Oh, this *is* a fine item, right here! It's made of the finest filth-resistant, damp-resistant and stain-resistant material—and if you buy it with the other display items, you'll get a discount!"

Penny smiled as she admired the accompanying items: a white ruffled blouse, a blue skirt that fell to just above the knee, and black leggings. The shopkeeper asked her if she wanted to try it on and she agreed with a tiny nod. With a wave of a pair of enchanted silver scissors, the entire outfit was swapped with Penny's clothes. The saleswoman flourished the scissors about to help expand and tighten the material in different places until it reached a comfortable fit.

Penny looked herself over with a shy grin. "I'll take it!"

Penny picked out a pair of boots and Hector selected a new shirt, a sensible green vest, and a pair of trousers. He milled about the shop, grabbing a few more items here and there and talking in a low voice to the shopkeeper. He found a set of satchels that had been enchanted so that the things placed inside were stored at a faraway location, which meant they could carry as much as they wanted and it would weigh next to nothing. They approached the register with their bags, wearing the new sets of clothes.

"Your total comes to three topaz, and one amethyst Yuebell, sir. We take transfer slips, as well," the bespectacled woman recited with a bit of cheer as she tallied the price up, using her enchanted scissors as a pen. Penny was enthralled as Hector produced a small sack from his pocket and plucked out a handful of little round stones, each no bigger than a marble. He counted out the correct amount and handed it to the shopkeeper, who gave a toothy smile and thanked them. Penny sauntered out of the store, enjoying the feel of her new clothes and the small relief of fitting in with the crowd that came with them.

"So those little jewels are the money of this world?" she questioned.

"Obviously," Hector replied with a hint of arrogance. "The color indicates the value. I discovered before that you can combine similar types of a lower value. The stones will draw together and change color. Tapping on it will also break them apart, see?" He showed Penny a handful of the brilliant stones. Tiny star-like points of light swam within the jewels like fireflies trapped in a jar. Hector pulled a single blue stone out of the sack and rapped the top with his finger. It shivered a little before springing apart into five yellow pieces. Penny watched in wonderment as he squeezed them back together before pocketing the Yuebells and resuming their walk.

They passed through another poorly lit alley where vendors watched them go by with hungry eyes, silently begging them to buy something from their carts. Penny could see more of the amphibian-like men crouched in groups in many of the alleyways.

"I think we passed a tavern a while back. This way," Hector said as he tugged Penny away from a cart covered with painted animal skulls and flickering candles. The man keeping shop had long pointy ears and cast Hector a dark look as they rounded the corner onto a wider and busier street. Steam-powered vehicles clanked by beside carts drawn by exotic beasts of burden.

They soon located the tavern Hector had mentioned. Hector explained that his glasses had been enchanted to allow him to read text from other languages and translated the sign post, identifying that the tavern was called *The Dancing Dragon*. Inside, a few grimy lanterns shone through the dimness and guests chatted amongst themselves. Every so often a peal of raucous laughter would rise up from the corner booth like a wave and die down again. Penny watched a tall woman with long chestnut hair and a small scar on the left side of her face wipe down glasses behind the bar while eyeing the crowd like a hawk. The wall behind her was filled with bottles of every shape and color. A faint, warbling tune whined out of a phonograph-like object at the end of the bar.

They managed to pick out meals that seemed remotely familiar from the menu, and the bartender brought them their food with the same cold unflinching look on her face. Penny was pleased with the quality of the meal; it was reminiscent of a pot pie, but full of vegetables she'd never seen or tasted and an unrecognizable meat. She did not care to know what kind of animal it had come from and went on eating while forcing herself to think of something else. After he was finished eating, Hector pulled out a thick strip of paper from his pocket and spread it out on the bar top in front of them. Penny leaned over in the dim light and saw that it was a map.

"I picked this up at the tailor's," he told her before she could ask. "It's a map of this world."

Penny gazed with a furrowed brow at the map, running her fingers over the creases and studying the unfamiliar territories with interest.

"It's called Elydria," Hector read the spindly text aloud.

"El-ee-dree-ahh," Penny repeated, testing the word out.

"I believe we are currently right—" Hector tapped his slender finger to a tiny dot on a continent on the right of the map, "—here... just north of the river that separates this country from the Nation of Elves. In the town of Dewthorne."

"Now, the most astute plan of action is to find as much information about Elydria as we can. We need to know how things like magic, energy, economy, culture, and politics work here. Perhaps their knowledge of other worlds is extensive. Our predicament may even be commonplace here. Knowledge is invariably the most important factor of success—and I must admit that I am rather delighted for the opportunity to closely study yet another world and lear—"

"Okay, okay. Got it. So where do we get information?" Penny snapped him out of his effervescent state. She resented him for being so ecstatic about their situation, and then remembered he most likely had no one to miss back on Earth.

"A library, of course," Hector said with the same smile he used when explaining a new concept in class. "And since there isn't a sufficient source of public literature in this town, according to my shop-keeping informant, we need to go from here—" he walked his fingers from the dot that was Dewthorne on the map across a painted forest, town, and river to a star at the top of the continent, "—to the capital. That's where we'll supposedly find a massive library simply brimming with books just waiting to be read. I'm certain we will find a solution to our problem there."

Penny thought about it for a while. A few inches on the map were sure to be long, arduous miles of dangerous and untamed territory. "It's a fair idea, in theory, I suppose. I'm not sure about this, Professor. But I'll trust you on this."

"Just Hector, if you don't mind," he said stiffly as he counted out several Yuebells in his palm and set them on the bar next to their empty plates.

Collecting their bags, Hector consulted with the bartender about lodgings and then led the two of them up to their assigned room. Inside was a single bed, and after an awkward silence broken only by some throat clearing and false starts from Hector, he managed to say he would be happy to sleep on the floor.

Penny retreated to the bathroom. After double checking that the door was locked, she took a long, hot bath, emerging in a cloud of steam and feeling much cleaner, but somehow more worried than ever. She was careful to avoid Hector's gaze as she scurried into the bed and burrowed under the covers. An overwhelming sense of exhaustion had taken hold over her body, but something prevented Penny from finding sleep. After about twenty minutes she saw the light fade from the room and listened to the muffled sounds of Hector curling up on the floor in a corner of the room. Penny sighed to herself.

The reality of her situation began to solidify in her mind, bringing a gripping feeling of nausea that refused to ease. Penny thought of her mother and her face screwed up as she suppressed a whimper. Thoughts of her warm quilt at home, her stack of unfinished books, and the smell of banana muffins in her kitchen exacerbated the spinning in her head to a state of acute discomfort.

How am I going to get through this? I can't. I'm not cut out for this; I'm not strong enough. Things like this shouldn't happen to people like me.

Anxiety fought to keep her awake and alert, but her eyelids grew heavier. The sounds of the night and Hector's soft breathing seemed farther away. In a half-conscious desire for comfort, her shaking fingers grasped the tiny silver pendant she had taken from her mother's store. Last night seemed like years ago. Penny drifted away, and for a few quiet hours, left behind the turmoil of feeling lost somewhere under Elydrian skies.

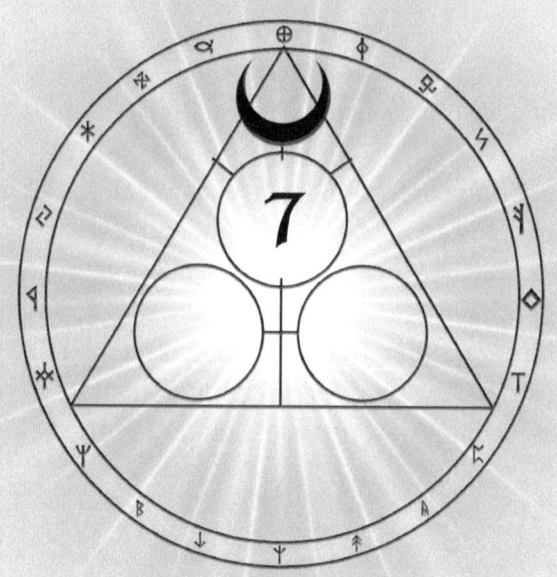

DEIMOS OF DEWTHORNE

The peculiar town came to life again the next morning, and as Penny ventured into the marketplace alongside Hector, she had to admit that Dewthorne was far less intimidating than it had seemed at night.

In the center of the town were a collection of stalls and a row of shops, all sporting a splendid array of goods. Penny and Hector bought some fresh glazed rolls to chew on while they wandered through the crowded aisles in search of useful goods to take with them on what promised to be a long and uncomfortable journey. Hector purchased medicines, cooking utensils, and blankets, as well as several other practical finds, such as bandages and a small knife for cooking. Nearby, a group of musical performers played a jangling tambourine, reedy pipes, and a huge, twisting horn that sang aloud in a melancholy voice. Captivated by their sound, Penny slipped away from Hector as he haggled with an irritable-looking man selling talismans.

"Mom would love it here," Penny said to herself as a dragon swooped overhead, landed, and went about inspecting some pottery.

Stepping under the shady canopies, Penny discovered an object so peculiar and beguiling that it startled her just to behold it. Laid out in a corner of the square on a dirty blanket, a man wearing a fancy turban and a shining sash over his face sat before a collection of wondrous stones, each in a different pearly, iridescent color. They appeared to be filled with vein-like cracks and fibers, and sparkled and hummed. She gathered up enough courage to speak to the man, feeling her usual awkwardness with strangers return.

"Erm, excuse me, sir—what is this stuff?" she asked, pointing at the cluster of stones. The man's expression grew skeptical, as if he were trying to tell whether she was joking or not.

"Do you not know raw magic clusters when you see them, Little Miss? Or are you trying to imply something about the quality of my merchandise?" his accented voice purred.

Penny frowned and lowered her head. "No, no…that's not what I meant," she shrugged. "I'm just—I'm not from around here."

"Indeed," the man replied with a nasty tone that said he did not believe her. "Anyway, it's fifty diamond Yuebells for the large clusters just there—and they're of excellent quality, I promise you that."

"*Fifty?* Isn't that a bit high?" Penny asked in awe.

The man seemed to be losing his patience. "Times are hard, Little Miss. Magic is growing scarcer by the day. The people continue to live wasteful lives, in spite of the shortage. But I expect a *foreigner* wouldn't know that," he said with a raspy laugh.

Not knowing how to react to this, she shrugged and walked away to a bench to puzzle over this strange form of magic. The air was rife with the crispness of early autumn, balancing out the sun's heat nicely.

Penny's rest was interrupted by vague noises of excitement in the center of the square. A man with an entourage was making his way through a crowd gathering around a wooden platform. At the same time, someone else appeared to be pushing in the opposite direction, leaving a trail of disgruntled people. The cause of the commotion emerged and Penny's jaw dropped. His cape and top hat made him easily recognizable as the magician she had met in the coffee shop.

It...it can't be Simon Shaw!

He stepped out from the wall of glaring people and straightened his clothes out, huffing. Penny charged in his direction.

"*Hey, you!*" she yelled in what she suddenly knew was English. Several bystanders glanced over at her outburst. Simon gave a little gasping scream when his eyes fell on Penny, and he broke into a relieved smile. His grin faded when Penny grabbed him by the front of his shirt.

"I *knew* you had something to do with this!" she snarled.

"P-Penelope Fairfax! I've been looking *everywhere* for you!" Simon sputtered, his voice high pitched and nervous.

"Care to tell me why? How did you get here?" Penny demanded.

"Oh, you have no idea what I've been through. It was awful," Simon moaned, grasping her shoulders. Taken aback, Penny broke away from him.

"Start talking. Now."

Simon's expression was anguished. "You and I are both in huge trouble...like the *we are probably going to die* kind of trouble. Please, you've got to help me. That lady—the one with the wings—the one who sent me here—she wanted me to give you something...s-so I could make up for getting us into this mess. She said you'd know what to do with it," Simon said in a frightened whisper, rummaging around in his pockets with trembling hands.

"Whoa—slow down. What are you talking about?" Penny stuttered.

From behind the crowd came the sound of brass instruments blaring fanfare. Out of the crowd, a tall man with a strip of gauzy cloth covering his right eye ascended the wooden platform and marched toward the center of it, waving as the crowd cheered. The man was dressed in finery and his long brown hair was pulled back into a bristled ponytail. Amongst the din of applause, Penny heard Simon give a terrified whimper and turned just in time to see his face drain of color.

"What's wrong?" she asked as Simon wobbled backward. Without attempting to answer her, he dashed away as fast as his legs could carry him.

"No, wait!" Penny rushed after him, making a desperate grab for his cape. Simon proved to be too quick and disappeared into the crowd.

The man on the platform was in the middle of announcing something to the crowd. "...and I promise each and every one of you the magic miners have been working grueling hours to find more resources. Word has been sent from His Majesty the King that we are to assemble—"

"Baron Deimos!" interrupted a voice from the crowd, and the man stopped speaking and turned toward the voice.

"Yes?" the man called Deimos replied in a silken tone.

"Please! Has there been any news about—about the wraiths?" the man yelped and a hush went through the crowd. Penny looked around, intrigued as she observed the disturbed looks on the faces around her. The team of men that comprised Deimos's guard muttered amongst each other and eyed the crowd. Penny looked his entourage over, and her heart skipped a beat.

Something was wrong with the man standing closest to Deimos. He wore a tattered hat with a green silk band over his messy mop of black hair, and his face was whiter than milk. One of his eyes was missing and in its stead was a deep, concave indent coated by metal and streamed with electric blue lines. This depression was covered by a thin sheath of glass fused into his skin. His remaining eye stood motionless, his face devoid of all life, and his right arm had been replaced with a steel, claw-like contraption. Penny felt a rather ominous throb in her chest that made her want to find Hector.

Deimos sighed and lowered his head. "I...do not wish to cause further alarm, but it seems we cannot keep this from the public any longer." He looked out at the crowd with the utmost seriousness. "The rumors are all true," he said, and a torrent of dread stirred itself into the mutterings and whispers.

"The number of wraith sightings has become more numerous than we could have ever anticipated. The claims can no longer be dismissed as rumors. We have begun to look into the incidents, though we can offer no definitive proof of a cause at this time. Please exercise the utmost caution when traveling in the hinterlands or close to any burial grounds. If you encounter a wraith, alert any town official immediately and we will call in the province's High Priestess to have it taken care of," Deimos instructed. "We are in constant communication with the capital on finding the source of the problem, so please be patient. In the meantime, please remember to keep all records of your Hidden Names well concealed and contained." Deimos broke off and his expression hardened; he looked as if he were having trouble speaking. "...And I must assure you that my brother is still properly detained and is in no way associated with the appearance of these wraiths."

"Of *course* not," a portly man near Penny breathed in a sarcastic sneer to a woman beside him. They exchanged dark looks.

"You really think it's his fault, don't you?" she asked in a hushed tone.

"How could it not be? The man's been convicted of using forbidden forms of Nomamancy before, hasn't he? He was the one who made a wraith out of the last baron some years back, remember? His own *father*, can you imagine? I heard he completely lost his mind because of it, too. They haven't got him in jail, no...He's locked up tight someplace *very* different. Or at least he *was*..."

"You can't think that he's escaped?" she whispered.

Penny was shaken from her eavesdropping with a start when a cold, wet nose suddenly pressed to her ear and sniffed. She yelped as she batted the nose away and turned around, finding herself face-to-face with a bizarre, yet charming, creature.

It had a dog-like snout, soulful brown eyes, a long, slender neck, and stubby horns that somewhat resembled a giraffe's. Its whole body was strong and muscular and covered in sleek, ebony fur that was silky to the touch. A saddle was hitched on its back. Penny marveled at it, and it stared right back at her, sniffing with curiosity.

"Things are going to be very difficult if you keep running off like this," said a familiar voice. Penny saw Hector standing next to the tall beast, holding its reins.

"What *is* that thing?" asked Penny as the creature whined, pushed its nose to the side of her face and tickled her into laughing aloud.

"Transportation," Hector told her, eyeing the beast with disdain.

"We get to *ride* on it?" Penny stroked its neck. The creature gave a contented groan. Penny broke away from this momentary distraction and turned to Hector. Hurriedly she told him about her encounter with Simon in the coffee shop and how he'd appeared again just moments ago.

"That's...odd. To say the least." Hector's expression was one of clouded wariness. "I daresay someone might be trying to target you in particular."

"Oh, you think?" Penny retorted and Hector frowned. "What gets me is it makes no sense, Profe—I mean, Hector. Why would someone go through all this trouble to attack me? Aside from the fact that I started producing all that magic, I'm nobody of any real importance."

"I haven't the foggiest, but if I were you, I'd stay away from that Simon fellow. It seems to me that following him would only lead to a trap. Come along, now." Hector gestured for her to follow and she did, the creature lolloping at her side.

The walk through town was a quick one; after only a few minutes they exited Dewthorne through the northern gate into the wilds. The long-necked creature galloped out and began snuffling at everything in the tall grass. Hector withdrew the map from his pocket and set about studying it.

"From the looks of this...and the signposts...it's going to be about a five-day journey to the next town," he said as Penny joined him and looked over the map rattling in the wind. "It's called Lindenvale. From there we can take a carriage into the capital, I believe."

Observing Hector trying to get control of the beast was a sight that reduced Penny to paroxysms of laughter. Hector was intimidated by its low growls every time he tried to get up on its back, and he had hold fast to the reins to keep it from bolting off. Once Hector's struggle to get up on the saddle was at last over, he helped Penny up behind him.

"Move, you blasted thing!" Hector shouted in frustration, tugging at its reins. The creature snorted and reared back. Penny grasped Hector around the waist as they took off at a mad gallop. The landscape jostled by as the creature's flat paws flew faster and faster through the yellow-green grass. Penny's breath came back to her after a few minutes and her grip on Hector loosened. They passed by an orchard, smelling the sweet fruit that had long since ripened. Lazy clouds wandered through the sky like huge white whales traversing the ocean. Brilliant firebursts of autumn leaves sailed through the air.

The ride through the grasslands continued for several hours. In the late afternoon they reached a seemingly endless field of lavender-colored blooms shaped like delicate bells. The beast was quite enjoying the romp, inhaling with loud snorts and then letting out a long, shuddering breath every so often.

"I wonder if they've realized we're missing yet," Penny shouted to Hector over the whistling of the wind. He seemed to think it over for a moment.

"Assuming that time follows the same flow as on Earth, it seems possible. It should be Sunday by now, so at least by tomorrow someone from the college will have noticed my unannounced absence. Will anyone have come looking for you by now?" Hector wondered.

"I don't think my mom has returned yet. She went to her mother's house for the weekend, so there's a good chance she's still there. Grandma, at least, will be pleased that I've gone missing. Maddie will probably just think I'm refusing to answer her calls 'cause we parted on iffy terms," Penny reasoned, feeling guilty and wondering if those were to be the last words shared between her and her closest friend. She thought hard, but could not remember if she'd even told her mother that she loved her before they parted. She touched the rune pendant that hung around her neck.

"What about your father?" Hector asked over the wind.

"I don't have one," she replied. "Well, I mean I *have* a father, I just never met him. He was some guy my mom met on her trip to Scotland—he ran off before I was born. It's why most of my family hates me; I'm their *shameful secret*," Penny said, and sighed. "I wasn't even supposed to be born, actually...my grandmother tried to convince my mother to...but Mom didn't have the heart to get rid of me, I guess. Oh God, why am I even telling you this?" Penny looked down at the pale purple flowers carpeting the meadow, feeling her face burn with humiliation.

Hector paused. "I'm sorry."

"Don't be—it's not like I care. How can I miss someone I never met, anyway? And the rest of my grandma's family combined hasn't got enough brains to fill half an eggcup, so why should I care what they think?" Penny said with a forced laugh, still aching with shame. *Stupid, stupid, stupid...*

Hector changed the subject to something less serious. Several hours later the sun began to sink and bathed the whole world in a golden-orange light. They stopped in the middle of a wide meadow and sat down under a tree laden with clusters of deep indigo blossoms. The fallen flowers created a blanket of radiant color underneath the ancient boughs and they both decided it would be a good place to spend the night. As Hector gathered up sticks for a fire, Penny roamed around the hills in search of a stream. The tall beast loped wearily beside her and she ran her hand across its soft fur.

"You'll need a name, I think," she said to the creature, as if it could understand her. The view was magnificent as she gazed out over the lost hills and spied a little creek. Penny stared into the creature's animated face. She dipped the basin she'd brought into the water and smiled as it came to her.

"You're to be called Humphrey from this moment on, is that clear?" she said to the beast in mock seriousness as she shouldered the heavy basin and made her way back to their camp under the tree, an obedient Humphrey following.

Hector and Penny set about roasting some vegetables they had bought from the market on sticks over the fire that Hector had little with a burst of magic. Jerky and bread completed their simple meal.

"Here you go, Humphrey." Penny scooped their dinner scraps onto the ground in front of the tall, happy beast and he greedily ate them up.

"Who is Humphrey, pray tell?" Hector asked with raised eyebrows. Penny was sure he already knew the answer, so she patted Humphrey with affection and tried to look aloof. Hector shook his head.

THE NEXT DAY they covered many miles and Penny observed the landscape getting greener and denser with trees.

They camped in a small, moss-blanketed glade. As evening fell, Hector produced large flares of energy from his hands, and when Penny asked him what he was doing, he acted shy.

"I'm practicing this spell. I realize that knowing no magic that could help in a life-threatening situation was a sore oversight on my part. We got very lucky last time—it might not happen again."

Penny watched with interest as he moved from energy fields to glowing discs of concentrated energy, noting that with each spell he conjured, her head grew dizzier. Humphrey watched the bursts of runes and light with his ears flat against his head, low growls rumbling in his chest. Seeing Hector's magic put Penny into a thoughtful mood.

"How come your world and Elydria have magic, but Earth doesn't?" she asked, staring into the campfire and furrowing her brow.

"Earth's got magic, too—something the inhabitants probably take for granted, I think," Hector said as he took a seat beside her.

"What do you mean?" she questioned, nonplussed, and Hector smiled.

"Dreams," he said and let her think about it for a moment. "Magic is expressed through dreams and the control over them in your world."

"What?" Penny wondered.

"It's true," Hector continued. "I was surprised at the concept of dreaming in the animals and people of Earth when I first came to Earth four years ago. I cannot dream, no one from my world is able to dream, and I doubt anyone in this world would be able to either."

"No way, that's impossible," Penny argued. "Isn't dreaming like…just a stress release mechanism or something? And how is it that people can't use dreams to perform all sorts of miracles or make things burst into flame or something?"

"They may *have* the ability, and the potential to develop it, but that sort of thing isn't considered credible in your world, therefore no one takes it seriously. Once something like that disappears from society, it becomes hard to replicate, much less master. Like a lost language. I've read books about the ancients of Earth manipulating the power of dreams, but it's classified as mere myth. You know, soothsayers, telekinesis, empaths, those who can communicate with the dead…I'm sure there are people to whom this power comes naturally, but they are dismissed as insane or fraudulent. Or perhaps they simply choose to walk among the world of dreams and don't care to return to the waking world. That's just my theory, anyway—take it with a grain of salt," Hector concluded with a shrug.

"Interesting…and you can feel the energy coming from us?"

"Precisely. When you dream, your aura gets replenished. But just as I expend the energy when I perform enchantments, people from Earth should theoretically should be able to harness the ability of raw dream material and use it however they'd like," Hector explained.

"So maybe even I could have the ability to weave dreams?" Penny smiled at him. He grinned at her little quip and nodded. Penny marveled at this concept for the remainder of the night. Lying beneath the canopy of whispering leaves, her eyes grew heavy and she fell asleep with a faint smile on her lips, hoping a dream would come to her.

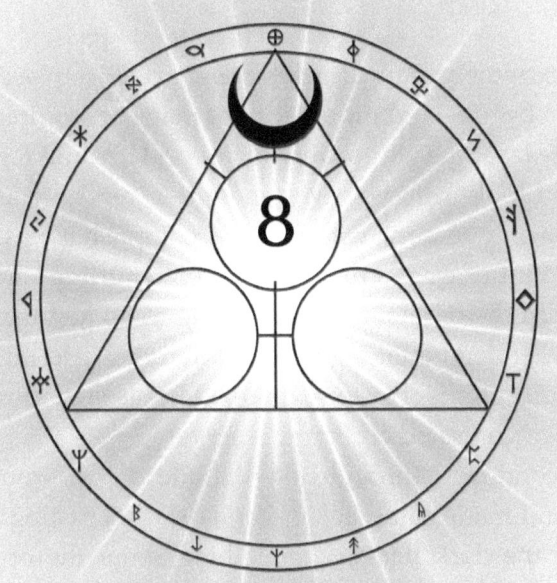

SPECTERS IN THE THICKET

Penny awoke to a sky of opaline white. The effects of sleeping outdoors, with only a few thin blankets for comfort and warmth, were catching up with her. A penetrating chill blew as Penny and Hector ate their meager breakfast and gathered up their things in a daze.

As the day wore on the wind picked up and the trees around them grew thicker and taller. Humphrey romped through the huge piles of leaves that littered the forest floor, and Penny and Hector spoke in soft mutters. Something about the quiet of the forest inspired a hushed tone.

"This place gives me the creeps. Why don't we just *teleport* like you did when we were stuck in the blizzard? Wouldn't that save a lot of time and energy?" Penny murmured to Hector, staring up at the high boughs. The canopy sent a shower of leaves down at a steady rate. "Come to think of it, why didn't you just teleport us away that night at your house?"

"It's extremely dangerous to teleport to a place you've never been before—and the amount of magic it requires is staggering. The last time we got very lucky, and if you'll remember, the magic I took from you was enough to render you unconscious. The only reason I was able to accomplish it was because of the amount of excess magic you were emitting—and as for that night in the basement, I was trying to do just that, but in my panic, I ended up taking us to a different world rather than a different location," Hector explained in his signature lecturing tone, which grated on Penny's nerves.

They continued through the solitude of the woods until nightfall and made camp again. Penny started casting nervous glances at the dark thickets; something about the oppressive hush of the whispering shower of leaves discomfited her. It wasn't at all alleviated by the fact that the nearby white-barked trees grew in such a way that they created the illusion of having eyes. She circled their camp and kicked at the dead leaves, trying to understand what was making her chest feel so tight.

Seeing the tangles and tendrils made her neck prickle and Penny tried to remember the words to a poem she'd read a long time ago. After standing for a while with the withered leaves around her ankles, the words sprang to her lips like a chant. *"Come away, O human child! To the waters and the wild... with Faery hand in hand...for the world's more full of weeping than you can understand."*

Hector stopped what he was doing and looked over at Penny. He smiled with a liveliness and earnest emotion that was rare. "That's—*The Stolen Child*. Yeats, if I'm not mistaken?" His eyes were bright.

Penny smiled a little and nodded. "I guess. I forgot the title," she shrugged.

"It's a lovely poem. The people of Earth truly have a way with words," Hector told her, then paused as if deciding whether or not to say something. He cleared his throat.

"I — I've always wanted to say…you impress me. You were always quiet in class, but the papers you wrote—they were quite insightful," he complimented. Penny blushed and turned her face toward the ground so he wouldn't see.

"Thanks for saying so." Penny couldn't stop herself from smiling. "I'm nothing special, though. People are always telling me I'm smart, but really my only real talent is following directions well. That and having no distractions—and by that I mean no friends." She shrugged and sat down across from him. "I shouldn't say that. I've got Maddie."

"Madeline Price? You mean that *loquacious* young lady who's constantly typing on her phone throughout my lectures?" Hector raised an eyebrow.

"Yeah, that's her." Penny smirked a little. "She's… not exactly the studious type," she offered as a half-excuse.

"So I've gleaned. It seems she's deliberately failed to complete several important assignments," Hector said with disdain.

"Maybe it's because you expect way too much from us," Penny combated. "Every other day it's another paper or six million pages to read. *I* can barely complete the work!"

Hector looked ruffled and smoothed his vest. "Oh, come now. That is the customary amount of work in Nelvirnee academies, I don't' see why the citizens of Twin Rivers should be given special treatment," he rebutted with self-conscious affront.

"Well, maybe on planet Arlington you can get away with that sort of slave-driving, but on Earth it's a different story," Penny admonished, still feeling defensive of her friend. "People can't deal with all that busy work. It's why half the class hates you—" she stopped and slapped her hand over her mouth, mortified. "Ah, I didn't mean that! I meant to say—"

It was too late. Hector's face grew stony and he stared into the flames with his fingers laced together. She could tell that she had touched a nerve.

"Hector, I'm sorry," she tried, "I—"

"You don't have to apologize, Miss Fairfax." His face remained expressionless. "I'm well aware of the opinions my pupils have of me. It's always been the same, regardless of whether I was home, or on Earth. I never seemed to acclimate well to the world of education—or to any other world, for that matter," he added.

Penny sat very still, trying to think of something to say. In the moments that followed, a strange emotion began to invade her mood. "If—if it means anything," she murmured in earnest, "I think you're a great teacher, despite all that."

She saw his eyelids flutter in her direction for a quick moment, then flit back down again. The majority of dinner passed in heavy silence and bedtime came quick. The emotion that Penny noticed earlier stayed with her deep into the night. Hours later, after Hector had fallen into a shallow slumber, she gazed over at him with worry swimming in her chest.

He always tended to seem out of place to her, like a traveler without a road to follow, or an empty bottle lost at sea. Penny found herself wondering what sort of life he must have led up until now, but felt as if she were intruding on his privacy by her mere speculation alone. As she rolled over onto her back and tried to get comfortable enough to relax, she understood the powerful emotion that had overtaken her. She felt sorry for him.

HECTOR REGAINED HIS brisk disposition by morning. Humphrey kept stopping to sniff the dried leaves and Penny and Hector had to strain together to get him to keep moving. Soon the path through the woods became obscured and they were faced with traipsing through the heavy underbrush. Penny was sure they were lost, but Hector dismissed the idea every time she brought it up. There were a few

instances where they happened across a number of uniden-
tifiable insects that sent chills up Penny's spine. Sometime in
the middle of the afternoon a deafening crash of thunder split
the air. Penny jumped and shrieked.

Hector looked back in shock. "What's the matter?" he
asked, concerned.

"N-nothing! Come on, daylight's wasting," Penny grumbled as she pushed past Hector. Minutes later it began to drizzle and soon the air around the forest was sparkling with rain.
Creatures could be seen scampering around trying to find shelter. Small furry rodents with bat-like ears and huge almond-
shaped eyes hopped about in the lofty treetops, and Humphrey
snapped at their bushy tails as they flitted about.

With every booming peal of thunder, Penny's body reacted
with an uncontrollable tremor of surprise. After several hours
of enduring the sudden flashes of light and sound that sent
spikes of fear into her heart, she was trembling all over. She did
not want Hector to know she was frightened of the thunder,
even though she was certain he had already noticed.

By evening, Penny was soaked and miserable. She shivered
from the biting air and waves of acute nervousness. Her throat
itched and burned as she sat down on a wet tree stump.

"Brace yourself, please," Hector said to Penny and she
straightened up in confusion.

An alarming amount of strength left her body in a rush,
and stars burst in her eyes as she almost fainted. Hector's hand
appeared on her back, prompting her to sit up.

"Sorry! It took a little more magic than I expected," Hector
apologized.

Blinking herself back into consciousness, Penny realized
that the rain had stopped falling on them. Hector had created
a huge invisible umbrella several feet above them. Rippling
walls of water flowed down like curtains of silk.

Penny was delighted. "Now we won't have to sleep in
the rain!"

Hector grinned and set about lighting a fire. In no time their tiny camp was drier, and they enjoyed a humble meal of grilled mushrooms and bread. After dinner, Hector resumed studying the map. Penny lay on her back and marveled at the glassy dome above, thinking once again of how much it would please her mother to see real magic.

"I can't wait to get home and tell Mom all about this," Penny yearned. "I'll bet you're also ready to go back home to Nel-whatsa, or whatever it's called."

"To Nelvirna? Not particularly, no. And even if I *could* go back, there's nothing there anymore," he muttered.

"What?" Penny sat up in surprise. "Nothing there?"

Hector looked up at her through the darkness, his face orange from the glow of the fire. Penny noticed for the first time that his eyes were a beautiful shade of hazel and looked away.

"The day I left my world," he said, struggling as if trying to think of the best way to start, "was the day Nelvirna was destroyed. It was something like a divine cataclysm."

"What happened?" Penny gasped. Hector shrugged a little and his expression turned muddled. He looked almost guilty as he considered his words.

"Well...It's all very foggy...I-I can't clearly recall much of what happened. The sky changed—as if great sections of it had been stained black with ink, and there were these...awful flashes of light. They burned away everything. All at once, everything came crumbling to the ground in whirlwinds of fire and smoke. I still don't know why it happened—all I know is that I escaped at precisely the right moment...quite like how it happened for us when we came to this world. One moment I was standing in my home watching the buildings and towers turning to dust, and I somehow slipped through that void and onto Earth." Hector waved off his serious mood. "Anyway, it's not important now. Even if I found a way to return to Nelvirna, I'm sure all I would find there are ruins..."

"So your home is—it's gone? Along with everyone you knew?" Penny breathed, even though she already had heard the answer. Hector flinched ever so slightly, then nodded, looking hollow. She couldn't think of any words of comfort that would help ease that sort of pain.

"It's all in the past. I've lived on Earth for four years now. Teaching there isn't much different than teaching in Nelvirna. It's a mite easier, in fact." His smile was almost imperceptible.

Penny remembered something. "Hey, that reminds me. Just how *did* you become a teacher on Earth, anyway? You couldn't have possibly gone to any college or gotten the credentials, in addition to a job, in such a short time, much less know the material well enough to teach it."

Hector smirked and cleared his throat. "It is surprising how efficient the application of a little practical magic can be. I can produce any legal paper or certification anyone might ever ask for with the careful use of mimicking enchantments. That, coupled with a considerable amount of reading, and you become one convincing imposter. I had to read the contents of several libraries and enchant my way into a few computer systems, but in the end I'd say I was successful." Hector looked a bit proud of himself and Penny's jaw dropped.

"You're a fake?!"

"Not *exactly*. I was a certified magical theory instructor back in Nelvirna and I have had proper training, but if you want to get into technicalities, I'm not *quite* as qualified as my diplomas might claim that I am. However, as you probably know litera-ture is a—a very *free-form* subject, and that is precisely why I chose it. Surprised?" He raised a brow.

"I have to say I am! I feel a lit—"

A blinding flash illuminated the night and the roar of thun-der exploded out. Penny screamed and leapt to her feet, her heart pounding so fast she heard a rushing in her ears.

Hector opened his mouth to speak but Penny anticipated him. "I'm fine!" she lied. She felt anything but fine, but she had no desire to discuss it.

Hector eyed her with confusion. "Look here, if it's frightening you, I can ju—"

"I said I'm *fine*," Penny snapped, and then regretted her outburst. Hector clicked his tongue and defeated shrugged in defeat.

"Have it your way," he conceded and moved over to his makeshift bed. Penny sat stewing in her anxiety for a while, then decided she had better do the same. For hours she stayed awake, shutting her eyes and whimpering as each crash of thunder and lightning pierced the woods. Nightmarish images from her past tried to flare up, but Penny held them at a distance with enormous effort.

It won't happen, again…It won't happen again…You're fine… it's only a sound…It's not going to happen again… Penny wanted to cry again, but once more she banished her tears and tried to tell herself to be brave. Feeling vulnerable, she reached over and found the cooking knife that Hector had bought at the market and brought it close. Somehow laying there with it clutched to her chest was enough to make her relax.

Defeated by her exhaustion, Penny fell into a troubled sleep. The haunting memories from her early childhood, resurrected by the voice of thunderclaps, seeped their malicious way into her dreams…

Penny lay snug in her blankets. The night was a warm one, and the rain that fell was humid, creating a humming static. Penny had heard thunder before and had always been enthralled by it. Through that entire stormy day, she had been seen scampering to the window every time the lightning flashed and breathlessly counted the seconds with her mother close by. When night fell, however, something about the thunder changed. It had been a deafening peal that roused Penny from her slumber that night. She teetered between the thin boundary of sleep and the waking world for some time until a sharp

*instinct shook sleepiness clean away. She sensed that she was no
longer alone.*

*Penny sat up in bed, her eyes glassy and her breath uneven. She
looked about her room for the intruder, but the darkness was too thick.
She wanted so much to call out for her mother, but even with her
child's mind she knew that whatever dark thing sidled among the
shadows would get her anyway.*

"W-Who's there?" Her voice was difficult to hear over the
sound of the rain pounding on the roof. Then came the flash
and with it the face that she would never forget.

She saw him for an instant: sublime, tall, and with a striking face that was so inhumanly beautiful it drove terror into
her heart. His hair was white and draped down the sides of
his body like waterfalls of diamond filament. Then the darkness came again.

Penny scrambled backward until her shoulders collided
with the wall. She tried to scream, but could not manage to
make a sound. He was coming closer.

"N-no!" she choked in a strangled plea. The thunder
crashed, reverberating about the room and rumbling in her
chest. Penny felt his fingers wrapping around her shoulders
and pulling her forward. The lightning came again.

The face, so abominable in its exquisiteness, was mere
inches from hers. His eyes were like two great white moons
stained with small beads of black that pierced straight through
her. As his hand scooped her away, the last thing she saw was
a flurry of feathers. Then there was only darkness.

Penny jerked awake with a gasp, then sunk her face into
her hands and gave a great sigh, trying to rid her body of the
last vapors of the nightmare. The memory of the most terrifying night of her childhood was still too fresh in her mind,
even though it had happened over a decade ago. The rain had
stopped falling while she slept and left the forest glittering
with crystalline beads of moisture.

Penny glanced over at Hector to see that he was still curled up in blissful sleep. Penny was about to lay her head back down when something moving about in the trees caught her eye. In a surreal moment, a soft glow fluttered out of the ferns and branches, and a human figured emerged into the clearing, radiating an unearthly light. Penny recognized the face of the person and clapped her hands over her mouth.

"*Mom?*" Penny gasped, springing to her feet. Several feet away stood Paulina Fairfax, pale gray in the light of the moon. She was wearing the same set of clothes Penny had last seen her in. Penny began to rush toward her and stopped, digging her heels in the rain-softened soil. Something was not right.

Before Penny could get a closer look, Paulina fled into the forest, a look of supreme fright on her face. Still holding the knife, Penny gritted her teeth. She couldn't let this chance go by.

She dove into the brush and pursued her mother, all the while calling for her to stop. Penny could sense the danger, but she could not let her mother disappear without at least speaking to her. Deeper and deeper into the trees she went until she burst out of the overgrowth into a small clearing with just enough space between the trunks to move about.

There in the center of the clearing stood an expectant Paulina smiling at Penny. Stepping forward, Penny observed it wasn't just the moonlight that had blanched her mother's skin and hair. Paulina's body had taken on a lustrous white coloring. Penny's stance turned defensive, her stomach feeling like she'd just missed a step on the way down a flight of stairs.

"Mom! Answer me! How did you get here? Why do you look so...weird...?" Penny whispered.

Paulina smiled again and held her arms open to Penny.

They stood frozen in their respective places, Penny not daring to break the eerie gaze her mother beamed in her direction. The look was enough to convince her that the specter was not her mother.

Turning to flee, Penny discovered with heart-wrenching terror that her foot was stuck fast to the ground. She cried out, realizing that a writhing bundle of snake-like vines had wrapped
their way around her ankles. Sharp thorns dug into her legs.

Penny struggled and the vines squeezed tighter, traveling
up her legs until they bound them together. Like dispersing
mist, the shade of her mother melted into a ball of light that
she now realized was attached to a vine. The vine had been
laced through the tree tops the whole time. Her eyes followed
the tendrils in a blind panic and with a sick realization she saw
it connected to a massive rose rooted some fifteen feet beyond
the clearing, with acid pink petals and several long, needle-like
protrusions emerging from the leaves below the bloom.

The vines that held to her legs yanked her to the ground,
throwing her turbulently side to side as Penny wielded the
knife, aiming for the tendrils. In a sudden surge, one of the
thorns shot out from the bloom and pierced into Penny's
shoulder. A blinding flash of pain ripped through her and
Penny howled, the knife slipping from her fingers in her
moment of weakness.

The thorns tore into her legs, leaving trails of blood that
shone black in the murky light. Something hot burned deep
inside her shoulder, seeping outward from the thorn. Summoning all her courage, Penny wrenched the thorn out from
her shoulder and tossed it away with a shout. The vines were
now halfway around her midsection.

I won't die here! Not like this! she told herself, fighting back the
urge to give into her fear. With one final burst of energy, Penny
flung her body backward and grasped at the knife that lay just a
few feet away in the grass. Her fingers grazed the blade and she
managed to take hold of it with a surge of fiery hope.

Penny slashed through vine after vine in a desperate
frenzy. Though she cut into her legs several times in her violent movements, her terror eclipsed the pain. Another thorn
shot out from the plant and landed with a thud in the grass

and just missed her abdomen. Struggling back up on her feet Penny fled, urging her feet to move faster as she heard the sounds of slithering vines follow.

Passing the clearing, Penny slowed her pace and staggered forward. Each gasp of air came with a jab of white-hot pain. The way ahead was obscured and it felt impossible to remember which path she had taken, but knowing that Hector could not be too far off kept her from sinking to her knees in exhaustion and despair. It seemed like an eternity of groping her way through the darkness until she recognized a pinpoint of light she knew was their campfire. Penny's heart ached with relief and she tumbled, gasping for air, through the shrubs and toward the camp. Stumbling to Hector's side, Penny collapsed in complete expenditure.

A drowsy Hector sat up, blinking. Catching sight of her, he gave a surprised cry and fumbled about for his glasses. "Penelope, what happened?" he gasped, still only half-awake.

Penny found she could only produce a weak moan. The light was fading fast. Hector pushed his glasses onto his face and gave a strangled shout. He lifted her off the ground and held her by the shoulders, his face aghast at the sight of her wounds. Penny let her head slump forward onto Hector's chest and the world melted away into oblivion.

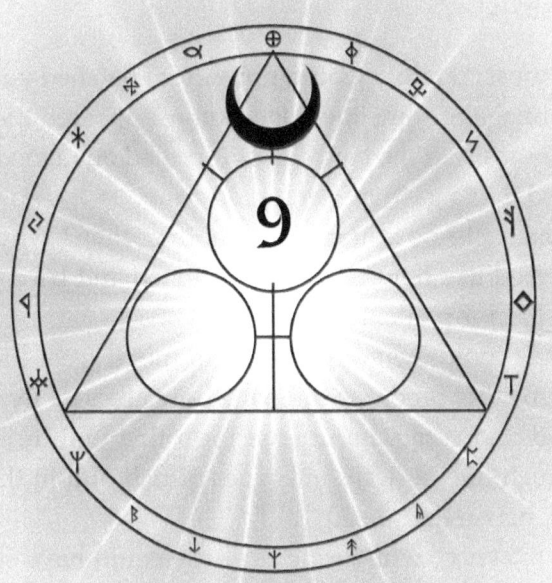

THE HIGH PRIESTESS

Penny's waking instinct was to sit up, but having forgotten the events of the previous night she was thrown back by a shock of pain. Hector came into view as Penny moaned.

"Penelope! You're alive—I-I mean awake!" Hector sputtered, looking her over with apparent dread.

"Wh-what happened?" Penny groaned, propping herself up on an elbow and looking her body over. One shoulder was buried in bandages and a dark, reddish-brown stain soaked through. Her legs and abdomen were covered in smaller bandages.

"I was hoping you could tell me!" Hector replied with evident concern. Penny eased down onto her back, and told him in a weak voice about the encounter with the ghost-like image of her mother.

"You're lucky to be alive. I don't know what you were thinking…" Hector scolded her and Penny scowled.

"If you saw someone you knew running off into the forest, wouldn't *you* follow them?!" she growled.

"No, I most certainly would not. After I patched you up last night, the image of someone I once knew appeared there too. I successfully resisted the bait." Hector pulled out a medicine jar and applied it to a gash on her leg. It stung.

"It came back? So you saw my mother, then? Why do you think it looked like her?" Penny questioned and tried to sit up again, but Hector pushed her back down.

"It didn't look like your mother to me. It was... someone else. It seems this predator can somehow access a living creature's mind and conjure a unique form that will lure it to its demise, much like how certain types of fish pull in their prey with the lights on their head."

Penny frowned, wondering how she could have stumbled into such an easy trap. "Who did it look like, anyway? That cute science teacher in the classroom beside yours?" she teased, wincing as Hector applied more of the medicinal balm.

"No," he snapped. "It was someone you've never met. Someone whom I know to be dead—that's how I knew it couldn't have really been..." he left off, his face betraying guilt. "It's beside the matter. How are you feeling?"

"I've been cut to shreds! How do you think I'm feeling?" Penny spat, and Hector gave her an annoyed look. "I'm a little woozy, too. I think that thorn had some sort of poison in it."

"Let me take a look," he said and unraveled the bandages on her shoulder. When the last strip of gauze had been removed, they both gasped. The wound had turned an unpleasant purple color and the veins around the area were swollen and dark. Penny tried to calm herself but found it quite difficult to do.

"Wh-what's—what's all that?" she stammered, working herself into a panic with little effort. Hector looked both repulsed and frightened as he examined it. He shook his head with an ominous expression, his face very white.

"We've got to get you to town. There must be some sort of doctor who can do *something*..." Hector whispered.

"It's that bad?" Penny choked. Hector looked uneasy as he tried to cook up a lie. A spiral of fear whirled through her. "I'm not gonna die, right? *Right, Hector?*"

Hector made a horrible attempt at a smile and shook his head. "You're going to be fine. We just need to hurry…"

Penny started taking quick, sharp breaths and clutched herself. *I don't want to die, I don't want to die…oh please, let it be a dream, oh please let me—*

Hector eyed her reaction with strained worry. "Maybe you'd better sleep," he suggested, then raised his hand, his index and middle finger extended. He put them gently to her forehead, and Penny tried to bat his hand away.

"No! Don't you dare, you stop right there Hector—"

A glowing ring of silvery runes bloomed from his fingers and touched her forehead, and sleep crashed over her.

VISIONS OF REALITY came in brief flashes. Her mind fluttered back and forth between foggy consciousness and absolute darkness. Penny could feel the jostle of riding on Humphrey's back, but could not quite break through the veil that seemed to cut her off from waking. After what seemed like mere minutes of dazed sleep, Penny felt herself lying against something rough and hard as water was poured into her mouth. She opened her eyes for an instant and could see a fuzzy sky filled with stars, and then became lost again in the softness of sleep.

The heartbeats of consciousness came and went six or seven times before she woke again, this time to the sight of a plain white ceiling. The room was dim, but a gentle breeze wafted in. Penny sighed with relief to think that walls were around her again, shielding her from the perils of the wilderness. She tried to move and felt blankets enveloping her aching limbs, and the pain flared up again. The gashes and wounds that spotted her legs seemed to have healed, but deep within her ribs there remained a terrible burning. It felt as if someone had sewn a hot stone inside her body, which continued to grow heavier by the moment. Soreness gripped her every muscle and her head pounded.

Penny tried to call out for someone, but managed only a groan. Her tongue was dry and puffy, and seemed to be blocking her throat. She heard someone moving across the room. Hector came into view through the hazy blue light and sat down at her bedside.

"Penelope?" he murmured, brushing Penny's bangs away from her eyes. Penny shut her eyes again and gave a shallow nod to show she had heard him. The sounds of early evening drifted in through the open window.

"Where are we?" she croaked, keeping her eyes closed tight. Even the meek light that shone from the twin moons of the Elydrian sky was enough to make Penny's eyes sting.

"I'm not entirely sure what to call it. Some sort of shrine, church, or temple. We've only just arrived, though. They should be with us shortly...or at least that's what they said about half an hour ago." He waited a few more minutes and then stepped out of the tiny infirmary, assuring Penny he would return with help.

The door creaked back open, and in shot a shaft of light, searing her aching head. She pulled the blankets up around her face to block the light and heard Hector talking with someone.

"Well, let's have a look-see," an optimistic voice said. The blankets were peeled away from Penny's face and a set of earnest, sea-green eyes peered at her in timid curiosity.

A girl who looked not a day over twenty smiled down at Penny. She had waves upon waves of honey-colored hair that flowed down her shoulders and back. Her face was oval-shaped and pleasant. A strange white bonnet adorned her head, from which hung two golden bells on either side. The girl wore a modest white and blue robe that matched her peculiar headdress.

"How are you feeling, my sister?" the young woman inquired. "I hear from your friend that you had quite the encounter in the Tarni woods."

Penny grunted in affirmation. The young woman faltered, and then continued on, "I am a Junior High Priestess and the resident alchemist of this sanctuary. You may call me Armonie, if you wish. Now, what is the nature of your displeasure, sister?"

"I feel like I'm dying. Everything hurts, I can barely move..." Penny croaked, unwilling to go into detail. Armonie blinked and looked over at Hector, nonplussed. Hector recounted the tale of Penny's run in with the monstrous plant in as much detail as he could. Armonie's face grew more and more somber as the story went on. The young priestess thought for a minute after Hector had fallen silent.

"Hm. Thank you for your help, big brother," she nodded at last to Hector. Penny did not care to lift her head to see what Armonie was up to, and was startled when she felt a dart-like pinch on her arm. Armonie gave an apologetic bow of her head as she lifted up a vial filled with blood. After bandaging Penny's arm, she bobbed over to the corner of the room, where the tinkling of glass vials and the heavy, rhythmic grind of a mortar and pestle could be heard.

"Oh, dear..." Armonie whispered after what seemed like a very long time. "I had better take these results to Madam Priestess at once. Please pardon me, friends. I won't be long." She fluttered through the door, her skirts rustling as she went. Penny looked at Hector with buzzing anxiety.

Minutes later the door reopened and a tall, graceful woman entered. Glossy, dark brown hair had been arranged in two loops around her ears. The woman wore the same sort of robe and bonnet as Armonie, only there were no bells that jingled as she went along. She was quite a bit older than Hector, but retained the radiance of youth. She took a seat beside Penny's bed and looked at her with great compassion. Penny realized she had been holding her breath since the tall woman had floated in and let it out.

"Good evening, my child." The woman's voice was deep and dulcet. Sadness hung in her gray eyes in a way that frightened Penny. The High Priestess turned back to the doorway to where Armonie was entering. "Would you mix a tincture of quillow bark potion for her, Armonie?"

"Yes, Madam Priestess," Armonie complied, bowing.

"Please, if you don't mind, can you…" Hector implored, wringing his hands together. The priestess turned to face Hector and put her delicate, light brown hand on top of his. He flinched a little at her touch.

"What name may I call you, brother?" she asked.

"Um…H-Hector Arlington is my name, but what—"

"Mister Arlington, I'm afraid that I have unfortunate news," she admitted.

Before Penny had time to feel another surge of fear, she felt ceramic touch her lips as Armonie poured a bitter potion into Penny's mouth. She swallowed, feeling a thick drowsiness come over her as some of the biting pain eased.

"What do you mean…?" Hector choked.

"We've found the seeds of the vententula plant in your friend's blood. The seeds use the flesh of living organisms for nourishment until they can sprout and grow into a mature plant," the High Priestess said.

This information sent Penny into a nauseating whirl. It didn't seem real to her at the moment, but somewhere beyond the amplifying, drug-induced haze of serenity, a chasm of terror had cracked open in her heart.

"*What?*" Hector took a sharp intake of breath, withdrawing his hand and clutching his chest. "You can't be—"

"I'm terribly sorry, but there is no cure for this condition. She won't have very long. The medicine Armonie gave her will help her pass into the Dawn Mirror without pain or fear. All you can do is stay by her side and comfort her, and if we can—"

"NO! I refuse to accept this. Please—there's got to be something I can do." Hector stood up, startling both Armonie and the High Priestess. His chest was heaving with emotion as he looked down at Penny. The whole scene felt distant to her, as if she was watching it on a movie screen at the end of a very long, dark hall. She could feel the rumbling of thoughts and frantic longings bubbling below the surface of clarity, but could not access them.

"Big brother, please try to stay calm." Armonie hastened to his side and tried to help him sit back down, but he jerked his arm from her grasp.

"I will not let this happen. You don't understand. She cannot die—I promised her that I would get her home."

The priestess drew a breath as if to speak, but Hector held up his hand to stop her. He glanced back down at Penny as if to make certain she was asleep. "I beg of you, is there nothing I can do?" Hector lowered his voice so that Penny could barely hear what it was he was saying. "This is my fault... she trusted me to take care of her...Madam, I—I've made so many mistakes in the past, Madam. Every day I regret I couldn't...I simply cannot allow this. I—I'd never recover. Please. *Help her.*"

The priestess faltered for one moment and looked at her shoes, her eyes bearing the weight of a difficult decision. She opened her mouth to speak, but Armonie stopped her, the young woman's eyes wide.

"Madam Priestess, you mustn't! What if you someone from the Cathedral gets wind?"

"Armonie, please hold your tongue. I am well aware of the consequences." The priestess shot her a look and Armonie fell quiet.

"What are you talking about? Please, Madam," Hector begged. The High Priestess hung her head. When she spoke it was in little more than a whisper, as if she were afraid of someone overhearing.

"Are you willing to risk your life for this girl?" she breathed to Hector, her clear eyes full of defiance. Armonie put her hands over her mouth and sat down hard. Hector nodded without hesitation.

"If you are fully ready to undertake a very dangerous task, then I will break a rule to save your friend."

"Madam, please! I want to help these people as well, but I—" Armonie interjected.

"Armonie, is it not the law of our Angelic Lord Nestor that we are to preserve life whenever possible? Would this child's blood not be on my hands if I were to let her die? Now please, her time is dwindling. Allow me to assist them unhindered, dear one." She turned from Armonie back to Hector. She lifted a pendant from around her neck and placed it into Hector's hands.

"One of my duties as a High Priestess is to guard the secrets and precious resources of my province. This pendant will allow you access to certain areas—secret places. Do you understand the seriousness of what it is I am doing?" Her gaze bore through him. Hector nodded again.

"Good. Long ago in this area lived an elf called Warwick. In his exploration of these lands, he came across a cavern in the woods. Inside it was a miraculous spring that could heal even the gravest of injuries. He chose to exploit it, selling the spring's water for profit. When the source of this miracle was discovered, the cavern was sealed off and the spring's water fell under control of the Order of Nestor. Now, as you probably already know, magical resources have been strictly rationed ever since the unfortunate shortage. Usage of this spring is very carefully moderated...however, tonight I'll make an exception," she whispered.

"To find the grotto you must pass through Lindenvale Cemetery, and I'm sure you know of the dangers that you may encounter in such a place," she added, giving him a meaningful look. Hector blinked a few times and shook his head no, which seemed to shock the priestess. "Why, you've not heard of the wraith sightings? I was quite sure that everyone must have become aware of the recent threat."

"I'm so sorry Madam, but we are strangers in this land. What exactly do you mean by wraith?" Hector inquired. He shot worried glances over at Penny to make sure she was still breathing. She felt miles away, watching the gravest of expressions come over the priestess's face.

"This is not the time to explain. Just please understand that you must proceed into that area with the utmost caution. If you see a wraith, you will have to defend yourself, do you understand?" the priestess warned.

"Y-yes—but how will I know one if I come across one?" Hector stuttered.

"You'll know," Armonie said in a hollow tone from the corner of the room. There was an oppressive silence for a moment, then the priestess proceeded to give a hurried set of directions to Hector. Penny could only make out her final words.

"You must go now. Take this poor child with you. She will need to be completely submerged to ensure that she is rid of all the seeds. You won't have long—she'll be gone before dawn breaks."

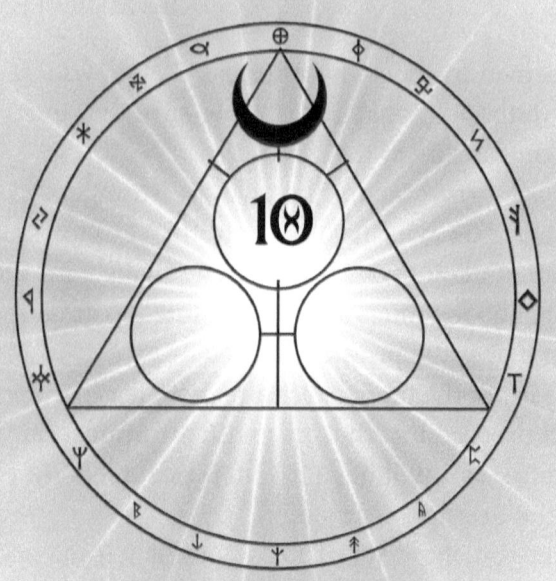

WARWICK'S GROTTO

Penny felt the bounce of Hector's step and heard the sound of his feet cutting through mounds of dead leaves, but the world in her eyes had become a mere pinhole in a heavy black sheet. She felt compressed, as if everything that she had ever been was being packed down into a tiny jar and forgotten.

Hector had enchanted himself before he set out so that he could be strong enough to carry her on his back, yet his breathing was harsh and his demeanor harried. With each jarring step he took, a little more life drained from Penny's limp body. Minutes slipped by all too quick. Time didn't seem so expendable a commodity when there wasn't enough of it left.

They passed under the iron gate and into the cemetery, the effect of the medicine Penny had taken fading. She could not stop herself from wondering how exactly the parasitic seeds in her blood were going about killing her, and the wondering made her sick with fear. Hector must have heard her soft whimpers, because he used what little energy he had to distract her.

"Don't worry. We're nearly there already. Think about something else, all right? Talk to me," Hector instructed as he took the first steps past the gnarled and weather-beaten gravestones, all carved in unfamiliar shapes. Their glassy black marble surfaces reflected the moonlight. The names of those long deceased were etched into the stones in spindly Elydrian script. Penny's eyes passed over each of them with a heavy heart.

"Penelope, talk to me!" Hector shouted at her, interrupting her morbid brooding.

"About what?" Her voice was weak and slurred to her own ears, and she shut her eyes.

"I don't know. Anything. Tell me about—a fond memory, how about that?" he said, and Penny shuffled through the memories of her life. Images of days gone by appeared to her like embers in a darkening hearth.

"There was this one afternoon my mom took me to a lake in the woods. I was—maybe eight years old, I think. I wore a little white dress with blue flowers on it and it made me feel so pretty. I remember we got there in the late afternoon—just when the sky gets that yellow tinge, you know? We ran along the shore and ate sandwiches. It was so warm and the lake reflected the sky like a mirror. No one else was there but us, and it felt like we were the only two people left in the whole world." Penny could see the day in her imagination like a dusty photograph. She could envision her lacy white dress and the ghost of her smiles.

Hector either didn't or couldn't respond and stopped moving. When a few long moments had gone by, Penny opened her eyelids a bit.

"Look," he breathed, gesturing with his head to the sky. Amid the swirling clouds of mist there floated a cluster of transparent, glowing entities. They reminded Penny of the deep sea creatures that bobbed with the currents of the ocean, sightless and delicate. The apparitions moved as if underwater, pulsing with a gentle incandescent light, wandering through the air without an obvious destination. Their frilled appendages fluttered, each one unique.

"What are they?" Penny whispered.

Hector shook his head and began walking again at a faster pace, still looking up in reverie toward the entities. After a few minutes of moving along through the clusters of dead leaves, a great twisted tree trunk loomed out of the mists. More of the ethereal creatures danced and weaved among the crooked branches like a string of lights hung on a Christmas tree. Grass swept high and wild around the gnarled trunk, obscuring the area. Hector laid Penny down with her back to the tree and tromped through the dry grass. Penny's eyes remained fixed on the sky, and she decided that whatever the beings above her were, they weren't dangerous. They seemed almost sad or lost. She took several deep, sharp breaths as a sudden and cruel wave of pain tore through her.

"I found it!" Hector cried from somewhere behind her. He emerged from the tall grass and proceeded to help Penny crawl through the overgrowth until they reached a tiny opening in a metal fence that bordered the graveyard. Hector forced Penny through, each movement digging into her like a hot knife. With effort, they emerged out the other side on a small path bordered by trees. A line of chalk-like powder was laid on either side of the road.

Hector picked Penny back up and hurried along. The opening of a cave sealed by a set of stone doors became visible through the gloom of the tree-lined path.

"Look, we've made it! You're going to be okay!" Hector shouted, sounding as relieved as if it were his own life that was about to be saved instead of hers. Penny could not muster enough energy to reply, the crawl through the fence having all but finished her off. The hot pain in her chest was growing unbearable, and her heart was skipping beats.

The doors opened with a grinding rumble the moment Hector pushed the pendant into the depression. When they stopped their trundling movement, all that was left was a vacuum of silence and the cold air that sighed out of the gaping throat of the cave, coaxing them as they twisted down into the cavern.

In the darkness, Penny could see luminous crystal formations growing from the ceiling and the sides of the wall. The tunnel seemed to be made of a sparkling mineral that glittered like thousands of miniature constellations. Another short turn through the tunnel and they came to the spring itself. The water was eerily placid and smaller than a pond, but it sunk deep and black. A few bits of old furniture were piled up in the corner, some covered with filthy sheets.

"We made it! Penelope, look!" Hector cried, scraping across the smooth stone and putting Penny down near the edge of the pool. It felt impossible to keep breathing; even the shallowest of breaths brought a jolt of agonizing pain. She was overpowered by weariness as Hector tried to shake her awake, and could not find the strength to move. In the furthest reaches of her perception, Penny became aware of a voice beckoning to her, as if someone was calling her from far away—a sound lost on high winds. She felt Hector pick her up again, cradling her in shaking arms and causing Penny an enormous amount of pain. She didn't want to take the plunge into the dark waters. What would come after that seemed as if it would be much more difficult than fading away in Hector's arms.

Before she could process another thought, she felt herself tumbling through empty space. She crashed like a bag full of stones into the icy water, the angry cold biting into her and refusing to let go. Penny's eyes shot open in shock and she caught a glimpse of Hector's distorted visage through the rippling surfaces. Helpless, she watched as the dark gathered with every inch she sunk into the pool. Her legs and arms immobilized, she was unable to fight against the water that seemed to be dragging her downward. Penny choked and had no choice but to suck in great mouthfuls of frigid water. It was a point beyond pain or fear; there was only the most sublime explosion of emotion—the last spark of a firework. Second later, her heart stopped and her eyes drifted closed.

But she did not see darkness.

There, on the very thread that separated life and death, flashed an image. Penny found herself face to face with a black iron mask, smiling mirthlessly atop a flapping black cloak. It was glad to see her. It was a cold face, devoid of humanity, yet so expressive it seemed alive. It welcomed her hungrily and without words, the tips of its cloak reaching out in anticipation for her.

I've been waiting for you...I've been looking for you, hissed a voice that sounded like dead leaves rattling across pavement. Sublime horror filled Penny and she was filled with a sudden desperation to live, so long as it meant escaping this masked entity. The trails of the cloak reached for her, winding around her ankles and pulling her downward.

I am yours, and you are mine.

NO! Penny screamed. With a soundless blast of retaliation, Penny's whole body jerked back to life. Her heart pumped as she clawed at the water toward the blur of light that offered her only escape. She had to move, she had to live. Death was no longer a comfortable form of noble defeat, but a hideous void where that grinning mask waited, patient and still. With every ounce of strength she possessed, Penny kicked her way upward and tore through the surface of the pool.

When she felt the dry, musty air of the cavern touch her tongue, Penny knew she had escaped from the masked entity's claws. Hector's voice echoed in the cavern as he pulled her from the spring and dragged her thrashing body out with a single powerful motion. For several long moments she kneeled on all fours, evacuating every drop of water from her lungs. Unable to stay upright, she collapsed in an exhausted heap, her head finding Hector's knee.

"Penelope!" he sputtered, wiping the thick masses of wet hair from her eyes. Penny looked up at him, her chest still heaving. She smiled at his look of relief, a light flutter of nervous laughter escaping.

They both laughed with unbridled relief, sharing the moment with shy elation. Penny closed her eyes again and sighed. Part of her was screaming to let Hector know what she had seen as she'd crossed the border of life — to warn him — but another part wanted to never speak of it, to keep it locked safe inside and let it be forgotten, though she could not imagine how she would ever forget that atrocious image.

"Do you think you're going to make it?" Hector inquired. Penny thought about it, taking her time to reply.

"I think so," she told him, her eyes still closed. "Everything's stopped hurting—Only, I feel really tired…like I've just run miles and miles without stopping. But it feels like— I don't know, I just want to lay here for a while, if that's okay…"

"Of course it's okay," Hector laughed with endearing warmth.

Whether she rested there for hours or for mere moments, Penny wasn't sure. Time seemed to have lost much of its importance since she'd entered the grotto, and a subtle sadness now ached within her, though she could not understand why. She would have stayed there through the night if something had not stirred her from her tranquil half-sleep. A noise reverberated in the tunnels. Alarmed, Penny sat up.

"What is that?" she whispered, looking toward the mouth of the grotto.

"Someone's coming," he hissed.

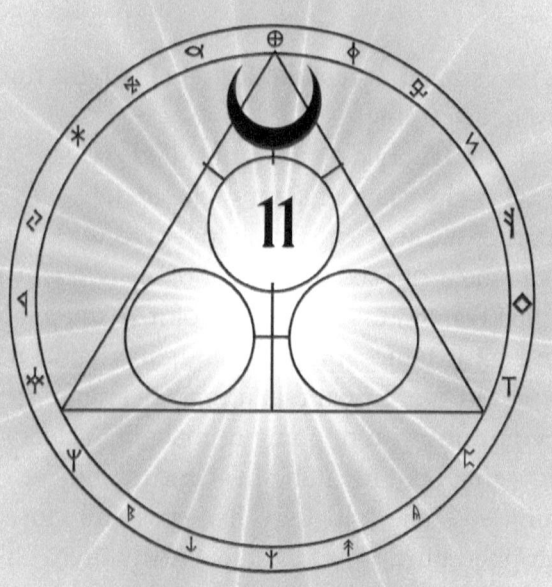

GILDED CHERRY PINE

"What're we gonna do? What—"

"Shush!" Hector hissed.

In tense silence they listened as the steps echoing throughout the tiny cave grew louder. Hector signaled for Penny to get behind him and she did, feeling a buzzing in the air followed by the now familiar tug of energy that meant Hector was pulling magic from her. They both waited, the air around Hector's fingers crackling with energy. Moments later a shadow crept toward them. Penny braced herself for the fierce break of tension as she studied the approaching shape on the cave wall. Whoever was coming wore a tall hat.

Penny's heart leapt as the intruder poked his head around the corner and peered at them. With a rush of disbelief and surprise, she recognized a familiar top hat and mustache. Hector tensed at her side, ready to attack.

"No! Please, I-I surrender!" Simon whimpered, throwing his hands up as he locked eyes with Hector and caught sight of his aggressive stance.

"What are you doing here?" Hector demanded, relaxing only a little.

Penny put her hands out too to assure him that all was safe. "This is that Simon person I was telling you about! The one from the marketplace, remember?" she told Hector and moved over to where Simon groveled. His once crisp clothes were now bedraggled with tears, tatters, and a number of stains.

"Oh, I thought I'd never find you again..." he whined. He rubbed at red eyes with the back of his hand and leaned against the cave wall. Hector shot Penny a bewildered glance and she shrugged. Simon seemed to be struggling to pull himself together and faced them, sniffing and looking pathetic.

"How in the world did you find us here?" Penny questioned as Hector crept closer, eyeing Simon with apprehension.

"I've been following you! And if it weren't for that blasted beast of yours I would have caught up miles ago! I *told* you I had something extremely important to tell you! Why did you just *wander* off?" He looked and sounded as if he had been through quite an ordeal, his voice hoarse and his face sallow and stretched.

"Um, let me think," Penny shot back. "I have no reason to trust you, for one thing—and for another, *you* were the one who ran away!"

Simon responded with a perturbed grimace. "I had no choice! The baron guy with the ponytail—if he had seen me, he would've killed me, so I had to get away as fast as I could! Did you hear me? *Kill me!*"

Hector shot him a skeptical look. "Kill you? Why would he want to kill you?" he asked, inching protectively between them.

"Because I wasn't able to murder Penelope like he told me to, but—" Simon shot without thinking, as if there were more important things to explain at the moment.

Hector grabbed him as Penny leapt back in fear. Simon squealed, trying to avoid Hector's grasp but failing.

"What did you just say?" Hector gasped, trying to look fearsome and not quite succeeding. It was still enough to make Simon cower back in terror, spitting out one frantic jumble of words after another. Hector turned to Penny with an uncertain look.

"Should I—" he started to ask, but Simon cut him off.

"No, wait! Let me explain, please! I'm on your side, really!" he sputtered. Hector looked at Penny for some sort of signal and she shrugged a bit.

"We might as well hear him out," she reasoned. It made sense to hear what he had to say, even if it was a complete fabrication.

Simon smiled and thanked her several times in the same breath, and she and Hector allowed the harried magician several moments to collect himself. When he spoke again, his voice still trembled.

"I know it sounds ridiculous, but I'll tell you exactly what happened to me—no lies or tricks. But after I'm done, will you *please* help me? I've been through hell. I don't know anything about this place or camping in the woods or how to get back, o-or—"

"Start talking, Simon, and we'll see," Penny said as she crossed her arms, trying to look tougher than she felt. He faltered for a moment and considered when to start, then launched into his story.

"A few days before we met, I came into that Podunk town I assume you live in to do a show with my partners. It was a cheap price to rent out that theater, and times are hard so we all figured we could make a few bucks while passing through. Just the same old card tricks, levitation, rabbit-out-of-the-hat crap, you know? Okay, so here was my problem. Though my partners really have the skill to put on an entertaining show, I myself haven't really got the materials or talent. As soon as they realize how much better off they'll be without me, I'm going to be out of a job—in other words, I was desperate." Simon looked back and forth from Penny to Hector with large soulful eyes, as if he were expecting some sympathy.

"That's all very unfortunate, but what does this have to do wi—" Hector began to interject.

"I'm getting there!" he retorted, looking indignant. The magician snorted and continued, "Anyway, I was handing out some fliers to advertise for our show and I ran into that baron guy with the ponytail. What was his name...Damien?" Simon stroked his mustache and goatee as he thought.

"Deimos. I remember it from the marketplace," Penny corrected. "Go on."

"Well, I handed him a flyer and he looked at me with such *great* amusement. He had this creepy guy with him, too, who had this weird eye, and his left arm was all mechanical-like, and—" Simon had been grimacing as he recalled the man, but suddenly shook his head. "It's beside the point. This Deimos... he made some small talk, asking me about this and that, and then he just pulled out a magic wand. A *real* magic wand. This wand, to be exact." Simon produced the same silver and crystal wand he had used in the coffee shop to transform the cards.

"After he proved to me that it really worked, I was shocked, but of course I was excited, too—if I could somehow use real magic in my show and dress it up to make it look like an illusion, I'd be more famous than Harry Houdini in a matter of months. Then it would be Oliver and Sam who'd be begging to stay a part of *my* show! He was offering me my *dream*," Simon emphasized.

"So, he showed me how to use it, and then he said if I wanted to keep it, all I'd have to do was dispose of someone in town named Penelope Fairfax. He told me that you'd be about twenty years of age, and that you lived in the area, but that's all he knew. So I told him I would and he disappeared but—" Simon stopped, cut off by an angry growl from Penny.

"You're telling me, in so many words, that you'd take an innocent person's *life* for your own personal gain? You slimy little—" Penny puffed up with rage, but Simon shouted back.

"I wasn't *actually* going to kill you! I planned to take off. I was going to use the wand to escape from him and to defend myself if he ever came around looking for trouble. That day, I came to *warn* you about him. I'd never be able to forgive myself if I'd been indirectly responsible for the death of an innocent, unsuspecting girl—and I had no regrets about double-crossing anyone who would wish for something so awful...So I tracked you down and found your photo online—by the way, you should really check the privacy settings on your profile. The point is, you should be *thanking* me for risking my neck to help you." His tragic attempt at nobility was almost laughable, but Penny couldn't muster a smile under the circumstances.

"That still doesn't add up to much, if you ask my opinion," Hector growled.

Simon frowned in exasperation. "Well, I *didn't* ask, and if you'd all stop interrupting, maybe I could actually get on with the convincing. *Anyway*, I was going after you outside of the coffee shop, when I ran into this amazingly pretty woman. No, not just pretty—she was *gorgeous*. It was almost scary how perfect she was. She had great big wings, too... looked just like an angel..."

The description disturbed Penny; it sounded much too similar to the man from her memory. *I was so sure that had only been a nightmare...what if that memory was all real? Stranger things have happened in my life recently—but Simon said it was a woman. The face I remember was definitely a man.*

"She appeared on the street beside me, stood there for a mere moment, then touched the side of my face—and just like that I fell straight asleep. When I woke up, I was in a beautiful garden, and it was the middle of the night. I was scared stiff at first...but I wandered around for several hours, and that's when she returned. But there was something different about her—her

skin was covered with these black blotches, and she was struggling to stay awake. She said that she didn't have much time.
She asked me why I had been following you and I told her
everything. It was like I was *compelled* to tell the truth. She could
hardly stay conscious, but she managed to give me this."

From underneath his cape Simon pulled out a small box
carved out of rich, lacquered cherry pine. The edges were
gilded in a beautiful design.

"She said that to make up for what I had done I'd have to
find you and give you this—she said it would help you. That
you'd know what to do with it. Then, just before she passed
out, she grabbed onto me and pulled me through—well, the
thin air. The world just sort of *melted away,* and I went through
this—this huge stretch of darkness. *Nothingness,* more like,"
Simon explained, looking as if he were still unsure exactly
what had happened. "When I came through, I was in that
town…and she was gone. Anyway, I suppose that angel lady
must've known you were nearby, because I found you the
next morning! You remember, in the market?" he prompted,
then sighed and looked distastefully at the box. "All that trouble just to give you this stupid thing."

Penny lifted the box from Simon's hands and inspected it.
"This has got to be a big mistake. I'm not who they think I am.
Why are all these people I've never even *heard* of trying to kill
me or—or help me or—"

Simon's face contorted. "Excuse me? Do you mean to tell
me that you don't have a *clue* about what's going on here? I
thought you were the one with all the answers! I need you to
protect me, to help me get back! And, if I may ask, who the *hell*
is this guy?" Simon gestured at Hector, who took mild offense.
"Who are *you,* Penelope Fair—"

"It's Penny, okay? And I just told you! I'm nobody. I've
done nothing to deserve this," Penny moaned. She looked
toward Hector. "*He* was my lit teacher. We somehow got tangled up in this together when a bunch of monsters attacked

me. *He's* the one who's special, not me. He's some magician or enchanter type teac—"

"I am the last surviving member of the Nelvirnee race and an enchanter of the Seventh Order of Seival," Hector corrected.

Simon blinked. "Well…there's *that*," he deadpanned, and it became apparent a lengthy explanation was in order. It took quite a bit of effort on Hector's part to convince Simon that he was indeed from a world other than Earth or Elydria, and it took even longer before Simon was able to understand the situation they were in. Hector demonstrated his abilities by casting the universal communication spell on Simon, and he was placated by this small miracle.

While Hector was elaborating further, Penny's gaze kept straying to the pool as an idea nagged at her. Amongst the collection of dusty paraphernalia littered about, Penny spied a small bottle that still had a stopper. She glanced over at Hector and Simon to see they were still in heated discussion. Satisfied that neither would take much notice of her, she inched over to the bottle and wiped the dust off on her jacket. The enchanted spring was so deep and plentiful, and it was a rarity to be allowed access to it. Penny decided to fill up the small flask as stealthily as she could.

Just a little couldn't hurt. We get into so many dangerous situations that this might come in handy at some point, she thought, filling it to the top and stuffing it into the deep pockets of her coat.

EVEN KNOWING ALL that they did, Simon remained skeptical and unsatisfied. "Are you sure that's exactly how it happened?" he questioned. Hector nodded, and Penny could tell his patience was ebbing.

"It's just that—don't you think it's a rather striking coincidence that you just *happened* to be Penny's teacher? I mean of all the classrooms in all the countries in the entire world, you two end up in the same one. The chances are phenomenal."

"Whatever the case, I think it's safe to assume that Penny is not just the ordinary young lady that she so ardently tries to convince us she is," Hector said, sliding his glasses back up his nose. "At first I thought you had somehow become the victim of a strange sort of magic surge, but in light of our recent discoveries I'd have to say that my opinion has changed. It simply cannot be a coincidence. All these events are happening for a reason—and I think they're happening because of you, Penelope," He proclaimed with such ominous decisiveness that Penny felt a stab of insecurity.

"Well, this is the worst thing that could've happened," he stated glumly. "I expected that you two would have all the answers—and more importantly, you'd know a way of getting back to Earth."

"We are currently looking into that. We're on our way to the capital where there's supposedly a large library that could be of some help. I have the ability to bring us back, I just need to figure out *how*," Hector told him with some misgivings. It was clear to Penny that he didn't trust Simon yet.

"Oh God, please, take me with you! I'll be butchered alive if I stay stranded here by myself. I don't belong in this kind of environment—I'm *sensitive*. You two owe me, anyway," Simon challenged, looking desperate.

Penny scoffed. "We owe you?" she cried. "For what? Promising to kill me, then chickening out?"

"I brought you that box, didn't I? You haven't even opened it yet! Maybe there's something inside that will help us find a way back," Simon urged.

Penny examined the box in her hands again. A little golden latch flipped up with ease when Penny tried it. She glared at Simon. "You didn't look inside this entire time?" She raised her eyebrows and he nodded. "Why do I not believe you?"

Simon's cheeks glowed pink and he cleared his throat. "Well, I might've tried to take just a little *peek* at one time or another. It wouldn't come open when I tried to lift the lid," he admitted, stroking his mustache.

Penny laughed dryly under her breath and focused her attention back on the box. She hesitated for a moment before flipping the lid back. All that lay inside was a piece of thick, cream-colored paper with fancy golden writing scribbled onto it. The loopy script was written in English and Penny scanned it:

My dearest Penelope,

Though you may not remember who I am and have no reason to trust my words, believe me when I say I have been your protector since before your birth. Though I tried to keep you hidden and safe from those who would wish harm upon you, the cautionary measures I arranged have been breached. It grieves me to face this, I do not have time or energy enough to relay to you the importance of what is to come. I have but a few moments left.

I must urge you to follow my instructions with the utmost haste; much more than just your life depends on it. You must travel to Mulgrith Woods on the continent of Crescia, which lies just south of the Goblin capital, Hulver. There you will find a witch who goes by the name Della. She will give you the information you seek. I truly wish I could tell you all that you are so desperate to know, and to personally ensure that you are safe, but I cannot. The consequences could be disastrous. I would give most anything to be by your side. Do not be afraid.

My blessings are with you,
Adrielle

P.S.— If you find yourself lost in Mulgrith, use this. I'm sure you'll know what to do with it.

Penny looked up from the note and blinked several times. *Use what?* She passed the paper along to Hector and noticed a golf-ball sized orb of glass hidden below the letter. It appeared to be full of clouds of shining dust, swirling in a constant tornado behind the glass. Penny picked it up between her index finger and thumb and rolled it around, peering into its depths.

"What is this thing? Is this what she was talking about in the note?" Penny wondered aloud. Simon and Hector watched her, their eyes shining with expectation. "I have *no idea* what to do with it."

"Keep it safe until you do, then," Hector advised her. Penny stowed the orb back inside the cherry pine box with care. Simon squinted at the note as Hector pulled his map out of his vest pocket.

"What does this all mean?" Simon asked.

"It means," Hector started in an astute tone, "that we are going to have figure out a way to cross the ocean, seeing as Hulver is halfway across this world."

"Hold it, hold it—we're just going to do what this note says—without thinking this through *at all?*" Penny demanded, wondering if the author of the note could indeed be trusted.

"Have you got a better idea? And didn't Simon say that Adrielle wanted to be a help to us?" Hector replied, folding up the map.

"I don't think I said anything like—" Simon started, but Hector interrupted again.

"Anyway, it says that this witch should be able to give us answers. I'm certain that means she'll know a way to get back to Earth. That's what you want, isn't it? And even if this whole thing isn't completely trustworthy, it's the only lead we have. As long as we proceed with caution, I believe it should get us somewhere."

"Oh, all right! We'll just *cross* the ocean, then! It'll be fun! Though I don't think Elydria's got any cruise lines running, but that's just a guess on my part. Hope you brought your floaties," Penny sneered.

Hector's expression turned venomous for a moment, but then he shook his head with confidence and grinned. "We'll ask Armonie and the High Priestess back at the sanctuary how to get there. They're bound to know," he told her with assurance.

"D-does this mean I can come with you?" Simon begged with an imploring smile. Penny and Hector looked at each other and considered. Simon removed his top hat and kneaded the brim in such a pathetic manner that Penny sighed.

"I'd feel sorta bad leaving you here," she shrugged.

Hector furrowed his brow. "All right, I suppose. But I shall be watching you very closely. At the first sign that you may be involved in any sort of trickery, I shall be forced to exercise extreme punitive measures—is that understood?" he warned. Simon gave Hector a somewhat incredulous look but nodded.

"Bless your merciful heart, you goddess among women. I am your humble servant," he purred, looking relieved and kneeling to kiss Penny's hand. She wrenched her wrist away.

"Don't touch me," Penny snapped. "Can we please go now?"

In silent agreement, they exited the grotto and began the long climb out of the tunnel, emerging from the cave into the blackest part of midnight. The light chill in the air had become a biting, blustering wind. With care, Hector removed the High Priestess's pendant from the notch in the door and it rumbled shut. The gateway to the Grotto now sealed, they wound along the gloomy forest path and fought their way back through the tall grass. Penny emerged into the cemetery and was greeted by the sight of the misty landscape. She smiled with grim determination.

Now all that stands between us and safety is the graveyard.

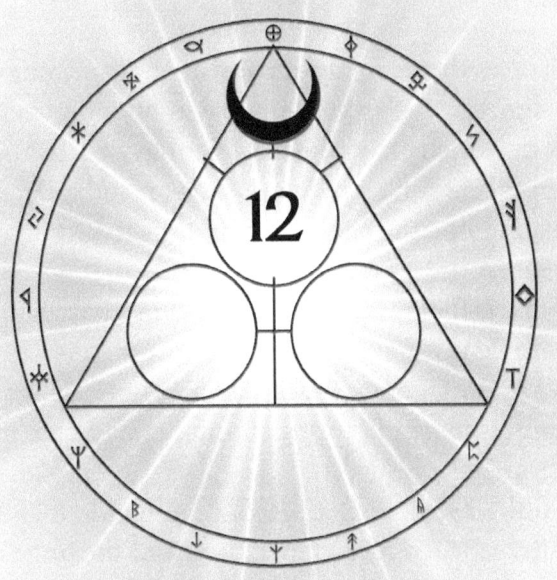

MOONLIT MONOLITHS

Discomfort struck Penny as she stepped among the grave-stones. The mists rolled by in ghostly billows. Something had changed. She looked up at the large tree beside her; it seemed empty and bleak now. Penny puzzled over it for a moment, and then it hit her in a bloom of confusion.

"Hey," she whispered, taking a few steps back until the tree was in full view. "Those—those things from before. They're gone."

Her eyes fell back on where Hector and Simon had frozen in place. Simon's face had gone white, and it looked as if he were gasping for air.

Penny craned her neck around, stumbling when she saw she was standing only yards away from an emaciated, limping figure shrouded in the mists. Scampering away at full speed, she took refuge between Simon and Hector. All three of them pressed close together, their backs against the weathered trunk of the tree as the figure stumbled closer.

Its gait was disturbingly inconsistent. The thing held its long, thin limbs away from its body in a weird and clumsy manner as it scraped along the road. Stringy, matted hair hung in filthy tendrils around a hideous, skeletal body. Penny could hear its rasping breath echoing through the night; it appeared to be in great pain.

"Wh-what is that?" Simon whispered in a horrified squeak, latching onto Penny.

"I don't know," Penny breathed back, not daring to move. Hector was poised, ready to strike, and Penny felt magic flowing away from her.

"Stay still," he instructed, lacing his hands together in a strange pattern. The figure grew closer, and the huge cloud of mist followed and enveloped them. Penny gripped Simon's cloak with all her might, listening to the rattling breath through the billows of mist that surrounded them. All at once the fog blew past and the creature stood only a few feet away, stark white and shivering with rage.

Penny swallowed a scream at the sight of its face; a mangled human visage that looked like it had been dead and rotting for several weeks. The mouth was carved into a hideous smile with several flat, yellowing teeth tearing through raw, red gums. The eyes bulged to twice the natural size and were rimmed in an angry scarlet flesh.

Penny felt a surge of magic around Hector. A flash of light and an explosion of silvery rune coils plowed into the earth in front of them. A shower of dirt burst upward, and Penny and Simon shielded their eyes as a cacophony erupted. When the racket subsided and the air cleared, Penny opened her eyes and blinked around.

Simon was still sputtering and coughing beside her while Hector stood panting, his eyes haunted and his hands trembling. On the ground where the creature had stood only moments ago was a round disc of stone, placed firmly within the earth. Penny gaped at Hector.

"What did you do?" she gasped, still trying to catch her breath. Hector wiped his brow.

"I sealed it inside the ground," he huffed, stumbling back and leaning against the tree, his entire body shaking. The spell must have been difficult to perform, Penny realized.

"You mean that *thing* is still alive?!" Simon wheezed in a high-pitched whine, scandalized. "Why didn't you kill it, for God's sake?!"

Hector looked down at his shoes, brushing the hair out of his eyes and gripping the tree trunk behind him for support. "I should like to avoid killing, if at all possible," he explained, his voice monotone. "I'm sure the priestess will know what to do with it. I've no doubt this is one of the wraiths she spoke of. Now if we don't get back this instant, I fear I shall collapse."

Simon stared at him, and then pulled out his wand. "I can help with that—I figured this little trick out while tailing you two. It doesn't go as fast as your beast, but it's definitely better than walking," Simon said, flourishing the wand. With a small crack, a shower of colored sparks combusted and a fluffy white substance began to form in the air. The puffy substance congealed until a cloud bobbed just a few feet away from Penny, big enough for the three of them to sit upon. Penny tested it with her hand and found it to be buoyant. She and Simon jumped on and helped Hector aboard.

"All right, here we go..." Simon announced. The cloud rose a few feet in the air, bucking and bouncing, and they all made a noise of surprise. "Sorry, I haven't really got the hang of this thing yet—you'd better hold on to something," he apologized.

"YOU SURVIVED...THANK Heaven," the High Priestess beamed out from behind the sanctuary doorway at the three of them. Hector bowed his head and handed the pendant back to her.

"Madam Priestess," Penny began, feeling shy and awkward, "I want to tell you how thankful I am, but I can't express my gratitude in words. I owe you my life."

The priestess laughed in a maternal way and ushered her into the sanctuary's lofty entranceway with a supportive hand on Penny's back. She latched the door behind her.

"Just to see you are safe, child, is good enough for me. There is no need to thank me," she told her, and then looked back to Simon. "And I see you've come back with a friend." Simon waggled his fingers in a half-hearted, nervous wave.

Hector shot him a quick scowl. "Yes. We've been searching for him—for some time now. It is very fortunate we crossed paths," he replied, staring at Simon.

"How fortunate, indeed," the priestess said, a hint of doubt in her voice. She took them into a side corridor off the entry chamber.

"M-Madam, I'm afraid I have some upsetting news," Hector began.

The High Priestess stiffened but turned with unwavering grace, waiting for him to continue. "It seems we might have run into one of the wraiths you described earlier," Hector said.

Her expression sharpened. "What did you do when you found it?"

"I sealed it inside the ground. It shouldn't be able to get out, but it was not harmed," Hector assured her. The priestess's expression softened and she breathed a sigh.

"Commendable decision, brother. Now I can properly send it on to the Dawn Mirror," she said with a smile, touching his shoulder.

"What does that mean?" Simon interjected. She glanced at him, seeming to find humor in his outburst. Her deep gaze passed over each of their faces for a moment, as if sizing them up. She gave a little musing laugh that sounded more like a hum.

"Where did you say you came from, again?" she asked, raising an eyebrow. Penny's heart leapt a little. They all glanced at one another and muttered some unintelligible sounds, trying to look as innocent as possible.

"As the province's High Priestess, I have the ability to help lost souls find their way to the Dawn Mirror, or 'spirit world' as you might think of it. You might've even come across some wayward souls in the graveyard this evening, I presume? It is because a soul generally stays near its earthbound body for a certain period of time after dying."

Penny thought of the pale, luminescent entities that drifted in the night sky. A meaningful glance from Hector told her he had made the same assumption.

"Mostly we just use this ability to help the lost ones make their way along to the Dawn Mirror when needed, and in some rare cases, help with a malevolent or disruptive soul. However, this ability can be used for another purpose, as well," she confessed, her face growing taut, "to release wraiths from their misery. Many Ages ago, a discovery was made in a particular field of magic—nomamancy, to be exact."

"Sorry, I failed out of school. Grew up on a farm—all that nonsense. Would you mind reminding me what nomamahhncy is, again?" Simon interrupted once more, and the priestess raised an eyebrow at his pronunciation.

"Noma*mancy* is the sacred art of name divination, or the manipulation of power over a name. It's generally used by our Order for emotional healing and guidance," the priestess told Simon, then continued on with what she was saying prior to his interruption. "However, three Ages ago, a very misguided nomamancer, Gilder the High Priestess of Trulle, began to study ways of misusing eidolorbes to try and capture the souls of the living or recently deceased against their will—" The priestess stopped, noting her audience's look of confusion and sighed, seeming frustrated with having to explain simple, everyday concepts. The priestess reached inside her pocket pulled out a crystal orb attached to a long, silver chain.

"This is an eidolorbe. It's a vessel for carrying souls. As I was saying, the misuse of these objects was discovered many hundreds of years ago. It is a twisted form of magic that abuses the very principles on which nomamancy is based. If one uses an eidolorbe to steal the name of a person, alive or recently deceased, one can take full control over the individual. The seizing of the name creates a schism between the body and soul, and the person's body is transformed into something frightful—an abomination, which we call a wraith."

"W-wait a moment," Simon stuttered. "Do you mean to say that someone is going around ripping people's souls out and turning them into monsters like that...*thing* from the graveyard...?"

The priestess nodded and Simon's skin took on a greenish coloration. "Sadder still, the wraith becomes an extension of the master, which means they can be fully manipulated to do whatever the master wills. Or simply be left to wander in unimaginable pain and rage," she said, her voice heavy.

The idea that the horrific creature they had met in the graveyard had once been human sent an unshakable chill up Penny's spine. She could not stop her mind from wandering back to the grisly images of the man in Hector's drawing room window. She had no doubt that he too had been turned into a wraith, and the idea made tears well up in her eyes.

"Naturally, using this type of magic is strictly forbidden and shortly after its advent, it was extinguished by the good and gracious Lord Nestor. The teaching or study of this form of nomamancy is punishable by death in the Six High Nations and all the outlying countries, as well. Of course, every hundred years or so, someone will come along who's able to figure out how to abuse nomamancy and will be able to create a wraith, but they are swiftly punished by their own deed. To steal the name of another living creature—this act breaks the psyche of a person, rendering them completely insane. He will be haunted by his own wickedness for the rest of his miserable life. What is so deeply troubling about the recent events in this region, is usually there is only a *single* person who creates a *single* wraith, and that's the end of it.

"Over the past few months, hundreds of wraiths have been seen infesting the Nation of Men, and have even attacked and killed innocent people. It doesn't make any sense how there could be *so* many of them." The priestess looked sick with worry. "It would be impossible for any one person to create that many wraiths and still retain their sanity." She took a harried breath and went on, her voice sounding thinner as she stared into the distance.

"I fear a very dark time is descending upon us. I thought the shortage of magic and the disappearance of the Angelic Lord would be the worst of it, but now we face the infestation of wraiths, as well. It feels as if the end-times are approaching..."

An oppressive air hung over their heads until the priestess shook off her cloud of gloom and faced them. "There's nothing to be gained from worrying about it, though. Let's not let these upsetting matters darken our hearts. I will take care of the wraith tonight—and you three best get to sleep. You'll find fresh clothes, a comfortable bed, and a hot bath down that hall." She gestured to a corridor across the chamber and turned, her lacy white robes fluttering as she exited, leaving Penny, Hector and Simon alone. The three exchanged troubled glances. They were silent until Penny dared to ask Hector the question that was weighing heavily on her mind.

"Hector, you don't think—those monsters that attacked us that night at my house, and yours—you don't think those could have been—"

"Penelope, I am afraid that is *exactly* what they were," Hector replied, sounding queasy. He stared at his owns hands for a moment. "And I killed one," he choked.

"Never mind that!" Simon squawked. "What were they doing on Earth? More importantly, we are all at risk for having our *souls* stolen! Does that not make you just a *touch* nervous?"

"Hey, we're okay as long as no one knows our full names, remember?" Penny piped up with blazing certainty. "I even heard that Deimos guy tell the crowd not to tell anyone your full name."

"Oh, of *course*. We can take his word for it, seeing as how he's such a model citizen and all!" Simon retorted. Penny was about to shoot him a snide remark when Hector commanded order.

"Calm down. Bickering about this isn't going to change anything. This affects all of us, so we might as well approach the problem in the most sensible manner possible."

"And what might that be, Professor?" Simon challenged rudely.

Hector cleared his throat. "Thorough research and study—I should think that would be obvious," he said and Penny rolled her eyes, aggravated. Hector glared back at the apparent discontent with his suggestion. "Well, *I'm* going to get some rest before I keel over, if it's all the same to you." He pushed past them and into the hall.

Just as the priestess described, all three found fresh robes that smelled fresh and were soft to the touch. A bath rejuvenated Penny after days of sleeping outdoors, but the hot water made her sleepy. After pulling the robe over her head, she bundled her clothes under her arm, stepped back out into the chamber, and made her way down the corridor. Only a few dim gas lamps lit the long hallway, casting flickering gray shadows in every corner. For a moment the strangeness of the situation overwhelmed her, and loneliness held sway. Normally after being cooped up with people this long, Penny would have been going out of her mind and desperate for privacy. Shutting out the world for days on end always made her feel safe, yet now she somehow felt she would be more at ease in the company of others.

Looks like they already went to bed, she thought, chewing on her fingernail as she tiptoed down the hall. She tried the door handle of the room closest to her and found a little chamber with two beds and a wardrobe. Moonlight cut in from the window and cast an eerie coldness into the room. She stepped in and sat down on the nearest bed.

Penny thought about lying down and letting sleep override her exhausted mind and body, but being all alone in the unfamiliar room made her feel too nervous to even try. Her mind was still plagued by images of the iron mask, waiting in the void she had so nearly crossed into. More visions of deformed visages of wraiths whirred in her mind, and the potential of the masked entity visiting her in troubled dreams was enough to force her back onto her feet and out into the corridor. Penny closed the door behind her, feeling a knot of anxiety in her chest. She tried two more doors until she stumbled upon the room where Hector lay.

He lay fast asleep in the bed nearest to the window. Glad to have avoided an awkward conversation, Penny crawled into the vacant bed, covered her head with blankets and pulled her knees to her chest. The coverlet was scratchy and the mattress hard, but even a plank of wood would have been good enough for Penny on that night. She wondered what Hector would say when he woke to find her there.

I'll just think of some excuse in the morning. She sighed, feeling herself slipping away. A voice jarred her from her momentary comfort.

"What are you doing?"

Or not…

"What does it look like? I'm trying to sleep," she grumbled. Hector didn't reply, and Penny peered out from inside her cave of covers. He was sitting up and looked weary and confused, but not angry.

"Why in here? There are probably sixteen other rooms." Hector lay back down, turning his back toward her. Penny snorted and retreated back into her cave. Before she could think of a lie, the truth came tumbling out.

"I'm sorry, but maybe I'm just feeling a little uncomfortable being on my own because *apparently* even the friggin' *plants* in this world want to kill me. Hope the blankets are safe! I apologize if I'm *disturbing* you, your lordship," Penny shot back. Immediate remorse followed, making her stomach ache.

Hector didn't reply for a long, stunned moment, and then spoke in a small voice that just penetrated through the wall of blankets. "Sorry."

His tone was so feeble that Penny emerged once more. She took a moment to muster up the courage to speak. "No, please. Don't apologize. That was a terrible thing to say after everything you've done for me. I just—I just get a little uncomfortable—"

"Displaying vulnerability?" Hector finished for her. "I figured as much."

Penny felt her face burn in the darkness of the room. "I guess," she replied at length. They didn't speak for a while, and Penny thought he might have fallen asleep, but she still had more to say. She chewed on her words for a second time, feeling her heart start to pound when she got them out.

"I really did want to thank you, though," she chanced, feeling her words echo in the heavy silence. There was something about the darkness that made it easier to talk. "I mean—you didn't have to do any of those things for me. You could've let me die or left me behind countless times. I can't even express how awful this all would've been if it hadn't been for you." Penny's voice shook, but she forced herself to keep on going, hoping that she wasn't saying too much.

"My whole life...I always expected people to be selfish and cruel. That belief was pretty much why I cut myself off from everyone. The things you've done for me, the kindness you've showed...you proved me wrong. So thanks for that, too," Penny stammered.

Only silence hummed in response to her carefully chosen words. Feeling as if her bravery had been wasted, Penny rolled over and shut her eyes, wondering if he had fallen asleep or was at a loss for words.

As her long-awaited rest drifted over her, there remained the faint worry that when she did at last sleep, she would be revisited by visions of the horrors she had faced that night. She found some solace in the fact that even if they did appear, they would only be the hollow pictures of faraway dangers. Still, Penny envied Hector, to whom no dreams would come.

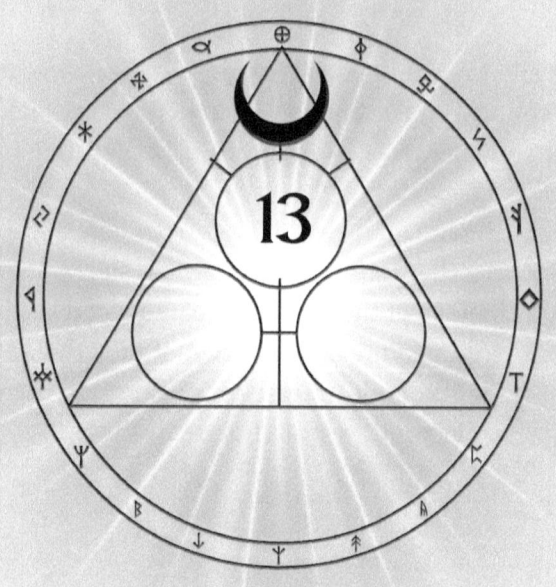

THE WANDERING WIND

S low down or you'll choke," Hector sighed, leaning back
in his chair as he raised a book up to his eyes. He turned
another page back, and Penny stopped mid-chew to glare
over at him. She swallowed the last bit of the spice bread
before replying.

"I haven't eaten in like—a *million* years. Leave me alone." She
glanced back at him, perturbed as he flicked another page aside.
"You read inhumanly fast. It's starting to freak me out."

"I'm cheating with magic. Now, hush," he retorted, and
Penny grumbled under her breath about how he had been the
one who spoke up first. "Fascinating…" Hector murmured,
turning another page with fervor. Penny watched his hazel
eyes flit back and forth behind his glasses.

"What is, Hector?" she drawled, not expecting an answer.

A comfortable silence ensued, until Penny heard muffled
voices in the hall that told her Simon and Armonie were coming. The door swung open and they bustled through, looking

ruffled. He'd been trailing around after her all morning, not bothering to veil his lecherous intentions in the slightest.

Penny shot Simon a warning glance, which he returned with a devilish smile. Armonie said good morning to each of them and set about placing a bundle of flowers on the desk by Hector.

"I trust you're feeling better, sister?" she asked with a genuine smile, holding several folded garments in her arms. "I brought you these fresh clothes." She laid the clothes on the table beside his Hector's untouched breakfast, and then moved over to Penny. Seeing that Armonie had handed her a delicate sundress a light shade of pink, Penny's face fell.

Before she could be stopped, Armonie collected up their dirty laundry and stepped out of the room, humming. Penny went to change in the bathroom down the hall, but didn't emerge for several minutes. The sundress was comfortable, but wearing it made Penny feel awkward. When she returned to the room, she received just the sort of reaction from Simon that she had been hoping against.

"Dear Penelope! You look so much more ravishing today than I have ever seen you before. Your beauty is like a shy bud, just waiting to be coaxed into full bloom! Do please allow me to—"

"Shove it," she retorted, crossing her arms and glaring. Simon stopped his suave banter and retreated back into his playful smile. "I'm going to go out to see Humphrey. Can you stop bothering Armonie? It's starting to get embarrassing."

Hector grunted in agreement to the request that wasn't directed at him without looking up. Fed up with the both of them, Penny grabbed her bag off the top of the wardrobe and left. The lofty halls of the sanctuary were flooded with light, which shone in through the decorative crystal windows and created shimmering rainbows on the carpet.

While exploring, Penny discovered that in addition to having an infirmary and guest housing, there were dormitories for the priestesses in training, several private meditation chambers, a kitchen, dining hall, library, laboratory, and an office for the High Priestess. Penny noted with interest that all the members of the Elydrian clergy seemed to be female. There was not a uniformed man in sight.

When Penny came to the largest hall in the facility, her breath shortened in reverence. The chapel's ivory ceiling was at least twenty feet high, and had been carved into smooth, rippling shapes. Stained glass windows looking like treasure chests full of precious stones faced toward the sunlight, bleeding vibrant colors all over the floor of the chapel. There was a round pedestal set in the middle of the room with curved wooden benches encircling it. She admired the room for a while, admiring the beautiful loneliness.

Outside the sanctuary, the day was warm and dusty. She tiptoed past the flowerbeds, ablaze with orange and red blossoms harmonizing with the autumnal leaves. The smell of straw and animals was heavy on the breeze, but the sight of Humphrey bounding up to the side of the stable to greet her was enough for her to disregard it. Penny patted him and fished out some food from her bag. He chomped on the oats she'd given him. Penny jumped with shock as several other beasts plodded over to the wall and sniffed at her. Delighted, Penny discovered two of them looked like Humphrey, except one was a rich tawny and the other speckled gray.

"More Humphreys!" Penny cried, and gasped as another strange animal crawled toward her. "Oh, and who's this?"

The newest creature was much shorter than the others and had a long snout that twitched and snorted in great puffs of air. Its body was thick and fat and covered with bristly gray hair, just short enough to show two glossy black eyes blinking out. Penny laughed at the sight and tossed it a handful of oats. The creature ate them up and whined for more. She watched the animals with a grin until a cheerful voice rang out.

"Visiting the anteloos?" Armonie's voice called. Penny turned to see her exiting the sanctuary with a basket in her hands. Armonie gestured at Humphrey and the others like him. She approached and leaned down to pet the squat, gray creature at the bottom of the stable. "I just came to feed her. Good morning, little one. Madam Elise allows me to keep a pet—it's very kind of her."

"What sort of animal is she?" Penny asked.

Armonie blinked at Penny. "Pepper is a heggol. Elise mentioned you were a bit unfamiliar with things, but you must be from a very faraway land, indeed, if you've not seen a heggol before..." she said, looking as if she hoped Penny would elaborate. Penny could see no way out, so she played along.

"Oh yeah, we come from *very* far away. It's—it's an island right in the middle of the ocean. We barely have any contact with the outside world! Our customs are completely different, you see. As is the—erm—wildlife." Penny shrugged, but Armonie furrowed her brow.

"Oh, really? Maybe I've heard of it. What's it called?"

"New...Jersey..." Penny unconvincingly answered. It was the first place that had come to mind.

"I...see." Armonie remained skeptical, but well-mannered. "It's fortunate that the fomorians do not threaten your people," she chirped.

"Right. We are *indeed* lucky," laughed Penny with a nervous smile, trying to imagine what a fomorian could be. Always polite, Armonie nodded her head, her waves of honey-colored hair rustling about as she held up her basket.

"I'm about to go to town to get some business done. Would you like to come along? I'd be glad of the company," she offered and Penny grinned in agreement.

Armonie led the way down a path beyond the stables, then on toward a tree-lined lane with its canopy of red and gold leaves. The lane went on and on for at least half a mile, leading out onto a winding path that weaved in and out of lush green hillocks. Penny spied a city that looked like it had been carved of ivory and gold on the horizon. Armonie told her that it was the city of Lindenvale.

Penny was at once mesmerized, drawn toward the pearly towers, eager to go and see it up close. Even from far away, it was a far cry from the cramped alleys of Dewthorne. On their way up the hill they passed several luscious villas nestled in the flora-rich landscape. Each was a secret, beautiful world sealed off by fine gates and high stone walls. Penny blinked in wonderment as they walked by a shady mansion almost hidden by the long vines of a massive tree that grew beside it. She peered over the gate to see water from a fountain playing in the light-dappled grasses, as well as a small swing that looked to be made from silver and silk.

"Many of Elydria's wealthiest reside in this city. It is the dream of many to one day live in Lindenvale. In the times before the Dragon Wars, it was the capital of the Nation of Men," Armonie told Penny, her bell-adorned bonnet jingling with each step.

When they arrived at the urban hub of Lindenvale, high atop the tallest part of the hill, Penny was overcome by the serene beauty as soon as they stepped onto the main street. Many of the houses were white and carved from shining stone, each one trimmed in gold and laced with ivy. Clear, clean water flowed through long, gliding troughs, which lined the city's paved roads and filled the air with the gentle sound of splashing streams. The chattering ladies who passed by were dressed in elaborate clothes, every one of them covered head to toe in satin, pearls and glittering jewels. Huge birds with radiant plumage hung in platinum cages in the windows of many houses and sang out to the passers-by in almost melancholy cries. Armonie pointed out such sights as the baron's house, shopping pavilions, and statues of the heroes and kings of the forgotten Ages. Penny was breathless with awe as she took in all of the grandeur.

"Armonie, I thought there was an economic crisis afoot…
the magic disappearing. How are they able to live so grandly?"
Penny questioned.

Armonie's face fell. "Those who are well-off refuse to stop
consuming the magic. The price goes up and up, and there is
irrefutable evidence that soon we will have nothing left. The
theorists have suggested we have only five years before all the
stored magic is used up, but the demand for it still exists. Nothing will stop them, and most of the world still lives in excess.
The poorest among us are the ones who suffer now, but soon no
one will be safe. It's as if they are ignoring the fact that the end
is hurtling toward us. Aside from a few feeble attempts to con-
vert magic-based machinery to steam-power, no one is doing
anything to stop it," Armonie explained in despair. "Come see
what I mean." She gestured for Penny to follow and led the
way to the center of the city, where they found a circular stone
dais, around ten feet in diameter. Standing atop this dais was a
huge crystal prism in the shape of an obelisk. A small crowd of
people was gathered around it, staring at the three faces of the
crystal, some debating amongst themselves.

"The news on the Sophotri Stones shows how bad it's getting," Armonie sighed.

Close up to the Sophotri Stone, Penny saw that below the
crystal's surface there seemed to be spindly paragraphs of
foreign text floating beneath the surface. Each of the articles
stayed visible for several minutes before shifting to another
news story. Armonie stood there contemplating the news, and
Penny started to pick up what some of the people in the square
were saying.

"The Mines of Olphinem have gone bare now, too? This is
an outrage. Baron Quent should be forming a plan of action,
not sitting up in his office and hoarding all the magic while the
rest of us suffer," one man complained to his friends who stood
around glowering. Penny watched him for a moment, but her
attention was taken by a shrill woman's voice near her ear.

"Shouldn't the *king* be the one doing something about all this?"

Penny and Armonie left the Sophotri Stone and walked side by side in silence over the cobbled road, the urban area growing less dense. Armonie led Penny out the opposite end of the city and sighed as they overlooked the valley below them. There were groupings of cozy cottages nestled in the tender green hills bordering the town. A brook meandered through the village and far in the distance Penny could see a group of children playing around the front of a school. Beyond the village were expanses of fields, stretching like a heavy quilt over the untamed land.

Armonie led her down the steep dirt road, and in twenty minutes they had reached the cottages. The tiny structures were shaded by terraces draped with clusters of damask blossoms, and bordered by gardens with a variety of strange vegetables and fruits, wells and water pumps. Massive trees whined and whispered in the afternoon breeze. Cream colored, foxlike creatures slept in the sunny spots of windows and idle villagers grouped around fence posts. The air was heavy with the scent of dinners cooking.

"I...really, really wish my mom could see this," Penny said, fighting back tears again with the thought of how Paulina's dreams seemed to be brought to reality before her eyes.

"You'll have to bring her here someday, then," Armonie replied. She took a left turn on the snaking road and went down a wooded path. They passed a bakery, a store that sold herbs and teas with magical properties, a toy shop with a window bursting with motion and color, and a gardening supply store. Each shop was cluttered with wares, both mundane and magical. Penny longed to inspect them all, but Armonie hustled her along.

At length they arrived at a light-blue house off the side of the main road. Armonie lifted the latch on the wooden gate bordering the cottage and it swung open, creaking. Armonie knocked on the front door and smoothed the front of her robes as she waited.

A woman poked her head out. Her face was plain and showed some of the signs of her age, but her eyes shone with a sweetness that exemplified her features.

"Hello, Cassandra! Madam Priestess has some things for you and asked me to see that you were doing well," Armonie recited.

The woman laughed and opened the door wider. "How wonderful. Come in, then. We'll see if I can't find something for you to eat since you've gone through the trouble of coming all the way out here. How does some cellanoa tea with some jam-puffs sound?"

After exchanging greetings, introductions, and small-talk, Cassandra brought them to her kitchen and poured a glass of crimson-colored tea for each of the girls. She set a plate of buttery round pastries filled with fruit jelly on the table. Armonie and Penny thanked her and ate of them heartily.

Penny could hear the shouts and gleeful screams of children in the house. Armonie drained her cup and unpacked the contents of the basket, setting some items out on the table. Penny saw that she'd brought Cassandra food, vegetable seeds, a few lengths of ribbon, and some cloth and needles. The last item Armonie uncovered was a small hunk of what Penny recognized as raw magic. Cassandra gasped.

"Oh, no, Armonie. The sanctuary can't spare this," Cassandra protested, but Armonie shook her head.

"No, please accept it. It's a gift from us in your family's time of need. We know that today marks the second year since…we just want you to know that our whole town is grateful for the brave work your husband did. It's only right that you have this." Armonie placed it into Cassandra's palm. Cassandra looked very touched and closed her thin white fingers around the stone.

"Bless you, little Armonie," she breathed, her face alive with emotion.

Armonie was silent for a moment as if she were considering something. "Of course. Has—has there been any news?" she braved.

Cassandra's face fell at once and she shook her head, her gaze distant. Armonie patted her on the shoulder and changed the subject. They talked for a short time longer, and then Armonie declared they had to be off to collect medicinal plants. Cassandra thanked her again, bidding Penny and Armonie a fond farewell.

Penny and Armonie made their way to the wide fields outside of town, wading about in the knee-high sea of grass as Armonie showed Penny which flowers and herbs she needed. In the distance, purple-gray mountains towered, the golden afternoon light highlighting the cracks and crevices of the aged stone. They hunted about the field until the sky turned amber, signaling evening was falling.

Penny studied the horizon with the wandering winds sweeping by her until Armonie roused her from her quietude. "You seem troubled. Whatever is the matter?" she inquired.

"I don't know," Penny said at length, her voice lost in the sighing gusts of the wind. "Things just got so out of control so quickly…" she hesitated, knowing that Armonie wouldn't understand her. The priestess looked over at her, somehow looking past her vague words and into the emotion behind them, which Penny had tried so hard to cover.

"I will pray for you, Penny, my sister," Armonie told her with empathy. Though her words did touch Penny, she couldn't help but scoff. Armonie looked ruffled at her reaction and Penny scrambled to explain herself.

"I'm sorry…I don't mean to be rude. I'm just not one to believe in that sort of thing." Penny shrugged, looking off in the distance to avoid Armonie's stare.

"Whatever do you mean?" Armonie sounded more confused than affronted.

"Let's just say I don't have much faith in any sort of God, no offense to Nestor or whatever his name is," Penny admitted, feeling as if she were entering a delicate conversation that she wanted to avoid.

"But...Lord Nestor is not a God, he's an Angel. Nor is his existence based on faith of any sort—he's real. I have met him myself—I've had an audience with him!" Penny looked at Armonie, disbelief apparent on her face. The priestess took the opportunity to explain further, "I made a pilgrimage to his palace on the Trinity Islands when I became inducted as a Junior High Priestess. He personally confirmed my loyalty to his Order."

"Wait, wait, wait. You mean to say that this Nestor is a real person—er, Angel?"

"But of course! Surely even on your faraway hometown, you *must* have heard of him. We people of Elydria owe our very existence to him. He was there at the beginning of this Cosmic Age. He shaped and named the world and made the laws of the land and sea—his work created us all! Humans, faeries, goblins, dragons, therios—even the anteloos and pofflins! He is both the sculptor and guardian of our world," Armonie declared, her voice full of deep devotion. Penny took a moment to digest what she was being told.

"So, you're saying that Nestor created Elydria and still lives to this day? He's immortal?" Penny questioned, wondering whether Armonie had been fooled by a charlatan claiming divinity, or if it could be something more.

"No, no. The matter that makes up this world was here long before any living soul can remember, including Lord Nestor. This universe is as old as the Dawn Mirror, which is as old as time itself. He only *shaped* Elydria into what it is today. Lord Nestor was born from the Mana Tree, and will one day die. When Lord Nestor was born, the world was a wild mess of chaos, left in tatters by the Angel of the last Cosmic Age. He brought order out of the ashes of the old world, and reassembled the lands so that life could once again come into existence. I am merely a servant of a great and powerful master. I am eternally grateful for my life and all the wonderful things in it. It is all thanks to Lord Nestor," Armonie proclaimed, her eyes shining in the dying sunlight. It was difficult for Penny to fully accept what Armonie was telling her, but her claims were intriguing. She was intent on finding out more when Armonie spoke again. "It is a source of infinite pain and despair that he has disappeared..."

"What are you talking about?" Penny questioned.

"Really, big sister, you must try a bit harder to get in touch with current events. These things are rather important. Lord Nestor has been missing for years—one day he was simply gone from his palace, from Trinity Islands...from the world. Even Cardinal Rhea has no inkling of his whereabouts, and she speaks to all of Elydria on his behalf. There have been rumors that he is moving from continent to continent. Occasionally someone will spot him in some corner of the world, but he is most definitely hiding. It is *very* strange, for up until his disappearance he was so concerned with the well-being of his children. He would grant boons to those in need, quiet political disputes, keep the world safe from disaster and maintain worldwide prosperity. That he would choose to desert us in this time of crisis...is..." Armonie did not have the heart to complete her statement. "This is not the time to give up."

As they left the field to return to the sanctuary and dark descended upon Lindenvale, Penny pondered Armonie's claims about Nestor. She couldn't wait to get Hector's opinion on this matter. The night was growing quite cold when they stepped down the tree-lined lane outside the sanctuary.

Just as Penny expected, Hector was still sitting in the exact same chair she'd left him in. What she did not expect was to find Madam Elise sitting in the room talking with Hector. Upon opening the door and seeing the two of them sitting alone and speaking in serious tones to one another, an odd and unexpected emotion erupted in Penny's chest, and she was at once aware of a vague illness. Penny greeted Madame Elise, irritated that her own voice sounded so high.

The High Priestess rose from the chair beside Hector to greet her. "Why, hello, little Penny. I must thank you for the information, Mr. Arlington." Penny's brow furrowed. "Little Penny, can you tell me where Armonie has gone, please? I must speak to her at once."

Penny offered directions and apprehensively sat down on the bed near Hector's desk as Madam Elise exited. She noticed with a chuckle that the stack of books on the desk had grown into a small tower.

"Enjoying yourself, I see?" she remarked with a wry smile.

Hector shrugged. "I suppose. I've discovered a plethora of valuable information that should no doubt be of use once we arrive at the capital," he mused.

"What have you found exactly? And can we please keep the pretentious technical jargon to a minimum, if you don't mind?" Penny requested and Hector narrowed his gaze, but none the less cleared his throat and launched into an explanation.

"Well, most of what I've learned today has to do with the way magic works in this world. Magic enters the world from the Dawn Mirror and is expressed in physical form. Basically this means it can grow into plants, rocks, wood, or can even be found in its raw state—but it's always found in tangible form," Hector explained, gesturing, then continued in his lecturing tone.

"Of course there are a staggering variety of ways magic can manifest, and certain types of life-forms in Elydria are born with magic growing inside their bodies. According to the text, there are several different types of these people, but the most common are known as crafters. They have the ability to shape and carve magic into any device or form that they desire. Basically, all that means is that they are the people who can turn the raw magic into working magical tools, which can be used by the common folk," Hector finished, his arms crossed. "Do you understand?"

"Yeah, I think I get it." Penny shrugged. "I don't see why it's so important to know, though."

"It's of astronomical importance! These theories suggest that, like matter and energy, magic perpetu—"

"So what did the priestess say?" Penny interrupted, hoping to bypass what was promising to become a long and complicated explanation that she was not in the mood for. Hector frowned at Penny as if she were a lost cause.

"She just wanted to hear the details about what happened last night." Hector shrugged, but then made a small noise to show he'd just remembered something. "Oh yes, I told her we needed to get to Crescia and she told me about an airship that travels from Iverton to Hulver about twice a week."

The door slammed open with a sweep of exuberant motion. Penny jumped back as a giddy Simon tumbled into the room, his hat sitting crooked on a head of disheveled hair.

"Evening!" he sang before flopping down on the bed with a contented sigh.

"What are you so happy about?" Penny demanded. Simon laughed. "This whole building is *filled* with beautiful young girls, if you hadn't noticed. I've been getting to know them all... I'd forgotten how innocent ladies of the religious persuasion can be. Little lambs, all of them..." Hector looked scandalized and shook his head.

"Oh come now, Hector. What's life without the simple pleasures? But don't you worry your little head, I was completely harmless. Besides, I didn't get any complaints—they didn't seem to mind at *all*." He grinned, overcome by another wave of devilish laughter.

Hector lifted his finger at Simon, but the arrival of Armonie carrying three plates full of dinner for each of them interrupted his reprimand. As the young priestess was handing everyone their own plate, she delivered surprising news.

"Madam Elise has asked me to relay a message. She wanted to tell you that she can no longer ignore the frequency in which the wraiths are appearing in the area and has decided that she and I are to go to the capital to request assistance from the Grand Cathedral," Armonie announced, as if reciting something Madam Elise had just dictated to her. She smiled at the three of them, adding, "…and we are extending a formal invitation to you to join us."

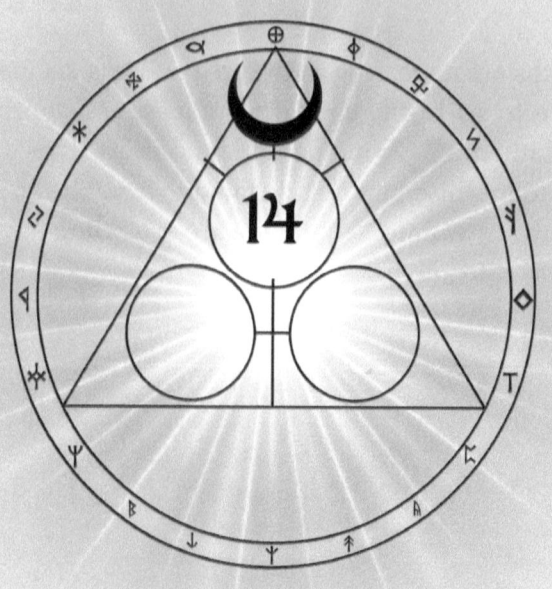

IVERTON

Penny leapt from the carriage as it came to a halt in the middle of a wide meadow. The long journey to Iverton was halfway over, and she was desperate to stretch her legs after being cooped up inside the tiny space, crushed between Hector and Simon. Elise and Armonie drifted out behind her, blinking in the sunlight. Penny wandered over to where poor, tired Humphrey, drank from a nearby stream. As she stroked his fur, Simon approached.

"You're really attached to this smelly beast, aren't you?" he asked, grimacing as he looked over Humphrey with apprehension.

"I guess. I can relate well to animals—or at least I like to think I do. Animals are honest in a way people aren't, you know?" she reasoned, running her fingers over Humphrey's back.

Simon stepped closer and flashed Penny a seductive smile. "Maybe you just haven't met the right person," he purred, extending his arm to touch Penny's face. She batted away his wrist, their hands connecting as a flash of light burst behind Penny's eyes and the world melted away, replaced by a strange, dreamlike image flooding into her mind faster than she could process what was happening...

A sixteen-year-old Simon stood on a stage. The theater was empty except for two men sitting in the front row, watching him with vague interest. Darkness clouded the windows outside of the dingy theater as Simon flipped cards into the air with flicks of his palm, a look of intense concentration on his face. The cards spun in midair for a few seconds before being drawn back to his hand.

The man in the front row gave a great laugh and Simon dropped his cards. The man who had laughed was tall and lanky with chocolate brown skin and a warm smile.

"What are you laughing at?" Simon glowered as the man tried to suppress his grin.

"I'll tell you what I'm laughing at—the string you're using to fly those cards around is a little obvious. What do you think, Olly?" he addressed the man sitting beside him. Olly grinned underneath his bushy mustache and rubbed his bald head.

"Let's see what else you've got, kid," Olly grumbled in a deep voice. Simon's heart flooded with shame and determination as he gripped his deck of cards. His mind raced to think of a good trick and he....

The scene was ripped from Penny's mind in a jarring instant as she blasted back into reality, her eyes still swimming with stars and cards. Simon choked as she stumbled back, trying to regain her balance.

The magician sputtered for a moment. "Wh-what was that? What did you just do?" he demanded, his voice pinched and frantic.

Penny looked at Simon with wide eyes. "I-I don't know! Could you see that, too?" she gasped, her heart straining.

"Of course I saw it! It was *my* memory...It was like I just re-lived it or something," Simon said, shaking. He staggered back to where Penny was leaning against the carriage, glancing over his shoulder at the others. Armonie, Hector and Madam Elise all seemed to be immersed in their various activities and weren't paying any attention to the two of them. Penny took a moment to calm down before speaking again.

"That was too weird...It happened when I touched your hand just then—it was like I was dreaming. I mean, it had that sort of dream logic. You know, where you know exactly what's going on for whatever reason, you know? I felt what you were feeling," Penny tried to explain.

Simon looked anxious as he smoothed his hair. "Has that— ever happened before?" he inquired, still shaken.

"No. Not ever."

"Try touching my hand again. I'll think of a memory," he said, offering his hand and closing his eyes.

Penny took a deep breath and steadied herself, then pressed her fingers to Simon's wrist, bracing for what was to come. The two of them stood still as statues for several long moments, but nothing happened. Penny let her hand drop and shrugged. Simon looked as baffled as Penny felt.

Armonie strolled up to the carriage. "What's going on? You both look awfully pale," she observed.

Penny glanced at Simon and they made a silent agreement to say nothing. Simon explained they were just feeling tired before making his way back into the carriage. Penny's head throbbed as she followed him inside.

They exchanged a few more looks before Madam Elise and Hector rejoined the company and the journey resumed. As the carriage shook back into its bumpy rumble, Penny shut her eyes, thinking hard about what had just happened. She couldn't remember experiencing anything like what she'd just seen. No matter how she thought about it, no answers appeared for all her questions, and her train of thoughts turned toward the future.

PENNY SHOOK THE glass orb, marveling that the encased sand didn't appear affected by the motion.

"The subtle approach you take to problem-solving is astounding," Hector teased, and Penny realized he had been watching her examination of Della's mysterious gift. She glared at him with narrowed eyes.

"Have you got a better idea?" she challenged, lips pursed in annoyance.

Hector plucked the orb from her hands with a swish of his bony fingers, and pushed his glasses upward to get a better look. He examined it for several long minutes before handing the tiny sphere back to her without saying a word.

"So?" she prompted, waiting for a response.

Hector cleared his throat. "I have no idea," he announced with a shrug.

Penny shook her head and went back to staring into its depths. The miniature hurricane of dust was hypnotizing. It drew Armonie's attention next.

"What is that?" she asked with curiosity, reaching her hand out to receive the glass ball.

"Maybe you could tell me," Penny said, tipping it into her fingers. Armonie turned it over and over in her hands, but only handed it back to Penny with a shrug. *Guess not*, Penny thought, and put the cherry pine box and its treasures away before settling in for a nap. The darkness that clouded her eyes was meager, but even through such a thin veil of sleep, a dream still visited.

Penny was marching down a street wearing a strange costume. The dusky sky was tinged with pink and purple clouds, and balloons painted with grotesquely comical faces floated in the trees. White sheets flapped in the wind.

Ahh, of course. It's Halloween! I've got to go meet Maddie.

Penny was at a door. She knocked and a man with a serious gaze answered. He was angry and seemed to be fed up with Penny. Was it already too late to trick-or-treat? Maddie couldn't come out to play.

Penny turned from the house, singing a song at the top of her lungs. It was cheerful and loud and felt magnificent as it reverberated in her throat. Then she saw the sky. Black. It killed the music. The ghoulish cartoon balloons didn't seem so funny anymore. She turned. A crowd of people rushed by, their faces obscured. Penny tried to catch a glimpse of one of them, but they were gone. Her eyes focused on the area they'd run from, and she saw it.

NO. NOT HERE.

The masked entity, the same one that Penny had met at the bottom of the Grotto's pool, stood all the way across the street, silent as mist. Its death-mask smiled back, peering at her with its ghastly visage that was just as terrible as she remembered. Penny's chest heaved with horror and the dream suddenly lost its thin quality. It was now cold and harsh and all too real, like nails and ice. The inky black of the sky bled down until there was nothing but darkness. Penny knew she was dreaming, but she couldn't make herself wake up. She struggled, her teeth grinding against themselves, begging her mind to let go as the void-like eyes of the mask stared deeply into hers.

It's hungry. It's starving.

She felt it speak, its voice like warm poison in her ears, "Life is but a dream...Life is but a dream."

Penny, her heart buzzing with fear, tried to move her arms and legs to no avail. She tried to scream, but something was stuck. A frantic burst of terror hit, and control flooded back into her limbs as she jerked awake with a whimper.

It was pitch dark all around her, but a midnight blue square of light provided a reference to where she was. The carriage was still bouncing. Clutching her chest, Penny caught her breath and stared out the window of the carriage, where night had fallen. Though it had only been a dream, sickness still clung to her body like a filmy sheet of gauze. Her panic was just beginning to subside when a soft voice spoke in the darkness.

"Is something wrong?" Hector sounded as if he, too, had been asleep mere moments ago.

"Sorry. It's nothing—I just had a weird dream, that's all," she whispered to him, rubbing her eyes. The spinning in her head worsened. She didn't notice Hector had drawn near to her until he put a hand on her forehead.

"You're fine. Go back to sleep, okay?" Hector comforted in the gloom. She nodded, feeling her dizziness rise to a crescendo as magic was drawn from her. Before she could realize Hector's intentions, her limp body was falling against the wall of the cab. There were no dreams this time.

The next thing Penny was aware of was the twittering of excited voices. Her eyelids fluttered open. The creaks and cracks of her bones told her that she had slept in the wrong position.

"Rise and shine, sleeping beauty. We're here!" Simon shouted at Penny, and she groaned in reply. The light from outdoors stung her eyes.

"How long have I been asleep?" she croaked.

"Ages." Armonie smiled at Penny for a brief instant as she pushed her way over Madam Elise's lap to get a look out of the window. Hector was also attempting to get a glimpse. Penny rubbed her sandy eyes until the sunlight was no longer an enemy, and turned her attention toward the window. Outside was a striking scene.

The languid, stretching grasslands had become a bustling cityscape. Peaked roofs split the cerulean blue sky, their tiled sides made of red clay that burned in the autumn sunlight. The plaster faces of the buildings were painted in soft pinks, yellows, and greens, oftentimes trimmed with bushels of flowering plants. Steeples, towers, turrets and domes rose high into the air all around the wide stone streets. Their carriage was traveling in a line of carriages, which cut through the middle of a crowded lane so wide it could've passed for a city square. Cars that ran on steam and magic-powered engines, street vendors with eclectic bursts of colored merchandise, busy pedestrians, and a vast assortment of creatures overflowed in the streets. Everywhere she looked, flags bearing the crest of Iverton waved in the breeze. Meticulous iron work decorated the signs and lampposts of the city, and flowering purple trees lined the sidewalks, towering in the alleys between the neat rows of buildings. A group of elves stood together on a street corner beside a lively café, and the terrace jittered with tiny birds the size of bees. People of every variety imaginable were enjoying lunch on the green pavilion in front of the café. Buoyant lacy parasols bobbed over the heads of the crowd.

"Look, faery nobles... Oh, what I'd give to have a gown like that," Armonie pointed out as she shook Madam Elise's shoulder. Penny expected to see tiny, sprite-like creatures, but as she followed Armonie's pointing finger she met a different image. The faeries stood beside each other with smiles on their faces that looked as beguiling as they were dangerous. The female had luxurious, thick black hair that hung to her ankles, and wore a crimson, embroidered silk gown paired with sheer sashes that wrapped around her body like colored fog. From her back projected a shimmering set of wings that reflected iridescent colors in the sunshine. The male faery beside her was easily six and a half feet tall, lithe, and gorgeous. His hair was just as long and grand, but grew in a bluish-silver that matched his eyes. His wings were a bit larger and had a darker coloration than his female companion's. Their dreamlike beauty made Penny's heart leap.

They rode on through the fantastic city, their eyes feasting on the wondrous sights until the carriage came to an abrupt halt in front of a colossal building. Both Penny and Armonie sprang out. Hector and Simon emerged blinking in the sunlight as Madam Elise spoke with the carriage driver. With sore, stiff legs, Penny darted around to Humphrey's side. He was radiating excitement, his wet nose twitching madly to draw in all the new scents around him.

Satisfied he was well, Penny turned to face the behemoth structure, easily seven stories high and crafted from a type of

stone that looked like alabaster. At the very top of the building, two star-shaped lamps stretched upward toward the
clouds and several flags bearing different insignias rattled in
the breeze. Patterns of knots and ancient lettering wove up and
down the side of the building. The entrance was almost a quar-
ter mile away, set above the rest of the city's plane by huge,
stone steps. Arched pillars marked the entrance of the building. Penny could just see a glimpse of sheer curtains drifting
about in the breeze and obscuring the doors. As she admired
the structure, she noticed Hector and Simon releasing Humphrey from the reigns of the carriage and tethering him to a
nearby streetlamp. Armonie took a few steps toward the stone
giant and sighed with adoration.

"Goodness. It's even more beautiful than I imagined,"
Armonie breathed, clutching her chest in wonderment.

High Priestess Elise drifted up behind her. "This is the
Grand Cathedral of Iverton, the official department for the
Order of Lord Nestor and the central bureau of medical stud-
ies. It is the largest sanctuary in all of Elydria," Elise told
Penny, then turned to her protégé. "Little Armonie, today will
be very special for you—it shall mark the first time you will
ever look upon our exalted cardinal." A proud smile lit her face
as Madam Elise looked at Armonie.

"Madam Priestess, I have been preparing for this moment…
since you took me in and adopted me into the sanctuary as a
baby. Thank you so much. I am overjoyed," Armonie said, and
looked it.

"Little Penny. This is where the Junior High Priestess
and I must part ways with you and your friends. Only sworn
members of the Order are permitted to enter the walls of the
Cathedral. It has truly been a pleasure to know you, my child."
Madam Elise extended arms draped in silvery robes and pulled
Penny into a soft embrace. Her voice and demeanor were so
maternal that, for a split second, Penny felt a twinge of emotion, almost imagining it was her own mother.

Armonie gave Penny a dewy smile and drew her into her arms, her waves of hair enveloping Penny. "I know we'll meet again, my sister. I shall await the day."

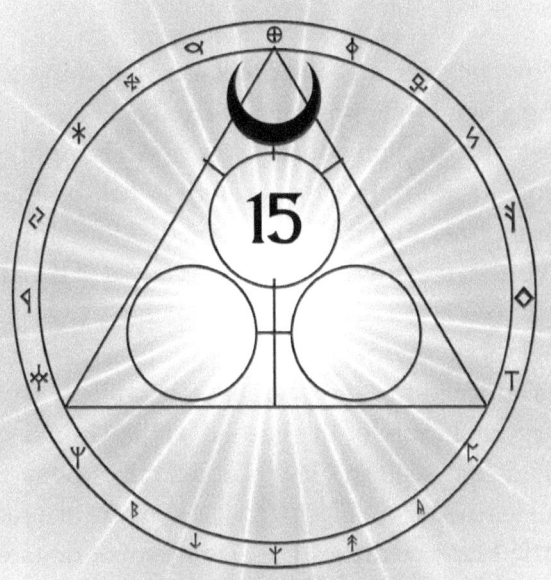

THE ARCHILLION

Penny, Hector, and Simon sat on the white steps outside of the Grand Cathedral, their bags beside them. They watched for a long time as the crowds and traffic rumbled by.

"What now, o wise leader?" Simon directed at Hector, squinting at him from beneath the brim of his top hat. Hector watched as Humphrey struggled with his bonds several feet away before responding to Simon.

"This is an enormous city. We ought to find some place to put that silly beast, and then set about finding the airship Elise talked about. According to her, that will take us to Hulver. From there we can go on and begin our search in Mulgrith Woods. It's just too bad we won't have time to visit the library—I did so want to see it." Hector looked wistful as he pushed his glasses up his nose.

"That is truly a shame," Simon retorted with a hint of derision. "But I'm of the mind that getting back to a world that isn't plagued by bloodthirsty demons is a *tad* more important than reading. Now, let's mosey," he proclaimed, leaping to his feet and offering a hand to Penny and Hector each.

They set off, dragging their bags and Humphrey along. After asking around, Hector located a nearby stable and checked Humphrey into it. They proceeded to roam the lively streets of Iverton, mesmerized by the vastness of the city. They wandered across a massive bridge stretching over a rushing river, past glass skyscrapers and alley shops. Colorful displays and posters adorned the city's white brick walls.

Penny spotted more of the horned, catlike humanoid creatures she had first seen in Dewthorne shying away from the masses, and learned from Hector that they were of a race called therios. Little black creatures the size of small dogs engulfed in sheets of fur shuffled about by people's feet, snuffling and puffing. Dragonflies zoomed through the air, leaving trails of radiant dust. More anteloos paraded by with their long slender necks bobbing.

Penny was drawn toward some crowded stores as Hector and Simon left her in search of a map, and window-shopped through an exotic array of magical home appliances, bottles filled with electric-blue liquid that might've been liquor, and steam-powered apparatuses while awaiting their return.

Simon and Hector returned with a brand new map in hand, and they found a bench and spread the map over their laps, three heads pressing together as they examined it. The entire city was built behind a massive wall and divided into different districts. Hector pointed out some of the things on the map, reading the strange text with his enchanted glasses so that Simon and Penny could understand. They had entered the town from the eastern gate, which had led them right into the Royal District. This particular section of Iverton boasted such prestigious establishments as the National Museum, the Royal Academy, the huge library Hector was so keen to visit, the Crafter's Guild, and of course the castle grounds.

On their way from the cathedral they had passed over a white bridge and crossed over into the Business District, which was in the very heart of Iverton. After a few moments of peering over the map, Hector spotted a tiny building labeled Airstation, and they all agreed that would be an excellent place to begin their search. The only problem was that it was several miles away in the far reaches of the Harbor District, which lay on the western edge of the city. Hector led them through the crowded Business District in search of a faster method of transport.

In the direct center of the Business District was another public Sophotri Stone, quite a bit larger than the one Penny had seen in Lindenvale. Off in the distance, a large coliseum-like structure loomed tall over the buildings. Beside the News Bureau of Iverton, which Penny guessed had a direct link with the Sophotri Stone, were lines of official-looking establishments. After a short walk past the industrial complex they reached a staircase that led underground. Hector read the gleaming green sign that hung above it and nodded with satisfaction, announcing they had reached the entrance to The Tunnels.

They descended the staircase, traveling deep underground. A thin, incense-like fragrance hung in the air and grew into a thick cloud of smoke as they went down the spiraling stairs. The way was lit with yellowing lamps in which luminous rocks were encased. The sounds of busy voices echoed from below and every so often a hurried person would push by them, headed toward the surface. They came into a shadowy chamber with many people shoving past each other. Several lines had formed, each one leading off into a different tunnel that connected to the central hall. Up against the wall was a collection of glass windows, each illuminated by an orangey glow. Hector went over to one of the windows. Behind it was another one of the amphibian-faced creatures Penny had seen on her first day in Dewthorne. Hector whispered to her that he was a goblin.

"Greetings, folks. Need a ticket?" the goblin asked, flashing his needle-like teeth. He wore glasses with inch-thick lenses and had a shock of green hair.

Hector squinted at a small list of prices that was tacked up beside the window before requesting three tickets to the Harbor District as he handed over a glittering handful of Yuebells. The goblin jabbed at a button on a board beside him and, with a hiss of steam and a clattering of machine parts, three tickets blossomed out from the slot on the top of the board. He handed them over and they went and stood in line underneath an illuminated blue sign with a depiction of little waves.

The Tunnels were humid, stuffy, and smelled terrible, but the wait was brief. They reached the front of the line, still not knowing what to expect. Another stout goblin collected their tickets and pushed them forward.

The trench extended into a tunnel on both sides, and it wasn't long until a rickety car, gleaming with gears and puffing out great quantities of perfumed smoke, came clanking up out of the darkness, its dingy lamps swinging. Propelled along by four golden legs that moved like a spider, the car came to a sputtering halt and collapsed in front of the platform. The doors were yanked open by an elf, and Penny and everyone behind her were shoved into the car. The doors shut, latched closed by a flimsy hook, and the car rocketed into the darkness. Exiting The Tunnels in the Harbor District, all three of them walked bandy-legged and gray-faced as they clutched their stomachs.

The Harbor District lived up to its name, and Penny was surprised to discover Iverton was built beside a vast lake. The lake, which Hector said was called Olveria, brimmed with clear, deep sapphire water. Aged docks stretched out into the churning waves and white-sailed ships bobbed on the currents. Paint-cracked shops and restaurants with rustic, seaside aesthetic were grouped together by the entrance to The Tunnels. A salty golden aroma hung in the air. As the scent tickled her nose and the briskness of the air banished the last of her motion sickness, Penny realized she was starving, but Hector told her they'd have to wait. They strolled along the boardwalk, past lines of fishermen who leaned on the wooden posts at the docks. More of the cream-colored foxlike creatures pawed at their catches. The boardwalk stopped after a mile or so and gave way to white beaches lining the lake's edge. Coming to the sandy shore, Penny caught a glimpse of their final destination.

The Airstation of Iverton was even larger than Penny had imagined. The entire structure seemed to be made out of glass and silver that shone like a mirror in the afternoon sun. She goggled, spellbound, at the most bizarre assortment of flying machines buzzing around, to, and from the gleaming building. The air was alive with whirring blades, colorful balloons, and mechanical wings.

"It's like da Vinci's notebook come to life," Simon commented as they climbed the steps to the entrance. They pushed the sleek glass doors open and entered the cool reception area. A black-furred therion, female and thus hornless, sat at the main desk and directed them to where they could find transcontinental travel. They moved along, their footsteps clicking on the reflective floor as they passed several halls reserved for recreational and inner-city transport.

A spirit of excitement was growing in Penny's chest as they approached the department where they could find the airship to Hulver. She was getting closer to Della, which meant she could be closer to getting home. The idea of riding on a magnificent airship above the foreign oceans of Elydria seemed rather romantic.

Hector bounced in his step as the transcontinental travel desk came into view. The woman greeted him and as he began to question her about the airship, Penny took interest in a mammoth, cerulean blimp tethered to the ground outside the window. Lettering and designs were painted all along its ribbed body, coupled with a splendid wooden compartment at the base.

Excited, she ambled back to where Hector stood, and felt a pang of dread upon seeing his face. His brows were knit together and he was rummaging through his belongings.

"Well, let me see..." she heard him mumbling, "Is there a more, erm—economic rate, by any chance?"

The woman shook her bushy blonde head. "I'm sorry, sir. The Airships that cross the oceans only run on magic, and with the shortage..."

Penny's heart sank. "How much is it to ride the airship?"

"A hundred diamond Yuebells—per ticket."

Penny's jaw dropped.

The clerk kept a straight face. "We take bank note or transfer paper."

"Um, isn't there a boat or something?" Simon interjected from behind Penny.

The woman raised her eyebrows as if she were trying to suppress a look of disbelief. "Um...no, sir. Sea travel is far too dangerous, as I'm sure you must know. Because of the fomorians, of course," she explained with a nod.

As they excused themselves, Penny wondered for the second time exactly what a fomorian was, recalling when Armonie had spoken about them in a spooked tone.

"This shouldn't be too much of a problem. Hector can just summon up the money? Right?" Penny prompted Hector. He shook his head at once and she grimaced at him. "Why not? You took all that money before, why should it be a problem this time?"

"Because last time I took mere pocket change from a large amount of people. Would you notice if fifty cents disappeared from your wallet?" He allowed a moment for her and Simon to think. "Now, would you notice if fifty dollars disappeared? And wouldn't you think it odd if fifty dollars disappeared from every person you know? I'm almost positive that someone would be able to track it back to us *somehow*—it might be a slim chance, but I don't want to risk getting thrown in jail."

"But how are we going to get to Crescia, then?" Simon frowned.

Hector remained firm. "Look, we'll find some way to get there. I'm sure with enough research—"

"Screw your research. I want to go home," Simon spat, breaking from their huddle and huffing down the hall. Penny shrugged at Hector and they followed.

Back in the harbor area, they all felt lost. After sitting by the lakeside in heavy silence for a while, Penny requested they find a meal of some sort. They wandered into a fishy-smelling restaurant on the boardwalk and ordered crispy fried fish with a mound of crunchy, bite-sized vegetable rounds. The food made clear-headed conversation much less laborious and they launched into a debate of what their next move should be.

Though there were many ideas between the three of them, nothing was to everyone's liking and they went on arguing even after they left the restaurant. They sat on the boardwalk, watching the fisherman pull in a number of alien fish, their shimmery rainbow scales flashing in the last light of the day. Then they busied themselves by asking vendors and shop owners if they knew of any other way to get across the sea, but learned nothing of value. At the end of a long and unproductive day, there was nothing to do but stand shivering in the chilly evening breeze.

The air above the horizon was illuminated by the ever-burning lamps of the city, creating a halo of light that diffused into the deep inky darkness of the sky. Penny rubbed her arms, trying to fend off shivers as she stared out at the rippling reflection of the twin moons on the lake. It became apparent they would have to stay somewhere for the night, and they moved through the dark district in search of an inn. The inn they found was shabby, but Penny didn't care. Her legs and feet ached from all the walking and she wanted nothing more than to collapse in a bed and forget everything.

Their room was filthy and noise from a neighboring public house blared in through the thin walls. The tub in the bathroom was so grimy that Penny was sure it would only make her dirtier if she chose to bathe in it. A single bed in the room was stained in places. Hector and Simon both refused to sleep on the floor, so they were all forced to squash together in the bed. Penny made a point of placing Hector in between herself and Simon, trying to avoid the chance that Simon might try to get a little too friendly in the night.

After a very uncomfortable night-long attempt at sleep, which contained an excessive amount of elbowing, they dressed and washed up as best they could. Still wooly-headed, Hector led them out into the brilliant morning.

"We are *not* staying there again," Penny proclaimed after they had eaten breakfast. Simon and Hector did not need to be told twice. They walked back to The Tunnels, and this time took a Spider-Car to the southern-most area of Iverton, the Shopping District. They emerged, reeling and yet exhilarated from the ride through the dark, subterranean world.

This district boasted the largest and most intriguing open-air market Penny had ever laid eyes on. Glittering jewels, sacks full of fragrant spices, animals both feral and friendly, fantastical balloons, lamps laden with mirror shards and dark beads, roasted nuts glazed with sugar, and fresh fish of every shape and color flooded her vision and bombarded her senses. They drifted through the stalls, gazes stolen by the clamorous bursts of motion and color that surrounded them. Hector tried to get Simon and Penny to move along, but they kept getting distracted by the various oddities. He gave in and bought each of them a sort of bowl-shaped cookie filled with ripe fruits and berries, drizzled with syrup, and topped with fluffy cream.

They ate their treats with contentment, chewing and wading through the dazzling crowds. After at least twenty minutes of traversing the narrow alleyways and escaping the inviting calls of salesmen, they emerged into a more manageable part of town. Hector used his map and brought them to a cozy looking inn with pink and violet flowers spilling out its windows, separated from the crowded street by a white fence. They all filed in, Simon and Penny talking in low voices, as Hector booked them a room.

The innkeeper was a plump man with a tangled red beard and spectacles. He told them for an extra few Yuebells a night they could have dinner alongside his family and the other guests. Simon agreed to this as soon as he caught sight of the innkeeper's daughter, who was young, tall, and had the same shade of luscious red hair, with cream-colored skin and an hourglass figure to boot. Penny frowned at the statuesque girl as she moved past them with swaying hips, sighing as she imagined how her own short, boyish frame must look in comparison.

When they got into their room, Penny sighed with relief when she saw they'd each have their own bed. Only a few hours after settling in, she wasn't surprised when Hector told her he was going to take a trip to the library, nor when Simon insisted on staying at the inn. Penny, curious to see more of Iverton, announced she was going with Hector.

Back outside in the lively Shopping District, Hector looked down at Penny. "Ah, I'm so happy that you decided to accompany me!" he beamed, strolling briskly forward. Before Penny even had time to blush at his comment, he continued, "Now I'll be able to use magic to read even faster!" She couldn't hide her look of dismay.

They passed through the central Business District first, and Penny noted with interest that the large coliseum she had spotted before turned out to be a theater. Posters advertising an upcoming play were plastered all around the entrance of the huge structure. South of the Sophotri Stone was a rather odd sort of post office. Mailmen with large red bags and cloaks entered in and left through the rotary doors, some riding atop griffins. They wore goggles with their crimson uniforms, clinging to the magnificent beasts with bravery blazing in their eyes as they took off from the dizzying heights of the post office's roof.

Hector and Penny found the large white bridge that connected the Business and Royal districts after a two hour walk, and decided to take a rest on the bench outside of the Grand Cathedral, speculating what day it would be back on Earth. Hector guessed it would be around the end of October by this time, and then gasped. Penny gave him a curious look and he explained that his birthday had passed and he hadn't even noticed.

"Oh! How old are you now?" she asked with a smile. He shook his head as he got up from the bench and helped her to her feet.

"Older than I was before," he told her with a shade of despondency, and they resumed their walk.

The colossal gray stone of the library soon poked out above the roofs and steeples of the district. The building itself was made of nondescript rock and was about the height of a small skyscraper. A large stone sculpture of a scroll and quill was set above the tall wooden doors and engraved with Elydrian writing.

"It's called the Archillion. Strange name for a library," Hector commented.

"You've got to enchant a pair of glasses for me so I can read, too," Penny pestered him as he strained to open the heavy wooden door. He looked at her and considered this.

"But your vision doesn't need correcting. It'll give you headaches," he told her as she scurried in. She thought about this and shrugged.

"I'm sure I can find a pair that'll work," she said, but Hector looked skeptical.

The Archillion smelled just as a library should: musty and dry with a hint of aged wood. A man sat on a raised stone desk, scribbling something with a quill. His face was tired and pale, and he wore an expression of agitation. He squinted down at Hector and Penny, perturbed.

"Can I help you?" he snapped, looking back down at his scribbles.

"I'm looking for books about magic, demographics, geography, law—" Hector stopped short when the man pointed to his left. Hector stared at him for a moment, realized he wasn't going to get any other help, and stalked away. Penny scowled at the man and followed Hector.

The bookshelves were packed with tomes, volumes, and lexicons aplenty. Hector weaved through them like a child in a candy store, plucking up heavy books and piling them into his arms. Penny helped him arrange them at the table where he was hoarding his collection. Stacked high with towers of books, Hector sat down to read, his eyes speeding back and forth for what seemed like hours.

"Do you need me to stay here so you can read at that unholy speed? Or can I go explore?" she asked, her curiosity getting the better of her.

"Just stay in the building."

Ambling off, Penny decided she'd try the next level, and endeavored to climb the rickety steps up to the second floor. When Penny got to the top of the stairs, she found the second floor identical to the first. There was not a soul in sight, so Penny began to hum. Some of the books she looked over caught her eye and she flipped them open. They were filled with spindly text, and few of them had pictures. As her humming threatened to turn into a full-fledged song, Penny noticed an old man farther down the aisle, studying her. Self-conscious, she stopped humming and wandered back to the stairwell. The third and fourth floor proved uninteresting, but Penny was pleased to discover the fifth floor had something new to offer.

Here most of the shelves were empty. It was a bit unnerving to tiptoe through the lonely bookcases; to Penny they felt like skeletons without any meat on them. For no real reason,

Penny felt unwelcome in this place. She was about to give up on exploration and turn back to find Hector, when something in the corner of the room caught her eye. From behind the barren shelves, a pair of dark, wooden doors loomed. Penny felt drawn toward them and found herself crossing the room with no conscious decision to move.

A small plaque sat beside the doors. Penny guessed it was some explanation as to what lay behind them, but could not read the fancy lettering. This only piqued her interest further, and with a quick glance behind her to check for the old man, she pushed on the door. It creaked open with no struggle.

This is a public place. I'm sure if I wasn't supposed to go in, they'd be locked, Penny rationalized. Behind the doors was a gray corridor that stretched on into darkness. With a leap of excitement Penny saw that oil paintings adorned the long and empty corridor, each one illuminated by weak lamplight and paired with a plaque. Feeling silly for being so apprehensive before, Penny entered the hall.

The first painting she encountered was a depiction of a tree in a snowy field. Penny considered it for a moment, trying to decipher its meaning, then shrugged and moved onto the next. Most of them showed chiaroscuro Angels, complete with flowing white robes and wings, always set in dramatic poses, each of them strikingly realistic. She stopped mid-walk as her eyes fell on a disturbing piece.

The wave of revulsion that spread over her was unexpected and caused her to inhale sharply. In the painting was one of the Angels, but this time he was not shown to be heroic or noble. The Angel stood above a mangled corpse, his hands soaked in blood, his expression hollow. The legs of the corpse had been torn off at the knee, as had the hands at the wrists. The head lay shrouded in darkness in the background, but Penny could just make out the stream of blackish-red flow coming from the mouth, and the absence of eyes. A huge hole gaped in the chest where the heart had been. Penny's gaze flicked over it for a few seconds before she turned away, her stomach clenching. She walked away, trying to wipe the image from her memory.

The next painting wasn't interesting enough to distract her from what she had just seen, but she stared at it anyway, trying to force herself to think of something else. It showed a stone door with three stone holes set into it in the shape of a triangle. Just as Penny gave up on it providing distraction and began moving onto the next work of art, a heavy hand fell on her shoulder. She shrieked and batted the hand away, turning to see who had grabbed her. With an overwhelming surge of horror, she recognized the old man from the second floor. He grabbed her by the front of her jacket and shook her before Penny could scream again, his expression just as terrified as hers.

"What are you doing in here?! How did you get in?" he rasped with a voice like dust.

"I'm—I'm sorry! It was unlocked!" Penny shrieked, trying to justify her honest mistake. The old man tossed her back, shouting in his harsh, sandy voice for her to get out. Penny scrambled away, her body shaking as she fled. The old man followed behind, wheezing as he gimped down the hall. Once she was out of the hall, he shut the doors behind him and locked them up. She continued running down all the flights of stairs, eager to distance herself from the sound of his footsteps, which were never far behind. Once she was back on the first floor, Penny cried out for Hector. She sprinted through the entrance hall, and the man at the desk stood up in shock and choked as the old man thundered down the stairs behind her.

"Pop! What are you doing?" he demanded of the old man.

"I found *her* on the fifth floor, Clyde. The *gallery* on the fifth floor," the old man spat. All the color drained from Clyde's already pale face. With a pounding of footsteps, Hector rounded the corner and rushed to Penny's side.

"What's going on here?" he shouted at the two men.

Clyde approached, his hands waving toward the entrance. "Get out, both of you," he said in a quiet rage, looking disturbed. Before he shoved them from the Archillion, Clyde looked at Penny and rumbled a low, dangerous warning. "Don't you dare tell *anyone* what you saw in there. I don't want to see either of you back here ever again!" The door slammed in their faces with a boom.

Penny's heart was doing jumping jacks in her chest as Hector looked at her in disbelief.

"What could you possibly have done to elicit such a reaction?" he breathed.

Penny couldn't find the strength to answer him and buried her face in her hands. The raw hostility of the old man and his son had shaken her. She felt tears threatening to spill over, but forced herself to swallow them.

"I...I just," she mumbled, lifting her face and looking toward the sky. She tried to fix her hair, but ended up slumping down on the steps. In a trembling voice, she told him what had happened. He pushed his glasses back up his nose and fell into deep thought.

"Hey—I'm really sorry. I didn't know it would get us thrown out," she apologized again.

Hector lifted his head and sighed, shrugging. "It's quite all right. Anyway, your well-being is more important than— mountains and mountains of glorious knowledge ripe for the taking..." Pain coursed through his voice.

Penny chanced a hopeful question. "Well, did you learn anything at all in there?"

Hector's look of despondency brightened a little. "Well, I had to connect the dots here and there, but I believe I've confirmed a theory that I've had for a very long time. Back when I began studying magical theory, I was originally was under the impression that there could be hundreds and thousands of different worlds in existence, but now I know there are only evidence of three—or at least three that are directly connected to each other. Here, let me try to explain…"

Hector reached into his pocket and pulled out a scrap of paper and a pencil. He drew three small circles, labeling the first circle *Nelvirna*, the second *Earth*, and the third *Elydria*.

"Now, here are our three worlds, yes? Supposedly, they are each connected by an invisible realm that cannot generally be reached in physical form. This is the place Madam Elise referred to as the Dawn Mirror. From what I've guessed, magic flows in a pattern through the Dawn Mirror, like this—" Hector scribbled three arrows onto the paper between the circles.

"You see, it's really rather exciting. When magical energy is expended here in Elydria, for example, the by-product will pass through the Dawn Mirror and into Earth, where it becomes raw dream matter. After being used up on Earth it travels to Nelvirna, my home. Then the process starts over until the magic comes back to Elydria, ready to be used again. The magic flows through our different worlds, constantly recycling itself."

Penny gasped as she realized something. "Hector, if this is true—you said your world was destroyed, right?" She waited to confirm the fact and he nodded. "If all the people on Nelvirna are gone… then according to this theory, there would be no one there to 'recycle' the magic and send it to Elydria, would there?"

"Precisely. I, too, came to the very same conclusion. This explains the shortage of magic in Elydria—the worlds have been thrown off balance. Soon, there won't be any magic at all here in Elydria because it's all staying built up on Nelvirna. Magic is the same as mass and energy—it cannot be created or destroyed, only transformed," Hector proclaimed with eyes ablaze.

"Well, this is great then! We can just tell everyone in Elydria why the magic has stopped appearing!" Penny clapped her hands together, but Hector shook his head.

"It's not that easy, unfortunately. No one would take this theory seriously, I'm afraid. You see, the existence of these other two worlds—our homes—they're still only legend. It would be like submitting a theory about UFOs or ghosts. No one has ever been able to travel between worlds like I can. The information gathered in those books is mere speculation and includes accounts given to the people by Nestor. Yes, the Angel," he repeated when Penny's face dropped in disbelief.

"Now, I…I must admit I know a bit more about this than I originally let on. This Angel that the priestesses serve is very much a reality. He is, in fact, a living, breathing entity. The truth is…back on Nelvirna, we had an Angel, too." He let Penny digest this for a moment.

"The Angel from Nelvirna was almost identical to this Nestor. He was likewise worshipped by our people as the divine creator of our world. I even saw him once as he addressed the people of my country. I was very young, but I remember it with great clarity."

Penny stopped him again. "What was his name?"

"Seival. He was a good and kind ruler to us—always, without fail or exception. I think it would be fair to say that he loved us… but then one day he simply disappeared. Notice a pattern yet?" Hector grimaced. "I was only around eight years old when it happened, but it still affected each and every one of us. We lived in hope that he would return to us again. Seventeen years later, we were still waiting. But he never came. Nelvirna was reduced to ashes before my eyes and I only narrowly escaped…I still don't know what happened to Seival," Hector finished, his face still and his voice monotone. They shared a troubled look.

HECTOR AND PENNY arrived back at the inn just as twilight was setting in. Neither of them was shocked to find Simon standing close to the innkeeper's daughter at the front desk. He leaned against the wall, keep his eyes glue on her. The red-haired beauty was trying her best to concentrate on her job, but kept getting sidetracked by the compliments Simon whispered. Hector yanked him away and Simon yowled in protest as they led him up the stairs. He gave up and blew the girl a tender kiss. She giggled and put her hands over her face.

"Well, that was uncalled for!" Simon squawked, straightening out his clothing once they were back in their room.

"Oh, stop your whining. You'll see her again at dinner," Penny scolded Simon. He seemed to be satisfied with the prospect of dinner and skittered over to the mirror to trim his goatee.

Something unfamiliar on the dresser caught Penny's eye and she picked it up, recognizing it as the same type of poster she had seen on the advertising board near the Business District theater. It showed a handsome man dipping a gorgeous woman with flowing, angelic locks of sleek blonde hair and porcelain skin down into a passionate kiss. Penny read it over, and Hector crept up behind her to read the title over her shoulder. He snickered.

"What is that? The Cursed Kiss of Anthony Adonis?" he dictated with a short, derisive laugh. Simon realized what they were doing and pushed past Hector, snatching the poster out of Penny's hands and hugging it to his chest.

"Don't you people have any respect for my things? You can't just go snooping around like that, it's rude!" he snapped at them, glancing down at the poster as he ignored their mocking looks.

"You stole that off the front of the theater, didn't you? It's only an ad for a silly play, you know that, right?" Penny told him with a gentle hint of ridicule in her voice.

Simon snorted. "Of course I did, and I *know*—but just take a look at her!" Simon flashed the poster in Penny's face and pointed to the doll-like beauty on the front. "She's *ravishing*. Absolutely astonishing! I've got to behold this unearthly loveliness with my own two eyes. I'll die if I don't..." he sputtered, patches of color glowing on his cheeks. Penny shook her head with a scoff.

Hector rubbed his chin for a moment. "I wonder if I might see that again," he requested.

Simon grinned at him, the light of victory creeping into his eyes. "Well, all right. But only for a second. It's mine, after all."

Hector raised his eyebrows and made an interested noise as he studied the poster. "This young lady *does* have rather captivating characteristics, I must admit. I wonder—"

Penny snorted in irritation, marched up to the two of them and ripped the poster away. Both Simon and Hector tried to pull it back, their expressions wistful.

"This is no time to be gawking over some bimbo. We need to plan our next move. Or did her *captivating characteristics* wipe that from your memories?" Penny snarled, tossing the poster aside. Hector blushed and pushed his glasses back up his nose.

"*Ahem.* You're absolutely right, Penelope," he agreed.

"Well, what's there to talk about? It seems to me that Plan-Man over here is fresh out of ideas." Simon jerked his head in Hector's direction. Penny sighed and looked over at Hector, hoping Simon wasn't right.

"I...am indeed at a loss of what to do," he admitted, and Penny exhaled.

"There has to be *something*." She was sure this couldn't be the end of their adventure, but Hector remained nonplussed.

Simon answered for him, looking as if he thought himself rather profound. "The only thing we can do is to keep going. We've just got to keep on living—and hope for a miracle."

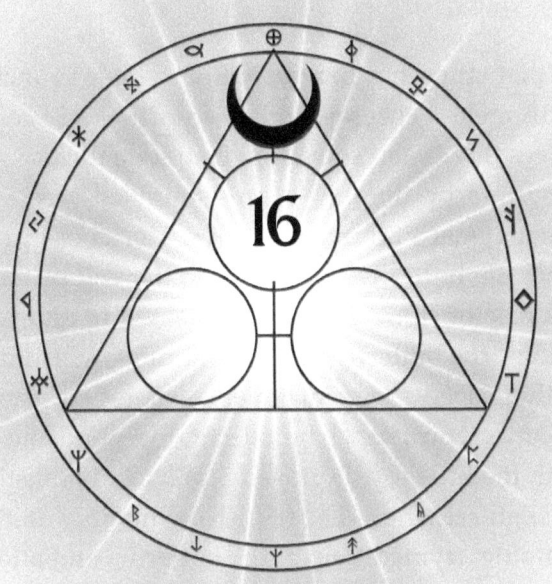

FINDING FREEDOM

The first few days at the inn were hard for Penny. The frustration of being stranded and not being able to do anything about it nearly drove her out of her mind, but somewhere in the blur that followed, that notion somehow lost its edge. Though her encounter with Clyde and his father in the Archillion had shaken her, she reasoned that a way forward wasn't going to come and find her, so she'd have to go looking for it.

She found it difficult to wander far from the inn at first, but within a few days her eagerness to find answers pushed her out the door. She fetched Humphrey from his stable in the Business District and transferred him to the inn's private stable, where she learned the proper way to care for an anteloo from Matilda, the innkeeper's daughter.

Penny wandered to the open-air market, which was just as alive and vivid as she had remembered. In two hours, she spent every last Yuebell purloined from Hector's private stash on useless trinkets and exotic foods, like a savory grilled mystery-meat that stung her tongue, vibrant green crunchy puffs stuffed with melted cheeses, and an assortment of refreshing, icy beverages that tasted something like soda floats.

In a toyshop by the inn, Penny stumbled across a number of phenomenal little magical toys. Her chosen purchase was a miniscule butterfly that acted on the will of the person holding its reactor stone. Penny was pleased to find when she held the stone, the butterfly made a charming whistling sound and brightly flashed every imaginable color. Out of spending money, Penny sat on a bench by a decorative pond and amused herself with the little toy. It moved and looked realistic, reacting to her slightest whim. The fat fish swimming in the pond started jumping, trying to nip at the butterfly, and after one of them came very near to achieving its goal, Penny decided she'd better focus on more important things.

Hector decided it would bring too much unwanted attention if they wore the same things every day, even if the magic sewn into the garments kept them pristinely washed, and bought new clothes for each of them. In addition to everyday wear, Penny persuaded him to get her a blue, feathered miniature top hat with a sweet yellow bow. To her surprise, he also presented her with a tiny star-shaped barrette that changed color to match her outfit. Though a modest gesture, the gift warmed Penny's heart and she treasured it.

With indulgences like these, plus the food and lodging expenses, their funds were growing more meager by the day. Hector, who Penny discovered had something of a sweet tooth, was disappointed when he realized how much he'd spent on sampling Elydrian confections. He had to perform his summoning spell once more, and felt guilty for an entire day afterward.

Simon and Matilda had become something of an item within their first week at the inn. In the same space of time, the magician became insufferable to be around, taking every opportunity imaginable to mention Matilda and his new romance with the certainty of a much longer relationship. Penny discovered with annoyance that Simon seemed incapable of answering a question or speaking as an individual; his singular pronouns changed overnight to plural.   Despite their determination to portray themselves as the ideal couple, Penny watched the attraction between the two of them fade in mere days. Penny suspected Simon's proclamations of happiness were aimed at convincing himself, rather than her or Hector.

Hector launched himself into a full investigation of how they would get across the ocean to Hulver. It wasn't long before he located a bookstore down the road from the inn and covertly read all he could in the dark corners of the shop, until the owners noticed and asked if he was planning on buying anything. He shared fascinating new tidbits about Elydria with Penny every day. His discoveries about the Ages of Elydrian history continued to awe her; the laws and customs of the six different races, nations, and countries across the world, and, of course, cutting edge discoveries in magic and steam technology.

Penny learned that Elydria was split into four major continents: Ciellios, the Borbarro Islands, Aulbaine and Crescia. Iverton was located on Ciellios, and ruled by humans in the northern region. Far to the west end of Ciellios was a mountainous area inhabited mostly by dragons, which Hector explained weren't the brutish, fire-snorting beasts from fairytales, but rather a civilized, albeit hot-headed, race with their own unique culture and history. Central Ciellios was where the Nation of Elves could be found, and far to the south was a country of plains and grasslands called Nern.

To the north of Ciellios were three islands dubbed the Trinity Islands, and it was here that Lord Nestor had lived before his disappearance. Even farther north from these islands was the continent of Aulbaine, origin of the faery race and the nation of Luarpok. The continent Crescia was quite isolated from Ciellios and Aulbaine due to a vast ocean, and it was there the Nations of Goblins and Therios sprawled. Penny also learned the fomorians were a race of brutal sea demons that made their homes in the oceans. They could not survive on land, or in warm or fresh water, but made sea travel and trans-continental trade and relations a challenge.

Yet another concern arose when Hector inquired about transport to Hulver one night at the dinner table, and the innkeeper's family grew stiff and anxious. The goblin and prideful therios races did not coexist harmoniously alongside human or elfin beings. The innkeeper told them in a hushed whisper about the rumors he had heard over the past months at the neighboring pub, explaining that the goblin owners were rumored to be linked with the appearance of wraiths in the Nation, and that there was talk the goblin monarch was responsible. Hector dismissed this later as a load of poppy-cock, but it didn't make Penny feel any better about Hulver being their final destination.

As the days grew colder and grayer, Penny's bravery increased and she began to explore the other districts of Iverton in hopes of finding something that would give her the infor-mation she sought. She rode Humphrey through the streets, stopping anywhere that looked promising or interesting. The first few attempts at mingling with the people in pubs or mar-ketplaces took great effort and left her with worn-out nerves. However, after engaging in small-talk with a dragon while standing in line to buy a book for Hector, somehow talking to strangers wasn't as frightening to her.

About two weeks into their stay, Penny attempted to visit Armonie at the Grand Cathedral. To her disappointment, she was not allowed past the opulent reception hall of the Grand Cathedral, nor was she permitted to send Armonie a message. She exited the colossal building and set out to explore more of the Royal District, visiting both the Royal Academy and Museum. The Crafter's Guild was a subject of great curiosity for Penny, and one day she trudged through a light rain to see it. Upon entering, she became fascinated to see a group of crafters at work. Their display was open to the public and Penny watched as a young woman with eyes a shocking shade of blue transformed a hunk of raw magic into a ring that would make the wearer's voice as loud as if they were speaking into a microphone.

Running out of ideas and knowing it was a long shot, Penny ventured to the castle. It was a stunning sight. She peeked between the iron bars the twelve-foot gates barring the castle grounds from the main streets and stood on her tiptoes to see the large gardens and orchards that it hid. Even from a mile away, the castle's height was staggering. The turrets and steeples rose high, silhouetted deep gray and navy blue against the dense, clouded sky. Penny tried to go inside, but found she was not allowed to enter the castle grounds without an official form. As she turned to start her journey back to the inn, an advertisement caught her eye. She could not read it and struck up a casual conversation with the castle guard to inquire.

"This is a notice for the King's Annual Jubilee Ball, little sister," the plump guard told her. "It's a celebration to congratulate our king for another successful year on the throne. All sorts of ambassadors and special guests come from all over the world—they have these sorts of balls in other Nations, too, but of course Iverton's is the grandest. You'll need an invitation, though." Penny thanked him, her curiosity sated as she made her way back to the inn.

Upon returning, Penny was surprised when Simon broke away from twirling a strand of Matilda's flaming red hair to follow Penny upstairs.

"Got a minute? I'd like a word," he murmured halfway up the staircase. Penny frowned, but agreed. They took refuge at the end of the corridor, and Simon shot a shifty gaze back before speaking.

"Erm, do you remember when we were traveling with Armonie and Madam Elise?" Simon mumbled, looking a bit nervous.

Penny knew what he was getting at and the memory hit her like a sack of heavy stones. Searching for clues in Iverton had driven the event from her mind, and the ease with which she had forgotten it disturbed her. Simon watched her expression and seemed to know they were on the same page. "I've been thinking about that quite a bit, have you?"

Penny shook her head. "It slipped my mind somehow. I've been meaning to tell Hector, but—"

"I, well, I actually told Hector myself," Simon admitted with a shrug.

Penny couldn't help but feel exposed, and a panicked buzzing started in her chest. "Oh," she replied. "Well, what did he think?"

Simon looked thoughtful. "Well, don't discard this theory as soon as you hear it. It sounds a little crazy, but hear it out, okay? Hector and I talked about it, and we both thought—" he fumbled, trying to find the right words, "What I mean to say is—you know how Elydria and Hector's world have types of crafters or enchanters or that sort of thing…" He gesticulated in a bizarre manner that must have made sense to him alone.

Penny thought a moment before answering. "Yeah. Hector told me people from Nelvirna could perform magic by using their intentions to do enchantments and crafters of Elydria can shape physical magic to whichever form they'd like, right?"

Simon appeared not too concerned with the details. "Yes, yes. Well, it only makes sense that people on Earth should have a certain natural magical ability, too, am I right?"

"Yeah, Hector mentioned something about that before… had to do with dreams, I think," Penny said, but Simon was explaining his idea.

"That thing you did—what if that was you… *using magic*? What if you saw my memories in a kind of dream?"

Penny was stunned for a moment, hating to admit that what he was saying sounded plausible.

"I think it could be a useful asset," Simon continued. "You should try and take control over it if you can."

Penny looked at him in disbelief. "I think you're getting carried away. That could've been a million different things. And even if I did have this *ability*, how do you suggest I use it?" she challenged.

Simon went very still, his face devoid of emotion. Penny thought she had stumped him at first, but felt a low rumble of alarm when he held the expression for a moment too long. She was about to ask him what was the matter, when he lunged straight at her. Penny yelped as she felt Simon's hands brush against her face. For a moment there was only bewildered panic, and then a familiar shock descended upon her. A flash of light exploded in her eyes and her vision was bombarded with unfamiliar sights, her heart filling with foreign feelings...

"SIMON! Look what you've done!" a frustrated female voice rang out. There was playful defiance in the young boy's heart as he watched his mother round the corner and bluster down the hall of a simple country home, her lips tight. He giggled and let out a shriek of wicked joy as he tried to escape from his mother's grip. She caught him, and he received a furious telling off, her relentless shouts forcing him into bearing a serious expression.

Satisfied that he had become still and respectful, Mother spoke again. "What have you learned, young man?"

Simon's youthful face remained grim for another second, then split into an impish smile. "That with enough glue—anything is possible!"

Mother did not appreciate this response....

The memory faded to darkness and before Penny could draw herself back into reality, another sprang up in its place...

...An even younger Simon trudged up a mound of dirt, surrounded by golden fields of wheat. There was not a building in sight, only seas of grain. Simon clutched a ragged bouquet of mismatched flowers in his fist, the sap congealing on his wrist. At the top of the mound of dirt sat a little girl in a gingham dress, with bushy hair and dirt on her cheeks. Simon marched right up to her and extended his arm, holding the flowers in her face.

"Julie, will you marry me?" he shouted at her, beaming.....

....It was the Simon from only a few years younger than the present. He was speeding down the highway in a vintage burgundy Camaro....

....*Simon from a year ago, blinding lights burning his eyes and a dove fluttering from his hands, a flapping silhouette against the powerful whiteness...*

Penny was flung back into her own head and leapt away, grasping for something to help her stay balanced. She steadied herself and looked back at Simon, her eyes narrowing despite his dazed and ecstatic countenance.

"Simon! What is wrong with you?!" Penny choked.

"I knew that was it. You were able to do it last time when I caught you off guard. I think it's a sort of defense mechanism! I am *so smart!*" Simon congratulated himself while Penny shot him venomous looks.

"That makes *no* sense. I've been threatened or caught off guard tons of times in my life. There's no reason why it should be happening like that now," Penny told him, but Simon remained smug.

"In your life *before.* What about after you started giving off all that magic? Or after you almost died?" Simon questioned and Penny bit her tongue. Once again, the frustrating notion that Simon could be right nagged at her. As her brain tried to work logic into the situation, Simon spoke again, this time in a gentler tone.

"I think we should try again. Do you think you could do it without having to be surprised?" Simon asked, putting a slow hand on her shoulder.

Penny eyed it. "Why do you want to do this? And why are you so eager to open up your own private memories like that?" she asked, feeling a bit skeptical.

Simon looked shocked. "Why shouldn't I help you?" he retorted, sounding indignant. "We're friends." Penny started a little when he said this, feeling a bristle of emotion. "And I don't mind sharing my memories, anyway. I've got nothing to hide. An open book, as it were," Simon added with a grin.

Penny looked at his guileless expression and shed her suspicions. "Well, all right, I guess. I'm not entirely certain this is a good idea, but it might be worthwhile. Only, let's not practice in this hallway," she suggested.

Situated inside their room, Simon extended his hand to Penny. She studied it. The whole thing seemed a little embarrassing to her. Physical contact of any kind tended to made her feel very nervous and uncomfortable. With a little prodding, Penny brought herself to grasp his hand, bracing herself to feel the shock of unfamiliar images drowning her eyes. Nothing happened. Penny shut her eyes and made a strained face, trying to jumpstart the blinding flash that would be the harbinger of success. The awkward silence made Penny feel self-conscious.

"It's no good," she admitted in defeat, relieved to break contact with Simon. He frowned, the tips of his mustache drooping downwards.

"You're not trying hard enough. Concentrate." Simon grabbed at Penny's hand again. She gave a vexed sigh and shut her eyes once more.

The attempts went on for an hour with no results. Hector arrived just after dark holding a stack of new books. They informed him about what they were trying to do, and Hector offered Penny a few suggestions, but there was still nothing that would trigger it. Penny was getting frustrated and hungry as the smells of dinner began wafting up from downstairs, and pleaded with Simon and Hector to let the whole thing go.

Hector rose from his desk and approached Penny from behind. "Come on, now. Just focus and clear your mind. Here, face forward—" he grabbed Penny by the shoulders and positioned her. As his hands cupped her bony shoulders, Penny felt her heart surge in her chest. When Hector let go of her, her hand twitched inside of Simon's and the blinding flash met her eyes again. She heard herself yelp with victory and surprise just as her consciousness was wiped away, met by another memory of Simon's.

...Simon leaned against the wall of a shady restaurant during the very last moments of twilight. A woman with a strained expression stood by him, her long, silky hair falling to her waist. Arms crossed in front of her chest, she was trying to avoid Simon's gaze and hopeful smile...

With a control she had never experienced before, Penny pulled away from the memory and back into reality. Coughing and stumbling backward again, this time she was caught by Hector and she felt her cheeks burn. She looked at Simon and shook her head.

"Typical," she remarked, referring to the memory she had just seen.

"You did it again!" he exclaimed. "I knew you'd be able to!"

WITHOUT FAIL, EVERY evening for the next two weeks when Penny returned from her adventures in Iverton, Simon persuaded her to practice with him. After a few days with little development, Penny had begged to end it, but Hector agreed that she should continue to work on controlling the ability. During the first week of what Simon dubbed her Dreamweaving Training, Penny dreaded coming back to the inn. The times she was able to succeed and witness one of Simon's memories made her feel as if she were intruding on something private. There was no control over which memory she would fall into, and that scared her. Thick humiliation and fear of incompetence also badgered her, as Hector insisted on watching most of the time. On top of all this, the training sessions left her feeling exhausted and unable to do anything besides lie in bed, too troubled to sleep and too tired to move. Every evening, Penny would lay enervated on the bed and listen to the sounds of raucous merry-making in the street below. In a little square a half mile from the inn, a band of street musicians assembled almost every night, creating bizarre and exotic melodies from their assortment of pipes and strings. Simon and Matilda often attended.

In the dead of the night, unquiet dreams would visit her. Visions of the masked entity floated in and out of focus, peeking out of the shadows of otherwise bizarre dreamscapes. To escape from the daily rigors of her training, Penny began to stay out later and later with Humphrey.

One evening Penny decided that rather than fall prey to Simon and Hector regime, she would visit the coliseum-like theater in the Business District. Arriving she noticed more posters of *The Cursed Kiss of Anthony Adonis* had been plastered up. Penny had grown accustomed to this poster, as Simon had taken it upon himself to collect as many of them as he could and paste them up on the walls around his bed. He claimed he was in love with the blonde woman in the picture and would stop at no lengths to meet and woo her. Penny and Hector didn't remind him he was supposed to be in love with Matilda.

The front of the theater was lined in blinking lights of every color. Penny inspected these to see that small, jewel-bright insects were trapped inside the glass spheres. Feeling sorry they had to be the living décor, Penny stayed with them a little while to commiserate their sad fate.

The box office was manned by an elf with graying hair and sharp, silvery eyes. Penny loitered around the entrance, studying the posters from past musical and theatrical productions, and noticed the blonde girl from *Anthony Adonis* appeared in many of them. Her male counterpart was also smiling out from a few. Other posters featured a woman with glossy, ebony hair cropped in an elegant style around her chin. The elfin man behind the counter rose from his seat and came to stand beside Penny as she studied the posters.

"Got any questions, little sister? Would you like to buy a ticket?" he inquired.

"N-no, just looking." She scratched at the back of her head, embarrassed. "These posters caught my eye, that's all."

The elf looked up at the wall of advertisements with satisfaction. "These are all the shows that have played here over the last couple of years. We've had quite a good run, I'd say."

"Do you...?"

"I own this place. Commissioned it to be built myself about seventy years ago, after I came here from Kelvou City, in elf country. Name's Aldridge, pleased to meet you," the elf said, nodding.

She blinked. The elf didn't look at day over forty-five. Still not feeling entirely comfortable speaking with strangers, Penny mumbled something about it being nice to meet him, too. Aldridge felt the emptiness in their conversation and grabbed a small pamphlet from behind the booth.

"Here, take one. This is info for our upcoming play, *The Cursed Kiss of Anthony Adonis*. Maybe you'd like to come see it? I wrote it myself, so I can guarantee the quality—*and* it stars Annette Deveaux," he added with a quick raise of his eyebrows. Penny glanced down at the poster bearing the now familiar image of the couple, wondering if the name should mean something to her. Aldridge laughed and pointed to the blonde women on the front. "You don't recognize her?"

"Not really," Penny admitted and the man scoffed.

"Do you live in The Tunnels or what? She's only the most famous woman on all of Ciellios, not to mention the most talented—and beautiful!" he almost shouted at Penny, clapping a hand on her shoulder. "My dear, this is an absolute crime. I won't allow it! You haven't lived if you've never seen my Nettie perform. How many people are in your family, little sis?"

"Erm, no family, just my two friends. But, sir, really I—"

"Three tickets, then! Wait right there!" he shouted, rushing back to his post and rummaging around the box office.

"Oh, please, I couldn't! It's really not necessary!" Penny protested, trying to catch his attention without being rude.

Aldridge either couldn't hear her or pretended not to as he continued to bumble around the booth until he produced three tickets. He sauntered up to Penny and laid the tickets on top of her palm, closing her fingers over them. "Please, I insist," he said. "You're in for a treat. Got the voice of a siren, she does." Aldridge stared at the image of the blonde girl with adoration. "Now, run along! I'll look forward to hearing your opinion of the show! Bye now!" The elf shooed Penny away from the box office and out onto the street.

Penny sighed, watching the metallic heaps of parts that were the steam-powered cars of the city roar by, clanking and sputtering as they went on their way. She would give the tickets to Simon, who'd enjoy the show very much. Seeing it at least three times didn't seem out of the question for his level of obsession with the actress.

Simon was waiting for her at the inn with a scowl on his face. She avoided his complaints about her absence by shoving the tickets in his face. His annoyance forgotten, Simon squealed and thanked Penny over and over as he floated around the room.

"Oh, I found out what your girlfriend's name is, by the way. Annette Deveaux," Penny articulated with mock pretentiousness. Simon repeated the name, treating every syllable as if it were a delicate treasure.

Hector snorted at Simon, then turned a shrewd gaze to Penny. "Don't think you're getting out of practice just because of this."

Penny groaned with disappointment and collapsed on the bed in a heap. "I'm *tired* of this!" she complained. "It barely works, and even if I was able to get the hang of it, it's completely useless. Besides, Simon's a pervert! I'm tired of bearing witness to the visual anthology of every girl he's ever hit on."

Lost in his daydream, Simon appeared not to have heard.

"Pursuing this could be of vital importance, Penelope. Don't you want to find out why you produce so much magic? This is also a vital step to finding out how magic works on Earth. I insist that you continue practicing," Hector implored.

Penny gave an enormous sigh. "Fine. But I'm done practicing with Simon. Let's you and me try, okay?" Without waiting for him to agree, she hopped off the bed and crossed the room to where Hector sat.

"I don't think that's such a good idea..." Hector protested, his face turning white.

She frowned at him. "What's the matter? Don't be shy, come on!" Penny urged, reaching toward Hector's slim wrist.

"NO!!" he shouted and cringed back from her outstretched hand in a spasmodic motion, leaping up and away from Penny and knocking his chair to the ground in the process.

Penny stared at him in shock, and even Simon looked up with alarm. Hector and Penny stood several feet apart, both staring at each other as he panted, the tension palpable.

Hector relaxed and hung his head in shame, pushing his glasses up his nose as his face turned pink. "I am terribly sorry," he whispered. Penny watched in bewilderment as he crossed the room and exited, leaving Simon and Penny alone in the oppressive silence. Penny glanced back at a wide-eyed Simon, perplexed.

"What was that all about?" Simon broke the silence.

"I don't know. He's never freaked out like that before," Penny stammered, feeling very guilty as she sat down beside Simon. She had grown so comfortable with Hector; his consternation came as a huge shock. It hadn't occurred to her that there were still high walls between them, and as she sat on the bed beside Simon, Penny came to realize his violent reaction had done more than scare her. The ashen understanding that Hector might never have trusted, or even felt as at ease with her, shook Penny. She trembled at the idea that she had overstepped her boundaries.

"Maybe he..." Simon was about to continue, then shook his head, dismissing whatever he had been about to say. Penny was glad of it. Simon was silent for a moment, and then looked up at Penny with kindness in his chestnut-colored eyes. "We don't have to practice tonight if you don't want to," he told Penny with an uncommon softness. She smiled back at him with gratitude, swallowing what was left of the shock.

"What should we do then? I'm not tired enough to go to bed yet," Penny admitted, intent on getting her mind on anything else.

With a flourish, the magician withdrew his old pack of playing cards from his pocket. "Know how to play poker?"

DREAMWEAVING PRACTICE RESUMED the next night as if nothing had happened, and it became apparent that Penny was gaining more control over her ability. With a solid two weeks of painstaking effort, she was able to more or less call upon Simon's memories at will. They next moved to controlling which memories she wanted to see, and Penny soon found she could at least target a general timeframe or type of event by concentrating before she made contact. Though her abilities were developing, she never asked to see Hector's memories again.

Even though she kept quiet about it, that moment had never left her mind. The question of what he could have possibly wanted to hide from her had been planted in her mind, and like a malicious seed it stayed lodged, waiting just beneath the surface. She mulled it over on nights when sleep wouldn't come, running over the possibilities, but never satisfied with the scenarios or explanations her mind offered. Penny tried to convince herself that Hector was just overreacting about something, but something inside her told her otherwise.

Though sleep brought relief from her worries, she would almost always fade from the peace of nothingness into nightmares, where the entity with the funerary mask for a face waited for her every night. Sometimes it appeared to her in different forms: a skeletal wolf with black eyes, an old woman with a wasted frame, a clock with a broken pendulum, an emaciated beast with hands like the withered branches of a dead tree. It would arrive guised as these varied phantasms, but it was never able to fool Penny. She could always tell what it was—she knew it was always there. She could feel it hovering, breathing, and beckoning her to at the crossroads where a dream would take the wrong turn into a nightmare. She awoke with a start many a time in the black night with the terrified delusion that the masked entity had been only inches away, or remained only inches away. After calming down, she would be lulled back to sleep by the rhythmic and comforting sighing of Simon and Hector in the beds on either side of her, and by daybreak the threat of the iron sarcophagus mask was worlds away. She felt no dread in daylight, not when the fantastic city of Iverton was calling her name.

Even with the disturbed dreams, life in Iverton was rich and sweet, like golden summer fruit. The days were full of wild breezes and soon-to-be memories painted in a thousand different colors, and the nights were lit by warmth and wonderment. Penny found freedom for the very first time in the shady pathways of the parks and by the diamond-white sands of the lakeshore. She'd felt it as she leaned out of the window listening to the whine of faraway music while she gazed at the distant constellations of the Elydrian sky. Each hour that swept past in Iverton was an earthy-rich wine, intoxicating her with the sense that she was already more a part of this world than she had ever been of Earth.

"WELL, I DID it," Penny announced as she threw the door open and tromped into their room at the inn. Hector looked up from his reading and Simon peered up from where he lay on the bed. Penny crossed the room to where Hector was leaning back in his chair and placed a pair of clear spectacles beside him. They were of the pince-nez variety, with circular frames joined in the center and no ear-rests.

Hector studied them for a moment and then looked at Penny. Simon lost interest and went back to his nap. Penny gestured again, and sighed with exasperation when Hector still didn't catch on.

"I found a pair of glasses with lenses that aren't meant to correct vision! They're just made from normal glass. Now you can enchant them so I can read, too," Penny reminded him, and a look of understanding dawned on his face. He smiled and shook his head in disbelief.

"I don't know how you did it. All right, clear away and I'll set up the spell." Hector set his book aside and began magicking silver designs directly into the table-top. The enchantment only took a minute to complete.

Excited, Penny scooped the glasses up as they faded back to their proper color and fitted them onto her nose. Hector handed her a book and she opened it with a quivering hand. Her eyes ran over the letters and she laughed out loud, seeing she could read them all. "Works! Works like a charm!" she cheered, skipping over to the mirror to see what the eccentric frames looked like on her face.

"Of course it works," Hector retorted.

Penny noticed Simon in the reflection of the mirror studying a piece of paper. "What have you got there?" She approached Simon and snorted with laugher when she saw he held the bundle of tickets for *The Cursed Kiss of Anthony Adonis*.

He looked up at Penny with a dampened expression. "It's playing tonight. Opening night," he said, his voice heavy and sullen.

"So go! I bet you'll have a great time—maybe you'll even get to meet that Collette Bordeaux," Penny encouraged.

"It's *Annette Deveaux*, and—and—" Simon stuttered, looking embarrassed as he tried to get the words out.

"What?" Penny prompted. Simon's face flushed deep red.

"I don't want to go alone! Please come with me!" Simon begged, clutching at Penny.

She threw him off and shot him a disgruntled look. "No way! I can't stand that romantical stuff."

Simon gave her a heartbroken look and clasped his hands together. "I'm sure it won't just be romance!" he whined. "It's not asking too much..." His eyes were wide and glistening with hope. Penny sighed, looking over at Hector, who was watching their argument out of the corner of his eye while he pretended to read.

"I'll go if he goes," she compromised, jerking her head in Hector's direction. "There's no chance I'm going to something like that alone with *you*. You're incorrigible enough as it is."

"I would not be completely averse to attending a theatrical performance," Hector injected, his eyes still fixed on his book. Simon leapt off the bed.

"Oh, Miss Annette! This shall be the most glorious night of our lives—it will be the day we meet!" Simon declared to the poster on the wall. Penny noticed that he had doodled a little mustache and goatee on the man who sharing a passionate kiss with Annette and wondered exactly what she was getting herself into.

Penny resigned herself to looking out of the window as Simon scurried into the bathroom to primp himself. She stared out at the velvet sky sprayed with clusters of stars, feeling the autumn breeze breathe in and shiver through her hair. The aromas from the nearby bistros and the hay from the stable below teased her nose. She didn't realize she was smiling until Hector spoke.

"My, don't you look different..." he remarked.

She turned to face him, crossing her arms over her chest. "What are you talking about?" she questioned, a feeling of self-consciousness rising in her chest. "You mean the glasses?"

Hector shook his head, a distant understanding in his eyes. He was silent for a long while as he organized his books. Penny was glad for the chance to ponder his words. Hector finished fiddling with his books and papers and rose from his chair, padding across the carpet toward Penny and joining her by the window to peer out at the frosty stars. He touched Penny's back for what she felt was almost too short a time. The reassuring contact caused Penny's face to burn once again. He spoke to her in a tranquil tone, a light, silver laugh laced into his voice.

"You look happy."

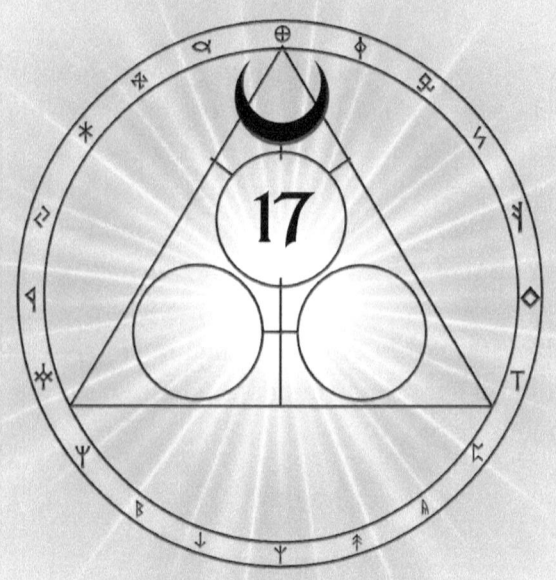

AN EVENING OUT

The excitement around the theater was so palpable it seemed to vibrate through the air, mingling with the misty glow of multi-colored lights streaming from the theater's front entrance. Richly dressed people, composed of mostly humans and elves, made a dull roar as they struggled to get past the gates. Hector and Simon flanked Penny, the professor frowning while the magician beamed. Penny grasped their wrists to keep from losing them as she plunged through the horde.

"What can possibly be so exciting about a silly play?" Hector complained.

After twenty minutes of waiting behind a woman in a satiny purple dress, whose hat was adorned with two huge, glittering, live beetles, they made it to the ticket gate to find a harried looking Aldridge assisting two young workers in rounding up tickets. He gave Penny a small nod of recognition and a wave, which she returned with an awkward grin.

The halls of the theater were decorated in deep red and gold, giving it quite a different appearance than its exterior of stone suggested. Huge staircases draped in the royal crimson fabric wound up and down the main hall, leading to different floors of seating.

It was captivating to observe the ocean of people, their various jewelries and fabrics glinting in the reddish gloom of the theater. Inside the noise level was more hushed and restrained, and Hector looked very grateful for this. They sidled through the aisles past a couple of therios in their lavish formal garments, and took their seats in the cushy theater chairs in a row near the middle.

Hector sighed in relief and took off his glasses. "I hope you're satisfied, Simon," he murmured, breathing on one of the lenses until it fogged.

"Quite," Simon replied. His eyes were locked on the stage, ready for the moment when the orchestra would announce the play's commencement. Penny leaned back in her own seat, flipping through the program. She stopped at the collection of cast members' biographies, and read with interest through one success story after another, ending up at Annette's section:

—Annette Deveaux—

This twenty-three year old darling of the performing world has been training in the arts since the age of five. She has often said that nothing makes her happier than giving her all for the grateful fans of Iverton. Miss Deveaux made her debut at the Iverton Central Theater at age sixteen, but didn't receive her breakthrough role as 'Elizabeth' in Aldridge Alenter's "The Shore Beyond" until four years later. Since then, she has been the shining beacon of Iverton's performing arts society, claiming the starring role in more than 10 different plays and singing in 14 musical festivals.

The illustration below the short biography showed the doll-like Annette flashing a charming smile. The next page offered another short summary about the leading man, Fredrick Weberforth, and Penny passed it on to Hector and turned her attention to studying the crowd. Many of the audience members were drinking fragrant beverages that smelled of alcohol, and Penny scanned the hall until she discovered a small bar in the top tier of the coliseum.

Noting her interest, Simon whisked away to get them both large glasses of the strong-smelling wine. Penny, who had never had alcohol before, drank it down with only a few gulps. Simon sniggered at her as her cheeks turned red and Hector gave her a scolding glare.

Feeling quite dizzy now, Penny resumed studying faces in the crowd. Farther down the row in front of her was a familiar person; a beautiful woman with black hair, cropped short in a chic style, and an unpleasant expression on her face. In her gloved hand she cradled a long cigarette from which plumes of sparkling violet smoke poured, accenting her low-cut, tight red gown. Despite all of her adornments and elegance, she exuded an air of trying to act and look younger than the telltale age lines on her face revealed her to be.

The lights in the theater started to dim, and Penny refocused her attention to the stage as a hush fell across the theater. The band began a merry overture as the curtains whipped open, revealing a set depicting a tavern. Simon squeaked when he spotted Annette standing behind the fake counter, dressed in a disheveled barmaid's outfit as she pretended to scrub it clean.

A peal of applause rang out for the starlet. Annette's voice rang through the amphitheater crystal clear as she started off her dialogue with another actor, who portrayed a regular at the bar. Annette's character had been stuck at the dead-end bar for years, with no way out and no future. Penny decided that Annette Deveaux appeared to be very deserving of her fame; her acting was charming, and she did her best to turn

the cliché script into something that commanded the attention of the audience.

The first musical number was nothing short of spectacular;
special effects reached a new level with the assistance of magic.
Penny was just getting drawn into the plotline when something
in the audience distracted her. She shot a quick glance back at
the black-haired woman, her face still maddeningly familiar,
and a heavy shock made her breath catch in her throat. Next
to the black-haired woman was Deimos; the very same man
that had tried to coax Simon into murdering her over a month
ago. The sound of her strangled heartbeat drowned out all the
dialogue from the stage and Penny stared at her knees, trying
to keep calm.

*All right, just remember...he doesn't know what I look like...
and it looks as if he hasn't noticed Simon's here, so we're okay...*she
reassured herself, keeping her eyes fixed on Deimos, watching as he whispered into the ear of the black-haired woman.
As he leaned, Penny saw that on the other side of Deimos sat
the disfigured, dead-eyed man she had seen in the square of
Dewthorne. Around his chalk-white neck was a metal collar
attached to a chain, which a bald man on his right clutched.
Penny's lips quivered and she was already moving to alert
Hector and Simon when something occurred to her.

Though it made her stomach twist with fear, she knew
what she needed to do. Penny stared at her hands, trying to
remember her evening practices with Simon as she stole his
memories away one by one.

Deimos is here at this very moment, and completely unaware
of me—Deimos who, for some reason, wants me dead—who
started all of this—who knows why this is happening.

Perhaps the wine she'd downed inspired reckless bravery,
but Penny had decided. She took another slow breath, trying
to quell the powerful thudding in her chest. She shot a covert
glance at Hector, craving his support, but knowing he would
never allow her to go down there. She knew as soon as Simon

got wind that Deimos was near, he would make a scene. This would have to be done alone.

Penny feigned interest in the performance as she formed a plan. Annette Deveaux stood in the middle of a faux thicket tinged a deep blue, fireflies floating around her as she sang a sorrowful song. Her face displayed such pure emotion and her voice was so clear and bell-like that Penny was distracted for a singular moment, captivated by her beauty and delicacy.

The Rune Pendant she had taken from her mother's shop still hung around her neck and Penny touched it as she shut her eyes. Her most forceful inner-voice whispered to her. *You've never once been brave, have you...? You've always been a coward. Just once, Penelope. Just once, be brave.*

Opening her eyes again and clenching her fists, Penny rose from her seat with shaking legs.

"Where are you going?" Hector hissed, looking confused when Penny rose from her seat.

"Bathroom," Penny whispered back.

Hector turned back toward the stage and Penny fought her way down the aisle, trying to be inconspicuous and silent. She spotted an empty chair behind the man with the metal collar and squirmed through the aisle to get to it. Once she'd sat down, she breathed a quiet sigh of relief.

With a rush of horror, Penny realized she could not reach Deimos from her seat. Her head swam as she tried to think of a solution. The disfigured man sat before her, his face slack and unfeeling, the missing eye covered with the sheet of glass fused onto his face. Up close, his features were nothing short of horrendous.

Simon said he saw this guy with Deimos on Earth...would he know the same things that Deimos knows? She juggled her choices. There was only one shot at this, and even if she succeeded there was no telling if she would escape unscathed.

Penny shot a furtive glance downward, locating the chained man's wrist dangling limp between the seats. With one final countdown, her hand shot forward, snaked between the seats, and grabbed the man around the wrist. His skin was like a corpse, and she willed herself to not let go as a wave of revulsion hit. Swallowing her fear, Penny braced herself against the flash of light that burst behind her eyes. Nothing followed. She gasped, the empty dream dissolving for a split second before she summoned it again. There was still only darkness.

Penny pulled away from the man's wrist and leaned back into the chair with a thud. She covered her mouth in terror, prepared for his inhuman face to turn toward her, trying not to imagine how his grotesque features would appear with outrage contorting them. She sat frozen, her arms stuck in an unnatural position for the longest minute of her entire life.

He did not move. He continued to stare off into the distance, motionless. Penny's vision blurred and she remembered that she would have to breathe soon. She ignored the curious looks she was getting from the walrus-like man beside her. Annette's song finished and Penny clapped with the rest of the audience, trying to organize her thoughts.

He's got no memories?! Maybe I was doing it wrong? Trying to keep her voice from trembling, she tapped Mr. Walrus on the shoulder and leaned up to his ear.

"Excuse me, sir, I'm so sorry. Would you mind switching seats with me? I *really* need to talk to him..." she pointed at Deimos, wishing she had even a scrap of Annette Deveaux's acting talent. The man raised an eyebrow, and then shrugged as he got up to shift his corpulent body into the seat Penny had vacated. As he moved past her, Penny was shoved against the back of the seat of the bald man that held the chain in his hand. For a heart-stopping second, he turned around in his seat and glared back at her, his white-blue eyes filled with such wild anger that Penny stopped in her tracks, wondering if he had somehow figured her out. When he turned back around, Penny slid into the still-warm seat previously occupied by Mr. Walrus.

Catching her breath, Penny summoned her courage back. This was it. Her gaze locked onto the back of Deimos' neck and his ponytail. She could not afford to miss.

Penny whipped her hand forward, her eyes fixed on her mark and her heart exploding with victorious relief as she felt the warm flesh of Deimos's neck connect with the tips of her fingers. She didn't allow him a second to realize what was going on as she focused on summoning an important memory and felt herself overtaken by the light and falling into Deimos's past...

...Deimos sat on a regal-looking couch crafted of pink silk and dark wood. He was filled with a powerful sense of satisfaction—how could he ever have gotten so lucky? From where he sat, he could see the black-haired woman lounging against the wall of a richly decorated home, smoking her token cigarette and filling the drawing room with its heady fragrance. Beside him was his brother, bald and smiling his crooked grin. He was just as pleased as Deimos.

"You're absolutely sure, Ms. Valentine?" Deimos spoke, his voice deep and serious with a hint of menace playing around his words. The black-haired woman smirked.

"Of course I'm sure, assuming what you said is true. It has to be...how else could that little fool have gotten to where she is without it?" Valentine sneered, her green eyes burning in her head. Even with the blush of youth fading, her beauty was intimidating. Deimos's gaze narrowed as his brother laughed a warped, high pitched giggle beside him, revealing a set of broken, yellowed teeth. Valentine shot him a look of disgust. Deimos gave his brother a warning glance and he relaxed back into a wicked smile.

"And you're certain you'll be able to get us to her discreetly? We cannot afford to be discovered." Deimos tone was even, calculating. He turned to his brother, wrath splintering from his tongue. "We can't have any more slip-ups—isn't that right, Phobos?" Anger still smoldered in his chest. Phobos returned his gaze with an even more belligerent scowl.

Valentine took a long drag on her cigarette and blew it through her scarlet lips. "Who do you think I am, huh?" she spat, insulted.

"I don't know who you think you are, but if a person like Annette Deveaux goes missing, I'm absolutely certain the blame is going to be set on someone…and if it's us, I promise you the consequences will be severe," Deimos hissed , his single eye narrowed to a slit. Valentine's face showed a flare of panic that she deftly hid.

"Don't you worry, no one will know." She was humorless now, her apple-red lips pushed into a pout. "Just do what I say and she'll be yours…"

"So we've reached an agreement then?" Deimos prompted.

Valentine considered, her emerald-bright eyes drifting in thought. Her lips parted for a moment before she spoke. "… She will suffer? You swear it?" she asked with carnivorous hunger. Deimos was still, a low murmur of incredulity shivered through his heart at the cruelness of her intentions. He was certain they far bypassed his own.

"More than even you could imagine," he told her in a flat voice, and an indulgent smile split her fearsome beauty, warping it into something monstrous. Deimos stood and saw another pulse of fear in her face. It sent a flurry of gratification up and down his spine to see her frightened. "Don't forget, now, you take orders from us. Because of what you know, you've fully committed yourself to this, and there is absolutely no backing out. We'll be staying with you at all times to see that your loyalty does not waver, is that understood?"

"You're the boss," she conceded, shrugging a little as if to say she didn't care.

Deimos laughed. "No, I'm not the boss, Valentine. You should know that by now," he reminded her, thinking with dread of the one who dwelt alone in the dark of the palace, waiting for them to return—to return with Annette Deveaux.

Penny felt her senses flooding back into her own body as she emerged from the dream. *NO! This isn't enough!*

With as much strength as she could muster, she willed the light to return and another memory to flood into her eyes. Images shot out at her through black smoke. Flashes of shining teeth, wretched wails and waves of ripping agony blazed past Penny's eyes in hot explosions, overloading her brain with bursts of terror as an unbearable pain erupted in her right eye. Recoiling from the shock, she wrenched her hand away from Deimos, desperate for it all to stop and gasping for air. Deimos let out a pinched yell and fell off his chair.

Valentine gave a ragged gasp and leapt up from her seat while Phobos grasped his brother's arm. Glances and whispers began blossoming all around. Penny rose from her seat and Valentine shot a fiery green glance in her direction. In that instant Penny realized with a start why she looked familiar—the dramatic posters from outside the theater had Valentine's face plastered all over them. Their connected gaze seemed to last an eternity as Penny stood paralyzed, until with a great surge of effort she broke eye contact, keeping her face down as she made her getaway. She pushed down the aisle, leaving a trail of affronted grumbles. Seeing her paper-white complexion and shaking limbs, Hector rose to help Penny keep her balance.

"We need to get out of here. Now," she whispered, and that was enough for Hector to spring into action. He gestured to Simon, already guiding Penny out of the aisle and toward the staircases, holding her by the elbow the entire way. A sense of safety and relief floated in her dizzy head as she felt Simon and Hector nearby, leading her down halls and away from danger. When they burst out into the brisk night air, the muffled echoes of noise from the coliseum rumpled the otherwise quiet night.

Situated a safe distance away on a bench, Penny felt clear-headed enough to relate what she had done and launched into a detailed account without stopping for air. Hector was just as upset as she knew he would be.

"What in the *world* possessed you to do something as *air-headed*—" Hector seethed, his composure angry and fear in his eyes. "This is why I don't drink!"

"It wasn't the wine, I had to do it! I've been searching this whole time for answers and now fate serves them up to me on a silver plate! I couldn't let that chance go by!" Penny defended.

Hector sighed with frustration. "Penelope..." he said, more gentle now, but it somehow made her twice as depressed.

"I was just trying to—" she sputtered. Her heart sunk even lower as she thought about her failed attempt to prove herself something more than a coward. It seemed so foolish in retrospect. "I don't know..." They fell into silence, each of their minds restless with thought and worry.

"Did you find out anything at *all?*" Simon asked with a trace of hope. Penny looked back and forth between the two of them. The gravity of what she was about to say already weighed on her.

"Brace yourselves..."

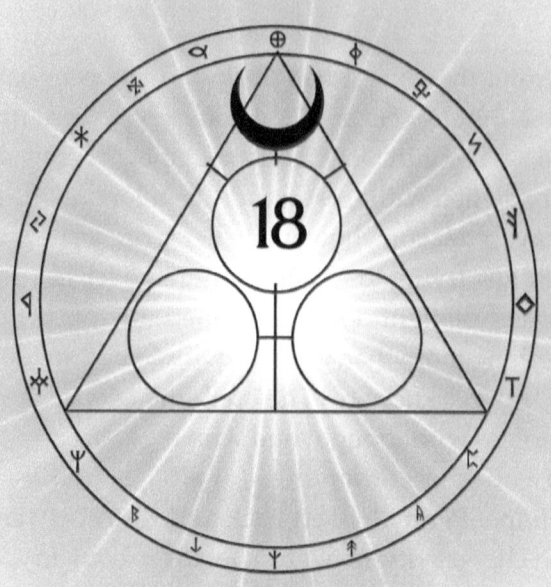

SILK AND SPOOLS

Simon was horrorstruck.

"You're—you're absolutely certain?" he sputtered, caught somewhere between bewilderment and denial. Hector looked troubled as Penny nodded. They'd made their way back to the inn while Penny relayed the stolen memory in a hushed voice. Even though they now sat safely in their room, the comfort and coziness of the place had gone.

"Reiterate exactly what you saw once more, please," Hector requested.

Frustrated, Penny took a deep breath tinted with frustration and she launched into an explanation for the third time. "I told you, already. Deimos and his brother were looking for someone—someone with a certain item, I suppose, and it turned out to be Annette Deveaux," Penny began, trying to force patience into her tone.

"Anyway, they went to that Valentine woman's house—she's an actress like Annette, I think. She was in all these posters on the theater's entrance. They're using her to get to Annette quietly—I'm sure Valentine must have some history with her, being in the same line of work and all. It sounded like they were going to do something awful to Annette."

"Deimos's brother was there; his name is Phobos—I'm almost certain that he was the one who was locked up several years ago for...for making a wraith. He's supposed to be shut away, or at least that's what Deimos told the crowd...and according to what Madam Elise said, he should be completely insane," Penny repeated.

Simon thundered to his feet, fists clenched. "How dare that monster try to harm my sweet Annette!" he snarled. "We've got to do something!"

"Wait a moment, let's not be rash," Hector cautioned. "To be clear, they're going to try to kidnap her and do—goodness knows what...to get something that she has?"

"Yes, and they're going to do it soon. Or at least that's what it felt like." Penny shrugged and chewed on her bottom lip, considering.

Simon looked between the both of them in shock. "Well, what are we just standing around for? Every moment that goes by that woman's life is in danger!" he protested. "We've got to alert the authorities—those ranger fellows, or whatever they call themselves!"

Hector shook his head. "No, we can't do that," he admonished, absorbed in thought. Simon looked outraged, but before he could sputter out an argument Hector explained his reasoning. "You have to understand, we're not supposed to *exist* in this world. We have no place in this society, no means of legal identification, no history. If we expose this kind of claim to the Rangers, we're almost certain to get into a lot of trouble—and don't forget all the money we've stolen. What's more, Deimos is a baron. There's a very strong chance that he could have connections with the law. Not a chance I'd be willing to take." Hector paced over to the window. Penny knew he was right, but felt irked nonetheless.

"Well, what *are* we going to do, Hector?" she asked in a stinging tone.

"I'm trying to figure that out, give me a moment," he mumbled. His gaze narrowed in consideration. "Let's try and talk this out. The same people who have it out for you also want this Annette Deveaux. Now obviously she's got something that they need or want badly enough that they'll go to any lengths to get it—even trust an outsider like Valentine. There is a huge possibility that this could be connected in some way. Now, Deimos has no idea what Penelope looks like, am I correct Simon?"

Simon nodded.

"If this is true, then there's no way he'll be able to connect what happened tonight with who he knows as Penelope Fairfax. For all he is aware, Penelope died back on Earth on that night he was there. In actuality, we've got the upper hand in this," Hector reasoned, though Penny thought he was being optimistic. Hector spun around to face Simon and Penny. "Morally we have an obligation to warn that actress about a threat against her life, and logically it would make sense to attempt to obtain information from her regarding the people who are after her. She must be aware, to some degree, of the reason they want to kidnap her."

"Whoa, hold up. Are you suggesting that we just gambol on up to a celebrity and try to convince her that some baron dude is trying to kidnap her? That's *if* we're even able to speak with her at all!" Penny challenged Hector, who frowned.

"I didn't say the plan was perfect, but it's definitely worth a shot. If what you say is true, she may not have very long. I can't sit by and let a person be harmed when I might have the power to save them," Hector told Penny with the utmost seriousness.

"Hector's right! We can't let her be accosted by those swine! Besides, if I save her life..." Simon smiled as he rubbed his mustache.

"I want to help her, too, but let's be realistic. Is this even feasible? How are we supposed to find her in a city this big?" Penny asked.

Hector grinned and lifted his hand into the air, showing off the golden sparks that flitted off his fingertips.

"I *do* know how to use enchantments, don't forget. I can locate her exact position with a simple spell—in fact, I believe I demonstrated the effectiveness of the locating enchantment back in Dewthorne?"

Penny remembered the golden thread that had found her in the clock tower. "Fair enough, but don't you think she'll notice the string coming out of her *chest*?" she pointed out. Hector shook his head.

"It will only become visible when we come within about twenty feet of her. Once we get her in our sights, I can stop the spell and she'll be none the wiser," he assured her.

"I guess it's as good a plan as any," Penny mused. "She'll never believe us, though."

"We'll do what we can to convince her," Hector replied. "Though it's a bit of a risk, I say we wait until morning. We all need sleep—and time to think."

Penny deflated back into a slouch, stewing in her anxiety and still shaken from the night. As Simon stalked off in agitation, Hector drifted up to her and ruffled her hair.

"It's going to be all right, Penelope," he smiled down at her. She wanted to believe him.

AS SHE LAY awake in the darkness that night, while the pale blue slice of moonlight crept across the wall at a snail's pace, Penny's wonderings shifted to Annette Deveaux. *Who is*

she? What has she got that Deimos wants? She shivered, thinking of Deimos's promise to make Annette suffer.

Night fluttered away into the stark chill of the early morning, and the swatch of light between the curtains faded to periwinkle. Penny's exhausted thoughts lost their clarity and became fragments of images and sounds. A dream awaited her as she passed into a restless sleep, starting without any clear beginning, the way most of her dreams did.

...She lay on the floor. The shadows of leaves skirted across an old wooden porch. Her body was tiny and weak, but a feeling of warmth and comfort enveloped her as she felt a pair of strong, familiar arms wrapping around her, holding her close. It had been such a long, long time since she was held in the safe grip of her mother's arms. Penny rubbed her face against her shoulder as they rocked. She could smell the familiar scent of lavender, a perfume Paulina often wore. Overjoyed that they had been reunited, Penny wanted to look into her face and broke away. With every inch she pushed off, the warmth drained out of the world and the amber light from the nearby garden became a bleak gray. Her face swept away from the shoulder and brushed against her mother's face, and she felt metal where a soft cheek should've been. Cold metal. Iron. With a plunge into an icy whirlpool of fear, Penny saw that it wasn't her mother at all. The sarcophagus smile was mere inches away, willing the life away from her.

"Die. Die for me. Death is easy, life is but a dream."

With a burst of panic, Penny forced her arms and legs to move and break free. The safe familiarity of the warm bed returned as she sat bolt upright, panting. Drawing her blankets closer, she caught her breath and lay back down. Not even the presence of Hector and Simon soothed her.

Waking up several hours later was just short of impossible. Penny slid out of bed, her head reeling and spinning like she had just gotten off a very intense roller coaster. After getting dressed in a stupor and scarfing down breakfast, the three of them trudged to the front of the inn.

Hector's plan was to cast the tracking spell and use Humphrey to get to Annette. Humphrey was not at all pleased about having to support the weight of three people on his back and made his opinion clear by rumbling one vexed bellow after the next.

"How exactly does this work?" Penny asked, pushing away Simon as he dozed against her.

"I just imagine her name and face, focus on trying to find her and—" With a fizzing sound, a shower of silver and gold sparks erupted from Hector's fingers, causing Humphrey to prance around. Comforting him with gentle pats, Penny saw that out of Hector's hand stemmed a fine golden thread, stiff like a wire. It pointed them in the direction of a cluster of shops to the north.

"There we are. It accounts for roads, so it won't try to lead us through a building or anything. Even more brilliant is this spell won't work if your intention is to hurt the person you're attempting to locate. Fascinating, isn't it?" Hector smiled crookedly.

Simon rolled his eyes. "Daylight is burning," he reminded them. Following the thin thread, Hector kicked at Humphrey's sides and the anteloo dove into the stream of traffic. Flustered, Hector tried to get Humphrey to follow the golden thread as it stood suspended in midair, but the beast was more concerned with trying to run alongside any other anteloos it met on the road. Penny took the reins from an extremely peeved Hector and coaxed Humphrey onward.

After a much shorter ride than any of them had anticipated, they arrived at the front door of a shop. Humphrey fumbled to a halt as Penny tugged on the reins. Hector undid the spell with a small *pop*, and the golden thread disappeared from the door. Penny withdrew her tiny spectacles from her pocket and fixed them on the bridge of her nose. She stared through the lenses to inspect the shop's weathered sign, which read "Silk and Spools" and sported a picture of a needle and thread. She slid off, deciding not to wait for Simon and Hector to figure out how to get off Humphrey's back, and pushed the shop door open.

The moment she stepped into Silk and Spools, a subtle mixture of age-old potpourri and the dingy smell of dust tickled her nose. Ribbons, threads, small pearly buttons, and various other sundries crowded shelves. Dried herbs and flowers hung from the ceiling, creating a bizarre canopy that made Penny feel as if she were inside a forest. It took her eyes a moment to adjust to the dimness and she stepped forward, her footsteps echoing on the wooden planks. Something about the smell was prodding at a long forgotten memory that, try as Penny did, she could not quite recall. The woman behind the counter uttered a lazy greeting before looking back to her book. The shop seemed quite empty as Penny searched for Annette, and she wondered if the locating spell hadn't made some mistake. Hector and Simon entered the shop with a muffled crash moments later, looking windswept. They joined her, asking in a whisper if she had found Annette. Before she could reply, her heart jumped as she caught sight of blonde hair.

Annette Deveaux browsed through a selection of ribbons, humming to herself as she plucked a pink bow from the wall and dropped it into a shopping bag, which bulged with other items. The actress turned away from the wall and her face became visible. Penny's heart sank a little; Annette was so beautiful it was almost unfair. Her healthy figure was complimented by a delicate dress drowning in pink bows, lace, and ruffles. A pair of green, teardrop-shaped earrings swung as she walked. The three stood frozen as the actress drifted by, leaving a tantalizing floral scent behind in the air and shooting an apprehensive glance back at them as she went to search through the buttons and lace. Hector leant down to Penny's ear.

"Go on, tell her!" he hissed.

She snorted. "Do you know how crazy that will sound? What am I even supposed to say? 'Excuse me, miss, but I believe a psychotic baron is trying to kidnap you!' That will *surely* sound like a legitimate warning."

The argument seemed to shut him up for a moment. "Well, do *something*! We didn't come all this way just to stare at her," Hector coaxed at last.

Simon looked as if he disagreed with Hector on that point, but kept quiet. Penny took a nervous step forward, trying her hardest to think what she could possibly say. The door swung open and a burst of sunlight flared into the dim shop. The silhouette of an hourglass figure moved inside with deliberation. Penny's heart skipped a beat. The sleek raven hair and smoldering green eyes were unmistakable. She rushed behind Simon and Hector, making sure to keep her face out of sight.

"It's Valentine!" she hissed in a strangled voice. Penny silently thanked her stars that Hector happened to be so tall and took refuge behind his skinny form as he pretended to look through the basket of yarn balls.

Valentine, a disgusted scowl staining her features, moved through the shop, her hips swaying with each heavy, high-heeled step. She peered around each corner, her venom-green eyes searching. Annette was too absorbed in her shopping to notice Valentine pressing down the aisle toward her. Though Hector remained still, Penny felt a great amount of magic being swept from her. Moments later Valentine's voice cut through the silence of the dreary shop, causing the unsuspecting Annette to jump.

"Oh, goodness. Fancy seeing you here!" Valentine spouted, oozing mock friendliness. Annette's eyes grew wide for a mere moment before her expression hardened into a perfect cross between misery and outrage.

"Though I shouldn't be *too* surprised to see you in a place like this, I suppose..." Valentine plucked a frilly bow from the aisle nearby and looked it over with a curled lip as she pinched it between two ruby fingernails. "You always did have such tacky taste."

Annette's eyes narrowed. "What do you want?" she retorted, still looking away from Valentine. The shopkeeper had set her novel down and watched the confrontation with rapt attention.

Valentine clutched her chest, indignant. "Why, I was simply in the neighborhood and I saw you through the window! I thought I might come and say hello to my dear little Nettie. It's been such a long time, hasn't it sweetie?"

"I said, what do you *want?*" Annette repeated, now looking up at Valentine. Penny was shocked to see tears swimming in Annette's eyes. A wave of ire seemed to pass over Valentine's face, and she quashed it.

"Not too happy to see me, hmm?" her voice lowered to a dangerous tremble. "Now that just breaks my heart. I only wanted to check up on you—to congratulate you, as well." Valentine laughed again. "Yes, I was there last night. I must say— you were very good. You didn't even make a complete ass out of yourself this time around. Bravo."

"Shouldn't you be busy drinking yourself into a stupor in some bar on the low end of the Harbor District right about now? It's almost afternoon, you know." Annette floated past Valentine, her shoulders straight and her head high as she made her way to the counter. She paid for her items as Valentine's smiling countenance flickered in rage. Annette turned to leave.

"You'll have to work on your manners if we happen to cross paths at the Jubilee Ball, or they might see you for what you really are—a spoiled brat, desperate for attention," Valentine called after her, causing Annette to swivel around on her heel as if she were dancing.

"Oh no, *you* were actually invited to the ball? I didn't think animals were allowed in the palace!" Annette smirked, her hands on her hips.

"I was rubbing elbows with royals before you could walk. Don't you ever forget who I am, you snotty little insect," Valentine snarled, turning tail and stomping past her to the door. She turned back before grabbing the doorknob. "I'll see you and your extra forty pounds at the ball. Toodles!" She shot Annette one last wicked smile and exited.

Annette stood still for a minute, fuming as glassy tears slid down her cheeks. She looked just like a fragile porcelain doll. With a stifled sob, Annette covered her face with her hands and rushed out of the door in a flurry of ruffles and bows. Penny, Hector, and Simon watched her run down the street and out of sight.

The shopkeeper was trembling with excitement. "She left her things…" she said, pointing to Annette's discarded bag of items that lay like a popped balloon on the counter.

Hector perked up, rushed forward and scooped up the bag. "I'll take it to her right away!" he told the shopkeeper and rocketed toward the door, Simon and Penny in tow. As he pushed his way out into the brilliant sunlight Penny stopped him.

"What are you doing?! She's long gone!" she shouted.

Hector flashed an exhilarated grin. "Get Humphrey, I've got a plan."

AMONG THE LILIES

Hector, Penny, and Simon left Silk and Spools in a mad rush, chasing Annette Deveaux's gold and ivory carriage through the Business District to a part of Iverton Penny had never been to. Situated at the northern-most point of Iverton, between the Business and Royal districts, was a tiny suburb that appeared to house the richest, most posh citizens of Iverton. The houses were tall and skinny, each towering around four stories high, with crystal windows and well-tended foliage creeping up the pale blue, blossom pink, creamy yellow, or daisy white homes. Each house was ringed by a lovely garden, some with tiny wishing wells, gazebos, and trellises. Trees lined the immaculate sidewalks at exactly ten foot intervals, each the same height and pruned to perfection.

They watched from a distance as Annette's carriage pulled up alongside one of the largest houses and over to a circular stone patio. The actress dismounted, her long blonde locks covering her face. She was greeted by a short, bonnet-wearing maid. Annette collapsed against the maid's shoulder as she was led indoors.

The manor was like a masterfully crafted, overgrown doll-house; picturesque and charming up to the very last roof shingle. The garden boasted several flowering trees, marble fountains that whispered and bubbled in the tranquil atmosphere, and a deep pond with floating lotus plants. They approached the door with hesitation, Hector refusing to tell them his plan until they were mere footsteps away.

"Now, take this." Hector shoved the shopping bag holding Annette's things into Penny's hands. "You pretend you merely followed after her to return it. Once you've got her alone, try and warn her, yes?"

Penny opened her mouth to refuse, but Hector was already yanking the rope that rang the doorbell. He rushed off with Simon, leaving Penny standing alone on the doorstep, feeling frantic.

"Come back! I don't know what to say! Hey! You guys—" Penny hissed, stopping as the sounds of somebody fumbling with the door latch became audible. The door eased open a crack and an unfamiliar person leaned into view, looking tepid and raising a sculpted eyebrow.

There was a second's worth of studying the stranger while Penny tried to figure out if a man or a woman stood before her. The individual's body was built strong with broad shoulders, a thin waist, and skinny, flat hips. He was very tall; Penny guessed about six-foot-two. His face was beautifully proportioned and done up with lipstick and delicate hints of makeup around his gray eyes, which were shaped like Annette's. He wore his ashy brown hair long and silky, secured with a lacy bow as it ended in an elegant wisp near the middle of his back. A pair of silver earrings dangled and flashed in the bright sunlight. He looked graceful in a long silk jacket set with lacy cuffs, myriad opulent jewels on his white fingers, and a fancy skirt; the picture of radiant, if not overdressed, beauty.

"Can I....help you?" he looked Penny up and down, towering over her measly five feet and two odd inches. She swallowed, not knowing what to say. She held the small shopping bag up like a shield between her and the tall man.

"Um, um—I..." murmured Penny, and the man sighed and rolled his eyes.

"I don't know how you found this house, but she is *not* giving autographs right now. Run along, now. Shoo." The man waved his polished fingers as if to sweep Penny away as he began to close the door. Mustering her courage at last, she stuck her foot in the way. The man shot a ruffled glance back.

"Erm, sorry but...is there a blonde girl who lives here? I think she dropped this. I saw her shopping and she got into some sort of fight with this other woman, and she left this at the shop. I'd—" Penny's stammering was cut off by the sound of another voice.

"Who's there, Gavin?"

Gavin looked over his shoulder as Annette approached the door like a mouse poking its head out of a hiding place. Penny noted with a pang of sorrow that her eyes were red and she looked exhausted. Gavin made an effort to shut the door again, but Penny kept her face in view of the actress.

"Oh, it's no one! Just a girl who's found something of yours, don't worry yourself. You shouldn't—" Gavin said in a coddling tone, but Annette wasn't listening. She moved past Gavin and took hold of the door herself, her blue eyes curious as they looked Penny over. Annette spied the bag that Penny clenched like a crucifix and gasped, putting her hands to her porcelain face.

"Oh, my goodness! I was so upset that I forgot this!" She removed the bag from Penny's hands, gratitude in her eyes. Gavin looked down on the scene in vague concern. "You brought it back to me—how kind. What's your name?"

"Um, it's Penny Fairfax..." she told Annette, feeling entirely out of her element. Annette smiled, and Penny could not think of what else to say, so she burst out with the next thing that popped into her mind. "Wh-what's yours?"

Gavin strangled back an incredulous laugh which he attempted to transform into an unconvincing cough. Annette looked shocked, but her expression changed into a soft smile.

"Just call me Annette," she told Penny with satisfaction.

Penny already regretted her words; there would be no hope of warning her now. The actress shared a meaningful look with Gavin before turning her attention back to Penny. "You've gone through so much trouble to bring me this, I must thank you! Please, would you like to come in and have some tea?"

"Nettie!" Gavin exclaimed, sounding scandalized. "You've got to get yourself cleaned up and start practicing for your show tomor—"

"Hush, Gavin!" she snapped. Gavin fell silent. Annette gave Penny an apologetic look. "Please excuse my cousin, he's just a bit of a worrywart. Come in, come in!" She yanked Penny inside by the wrist and shut the door behind her. "Gavin, ask Auntie to make us some tea and snacks. Millie can bring it to us in the Sun Garden."

"Nettie—is this really the best ide—"

"It's my day off!" she said, her smile firm. He sighed and shuffled off down the hall.

Penny looked around, taking in the huge staircase that wound up three floors to a dizzying height. Rich wood, silk wall panels and original oil paintings decorated the halls. Expensive furniture dotted the room and the smell of jasmine hung on the air.

"You live here?" Penny asked Annette, breathless. "It's beautiful!"

"I'm glad you like it," Annette replied. Annette led Penny through the cavernous house, stopping only to hand off the shopping bag to Millie, the cheerful maid Penny had spotted outside earlier.

Annette led Penny through a few sitting rooms and down a long corridor lined with frosted lamps. At the end of the hall was a door that led to a hexagonal greenhouse, with the roof and walls made completely out of glass panels and crowded with a veritable forest of house plants. The room was warm, so filled with flora it felt alive, almost as if it were growing and breathing softly around them.

Annette led Penny over to a garden table and chairs. The sense of being inside a very large dollhouse grew more intense as Penny sat down across from Annette at the table. Delicate white lilies grew nearby and the noise of running water splashed, creating a tranquil ambience. Penny tried to peer out of the windows and see if Hector and Simon were watching her, as they'd promised.

"This is the Sun Garden," Annette explained with pride. "It's a product of my own design...I hope you find it to your liking."

"Is this your aunt's house?" Penny grasped at a conversation topic, feeling more than a little awkward. Annette looked shocked for the second time and giggled, the sound tinkling like silver.

"No, no! This is *my* house, Gavin and his mother live here to keep me company, that's all—it wouldn't do at all to live here all alone. My parents and sisters are out traveling as usual, so it can get a bit lonely," Annette answered.

"You bought this house all on your own? That's amazing!"

Annette leaned on her thin white wrist, studying Penny. The silence stretched on for a little longer than Penny liked and she averted her gaze, embarrassed.

"You've really never heard of me, have you?" Annette prodded in a contemplative, yet pleased tone. It struck Penny as odd that the actress seemed happy about being unknown, but she could only shake her head.

Millie bustled in, pushing a cart laden with a collection of treats and a dainty tea set. She set the steaming tea pot between them, adding two splendid teacups and saucers, followed by sugar, cream, and a silver spoon each. Penny's mouth watered when Millie set up a tiered arrangement of delectable-looking food: tiny tea sandwiches of every variety, crumbly scones, miniature tarts overflowing with sun-ripe berries that sparkled in a sugary glaze, tiny cakes frosted in springtime colors with spun-sugar flowers decorating the tops, and powdered cookies, glistening with jam. Annette clapped her hands together.

"Ooh, Auntie has outdone herself! Wonderful! Please, don't be shy, Penny, have as much as you like!" Annette coaxed as Millie poured a cup of tea for each of them before disappearing back into the hall.

Surprised by Annette's amiability, Penny found she was quite enjoying their time together. Each dessert was its own sensory experience; Penny was almost a little sad as she took the last few bites of tart, knowing it might be a long time before she got to taste anything half as wonderful again. She wished that Hector could have tasted them, knowing how much he loved sweets.

Penny inquired about the different plants in the Sun Garden, surprised to discover that gardening, embroidery, and sewing were just a few of Annette's many beloved pastimes. Annette seemed happy to discuss her hobbies and interests with Penny, but avoided more personal and direct questions with surprising tact.

Her open nature confused Penny at first, until it dawned on her that everyone in Iverton must know everything about Annette, and it had probably been a long time since Annette had been able to share herself as a person and not a celebrity. Penny listened intently, genuinely interested in what Annette had to say despite the alarm building in her chest. The whole ordeal was very much like the kind of dream she wished she would never wake from.

Annette's stream of conversation halted. "My goodness, listen to me! I've gone on and on, how rude of me. Please, tell me a bit about yourself. I'm guessing you're not from around here?" Annette prompted, her eyes sparkling. Penny scratched at the back of her head, trying to think of ways to lie as little as possible.

"That's true, I came from Oreg…a very distant place and I'm here visiting with my two friends, but other than that I'm really not very interesting," she told Annette, offering a mental apology for her plainness. It was becoming harder to deceive Annette. Penny liked her. She did not know what she had expected the actress to be like in person, but this certainly wasn't it. It was almost impossible to imagine why anyone would want Annette to suffer.

"I'm sorry, what was it that you said you did? I must've missed it…" Penny asked, congratulating herself for sounding so convincing.

Annette's expression dampened. "I was afraid you'd ask that," she said in a small voice, her gaze moving from the tea set to the lilies that surrounded them. "In truth, I'm an actress and a singer. Actually, it might sound bad—but half the reason I invited you in here was because you don't know who I am. You don't know how tiresome it can get…being stopped on the street all the time, keeping up an image, entertaining everyone all the time, not knowing who wants to be my friend just because I'm famous…"

Penny did her best to look shocked as Annette's head drooped, a bittersweet smile on the actress's face. A rush of emotion hit her knowing that her assumptions about Annette's loneliness had been quite correct, and the spike of guilt buried itself deeper in her chest.

"Just now, in the store—I mean, where you dropped your things…" Penny began, having every intention to tell the truth, but Annette interrupted, pouting.

"So you saw that, huh? That was Valentine Frost—" she scowled, an undercurrent of deep anger in her voice, "She—"

"She's awful," Penny said at once, losing her courage to tell Annette what she needed to. Annette flashed a mischievous grin.

"She's *is* awful, isn't she? Just a bitter, old has-been with an inflated ego," Annette snickered, then added, "Oh, would you like to see to the rest of the house?"

Against her better judgment Penny nodded and Annette led her back down the hall, opening doors and showing off a few guest rooms that would have sufficed as master bedrooms most anywhere in Penny's hometown. Annette showed her a few sitting rooms, telling Penny amusing stories of incidences that had occurred in each one of them as if they were old friends. They explored the kitchens, which were well-equipped and large enough to supply food for a restaurant.

"Auntie spends a lot of time in here—she loves to cook," Annette told her, skipping around the stove. "Come on, let's go see the dining room. The king even came to eat here one time!"

Annette swept her through the rest of the three-story house, and after some careful consideration invited Penny to see her bedroom. With a light footstep, Penny entered Annette's private sanctum, wondering how many people in Iverton would give everything just to be in her place right now.

A huge closet set against the back wall overflowed with dresses, each of them designed with lace, ruffles, bows, and charming prints. Annette's four-poster bed was carved of white wood and draped in sheer pink curtains, an assortment of stuffed animals and pillows spilling over the sides and onto the floor. Toys and sparkling trinkets lay all over the place, some even cluttered on a regal-looking desk, and the vanity was so covered with makeup products Penny could hardly see the surface. A jar of tiny translucent stones cut into the shape of stars sat on the center of the desk beside a hand-painted music box, a miniature carousel, and a collection of fancy dolls.

"Come see the view!" Annette rushed over to her curtain framed window and looked out at Iverton stretching before them. Penny joined her at the window and smiled as Annette looked at her. "You don't talk much, do you?"

Penny laughed, feeling self-conscious. "No…not really. Truth be told, I don't have many friends," Penny admitted. Annette gave her an understanding smile, which said more than any verbal sentiment could have possibly communicated. Gavin called for Annette then, and they left Annette's sanctum to see what he wanted.

They entered a chamber on the floor below and once again Penny was dumbfounded. Wide, tall windows lined the back wall, offering another panoramic view of the city. In the center of the room was a large instrument that bore a striking resemblance to a piano, made of the same white and gold carvings that seemed to be a central theme in the house. Several other musical instruments, some stringed and some made of bronzy metals, were displayed on their respective stands. Bookshelves packed top to bottom with musical scores and compositions were pushed up against the walls. Gavin was digging around in one of them, searching for a score that Annette helped him find in under a minute.

"This room—it's amazing," Penny choked, stepping up to the keyed instrument in the center, and trying a few of the keys, enjoying the sound that filled the air as she did. "Can you play *all* these instruments?"

"Oh, no! I can sing, but I'm miserable when it comes to these things. Gavin's the real genius between us," Annette laughed, her china blue eyes filled with affection for her cousin. He smiled at her compliment and tossed his wispy hair.

"Go on, Gavin dear, play something for her," Annette urged.

Gavin sighed, a light smile still playing on his lips. "Well, if you insist," he conceded, sliding down onto the bench. His strong, wide hands positioned themselves expertly above the keys. Everything was quiet for a split second before Gavin's fingers came to life over the keys, filling the room with an exquisite song. Annette had not been flattering him when she called him a genius; he played the complex, romping melody with confident ease. The music swelled and spun over their heads, making Penny's heart dance. When Annette's voice sang out clear and pure, Penny closed her eyes and let the music envelope her.

Annette and Gavin were perfectly in time and tune with one another, working together as if they could read each other's minds. Annette was everything Penny had always wanted to be, and seeing her stand so carefree and perfect made Penny realize how mismatched she felt in their world. The guilt at having not conveyed her warning to Annette deepened with a painful ache. When the song was over, Penny erupted into excited applause. Annette laughed and Gavin took a sweeping bow.

"That was *wonderful!*" Penny exclaimed.

"Well, thank you. All credit to Gavin, though—I'd be nothing without him. He taught me everything I know," Annette told Penny. Gavin excused himself, and Penny's stomach squirmed. It was past time to explain.

"Annette," she started, feeling her voice tremble, "Listen, it's been really fun visiting with you today. I feel so honored to have met you…"

"I know, I'm so glad we met! Maybe—maybe you could visit me again? I wish I could come out and meet you and your friends somewhere, but…you know…" Her honesty and kindness were almost painful to Penny.

"I'd—I'd really like that, but—I feel terrible…I've been meaning to tell you something—" Penny stammered, feeling her voice crash into a diminuendo. Annette picked up on her remorseful nature and drew back, looking disturbed.

"Huh?" she breathed.

"I haven't been completely honest with you, and before I say anything I want you to know I'm extremely sorry for it," Penny said, staring at her feet in misery.

"What are you talking about?" an ashen Annette demanded.

Penny balled up her fists and prayed for strength. "Listen, I know how this sounds—but that Valentine woman is—she's trying to hurt you. Someone is going to kidnap you, and she's helping them. It's all going to—"

"What?" Annette yelped. "How could you possibly know th—you *lied* to me?"

"Please, you've got to hear me out," Penny tried, but Annette's eye grew fierce. All her childlike sweetness was gone. Annette's lips parted and she spoke in an odd tone that seemed to vibrate in Penny's ears and shiver in her body.

"*Sit down,*" she ordered, and Penny felt their power as if she had screamed them.

Something was very different about her voice now; something was wrong. Penny's heart thudded in her chest as her body began to move of its own accord, drifting into the chair that stood by the piano. Annette fluttered over and shut the door with a resolve in her countenance that scared Penny. She struggled to stand back up, but her legs would not allow her to move.

Annette turned and spoke again in her bizarre, authoritative voice, "*You will not move from where you sit. If you have any intention of harming me or my family, you will immediately be rid of it. You will not be able to lie from this moment on, do you understand?*"

Penny nodded, realizing with a sick whirl of fear that she was unable to disobey Annette Deveaux's commands.

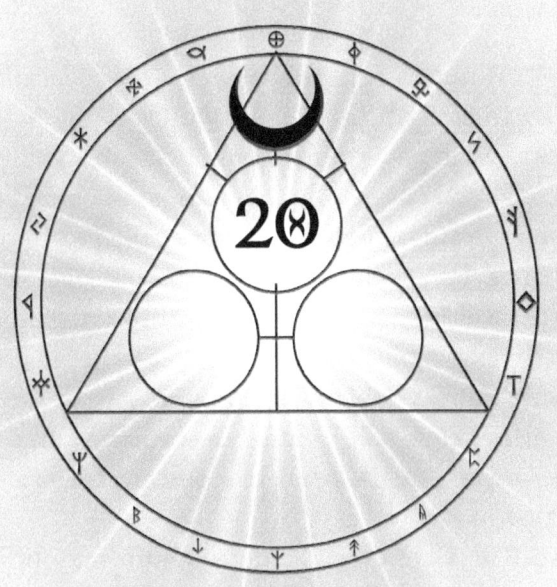

AN AGREEMENT

Waves of fear tried to shake Penny as Annette stepped up to her, but her body felt as if it were bound by invisible cords at every joint. Panicked, Penny looked around, trying to rationalize what was happening to her. Drawing up a chair, Annette sat down across from her without breaking eye contact.

"What's...happening to me...?" Penny struggled to speak.

"Quiet, please. I'll be asking the questions for now," Annette told her. "Now, tell me what you're doing here?"

"I—I came here to warn you, just like I said. Valentine is trying to hurt you," Penny repeated, feeling her lips move without her consent. The loss of control made her head spin. Annette's expression rippled with shock.

"So you *were* telling the truth..." she mumbled, half to herself. "How did you find out about Valentine's plan? Don't leave out any details."

"A-A—" Penny struggled against the sensation that tempted her to spill all her secrets and lost the battle. "An elf called Aldridge gave m-me some tickets to your show. I had never seen you before, my friend Simon persuaded me to g-go. When I was there I s-s-saw a man called Deimos Geller in the audience. He's trying to kill me and my friends—I don't know why. It was because of him I was forced to come to this world and I was curious to see why he was after us, so I tried to steal his memories—"

"Wait—*what?* Stop, stop! Didn't you hear me when I said *no lying?*" she stressed the last part in a powerful, vibrating tone that resonated in Penny's ears.

"I heard you, I can't lie," Penny's mouth said for her. She could not remember ever feeling so powerless. Tears burned in her eyes and she bit her tongue to stop them from coming. All the color in Annette's face drained as she processed what Penny had just said.

"No, something must be wrong. That's impossible...there's no such thing as other worlds—and isn't Deimos Geller the Baron of Dewthorne? This can't be. You've got some way of rendering it useless..." Annette spoke to herself, a hand on her forehead as she stared at Penny.

"What did you mean when you said you 'tried to steal his memories'?" Annette questioned, bemused. Before Penny could answer, a loud thump rang out from downstairs and somewhere Gavin cried out. Both Penny and Annette jumped. Dread soaked through Penny as more shouts sounded in the hall and thunderous footsteps clamored on the stairs. Annette jumped to her feet, her face pale. The door slammed open and Hector burst into the room, followed by Simon.

"Penelope!" Hector exclaimed, winded. His hands emitted silver and red runes as he prepared to perform a spell. Annette made a guttural gasping sound and caught her breath.

"*STOP!*" she commanded, pointing at Hector. Penny's heart sank again as Hector's arms fell to his sides and his eyes grew terrified.

Annette ran to the center of the room just as Gavin skidded in. "Nobody move!" she hollered, stamping her foot. Simon, Hector, and Gavin became motionless as Annette peered around at them all, her breath ragged. She swallowed.

"Now...we will all *calmly* go down to the drawing room... and someone...is going to explain to me what is going on here..." Annette looked to each of them in turn, and then gestured for everyone to follow her downstairs. Penny's body was lifted from the chair, as if tugged along by invisible strings. Simon and Hector followed behind with Annette leading the group, her face set into a hard expression that was discredited by her trembling shoulders.

In the drawing room Annette directed Penny, Hector, and Simon to sit down on a blue satin couch. She asked Gavin to leave, and he protested with an indignant squawk, "But, *Nettie!* I can't leave you alone with them! I don't even know who they—" he cut off when Annette pouted.

"Gavin..." she begged, her voice subdued and meek. Gavin's face fell.

"Will you at least promise to tell me later?" he tried to whisper, but they all heard him.

"Not everything, Gavin, but most things, I promise. Now go tell Millie and Auntie that everything's okay, and not to worry." She spun him around, pushed his towering form through the door, and shut it behind him after catching one last forlorn glance from Gavin. Annette swiveled back to face Simon, Hector, and Penny, all whom wore identical expressions of dread.

Simon began to squirm against his intangible bonds. "Please, don't hurt us! Or at least don't hurt me! It was their idea, they *forced* me to come along, I never wanted to—" he pleaded, but lost his voice when Annette stopped in mid-step and broke into a weak smile.

"I'm not going to hurt you," she reassured him, patting his shoulder. His face turned a warm pink and he let out a little breath as Annette withdrew her fingers and stalked toward the center of the room, deep in thought.

"From—from what Penny has told me, it seems you're all trying to help me, and I appreciate that—I really do. I just need to use certain safety measures to make sure no one is lying to me. I hope you all understand," she explained at last, still pacing back and forth, her frilly skirts bobbing with each step.

"Miss Deveaux, might I express my sincerest apologies for barging into your house like this?" Hector spoke up, and Annette stopped pacing to consider him. "Penelope was gone for so long, we thought she was in danger. But now that you have made your true intentions clear, I feel rather foolish. I acted out of fear, please forgive me."

Penny felt a strange twisting sensation in her chest at Hector's words, but her face remained still, waiting for Annette's reaction. To her relief Annette nodded at him in understanding.

"You may, and you are forgiven. Now, you seem to know what's going on, so please...tell me everything—every last detail. Also, *no lying allowed*." Her last command shook with ethereal vibrations and Penny knew Hector would have no choice but to obey. She now understood why Deimos so coveted whatever it was Annette was using to control them. Hector cleared his throat.

"Well, it is a rather long story, you might want to get comfortable," Hector forewarned. Annette took his advice and seated herself on a satin blue loveseat, only a low, elegant coffee table separating them.

"Well I suppose I'd better start with Nelvirna, then..." Hector sighed, displaying the usual disheartened look he got when thinking about his home. In his usual meticulous manner, he relayed to Annette everything that had happened and all the information that they'd learned from the time he arrived on Earth, up until the events of that morning.

As the tale wound on, Annette seemed much less confused and panicked. Her expression changed from intense concentration to astonishment now and then, but she never interrupted to question the credibility of their tale. Penny decided that she must either be confident that they were unable to lie, or completely gullible. By the end of Hector's explanation, Annette's face seemed to have aged; earlier it had been so vibrant and full of joy, now she looked strained as she mused over their information.

Penny, Hector, and Simon waited, no one daring to say anything more. Annette rose and drifted over to the window, distress clear on her face. Penny noticed the light outside had become weak; twilight was upon them. Annette turned back and cut through the uncomfortable silence.

"I knew this would happen eventually, I knew someone would—" her voice left off in a tremble. She looked at them, shaken. "I've been trying to hide—to disappear into my own little world, but—I have this awful feeling it's all about to come crashing down." Penny admired Annette for being able to so share her innermost worries with total strangers, something she was unable to accomplish even with her closest friends. "I—I'm so very grateful that you all went to such lengths to help me, even though I'm a complete stranger."

"Miss Annette, I would go to *any* lengths to ensure your safety!" Simon rose and proclaimed with melodramatic nobility. Penny was a bit shocked to see he was free of the invisible bonds, and discovered that she too could move and speak of her own will again. Annette was taken aback by Simon's outburst and looked as if she were about to laugh when something struck her.

"Are you—quite certain about that?" The light of sudden inspiration flickered in her china blue eyes. This threw Simon for a loop. His dashing smile faded and he fell speechless.

"What do you mean, Miss Deveaux?" Hector asked.

"Before I ask anything more of you, I feel I should make it clear that I do not intend to let you go. You know much too much about all this, about *them* and about...other matters," she said, indicating that this was all she would share about her curious ability. "If anyone were to know—well, my career and reputation would be tarnished. I hope you understand, but I'm not going to allow you to leave."

"Wh-what? You can't just—" Penny exclaimed, but the actress cut her off.

"Oh, yes I can. Anyway, it's safer for you here than out there. From the sound of it, Deimos isn't playing around, and if he's in town, you'd better be careful. It seems to me like our paths were destined to cross eventually. After all, some of the best friendships are formed out of sharing enemies. Of course, we'll treat you all wonderfully! And...it'll be nice to have a little company."

"B-but, we need to get to—" Simon blubbered.

"I know, I'm getting to that, don't worry," Annette assured him. "You need to get to Crescia, and I certainly don't intend to be kidnapped or murdered by anyone. I think we might be able to work out a way to make everyone very happy." She paused, gauging their reactions.

"Go on," Hector replied, still quite skeptical.

"Well, you'd be able to recognize this Deimos, right? You'd be able to stop him if he tried to get at me? I saw the magic you did before...could you protect me?" Annette addressed Hector, feigning innocent helplessness as she looked into his eyes. Simon scowled as Hector cleared his throat a little and loosened his collar.

"Erm, I suppose. I'd certainly be able to hold him off, if that's what you mean—but as I explained, I'm not adept at combative spells as—"

"I knew I could count on you, big brother!" Annette gushed, and Penny felt an unexpected, powerful burst of irritation toward them.

Really, Hector? I'd expect that of Simon, but not—

"W-wait a moment, I'm not quite sure what you want me to do," Hector stuttered, looking uncomfortable. Simon was still glowering.

Annette smiled, her hands on her hips. "I'm sure of one thing: they're planning to try something at the King's Annual Jubilee Ball. Valentine hasn't so much as looked at me for about four years. Her comment today about the ball was just *too* obvious. She wanted to make sure I'd be there, or give me a reason to show up by taunting me. I'm certain of it. She's just the kind of vicious little—" Annette stopped, looking a tad embarrassed at her outburst. "Anyway, I'd like to form an agreement with you all. The ball is two weeks away. If you stay here until then and escort me to it as my bodyguards, I promise to get you all tickets for the airship to Hulver. That way, I won't have to hire any outside bodyguards, which eliminates the chance of information being leaked by them. Hulver is a cesspool of rumors, so even if you told this entire story to the King Yulghrat himself, no one would believe it. How does that sound?" she offered.

We don't have much of a choice, do we? Penny thought cynically.

"I think we'd better take some time to consi—" Hector began, but Simon jumped up and clasped Annette's hands in his own.

"Miss Annette, I would be proud to lay my life down for you," he almost shouted. Hector frowned and sighed, sharing a worried glance with Penny. Annette twittered, extricating her hands from Simon's affectionate grip.

"Wait a minute," Penny interjected, "What will you do after we're gone? Assuming Valentine doesn't try anything at the ball, where will you be then?"

"If that's the case, well—I suppose I'll cross that bridge when I come to it. But I'm completely sure that's the night, and when her plan is cracked wide open, the Rangers will arrest them all and I'll be safe for good!" Annette chirped, wobbling a little. Penny sighed, knowing that there was no way her plan would work out as well as she hoped.

"Sorry, but are you feeling all right? You look a bit peaky," Simon interrupted, looking over Annette's graying complexion. Annette nodded, holding her forehead in her palm as she flopped back down on the satin loveseat.

"I'm just tired—I think I'd better turn in early. This news has been rather upsetting to me." Annette assured him. She got up with shaking legs and crept toward the door. "I'll send Millie to pick up your things and your anteloo from the inn, just give her directions." She stepped out of the room, then turned back to them for a final, chirping word. "Oh, and don't try to do anything silly, like leaving the house! You know what that will force me to do. Let's just all agree to be friends for now — it'll make everything so much more pleasant."

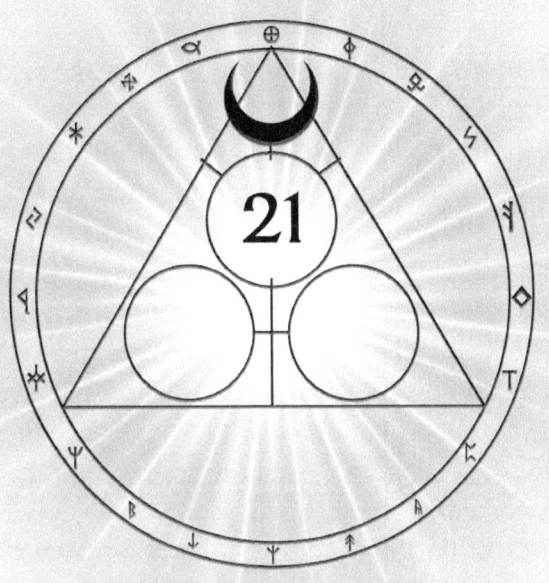

TRUSTING HECTOR

Penny, Hector, and Simon could not muster courage enough to leave the sitting room. Once night had come, Gavin interrupted their quiet by opening the doors and peering in with an uncertain smile.

"Good evening," he greeted them. "Nettie has gone to bed, I'm sure you know. She was able to make the situation clear to me beforehand, so I thought I'd take this time to formally welcome you to our home," he explained, not without apprehension. He seemed jumpy, perhaps worried that one of them might spring up and attack without warning. Simon was staring at him, every so often glancing down at the skirt he wore in blatant confusion. Penny noticed his rude reaction and gave him a sharp elbow to the ribs with a warning glance.

"Thank you very much, we really appreciate everything you're doing for us," Penny told Gavin, and he seemed to relax a mite.

"My mother's made some dinner, if you'd like to join us..." he offered.

"Good lord, yes! I'm starved!" Simon sprung to his feet, losing all prior misgivings with the mention of food. Gavin led them to the furnished dining room where several steaming dishes were waiting. Gavin's mother was a short, plump woman with half-moon spectacles and flossy white hair tucked in a bun. The woman beamed as her guests wandered into the room with wide eyes, welcoming Penny and her friends and introducing herself as Aunt Wendy to them. When they had all been seated, she encouraged them to keep filling their plates, stressing particularly over her son.

"Look at you, darling—you're like a walking skeleton! Here, have some more rolls." She piled a few more on Gavin's plate and he flushed a rosy hue.

"Mother, please..." he said through gritted teeth, and Penny giggled to herself. The food was nothing short of exquisite, rife with an authentic, homemade quality. Wendy was full of questions and compliments for each one of them, and though her attitude was warm, her attention seemed vague and fleeting. For dessert Wendy brought them a homemade spice cake frosted and bejeweled with autumn-time berries. Hector was beside himself with joy.

The night passed quickly, but the feeling of tension remained. Millie fetched their luggage and showed each of them to a separate guestroom near the Sun Garden. Penny's room was spacious and furnished with a writing desk, dresser, an almost humorously large bed with a powder-blue satin coverlet, matching silk pillows, and her very own bathroom.

Penny flopped down on the elegant covers and sighed. She had forgotten how nice complete privacy was after spending so long rooming with two men in cramped quarters. She went about putting away her clothes and possessions, setting her little butterfly-shaped toy on the dresser beside her cherry-pine box. A quick check of the delicate glass orb showed that it was the same as always.

Penny looked herself over in the gold-framed mirror, surprised to see her face looked older than she remembered, and her hair had grown quite a bit. Hearing low murmurs coming from the wall she shared with Hector, Penny abandoned her reflection and tiptoed down the long dark hallway, opening up the door to his room with a small creak.

Simon was sitting at Hector's desk while the bespectacled man sat on the bed, his back resting against the headboard and his arms folded across his chest. They both looked toward Penny as she entered, stopping in mid-conversation.

"Let me guess, doing some male bonding?" she joked, shutting the door behind her.

"Riotously witty as usual, Penelope," Hector drawled as she joined them. He continued on as if Penny's entrance hadn't occurred, "But *why* does Valentine have such a powerful distaste for Miss Annette?"

Simon shrugged and snickered. "Well, it's obvious, isn't it? She's jealous of her youth and beauty." He sighed, looking content. "Elydria is blessed with such lovely ladies, I've never seen so many grouped together in one place..." His face changed, showing he had just remembered something. "Oh no...If I'm trapped here, I won't be able to say a proper goodbye to my Matilda..."

Seeing he wasn't very bothered by that revelation, Penny shook her head in disdain. "Shouldn't we be more concerned with what Annette was doing to us? I'm sure you felt it..." she reminded them. "She must have something really powerful to be able to control people like that. It's got to be what Deimos is after. Imagine what a thing like that in the wrong hands could accomplish."

"I'm not so sure it's a *thing* at all," Hector mused as he nibbled the end of his fingernail in thought, his hazel eyes fixed on something faraway. "I never saw her using any sort of tool. She wore no rings, no jewelry except that pair of earrings. She may be doing it of her own accord."

"But doesn't that contradict everything we've learned about magic in Elydria? It doesn't make sense that she would just develop a random ability. That's impossible." Penny crossed her arms.

"Impossible? You can weave dreams, and I can travel between worlds. How does any of *that* make sense?" Hector raised his brows, and Penny frowned, feeling patronized. "Oh, don't get all huffy—I'm just reminding you that anomalies do occur—"

Hector was interrupted by a small cry accompanied by a loud crashing sound as Simon leaned too far back in his chair and tumbled to the ground. Penny and Hector watched as he untangled his limbs from one another and scrambled to his feet.

"Maybe we'd all better get some sleep," Penny suggested. "Simon's liable to hurt himself if he stays awake much longer." Though Simon was miffed by this remark, Hector agreed and shooed them from his room with a curt goodnight.

Penny prepared for bed, enjoying the wonderful sense of aloneness that she had quite missed. Mere minutes after she sunk into the heavenly softness of the covers, she fell into a quiet and untroubled sleep. Though she slept through the night without disturbing visions in her dreams, threatening voices echoed in the corners of her mind. She awoke the next morning, a phrase in her mind repeating like a song.

Death is easy, death is easy... Life is but a dream.

THE NEXT MORNING, Penny joined Hector, Wendy, Gavin and Simon in the dining room to find another wonderful breakfast tea spread waiting. After Millie had cleared the dishes away, Gavin asked for Penny's help in tending to the plants in the Sun Garden since Annette still wasn't feeling well. As Gavin and Penny strolled among the plants, Gavin told her more about himself.

"Before, I was a pianist for one of the fancier restaurants in the Royal District, but I came here to take care of my cousin after her first big play several years ago. She…she needs us. I help her practice for her shows, keep her in a routine, arrange business affairs, manage finances—that sort of thing. She's twenty-three years old now, but she would be completely helpless without me and Mother. Her parents never taught her many life skills; they're always off gallivanting wherever they please without regard for others. She's still so innocent and sheltered, the dear thing," Gavin sighed and once again Penny took a moment to admire his dedication. "Though I wouldn't call living in this house a burden, by any means." He gave her a small wink and her heart did a somersault.

Annette awoke an hour before her performance that night and left in a flurry of lace and perfume, her carriage pulled by a white anteloo named Serafee. Early the next morning, Penny heard her singing in the Sun Garden.

"Is this what you usually do on your days off?" Penny asked as she joined the actress soon after, observing the clusters of tiny pink blooms Annette was tending to.

"Yes, in the mornings. I sometimes go shopping later on in the day, but it gets a little tiresome giving out autographs and such, so I generally stay at home. I'm usually alone except for Gavin. To be honest, I haven't got many close friends…" Annette trailed off, a look of impishness in her eyes. A broad smile crossed her face. "Penny, how would *you* like to spend the day with me? I'm certain between the two of us we can think of something simply wondrous to do!"

The two of them spent a good part of the day wasting time with Annette's various oddments. Annette was very curious to learn everything about Earth and Penny's life there. She was transfixed with Penny's descriptions of cars that ran on gasoline, computers, and smart phones. Annette was astounded that people on Earth got on without magic, but more per-plexed when she found that humans were the only highly intelligent species which inhabited Earth. Penny stopped the routine of endless questions and explanations when her eyes fell on Annette's bookshelf.

"Wow, are these all novels? I've been dying to read some-thing good for so long now—all Hector brought back was bor-ing stuff about science and magic theory," Penny said, plucking a dusty volume from the shelf and flipping through the pages. To her delight Annette granted her full access to all of the books, even recommending some of her favorites. Penny was surprised to find herself bonding with the actress with an ease and open-ness that she had never felt, even with Maddie.

Thoughts of Maddie made Penny think also of her mother, and her chest ached with homesickness. It was too much to imagine Paulina wandering around their house alone, haunted by vestiges of the life Penny had left behind. She pictured her mother sitting alone at dinner, chewing her food lifelessly as she stared at the chair which Penny had almost always filled. She wondered if Maddie even bothered going to school any longer. Thoughts of the remains of Hector's makeshift life occurred to her, and she remembered she'd told Maddie that Hector—back then he was called Professor Arlington—had been doing some-thing questionable.

Has he been blamed for my disappearance? Are Maddie, the police, and my mom under the impression that Hector stole me away in the night and did something unspeakable to me? Does Maddie blame herself for not believing what I said that day?

Penny sighed, feeling the paralyzing effects of these ques-tions. It came as something of a surprise that thoughts of home had been absent from her mind for this long. Her old life seemed so distant and miniscule as compared to now. She almost let the feelings of guilt and grief swallow her up, but when she looked over and recognized true contentment on Annette's face, they were swept away. Penny could see why it

227 THE ANGEL OF ELYDRIA

was so easy for Gavin to forgive Annette of her flaws. She over-flowed with an uncommon affection for others and a joy for life that was unstained by the vices and cruelties of the world.

There'll be time enough for worry and sorrow, but not now. Not today.

These first two days set the stage for a wonderful week. The next day Penny dove straight into the books Annette had lent her, finding the stories a refreshing return to her most beloved of hobbies. The next day Annette was home, and she and Penny discussed the novel with enthusiasm.

Simon was eager to try and get to know Annette as well, though Penny was sure it was for a very different reason. Annette was civil toward him, but his suave pick-up lines and dashing smiles were not as effective as he'd hoped, which frus-trated and disheartened Simon. When he wasn't hounding the beautiful young actress, he spent time in the kitchen pilfering food under the pretense of helping Wendy prepare meals.

Hector's urge to learn new things didn't stay suppressed for long. After a few days, he asked Gavin about the collec-tion of instruments he kept, scoring music lessons from the flattered man. Gavin taught him how to read Elydrian music and the basics of each instrument. One afternoon, Penny was somewhat shocked to hear him singing a soft lullaby to him-self in Nelvirnee while trying to accompany himself on a small stringed instrument. His voice was unsure and quiet, but he sang in a pure tone that made Penny's heart ache with a pain-ful sweetness.

Each night Penny read until the dawn broke through her window with a misty, indigo light. She had done this back on Earth, too, but for a very different reason. Whereas before Penny had been drawn in by the plots of the books she loved, now it was a way to keep from sleeping.

Every night, without fail, she dreamed of the masked entity in its various apparitions. It waited for her, haunting sepulchral halls as its empty, soundless voice echoed over and

over. The chant would ring in Penny's ears, becoming a terrifying mantra. The dreams seemed to last for hours at a time,
and on occasion Penny found herself trapped inside them for
an excruciating long time, all the while aware she was dreaming and wondering if she would ever wake up again. Every
time she awoke from the nightmare, her limbs felt heavier
and her body weaker. Penny attempted to chalk this up to the
possibility she had a cold, but she knew this was not true. She
was beginning to fear the dreamtime horrors, but could think
of no way to bring them up to others. Each time she tried to
open up to Hector, Simon, or even Annette about her nightmares, she shut down, telling herself they could do nothing
to help. She thought it likely Hector and Annette wouldn't be
able to comprehend the idea of a nightmare.

By the end of the first week of their stay, Penny observed
a noticeable change in the young actress. She had lost some of
the painful loneliness that had troubled her gaze when Penny
had first come to stay in her house, though she retained her
guarded look. One evening as one of Penny and Annette's frequent talks were dwindling down and they both lounged in
the comfortable drawing room, Penny considered asking a few
of the questions she wanted answers to, wondering if it might
lead to a precarious situation. She had shared quite a bit about
herself with Annette, and though Annette was keen on chat-
ting about books and humorous anecdotes, she never seemed
to want to share anything about her past.

"Annette..." Penny started. The wind was howling outside, thick clouds had rolled in, and the days had all but lost
their warmth. Winter was threatening to do away with autumn
for good, but had not quite won the war. Annette made a small
noise to show that she was listening, but didn't open her eyes,
seeming very relaxed.

"I...wanted to ask. What is it between you and Valentine?
Why does she hate you so much?" Despite her gentle tone,
Annette stiffened and her eyebrows furrowed.

"Why would you want to know something like that? She's just a pathetic old drunkard who takes out her bitterness out on the world, that's all," Annette said with forced casualness.

"Well, it's a bit strange to me—why she would want to go to such lengths to hurt you? And for that manner, why is Deimos looking for you?" Penny asked, hoping that she could breach some of the taboo topics that had been nagging at her. Annette sighed and pulled herself into a sitting position, looking serious.

"There *is* a reason—I'm sure you've figured that out. But..." Annette looked over to the corner of the room as she blinked her eyes several times. "It's too painful. I don't want to talk about—I don't want to think about it. Can we just forget about it? Is that okay?"

Penny nodded, disappointed.

OVER THE NEXT week the cold began to sink in deeper and deeper. The clouds remained as an impregnable layer above Iverton, erasing all memory of the carefree blue skies. Two days before the ball, the rainstorms started, beginning as heavy mists of thick perspiration and evolving into icy bullets that crashed down on Annette's manor. Penny watched Humphrey and Serafee try to keep dry in their stable and was pleased when Gavin brought them a magical lantern to keep the beasts warm throughout the stormy night.

Annette decided it was time to select their formal attire for the ball and loaded everyone into her carriage, and they rode into the Shopping District. It was much less a shopping trip than an occasion for Annette to force them into clothing she approved of. She decided on a white-gold dress for herself and a snowy blue gown with a gem-frosted bodice and a sheer, fluffy skirt for Penny. Hector agreed to a smart-fitting outfit that was modest enough for his tastes, but Annette could not persuade him not to wear his glasses for the event. Simon was beyond elated to have Annette fussing over him and undressing him to try on different types of coats. Once their attire was decided upon, Annette purchased all of the clothing for them, arguing that it was because of her that they had to buy it in the first place.

After lunch at an upper-class restaurant where Annette was approached by no less than thirteen devoted fans, all to which she graciously gave autographs, they returned to the manor, everyone sopping wet from the torrents of rain that crashed down relentlessly on the city. Wendy was prepared with a toasty fire and a cup of sweet, steaming milk for each of them. They dried off in front of the roaring flames, wrapped in blankets and sweaters, talking and listening to the rain coming down outside.

In the midst of a comfortable lull came a blinding flash of light from outside, followed by a sound so loud and deep it seemed to shake the house. Penny felt her shoulders tighten and stifled a scream as the thunder crashed and died away. Annette hopped off the couch and ran to the window.

"Oooh, did you see the lightning?" she marveled, standing on her tiptoes to get a better look out of the window.

Penny tried to catch her breath, hoping that no one had noticed her reaction. Her head spun and she found herself busy bargaining with higher powers not to let the lightning strike again. But it did strike again, and Annette shrieked with delight. Simon joined her at the window. Penny started to feel sick, wondering if she could contain her fear any longer. Hector glanced at her from the corner of his eye and she gritted her teeth.

When the third deafening crash rumbled through the house, Penny sprang to her feet, her legs shaking. She made for the door, ignoring the sounds of confusion behind her. She rushed down the hall past flickering lamps and dove under the covers on her bed, covering her ears as she tried to calm her thumping heart. Another thunderclap snarled at her and Penny whimpered, filled with as much self-hatred as fright; she was ashamed of her irrational cowardice. For what seemed like eons she shuddered in the dark sanctum, begging the thunder to stop as she willed away images of the beautiful, nightmarish face from her childhood. Then came a sound closer than the thunder—the door was opening.

Penny tensed, her heart resonating like a bass drum in her chest. She heard the handle click and the door creak. Someone was in the room with her.

At first she could not restrain the terrified delusion that the man from her past had returned. She had imagined it happening so many times; reliving the moment of terror again and again, as if in an unstoppable loop.

"Penelope?"

Penny's heart dropped. Her cheeks burned.

"Yes?" she replied through the blankets, trying to force as much normalcy as possible into her tone. She recognized Hector's laugh and clenched her jaw tighter.

"Why are you under there? Come out." She felt the weight on the bed shift and tremble as Hector sat down beside her. Penny cleared her throat.

"No thanks. I'm quite comfortable right where I am," she said with feigned haughtiness. She tried not to think about how ridiculous she sounded.

"It's the thunder, isn't it? You don't like it, do you?" he coaxed.

Penny was somewhat touched by his interest, as well as comforted by his presence. She drew the blanket fortress away from her head and pulled it around her shoulders with a sullen nod. Hector smiled but didn't speak for a long time, which made Penny anxious all over again.

She broke the silence. "Go ahead and laugh. I'm pathetic. I'm a coward. I'm acting like a child. I already know how much of an idiot I am, but please—don't be shy. Laugh it up—I don't mind," Penny spat, checking out of the corner of her eye to see his expression. It showed only patient kindness.

"You do know that thunder cannot harm you, correct? It's merely a by-product of the lightning as it stri—"

"*I know what thunder is, okay?*" Penny snapped, feeling patronized even though she knew he had not intended it that way. A look of affront crossed his face as she regained her composure. She gave him an apologetic glance, feeling that she owed him at least a small explanation.

"It's not *really* the thunder that bothers me—it's just the memory—of—" her voice died in her throat as she found it too difficult to continue.

"Memory of what? What do you mean?" Hector urged. Penny fell silent as she stood at a crossroads in her heart. She wanted to tell him, though she couldn't understand why. Her eyelashes fluttered as she looked up, deciding to test him first.

"I haven't ever really told anyone, you see. My mother begged me not to say anything to anyone else. You've never met her, but she's…well—eccentric might be a good word to describe her. We own a shop filled with all sorts of junk to do with occult interests and witchcraft and whatnot, so that might give you a good idea about what she's like. A long time ago, my grandmother tried to have her locked up in a psych ward for things she said and believed in, so at that time she was try-ing to protect me, as well," Penny explained.

"I will not so much as insinuate that you are of unsound mind, you have my word," he assured her, watching Penny contemplate.

She cleared her throat, her gaze fixed on the sheets. "I suppose it wouldn't hurt to tell you," Penny decided. Hector waited with an unassuming expression for her to continue. She sighed and struggled to think of a place to begin.

"It happened back when we lived in Montana. That's where my grandmother lives, and where my mom grew up. I was only five years old, and I remember it was raining hard that night.

I fell asleep, but when I woke up—when I woke up, someone was there with me in my room." It made Penny shiver to hear the words uttered aloud and Hector's brow pinched in a worried line. Penny swallowed.

"I had no idea who he was or how he got in, but I felt him standing there, just in front of my bed. When the lightning flashed, I saw his face." Hector looked very worried and uncomfortable now, as if he had been expecting anything but this. Penny realized she'd been gripping the blanket until her knuckles were white and quickly let go.

"He looked like a—like a beautiful nightmare. He was beyond perfect, but terrifying because of it...he had these waves and waves of long white hair. I didn't even have time to scream, I just felt him grab me."

"Wh-what happened after that?" Hector shivered. Penny frowned and ran her fingers through her hair in frustration.

"I can't remember—that's the worst part. It could've been *anything,* but to this day I have no idea. I woke up in the rose garden in front of our house the next morning. I didn't feel hurt, but I was scared so badly I could hardly function for months afterward. I made such a big deal about it my mom moved us to Oregon. I remember she tried to fool me into thinking it was just a bad nightmare, and sometimes I try to believe that...but..." Penny left off, looking off into the corner of the room as she pondered it again. "It doesn't bother me most of the time, just when the thunder comes back. I'm afraid that—well, that—"

"That he might come back?" Hector guessed and Penny's heart jumped at hearing her most powerful dread articulated. She nodded again, hanging her head.

"You must think I'm such a coward, letting a silly thing like this reduce me to such a mess..." Penny whispered, trying to bridle in her emotions, wanting to keep everything inside, safe and hidden. When she chanced a look at Hector, he shook his head. They shared a long gaze in which Penny realized he understood her irrationality and emotional scars more than she could ever know. For a brief moment she felt she could grasp at the aching misery that lay behind his unguarded gaze, but then it slipped from her fingers like grains of sand, falling back into darkness.

"Why didn't you tell me this before? This is—"

"I know!" Penny cut him off, feeling foolish. "I know it could be relevant to why this is happening to me, or important information otherwise. I just didn't really feel—"

Hector interrupted her admittance with a vehement shake of his head. "I was going to say it's not something you should have to deal with by yourself," he said, his comforting words ringing in her ears. Penny had never felt so vulnerable and her heart pattered away like a runaway train. She found she could not look at Hector until he made a small movement toward her.

Her eyes fixed on his face in exhilarated nervousness as he reached toward her. For a moment she thought he was trying to embrace her and her heart leapt straight into her throat, but instead he placed a hand on either side of her head, covering her ears. Frozen in confusion, Penny stayed still until she heard and felt the crackle of magic. It flared around her ears for a short moment and died away, like a sparkler going out. Hector withdrew his hands and gave her the smallest of smiles. She blinked.

"Wh-what did you just do?" she patted her ears to make sure they were still attached to her head. Nothing felt out of the ordinary. Hector stood up briskly from the bed.

"I made it so you won't be able to hear the thunder tonight— but it will only last until morning. Let me know if you need it again, it's no trouble," Hector told her, crossing his arms over his chest. Overjoyed, Penny was at a loss for words. Hector laughed at her stunned expression.

"Thank you for telling me, Penelope. It was…it…well, you know," he finished with a gesture of his hands. She smiled, pretending she understood what he meant, too overwhelmed by emotions to do much else.

Hector coughed, looking shy. "Get some sleep. The ball will be here quicker than you know it. Goodnight."

Penny sat in silence for a moment after he left, then realized she had not spoken her gratitude. "Thank you! Thanks, Hector!" she shouted at the wall, hoping he heard her. There was no reply, but she was sure he must've heard. It was quiet now and the sound of the rain had become less menacing. Penny stared out the window at the midnight blue smears of water that rippled down the window. When a flash of light came, only a small shiver of fear licked at her heart.

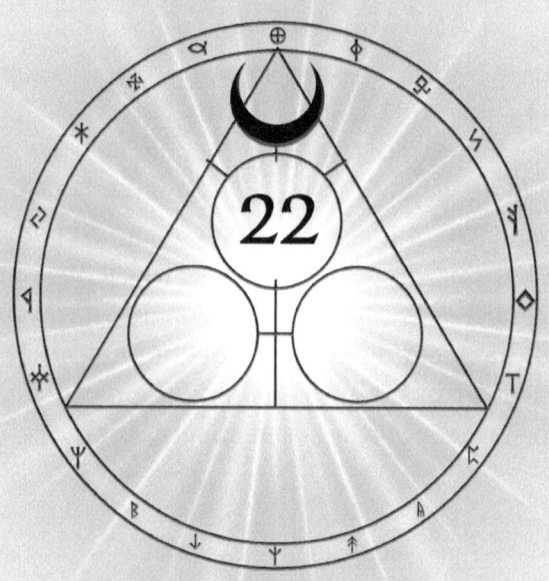

THE JUBILEE WALTZ

The castle looked like a mirage shimmering through the light drizzle that hung like a diaphanous curtain in the air. The tops of the trees were frosted with moisture, glinting in the lights streaming from the castle and its magnificent gardens. One by one the carriages rolled up to the gates, all number of strange feet clicking, padding, and plodding over the rain-slicked road. Above a patchwork of clouds cluttered an otherwise brilliant purple, star-speckled sky.

Annette was breathless with excitement. "Ooh, the decorations are phenomenal this year! Time to go, time to go!" she trilled, clapping her hands. Annette led them down the winding garden path, pointing out a collection of fine topiaries, elegant fountains, and carved statues of mythic maidens and beasts of legend. Tiny glowing insects trapped in crystal orbs hung from the limbs of trees, hid in bushes, and floated on the surface of the fountain's water.

The castle entrance was a yellow-orange mouth, radiating warmth and cheerful voices. Two more guards stood in front of the behemoth doors, and when Annette curtsied to them, they escorted the entire party inside the castle without needing to check the guest list. Penny detected a hint of excitement in the guard's eyes.

"Right this way, if you please…" The second man bowed and led the group up an indigo carpeted staircase and down a cavernous hall toward the ballroom. Even from the end of the hall, the ballroom was ablaze with spinning and glittering movement. Diamonds and emeralds adorned noble ladies, shining like they each contained a galaxy of their own. The entire dizzy scene was lit by a gargantuan chandelier that hung above like a spider made from thousands of pieces of ice. Tantalizing smells of the rich buffet hit, the prepared food so enticing it alone could have served as decoration. Girls in white dresses drifted by like merry ghosts, weaving between the cloth-covered tables sprinkled with a variety of regal centerpieces. They entered the ballroom with their escort, who cleared his throat to address the crowd, many of whom stopped dancing to see who had arrived.

"Miss Annette Deveaux, Master Gavin Deveaux and entourage," the man proclaimed, bowed again, and departed. Annette curtsied as the ballroom broke into applause; Penny felt very small watching Annette and Gavin take their respectful bows.

Sifting into the crowd, Annette greeted all the important party guests with formal exuberance. Hector and Gavin drifted away to find somewhere less chaotic, while an uncomfortable Penny and Simon hung around Annette as she socialized with various leaders of provinces. Not ten minutes into the party, Penny noticed Simon had his eyes set on two identical young women. Forgetting his duty, he trailed after them. Penny watched him go, inadvertently catching the glances of a group of goblins huddling near the corner of the ballroom as they glared about at the partygoers. Looking far less intimidating was a crimson dragon with cobalt hair and eyes, socializing with other party guests. Penny stared at his ruby-bright scales as he popped a pofflin leg in its mouth as if it were a malt-ball.

"I think that's Ambassador Farful. He's been working to better the way dragons are treated in the Nation of Men... things are still tense, even though the Dragon Wars ended a century ago," Annette whispered, and led Penny off on a tour of the room, pointing out some of the more prestigious guests in the crowd, including brilliant scholars of magic, mechanists, scientists, famous artists, crafters, and historians. Annette tried to locate the representative from Trulle, the capital city of the-rion Nation, but she could not.

"Therios aren't usually ones to rub shoulders with humans, and even though many of them are invited to the ball every year, their representative rarely shows up. Oh, over there! That's Cardinal Rhea!" Annette hissed, pointing across the room. Penny caught a quick glimpse of a woman in a long cloak wearing a metal blinder over her eyes and a silver headdress over her inferno of wild red hair. She remembered Madam Elise speaking about this woman and tried to get a better look at the Cardinal, who was the leader of the priestesses. Annette made a small noise of interest.

"Funny... she rarely leaves the Grand Cathedral. Still no sight of the king, either...or Deimos..." Annette mused.

"Maybe we should meet up with the others," Penny suggested, spotting the top of Gavin's head and working her way through the thick crowd to his table. Simon was also sitting at the table with the twins he had spied earlier, a dashing smile on his face as he performed little tricks with the help of his magic wand. Hector was eyeing him with distaste from across the table.

The moment Penny and Annette sat down, the twins erupted in a chorus of squeaky giggles as Simon produced a bouquet of roses and irises from within his cloak for each of them. Penny wondered if they were in fact laughing that he was performing everyday magic under the pretense that they were fantastic wonders, but decided not to say anything. Their enthusiasm died when they noticed Annette, and Penny watched in amusement as they gaped at the famous actress. Annette broke the awkward silence and introduced herself. Penny shot a glance toward Hector, who gave her a tired smile. She was about to speak when a cold, satiny voice crept up behind them.

"Why, Nettie. You decided to come after all!" the voice cried. An electric shock went through Penny. Valentine leaned against the back of a chair, clad in a scanty black silk dress that displayed most of her ample bosom. Penny felt magic being sucked from her body and saw from the color running out of Simon's face that Hector had drawn some from him as well. Gavin narrowed his eyes at Valentine, a protective scowl on his impeccable face. When it became apparent Annette wasn't going to reply, Valentine looked over Gavin's effeminate ensemble with a raised eyebrow.

"My, aren't you brash, Nettie. Showing up to a distinguished event with your manservant looking like such a joke. There *is* a dress code, you know…or does fashion confuse you as much as your own gender issues, darling?" Valentine taunted as Gavin blanched and cast his eyes away. Annette was on her feet in an instant, shaking with rage.

"How *dare* you…" she hissed in a low voice, so as not to disrupt the cheerful spirits around her. "Get out of my sight this instant or I promise you I'll find a way to have you thrown out. And I think you of all people wouldn't want to be embarrassed in front of all of Iverton again, am I right?"

Valentine took a lazy puff of her scented cigarette and blew a cloud of purple smoke in Annette's face. Penny saw her eyes water, but Annette's face remained locked in the same fierce scowl. Valentine shrugged, turning tail but still looking back. "As you command, princess…" She flipped her hair and sauntered off to mingle with the crowd.

Annette collapsed back in her chair, still livid. An intense silence floated over the table for a minute or so after Valentine had gone.

"I should've...I can't believe she'd even—" Annette snarled, but Gavin held up his hand.

"Oh, Nettie, dear. Don't give a second thought to a trollop like her. She parades around with the vile arrogance of high society and has none of the importance to match," he scoffed with an unfazed grin. Despite his attempts to comfort her, Annette remained reticent.

"Miss Annette, please. Whatever you do, don't antagonize her. Remember..." Hector warned, and she nodded, understanding his unspoken meaning. Simon looked between his two twins, who both seemed uncomfortable now. He stood up, taking each one by the hand.

"Come with me, ladies. Let's go get some drinks, hmm?" He led them away, moving an arm around each of their slender waists as they made for the bar.

Annette frowned. "Some bodyguard he is," she drawled. She remained sullen until a young man with wavy locks of golden hair slid up to the table. Annette squealed with delight as others swarmed them. Penny recognized the group as the cast of *Anthony Adonis* and listened as they chattered away about the ball and the latest scandals between mutual friends. After a short time, Annette's male co-lead, Fredrick, cocked his head to the side.

"Come on, love, let's go greet the others, hmm?" Fredrick smiled and an energetic Annette stood up and grabbed Gavin by the hand, stopping to address Penny.

"You don't have to follow us around now if you don't want to. She won't dare try anything while we're all in the open— she's too crafty for that." Annette waved and joined the rest of the cast. Though Penny had no interest in shadowing Annette while she gabbed with the egotistical actors who fawned over her, it still stung a bit to be dismissed. After half an hour of watching Annette from a distance, Hector rose.

"Where are you going?" Penny asked in surprise.

"To find something sugary and smothered in whipped cream," Hector told her, and she rose to follow.

Penny lingered behind Hector as he selected several sweets from the spread on a table. Near the buffet a disgruntled looking man in his late twenties barked orders at his underlings, instructing how to set up the plates of food.

"Do you think Deimos will dare to show his face…?" Penny wondered aloud as they returned to the table.

"I'll bet he's here somewhere. I doubt Valentine has the wherewithal to abduct Annette on her own, but still, keep your eyes open, Penelope," Hector reminded her as he chewed his éclair. Simon returned to the table, a dejected look on his face and a glass filled with amber liquid and ice in his hand. Penny knew better than to ask what had happened.

A loud fanfare of music blasted over the chattering of the partygoers. Penny watched the crowd shift away from the center of the ballroom and she tried to peer over heads to see what was happening. Somewhere, an official-sounding voice roared over the crowd.

"Esteemed guests, please enjoy this rendition of the Fille-niese Waltz, demonstrated by His Majesty the King and Cardinal Rhea." Music soared from the live string quartet in the far corner of the ballroom. Penny caught flashes of Cardinal Rhea's flaming mane of red hair through the gaps in the crowd, but little else. The joyful tune was short, and the crowd erupted into thunderous applause as it ended, breaking ranks and milling toward the dance floor. Simon sprang up from his chair as the music started again and charged toward Penny, his hands outstretched. Her heart sank, knowing what he wanted.

"Penelope…dear, sweet Penelope…might I have this dance?" He swept her hand from her side and held it in a delicate grasp. She pretended to laugh, feeling her chest tighten up as she thought of an excuse.

"I'm really not much of a dancer. Besides, don't you want to ask Annette to dance before that Fredrick guy does?" Penny jerked her head in the direction of man who'd played Anthony Adonis, pleased at her own quick thinking.

Simon's eyes flickered, and he nodded with resolve. "Wish me luck!" he said, cutting through the crowd, bumping into people left and right without apologizing as he made a beeline for Annette. Penny's eyes turned to the dance floor, where couples draped in jewels and fine fabrics twirled and laughed as they spun to the beat of another lively waltz. They all looked so carefree, fluttering about as light as if they drifted on balmy gusts of wind. Madeline had tried to educate Penny in the art of dance since the early days of their friendship, but Penny had never been coordinated enough to succeed. She felt a hand on her bare shoulder and jerked around to see Annette looking at her, breathless and stunned. Penny surged to her feet, ready to strike.

"What happened? What do you need? Where's Deimos?" Penny grasped her by the arms and looked her over, and Annette's face melted into a smile. She giggled a little and shook her head.

"Sorry I scared you! It's nothing important, but Simon's asked me to dance and—"

"Of course you said no?" Penny finished for her and was dumbstruck when Annette shook her head.

"I wouldn't refuse a dance to a friend! I just don't want to go up there alone with him, you know? People will start stupid rumors...if we all go together it'll be easier," Annette urged and Penny's stomach twisted. She had known from the first mention of the ball that this was bound to happen.

"Ah, um... I can't. I'll look like an idiot up there without a partner."

Annette huffed and looked around the room for someone; spotting Hector sitting by himself, she gasped as if experiencing a small epiphany.

"Dance with Hector. Go on, ask him." Annette pushed her toward the table where Hector picked at a slice of cake. Penny tried to dig her heels into the ground, protesting that this wasn't the solution she had in mind. Penny fought her until Annette called out to Hector to come join them.

He rose and trudged over, looking suave in his new suit. Penny whispered one last plea, but Annette would have none of it. Hector stepped up and stood in front of Annette, awaiting orders. Annette slunk behind Penny and gave her a hard push from behind toward Hector. Penny could feel her cheeks burning and cursed Annette.

"Hector! Penny wants to dance with you, but she's too shy to ask!" Annette sang. Penny looked at her in horror, feeling humiliated even as she caught Hector's surprised expression out of the corner of her eye.

"Beg pardon?" he stammered.

Annette beckoned to Simon to come join her as the song came to an end and the couples on the dance floor bowed and curtsied. Simon floated up, took Annette's hand, and the two of them stepped onto the dance floor. He appeared quite happy with all the pairs of eyes now glued to them. Penny thought she could see Valentine sneering at them both and was caught off guard when Hector touched her elbow. She shivered and shook her head.

"Oh, no, no! Annette was just being silly— I—" she tried to protest, but when she caught sight of Hector's smile the words died in her throat.

"Humor me?" Hector requested, taking her by the hand and drawing her toward Annette and Simon.

Penny let herself be pulled along, giving one last excuse. "But I honestly can't dance! I'm not trying to be modest, or—"

"Good thing I'll be leading then," he teased with a hint of a smile as they took their place beside Annette and Simon. Penny's face was hot with embarrassment.

The music started, and Hector led Penny around in perfect time, his hands clutching her waist. She had trouble fitting her hands around his high shoulders and strained to make herself taller. He led her through the complicated movements, laughing at Penny's lack of finesse. She told him rudely to shut up, which only made him laugh harder. He looked at her and smiled.

"You're wearing that thing I bought you," he observed, eying the star-shaped barrette that had turned a periwinkle blue to match Penny's gown. Penny was surprised he had noticed. They danced in silence for a while, and as she got used to being swept around, Penny had to admit there was something enjoyable about the twirling of a waltz.

"Tell me, how does a humble professor know how to dance so well?" she teased, but her question held genuine curiosity. He grinned and leaned closer to her ear.

"That, my good lady, is a secret," he whispered and spun her, making Penny feel even dizzier. His answer aggravated Penny, but she suddenly lost her burst of annoyance when he dipped her effortlessly.

In the final moments of the lilting tune, Hector drew Penny closer in until her face was up against the folds of his shirt. Penny could clearly hear his heart pounding an irregular beat in his chest. She realized with a start that Hector was probably just as nervous as she was and for whatever reason, this somehow relaxed her. She shut her eyes, feeling his arms poised on her waist as the song slowed. Penny inhaled, discovering that Hector smelled very nice, like sweet cedar pines and freshly done laundry. Without her permission, a rose-colored feeling swept through her, both wonderful and terrifying. They broke apart as the song faded, Penny's heart feeling like it was galloping away faster than she could follow it.

THE WALTZ OVER, Penny wandered around the ball-room, her head reeling and spinning as she meandered through the sea of cackling party guests. She squeezed through a par-ticularly large group and popped out the other side, colliding with someone so hard she fell to the ground as a deafening crash echoed throughout the ballroom. With a rush of horror Penny realized she had run straight into the angry-looking man who had been shouting orders at the cooks earlier. Scat-tered around her on the ground were the remains of a food tray that had been on its way to the buffet table. She choked as she scrambled to her feet, apologies flooding out. The man steamed with anger.

"Do you *know* how long it took me to make those?! Ruined, *ruined!* All ruined!" he raged, looking at the destroyed food.

Penny knew she was blushing again, but this time it felt painful. "I'm so, so sorry. I didn't see you there, I swear! Please, forgive—"

"*Sorry* does not get back the *hours* of back-breaking work, does it?" he shouted, anger staining an otherwise handsome face. Penny opened her mouth to beg for forgiveness again and felt a heavy hand land on her shoulder. She glanced back to see a man standing behind her, looking at the mess with a raised eyebrow. She wondered if she was in even more trouble as he surveyed the scene.

"Flynn, what's all this about?" he asked. Penny guessed from his fine attire that he was a ranger or military officer who was high up in the ranks. His voice was pleasant: husky and low, soft but domineering. The disgruntled cook ran his dark, olive-toned hand through his dark curls.

"This…*guest* just destroyed my wine-steamed kelru, that's what," he snorted, though he sounded much less spiteful now.

Penny was about to explain herself when she got a good look at the military officer. He was stunning; handsome and well-groomed, with rich blonde hair and eyes the color of the sea in the morning. Behind him stood a much taller unsmiling man clad in the same impeccably clean military uniform, with coffee-colored skin and dreadlocks tied back by an elegant gold chain.

"Flynn, you've gone and upset this Little Miss. It was an honest mistake," the golden haired man soothed, looking over Penny with kindness.

"Chivalrous as always, Noah," Flynn sighed to the golden-haired man.

"Won't you please excuse his behavior? He's under a lot of stress...It's no easy task to manage the kitchens," Noah requested, eyeing Penny with interest.

"Of c-course," Penny stammered, her eyes transfixed on the alluring man, feeling that whatever he asked of her she would be powerless but to agree. He extended a muscular arm to Penny and took her hand in his, exacerbating the dizzy sensation flooding her.

"It is truly a pleasure to make your acquaintance," Noah said with a bow, kissing her hand. "Might I ask your name and whom you are here with?"

"U-um, I'm Penny. Well, actually it's Penelope, but Penny—well, most people call me that, you see...erm...." she stammered, wanting to slap herself in the face. *Get a grip, Penelope. He's just a guy.* "I'm here with Annette Deveaux. We were introduced as her *entourage*, I think." She smiled, making an attempt at humor.

Noah laughed; it was a heartbreakingly perfect sound.

Flynn rolled his eyes at this and collected his fallen tray, leaving the scene as he shouted at several palace servants to begin cleaning the mess. Noah pulled Penny away from their work with genteel assertion, the silent man in the military coat following.

Penny could not take her eyes off the gorgeous Noah as he led her away while asking questions about where she was from, why she was in Iverton, her age, and her thoughts about the party. She answered each with as much truth as she could, lying here and there to avoid sounding insane. Penny joked with him in an attempt to diffuse the questions — his laugh was so pleasing to the ear.

Noah was not detained for long. "Now, I didn't want to say anything, but did you say you were here with Annette Deveaux? Do you mean to say that you know her person-ally?" he asked, looking a shade impressed. Penny smiled, feeling a bit braver.

"Yes. In fact, I'm staying as a guest in her house right now," Penny revealed, trying not to sound like she was bragging.

Noah contemplated this. "I wonder…if you aren't otherwise engaged with your entourage duties, would you care to join me outside? I'd be thrilled to show you the view," he offered in a way that suggested he knew she would not refuse him.

"Oh, that sounds wonderful, but Annette needs—" Penny stopped, confused as the man who had been trailing behind them laid a hand on Noah's shoulder and gave him a warning glance.

"We'll only be on the balcony, Damari. If I'm needed, I'll only be a moment away," Noah told him.

Damari considered this for a moment, and then nodded and stalked away, shooting suspicious glances at Penny as he went. Noah looked back at Penny, his gray eyes reiterating his prior request. She knew she had to protect Annette, but found she couldn't refuse Noah.

Penny flashed a quick glance back to see Annette at their table, surrounded by Hector, Gavin, and Simon. Convincing herself that Annette would be safe enough with them, Penny nodded. She stiffened as Noah led her through the ballroom and toward one of the doors that led to another part of the cas-tle, concerned she would lose sight of Annette.

Noah ushered her through the doors with a hand on the small of her back. Beyond the doors was the promised balcony. Outside it had stopped drizzling and the air was filled with a brisk bite and a dusting of mist. From the balcony's leafy railing Penny could see the city stretched out underneath the midnight sky. She floated to the edge, shivering, and spotted the Grand Cathedral, the Airstation, and the Sophotri Stone in the center of the Business District.

"The city looks so different from up here," Penny said, enthralled. She had come to love the city of Iverton, and being able to view it with such mysterious and charming company was nothing short of exhilarating. Noah stepped beside her and leaned over the balcony.

"Indeed, it does," he agreed, looking over the vast cityscape. "If I might ask…how is it that you know Miss Annette? I hear she's something of a recluse."

"Oh, I—" Penny's mind raced as she thought up something plausible. "I'm—I'm teaching her Elvish. She wants to go on a tour to the Nation of Elves—you know how popular Mr. Aldridge's plays are there."

Noah's eyebrows raised and he looked at her with sparkling eyes. "You speak Elvish?"

Penny laughed, her cheeks growing hot as she pushed her hair behind her ear. "Oh, my dear sir—I can speak pretty much every language in the world," she said, trying to channel Simon's flirtatiousness, doing her best to be alluring and sound Elydrian at the same time. It seemed to impress Noah, though he remained skeptical.

"Ah, is that so?" he tested and Penny detected his voice speaking in Elvish.

"Quite so," she answered him back in the same language with confidence. Noah nodded at her and continued his test, not satisfied until she had demonstrated fluent Fae, Gobblish, Therosian, and Old Andronian. Awed, he burst into applause.

Their conversation took off as Noah asked Penny about her education and roots, and she answered everything to the best of her ability, inserting scraps of truth wherever she could. They shared opinions about favorite foods, styles of music, and talked about the books Penny had been able to read while she had stayed at Annette's house. Noah seemed to be drawn to Penny's unbridled passion for Elydrian culture, oblivious that her enthusiasm stemmed from having just been introduced to what she thought of as exotic wonders.

Penny found herself quite enjoying the conversation despite the frequent lies, but her heart dropped when Damari appeared from within the ballroom and whispered something in Noah's ear. Noah nodded and turned to Penny, looking a little disappointed.

"Duty calls. It was enchanting to have met you, Penny Fairfax," he said and kissed her hand. "I hope you won't think me rude if I come by Annette's home at some point in the future to visit you both? I should very much enjoy seeing you both again."

Once again his words sounded like more of a statement than a request. Penny blinked. "You know Annette? Why didn't you say so?" she mumbled, surprised.

He laughed and let her hand go. "You are quite a funny one, indeed," he repeated and disappeared into the ballroom, melting into the crowd. Penny stayed motionless on the balcony for a long while, looking off in the direction Noah had left. She was almost sad when she thought of Noah dropping in on Annette only to find Penny had left for Hulver, but forced those thoughts away and looked back over the city, her heart pattering with contentment.

She only remained a moment longer before rushing back to the ballroom to find Annette. Penny was eager to tell Annette what had happened and ask her a flurry of questions about the mysterious Noah.

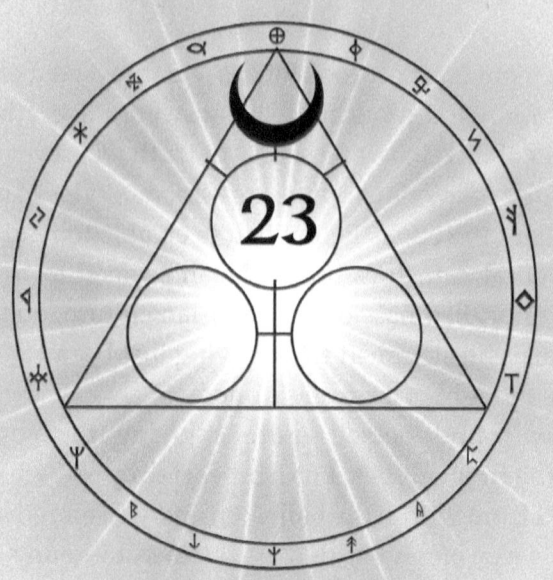

THE SHATTERED CHANDELIER

Back in the ballroom the party was still effervescent with activity. The dragon called Farful swung around the middle of the dance floor, his tail often smacking into guests. Penny peered around the room, and realized with a start that she could not see Annette anywhere. She circled the ballroom until she spotted Hector, Simon, and Gavin at the table where she had left them. Penny slammed her hands down on the table, jarring them from their conversation.

"Where's Annette?" Penny cried. Gavin looked back at Annette's group of theater friends as if expecting to see her. He went still.

"She was there *just* a second ago! I literally *just* saw her!" Simon insisted, panicked and getting to his feet.

"She's not in the ballroom, I've looked it over three times," Penny said, attempting to restrain her panic. They all exchanged fearful glances.

Gavin gasped. "I don't see Valentine anywhere, either…" he breathed, his gaze jumping from face to face.

"Come on, let's spread out and find her! She can't have gone far! Hurry!" Penny yelled as she rocketed away from the table toward the ladies' restroom. She pushed her way inside and called out Annette's name, but the only answer was a rhythmic dripping of water. Penny sped back outside, sick with guilt and frustration at the horrifying notion that her frivolous time with Noah had endangered her friend.

Penny bumped past two faeries as she made her way toward the exit. Seeing no one in the hallway leading to the main gates, Penny turned back toward the ballroom to face the multitude of guests. The loud music and tramping of feet on the dance floor flooded her mind and hindered her concentration. Her focus flicked over different things…a feathered fan, a tall pinstriped hat, a grinning face, a sloshing drink, a swatch of black silk, the chandelier, the—

Wait! Penny thought with a surge of emotion as her eyes flew back to the black silk dress she had seen. Sure enough, it belonged to Valentine.

Valentine was sauntering out of a side room Penny suspected wasn't intended for guests. She shut the door behind her, taking care to see that no one was watching. Penny hid behind a nearby column as she watched Valentine sidle through the crowd until she stopped behind a man in a white coat with long hair tied back into a ponytail. Penny saw the patch over his eye and her heart plummeted. It was Deimos.

Am I too late? Penny wondered, shuddering under a wave of icy horror. With a quick glance back at the door that Valentine had snuck out of, Penny slunk toward it, weaving between the swarms of people. A moment later her hand was on the knob and she looked through the crowd to confirm that Valentine was still in deep conversation with Deimos, completely oblivious to Penny's actions. Knowing she might only have seconds,

Penny grabbed the handle of the door, gritted her teeth, and slipped into the room.

She shut the door behind her and spun to face the rest of the room, coming face to face with a dead eye and a slack expression. Penny gasped and leapt back, fear coursing through her. The man with the chain around his neck stood before her, still as a statue and unblinking.

"I-I'm so sorry! I didn't mean to barge in here like this, I was…I was just…" Penny's stream of frantic apologies slowed in bewilderment when the man made no movement whatsoever. His one organic eye had not so much as twitched when she had nearly crashed into him. Penny caught her breath and took a quick look around the room. It was a simple sitting room with a mundane set of sofas and a small wardrobe in the corner, and a wide window on the far wall. Not seeing any sign of Annette, Penny crept toward the man, her body braced and ready to run.

"Can you hear me at all?" she whispered, somehow still expecting him to answer. His skin was the color of ash and he had dirty, unkempt black hair. Penny noticed for the first time that he had no eyebrows and more of the glowing blue lines were traced in angular patterns on his face. His left arm was made of a strong but thin metal, ending in a razor sharp set of claws. Penny's eyes wandered over his organic arm and she noted with shock that an eidolorbe hung from his motionless hand, the string woven around his fingers and wrist. With a start, she remembered Madam Elise had told her that this was the object that, if abused, could create a wraith.

Horror exploded in her chest when she heard voices, hurried and low, approaching the door. The handle jiggled and without thinking she sprang across the room, threw the wardrobe door open with trembling hands, and dove inside.

She shut the door to the wardrobe just in time. Penny put her back up against the wood, bracing her shoulders so that they would not shake. Through the tiny hairline opening between the wardrobe doors, Penny could see Valentine tromp inside with Deimos and the group of whispering goblins Penny had seen earlier.

"Hurry! Get inside!" Valentine hissed, gesturing for them to file in faster and closing the door with a snap. Deimos and Valentine faced each other, both looking edgy. There were three goblins — two awaited further orders, while the third went up to inspect the chained man just as Penny had done.

"This is a strange human, isn't it, Lorn?" the goblin commented in its native tongue. The goblin called Lorn gave the other one a smack on the head and snarled.

"Don't touch it, idiot. Can't you see there's something wrong? That's obviously defiled magic," he grunted back in Gobblish, eyeing Valentine with suspicion.

"Shut it, all of you," Deimos snapped at the goblins, his one good eye blazing.

Lorn frowned, showing off his crooked, needle-like teeth. "Then let's get on with what we came here to do. We've been standing around all night," he responded. Deimos's eye narrowed to a slit and he stalked out of Penny's vision.

"We'll start soon enough," Valentine cooed. "And all you *have* to do is stand around. That shouldn't be hard too hard, even for a goblin." The goblins shared a short, irate glance. During the long silence that followed, Penny could barely keep her terror contained. She was frantic to escape, to find Annette, but all she could do was force her breathing to stay quiet. When it began to seem as if Penny would be trapped there for an eternity, a loud rap sounded at the window and Penny almost jumped.

"He's here," Penny heard Deimos's stark voice, followed by hurried footsteps and the sliding of glass. Several more loud bangs and grunts trailed and then a hurried puffing of breath.

"Sorry, brother. It took longer than expected. Everything proceeding well here?" It was Phobos's voice, high and whiny.

"Yes, but we're cutting it close," Deimos worried. There was a flurry of movement and all of them formed a ring in the middle of the room, sharing the same identical expression that was a cross between deliberation and dread. Phobos took up the chain that bound the chalky-faced man as Deimos started to speak.

"All right now. This needs to go flawlessly, otherwise we're all better off dead, understand? Phobos, you take Cyrus and the goblins to the hall, yes?" Deimos gave him a hard look as if to say something more than words could express. Phobos seemed to get the message and smiled.

"Once you are *ready*...Valentine and I will grab the actress and bring her here. Phobos, you've got to get back quickly, understood?" Deimos ordered.

Penny's heart pumped with a mixture of fright and relief. Annette was still safe—but not for long. Deimos approached Phobos swiftly and whispered into his ear. Penny caught the word 'names' and in an instant made the connection.

Of course it's them, of course they're the ones making wraiths. Phobos obviously knows how to do it and they're using that man... that thing...to help them. They called him Cyrus...Why couldn't I have seen it before? He's going to turn those goblins into wraiths... The realization hit her like lead bullets.

Phobos moved toward the door with the three goblins, jerking the chain around Cyrus's neck, whose dead arms and legs shook into an unnatural, shuddering motion, his head lolling and bobbing as he moved. Penny wanted to jump out of the wardrobe screaming and warn the goblins, to try and stop the plan from going into motion, but she knew revealing herself would mean certain death. Time stretched by, second after agonizing second.

"How will we know when?" Valentine breathed, looking tense. Deimos turned his head, the corners of his mouth twitching up into a malicious grin as a terrified scream pierced the air, audible even from within the wardrobe. Penny jumped, but

Valentine and Deimos were too absorbed to notice. This first scream was followed by another, and another still, increasing until a cacophony of terrorized voices resonated throughout the entire palace.

"Now!" Deimos commanded, pushing the door open and charging out with Valentine behind him into the screaming mass of bodies. Penny kicked open the wardrobe door and caught a glimpse of people trying to escape the ballroom beyond. The lights were flickering now, adding to the catastrophic events. Penny could see strobing images of people getting knocked under the feet of the stampeding crowd and bursts of flame shooting from the dragon Farful's mouth. She watched through the open door as the dragon rocketed off the balcony and away into the night. Witchy moans and screeches emanated from the hall at the end of the ballroom — sounds Penny recognized as the voices of wraiths.

Penny was about to run from the sitting room and into the raging crowd when a very unwelcome face came out at her from the hazy darkness.

Phobos was recognizable in the flickering darkness by his shiny bald head and the chained figure trailing behind him. He spotted Penny and charged forward, overtaking her in seconds, the blinking lights illuminating his crazed, gleeful grin.

"Look what I've caught!" he cackled, gripping her wrist with vice-like strength and crushing it in his massive mitt until Penny screamed out in pain. Still holding Cyrus's chain in his other hand, he shook Penny until she fell to her knees, crunching the bones in her wrist.

"Why, you look like a quivering little grub, cowering like that!" He pushed his face closer and laughed into her ear. "What were you doing in here, little grub? Snooping, spying? Dear, oh dear…" His sour breath burned at Penny's nostrils and she sputtered with mutual fear and disgust. Phobos shook her about again and laughed his high-pitched, malcontent chortle.

Valentine emerged from the chaos, her face white and exhilarated as she called for Deimos, who joined them carrying a thrashing Annette over his shoulder. He came to an abrupt halt when he saw Phobos and Penny.

"What the hell is going on in here?!" Deimos barked, dumping Annette onto the ground. In the dim light Penny could see Annette's face shone with tears, and she whimpered when she spotted Penny. Their eyes locked for a moment, both aware of what was going to happen to them. With a sharp kick to Phobos's shin, Penny broke free of his hold and scrambled over to where Annette lay shivering on the ground.

"I found her in the wardrobe! She was watching us," Phobos said, unfazed by Penny's feeble attack.

"I'm so sorry, Annette," Penny whispered in anguish, keeping an eye on Deimos as she clutched Annette. Deimos knelt down and clamped Penny's face in his hand, scrutinizing her.

"What did you hear? Who are you?" he demanded, gesturing for Valentine to head toward the window. The biting night air was still blustering in from the open window and outside fluttered a gigantic moth that was easily big enough to fit four or five people on its back. Penny realized this must have been how Phobos had gotten himself in, and how they were planning to escape. She looked at Deimos with wide eyes and a chattering jaw, unable to speak. Without warning, he slapped Penny in the face with such force it knocked her out of Annette's arms.

Annette screamed. Deimos advanced on Penny with a fierce expression as she shuddered on the floor. "I said, *who are you?*" he hissed.

Penny wobbled to her feet and tried to stumble away, but Deimos withdrew a dagger from his belt and pinned Penny to the wall. Annette leapt to her feet as both Valentine and Phobos made a rush for her, leaving Cyrus motionless by the window. Annette took a huge breath, her chest expanding as they tried to bowl her over.

"*Someone please help us!*" she screamed at the top of her lungs in that strange resonating tone that Penny could feel more than hear. Both Valentine and Phobos crashed into Annette, causing her to yelp with pain. Deimos pressed harder against Penny, his face inches from hers, his dagger cold against her neck. Penny had no doubt he would slit her throat wide open just to save time. She felt the edge of the sharp metal sting into her throat and the warm rush of blood that followed as he started to draw it across her neck.

The sound of footsteps sped toward the door, and Penny saw the tall man in the military coat, the man she remembered as Damari, explode into the room with three rangers. Two of them made a grab for Valentine, but just as they took hold of her arms, Phobos pulled a heavy metal hammer from his belt and whipped it across their skulls.

It struck twice with heavy, stomach-churning crunches, but Damari was too quick. He flew behind Deimos, drawing a shining saber that flashed in the darkness. Deimos had but a moment to block. As he yanked his knife away from Penny's throat, she felt the razor-edge rip deeper into the wound and collapsed in a twitching heap, clutching her neck as blood oozed out. Her head was spinning at a hundred miles a second as she watched the dire fight between Damari and Deimos, their movements too swift to follow. More rangers were flowing into the room, drawing blades, flintlock pistols, and elongated golden rifles that looked something like blunderbusses. Valentine, Phobos, and Deimos drew together, each baring their teeth and gasping for breath.

"Jump!" Deimos bellowed, diving for the window with Phobos and Valentine at his heels. Damari was the first after them, grasping after Deimos's frock coat with fierce determination. Several guns went off, filling the air with choking powder. Deimos scooped Valentine up with one strong arm around her waist and she screamed as he leapt headfirst out of the window, followed by Phobos, who yanked Cyrus along with such violence that Penny was sure his neck would snap. The four of them plummeted out of the window, leaving the rangers gaping in confusion, only to realize Deimos and the others were making their escape on the back of a huge moth.

"Alert the Griffin Unit! Go, now!" Damari shouted, and a ranger sped off on his orders.

Annette crawled across the floor to Penny, who was trying to stay as still as she could, fearing that any movement would cause her to bleed out and die in a matter of seconds. She pressed hard onto the wound, feeling her own grip suffocating her.

"She's hurt! Help her!" Annette cried.

Damari rushed over and put a strong arm around Penny, speaking in a deep, comforting voice, which somehow didn't match his serious countenance. "Let me see," he requested with gentle urgency. Without waiting for her compliance, his strong hands pried her trembling ones away from her throat and he inspected her wound in the gloom with squinted eyes. He patted her shoulder and pulled a handkerchief from his coat pocket, pressing it to her neck.

"Hold this here, you'll be fine. It's only a tiny cut," he assured her, helping Annette and Penny to their feet. "Get to somewhere safe, but be careful—there's still one wraith out there somewhere. I shot the other one," he cautioned. Penny nodded and ran out of the room, still clutching Annette's trembling hand.

In the ballroom they shot head-first into the mess of screaming people. Penny's stomach did a somersault when she almost tripped over the body of a trampled faery noblewoman, lying still and beautiful on the ballroom floor. She regained her balance and continued on, dragging Annette behind her.

"Hector! Simon!" Annette screamed over the tumult. "Gavin!!"

Penny pushed past a few shivering girls, wishing she could move faster but feeling she had to protect Annette. She was sick with dread at the thought of seeing Simon's crushed body on the floor or Hector lying dead against the wall, gored by a wraith. Reaching the center of the room they became trapped in the mass of people, unable to move. Annette's face fell onto Penny's shoulder, her tears mixing with the blood from Penny's wound.

"Penny...Penny..." she howled, her entire body shaking in tremors. Penny rubbed her back, looking from one frightened face to the next, her panic rising to the verge of insanity. She couldn't think what to do next, and then her chest filled with relief at something shining in the gloom.

A trembling golden thread was sprouting out of her chest. Within moments Hector came fighting his way toward them, Simon clutching at his sleeves and Gavin's pale face bobbing behind them. When Gavin saw Annette, he shoved a man out of the way and tore her from Penny's arms, pulling her to his chest. Hector went straight for Penny, his eyes swimming with nauseated fear as he spied the blood-stained cloth Penny held to her neck. He took her by the shoulders, unable to form coherent words.

"I'm okay, it's just a cut," she sputtered. Hector exhaled, pulling Penny into a one-armed embrace and shielding her at his side amidst the sea of people. Simon clung to her other side, looking as if he might be sick at any moment.

The group of them huddled together. Now that the people had started to move, they were all making a mad rush for the exit. The ballroom was clearing and some of the rangers were calling orders into the crowd to try and get the party guests settled. Penny was about to ask if they had caught the remaining wraith when a shrieking wail answered the question for her. The sound came from the cavernous end of the hall and the river of evacuating guests came to a sudden stop and then launched into reverse, desperate screams beginning anew. Hector's chest heaved against her ear.

"Annette!" Hector called over the frantic cries. "Make everyone but us back up against the wall immediately. Simon, get your wand out!"

Simon nodded, withdrawing his wand and biting his bottom lip to stop his teeth from chattering. After telling them all to cover their ears, Annette once again took a mighty breath with her trained, songstress's lungs and let out an ear-piercing yell.

"*EVERYONE, GET AGAINST THE WALL!*"

The trampling feet slowed and began moving in a uniform pattern, eyes huge as the guests pressed themselves against the walls. Annette joined them, blending in like any other guest.

"Penelope, brace yourself!" Hector shouted, gripping her shoulder with a near-painful force as Simon raised his wand. All was quiet for a fraction of a second until, without warning, a malformed beast exploded into the hall, roaring and snarling. It had two milky white eyes, resembling the goblin it had been made from, and the same needle-sharp teeth, but they were long and pierced through its own flesh at odd angles. The body had grown large and deformed and had sprouted sharp bones and claws that coursed slick, black blood down its back. The wraith tore with inhuman speed toward Hector, Simon, and Penny, its black mouth open and ready to tear them to shreds. Penny could smell its rotten breath and see down its long, deep esophagus, the teeth and splintery bones poking out down every inch of its quivering, ebony throat. Mere seconds before it reached them, Penny felt all the magic drain from her body.

The chandelier exploded. Glass broke from every inch around them with an ear-rending sound of splintering crystal. Hector's hands alighted with fireworks of red and silver runes, which wrapped around the shards of glass that filled the air like acid rain. Vortices of fiery magic overtook Hector's entire body as a million gleaming fragments showered down upon the wraith. Hector shouted and threw his hands out in front of him, Penny still clinging to his body, willing all her strength into him as he directed every shard of glass at the wraith.

"*Simon! Keep it steady!*" Hector shouted, squinting through the glass storm that threatened to cut them all to ribbons if Hector made a single wrong move. Simon flicked his wand in the direction of the wraith, which seemed to slow its movements. One by one, the glass from the windows exploded and joined the torrent in the center of the room.

The shards began to form a glass prison around the wailing and spitting wraith as blobs of black blood dripped out of the creature. With a final twist of his hands, Hector forced the shards to solidify around the body of the beast and form an unbreakable sphere of ten-inch thick glass. The glass sealed itself with a deep cracking noise, trapping the wraith within. Enraged howls were now muffled behind the walls of glass along with the screech of bone scraping against the sides as it tried to claw its way out. Simon struggled to keep the spherical prison suspended in the air with his wand.

The crowd was deathly silent, their eyes traveling from the wraith to Hector and back. Penny looked up at Hector's face. He was paler than a ghost, and his eyelids fluttered. His legs went weak and he stumbled to the ground, passing out. Penny shouldered his weight and eased him to the ground.

A lone figure stepped out from the crowd, his strong shoulders thrown back and his head held high.

Penny recognized Noah with a start. He grasped a beautiful sword encrusted with emeralds in his hand and addressed the crowd.

"You there," he pointed to a man in a red ranger's coat. The man hurried from the huddle of the crowd and saluted Noah. "Find Captain Baldera, and see to it that he has secured the goblin survivor and prepared him for questioning. Tell him I'll be with him shortly."

"Yes, your Majesty!" the ranger cried and scrambled out of the room as fast as he could.

Your Majesty? Penny wondered, and understanding hit her like a locomotive going at full speed. Noah turned back to the crowd.

"Cardinal Rhea. Please…" he beckoned, and Cardinal Rhea stepped out from the crowd, her eyes still covered by the metal blinder. With great precision she stepped up to the glass prison and, pulling a silver flute from her cloak, began to play a low, melancholy song. The wraith's shrieks grew fewer and weaker, collapsing as death swept over it at last. Simon lowered the orb to the ground. Penny was shivering again as Noah turned toward her and her friends.

"You five—yes, I said five, Miss Deveaux," Noah pointed over at Annette and Gavin in the crowd, "Please come with me."

A PROMISE KEPT

A loaded silence filled the room. Hector lay motionless on a couch, so soundly asleep he appeared dead. Penny and Simon sat on another couch while Gavin paced from one end of the room to the other. Annette leaned up against the wall, tapping her foot with arrhythmic irritation. Simon covered his face with his hands and moaned.

"Why is he keeping us waiting like this?" he groaned. "It isn't right to just dump us here with no word of what's to become of us. What could he possibly be doing?"

"Some people just died, Simon. Part of the palace was destroyed—there are questions that need answering. Just give him time. It's lucky we're able to make our case directly to the king instead of being thrown in a dungeon to rot or something," Penny said, not taking her eyes off Hector. His complexion was pallid and his breathing seemed shallow.

"Maybe you two had better let me do the talking once the king finally gets here," Annette suggested, sounding exhausted. Penny and Simon both nodded, neither of them eager to explain this messy situation.

The door handle turned with a small click, and everyone but Hector straightened. Gavin sprinted across the room to join Annette. Four pairs of eyes fixed on Damari as he entered the room and cleared his throat to speak.

"His Majesty will see you now. Please act respectfully and speak only when spoken to," he instructed. Penny might have imagined it, but she thought his eyes lingered on her a moment longer than the others and she looked down at her knees. She wanted to leap up and explain that she hadn't known who Noah was before, but kept silent as Damari trudged off, leaving the door open behind him. Moments later Noah stepped into the room, a troubled expression on his face. Annette gestured for Simon and Penny to get to their feet and they obeyed.

"Good evening, Miss Deveaux, Mr. Deveaux, Miss Fairfax," the king greeted each one of them with a nod of his head, stopping at Simon, who provided his and Hector's surnames.

Annette looked a bit alarmed. "I beg your pardon, Your Majesty, but how is it that you know Pen—"

"I met your language tutor earlier in the evening," he said, looking at Penny. Annette blinked, piecing together the information. Noah continued, "Let's not waste time with trivialities…I need some answers from you. And don't bother with all the 'Your Majesty' nonsense. Please, be seated."

"I'd be more than happy to explain everything," Annette complied, subtle charm underlying her words.

"Why were you attacked by Valentine Frost and Baron Deimos Geller? How did Phobos Geller escape and how has he overcome his madness? How did your friend here perform such brilliant magic without the use of a tool? And most importantly, how did the wraiths get into the castle? The goblin prisoner isn't talking, but at least we know that the goblins must have some hand in this. I wonder if you might shed some light on this."

Annette remained motionless, her expression a perfect mask as she thought. Penny prayed she knew what she was doing. At long last Annette seemed to have found the right words.

"Two weeks ago while attending my play, Penny overheard Valentine speaking to Deimos about a plan to try and abduct me and warned me about it," Annette began, slow and deliberate. Penny knew from her careful omission of Penny's abilities that they were not to speak of their coming from Earth. Noah seemed to accept this and Annette continued.

"I wanted to keep this whole thing quiet. I'm sure you'd understand what going public with this sort of thing might entail, and Mr. Arlington here is gifted with the ability to perform magic without the use of any tool, so I hired him as my private bodyguard."

"It makes sense, I suppose, though you should have alerted the authorities," Noah reprimanded her. "But that still doesn't explain why Valentine would want to kidnap you." Annette's eyes glazed and Penny knew she was no longer acting or calculating her responses.

"She's hated me ever since I was young. It's because of our petty rivalry," Annette admitted.

"Very well, then. Do you know anything about the wraiths? Or the Geller siblings?" Noah pressed. Annette started to shake her head when Penny looked up. Noah looked at her with surprise.

"Penny? You know something?" he prodded. Something about the way he said her nickname made her heart flutter again and she cleared her throat.

"Erm, I might," she confessed, taking a deep breath. "I saw them coming and hid when I heard them come into the room— just before the wraiths appeared," she explained, hoping that she wouldn't hinder their release for admitting this. "The big bald guy, Phobos—he took this man away with him—he had a weird eye and a metal arm. I think he called him Cyrus—he had an eidolorbe on him. Phobos and Deimos also knew those goblin's full names," Penny stated, and she watched Noah rub his temple as he thought.

"Erm, please. What exactly happened with those two? I mean, didn't Phobos make a wraith before?" Penny questioned.

Noah looked up, surprised. "You don't remember? It happened only a few years back; it was all over the Sophotri Stones."

Penny shook her head, waiting for him to continue.

"According to Deimos's testimony, Phobos had been studying all types of dark magic...he was heavily involved with crime syndicates in the Dewthorne district. Their father, who was baron at the time, had been hunting his son for years and finally got proof enough to lock him away. Regretfully, before he could complete this, Phobos turned his own father into a wraith.

"Deimos tried to come between them, was attacked and lost his eye, but there was nothing he could do to help either of them. Phobos completely lost his mind, and was taken to an institution for the criminally insane, while Deimos inherited his father's position as Baron of Dewthorne. He's been doing a fine job. I would have never suspected him of something like this..." Noah shook his head. "But it still makes no sense. How did he escape from the institution? Phobos shouldn't be able to form so much as a coherent sentence." The king looked troubled as he pulled a small coin-shaped object from his pocket. "Miss Deveaux, you seem to be privy to all of this...I wonder if I could have a few more words with you in private regarding some of these matters? I'd like to verify some of these claims and ask about the backgrounds of your associates, that sort of thing," he requested and Annette rose without missing a beat.

"Of course, Your Majesty," she agreed. They left the room together. Almost two hours later they returned, Annette looking ready to collapse with exhaustion.

"Well, now I've got the full story, I suppose that's that. Thank you all for being so cooperative. I'll have some trusted men sent to protect you, Miss Deveaux. I suppose the only thing we can do now is to send a goodwill messenger to Hulver and speak with the King Yulghrat. That way we can get some information about the Goblin Nation's possible involvement," Noah said, half-speaking to himself.

Annette sprang back to her feet, and Noah looked at her in confusion. She was speechless for a moment, and then beamed. "Send us? That's a wonderful idea, Penny speaks Gobblish perfectly!" she cried.

Penny did a double-take, wondering if the exhaustion was starting to get to Annette's head. Noah's brow furrowed, his face showing complete befuddlement. Annette's chest was rising and falling with exhilaration, but her gaze remained steady.

"E-excuse me?" Noah asked.

"You … you just said you'd like to send us all to Hulver as your messengers, seeing as how these three are brilliant at speaking foreign languages — and since I'll need a clever place to hide anyway, it's a great plan," Annette said, her voice vibrating with her mystical power.

Noah's eyes glazed over as her words worked their power over him. For what seemed like several very long minutes, the only sound in the room was Annette's aggravated breathing. Penny caught Annette's eye and Annette shook her head, as if to stop Penny from doing anything that might get in the way.

Noah touched the side of his head, still looking lost. "Why—I suppose I did, didn't I?"

"Yes, of course you did! You said you trusted us and felt we would be able to do the job best. You were feeling very confident about it, don't you remember? It only happened a moment ago," Annette coaxed, still forcing her power upon the king. Simon's eyes grew very wide and Gavin was trying to hide his look of horror. Noah seemed to be trying to dislodge the haziness in his head as he shook it from side to side, his golden hair fluttering like a lion's mane.

"Yes, I remember, now. That *is* a good idea," Noah said, now brimming with certainty. Penny exhaled in relief and Annette smiled, still stunning despite the harried look of fatigue she wore. "Excellent, I'll send word down to the airstation to prepare the Royal Dirigible for five passengers."

"Oh, only four. Gavin will need to stay at home to take care of some important matters, after all," Annette said, holding up a finger. Gavin's jaw dropped, but Annette ignored him, still staring at Noah with her most charming smile.

Noah nodded. "I'll send word at once. Will you be able to leave by the day after tomorrow?" Annette nodded, looking very pleased.

"Well, this has been most enlightening. I'll see you again before you depart. Goodbye until then." Noah bowed and exited the room. Once the door was closed and he was out of earshot, chaos broke loose.

"Nettie! How *could* you leave me out of this? I can't be sitting at home, not knowing if you're alive or dead or—"

"Miss Annette, that was astonishing! You truly have mastered the art of—"

"You can't be serious, Annette! What if you—"

They all shouted at Annette simultaneously, but she simply ignored them and sat back down, looking as if she was about to follow Hector's example and pass out. After a minute of everyone shouting at her she held up her hand, looking stern.

"Listen! I'm going with you whether you like it or not! I kept my promise, didn't I? I got you all a way to travel to Hulver, but I never said that I wouldn't come along with you. Valentine isn't going to stop trying to get to me, and the first place she'll look is my house. I'll be putting you, Auntie, and Millie in danger if I stay. I won't allow that. The last place they're going to look for me is on Ciellios," Annette said with confidence.

SAFE BEHIND THE doors of Annette's manor that night, Penny dreamed of home. She felt her feet hitting each step as she bounded upstairs, calling out for her mother. She rushed down the hallway, checking her mother's bedroom first, then the bathroom. Opening the door to her own room, she was struck with deep fear. Her entire room was covered in filth and cobwebs with dark, black mud splattered on the floor. Gatherings of dead insects and dried leaves lay in piles all around her room, covering her desk and staining the sheets of her unmade bed. She wanted to scream, knowing what was coming; she could feel it. It hung in the grime that befouled her most comforting sanctum, singing to her in a chiding voice.

Come die, Penny. It's so much easier than you think. Come die, right here. After all—

Penny jerked awake, sweat clinging to her forehead. Bright light blinded her eyes as Millie opened the curtains.

Life is but a dream, Penny thought, falling back onto her pillow with a relieved sigh.

Penny was shooed into the kitchen where a worried Wendy waited with a breakfast so large it could have fed three people. She did her best to eat at least half of it, and learned from Wendy that Gavin had announced he was no longer speaking to Annette.

Penny observed Gavin as he made several calls regarding Annette's upcoming absence using a miniature type of Sophotri Stone. It was interesting to watch the faces and voices of strange and unfamiliar people speaking through the clouded prism.

A palace official arrived with their royal messenger badges, directions, and dirigible tickets. Their new marks of identification reflected the fabricated backgrounds Annette had told Noah the prior evening. Penny had to applaud her quick thinking.

When both Annette and Hector's condition hadn't improved by evening, Millie put in a call via the small Sophotri Stone to the Grand Cathedral for a priestess to come visit, requesting Armonie on Penny's behalf.

An hour later a knock came at the door and Penny rushed to answer it before Millie could get there. Opening the door, Penny was tackled by a storm of fluffy hair and robes as the jingling of bells filled the air.

"Ack, Armonie! I can't breathe!" Penny choked out, smiling. Armonie let go, tears swimming in her sea-green eyes. She grasped Penny's hands and smiled back at her.

"Oh, big sister. I missed you *so* much, I truly did. The Cardinal was there last night and she told Madam Priestess about what happened—when I heard what danger you were in I nearly fainted on the spot. I was overjoyed when I heard that you had called upon me...and to be able to treat Miss Deveaux! You have honored me greatly," Armonie beamed, and Penny led her inside to where Annette was relaxing in the drawing room.

Armonie lugged her portable alchemy case into the drawing room and set it on the table before introducing herself to Annette. The young priestess seemed rather star-struck at first, but after being exposed to Annette's lighthearted nature, she grew more comfortable and examined Annette for any injuries. Seeing nothing, she rummaged around in her alchemy kit and pulled out a vial of ruby red liquid.

"You're probably just exhausted after all of that stress. Get a good night's rest and drink this in the morning, you should feel completely refreshed!"

Penny took Armonie to see Hector next. They crept into his room and turned up the magical lantern to a dim glow, and found him still sleeping. Armonie woke him and Hector gave a weak smile at the sight of her.

"Armonie...what a surprise..." he croaked, shutting his eyes again. Armonie asked him a few questions and conducted another quick examination. Many of the flying glass shards he had used to seal the wraith had given him an assortment of small cuts and gashes, and she administered a strong-smelling gel to the wounds. Before she put the gel away, Armonie applied a daub to the horizontal slash on Penny's throat. The medicine stung, but Penny felt immediate relief. Armonie left them with two more vials of the ruby liquid, with instructions to take it in the morning.

"You all were very fortunate to get out with only scrapes and bruises. So, I suppose you'll be taking it easy from now on?" Armonie asked Penny as they walked downstairs.

"Actually," Penny faltered, "We're flying to Hulver tomorrow."

Armonie stopped, shaking her head. "May Lord Nestor protect you. My sister, you seem to be a magnet for trouble. I'll be praying for your safety." They reached the foyer, and she pulled out a little purse, calculating something. "The medicine costs one emerald Yuebell."

Penny's pockets were empty, so she called for Gavin. He arrived in a fluster, thin-lipped and huffing, but came to a quick halt when he saw them. He looked alarmed as Armonie spoke to him, so much so he dropped a few Yuebells from his wallet while trying to hand her the correct amount. Armonie seemed to be curious about his clothing, but she kept quiet as she accepted the fee.

"Goodbye, my sister," she said to Penny, smiling and grasping her hands once more. "Please let me know when you've returned, it will ease my mind to know you're safe." The priestess gave a timid nod to Gavin. "G-goodbye, sir." Gavin lifted his hand, trying to smile.

As she went to sleep that night, Penny's thoughts drifted to whether she would return to Annette's house, or even to Iverton. Della was supposed to have all the answers for them and would know how to send Penny and Simon home.

Penny came to the glum realization that she was going to miss Elydria when it came time to leave. She was going to miss all the exotic foods, the beauty of the world's antique aesthetic, Humphrey, and most of all the friends she had made while staying here. Her thoughts drifted back to the smoky campfire in the woods months ago when she had asked Hector about his plans after returning. He had said that he would not go home to Nelvirna, even if he could, but Penny somehow doubted he would want to return to Earth. She could not imagine him trying to make a new life somewhere else with a new name, trying to pass the days in another old, drafty house, rattling around in it alone like a coin inside a tin cup.

The idea made Penny feel sick and she crawled under the covers, forcing herself to think of other things. She fell asleep without much effort, but dark dreams came to her nonetheless. Her dream was an uncanny repeat of the one from the previous night, though this time there was no feeling of joy at returning home. She wheeled up the stairs and found her room in a state of horrific disarray again. This time, however, there were bones, blanched and dry, lying in the corner. She took several steps forward, leaning toward her bed and feeling painfully tired. To lie down would be so nice. The sheets were stained and soiled with mud, sand, and tar. The last thing she remembered seeing was her ruined sheets before the humming started, and the song echoed inside her skull long after dawn broke.

IVERTON'S PARTING GIFT seemed to be one last glorious sunny day. Arriving at the airstation, the group flashed the badges that had been delivered to them and were led inside, where they found Noah and Damari waiting. Noah greeted them each with a broad smile and a firm handshake, while Damari nodded a hello.

A faery in purple uniform collected their tickets and checked their badges once more, and the group was led to the runway. Penny stumbled at the sight of the gargantuan zeppelin. It loomed over the other airships, making them look like mere toys in comparison. The body was a rich plum color and lined with the finest gold trimmings; even the propeller and wings that stuck out from the massive shape were shining gold in the glaring sunlight. Below was a compartment for housing passengers the width of a cottage, but almost three times as long. Another staircase led from the compartment down onto the runway.

"It's—it's glorious!" Annette cried as she jumped up and clapped her hands, beholding the behemoth airship.

Noah stepped to Penny's side. "It's made by the finest mechanists and crafters Iverton has ever seen," he boasted with a smile. Caught off guard, Penny had to look away from his expectant gray eyes. She coughed a bit before answering.

"It's unbelievable. I've never seen anything like it in my life," she told him, lacing her fingers together behind her back.

"I'm very pleased to hear that. I went to some lengths yesterday to see that you'd be comfortable," Noah explained, putting strange emphasis on the word *you*. Penny avoided his gaze.

Next to the golden stairs Penny saw a man leaning lazily against the railing. His mess of coffee brown hair was pushed back by a pair of aviator goggles. He groaned as they all approached, gesturing for them to hurry.

"Ah, Noah. Wasting my time as usual, I see?" The man stepped up to Noah and clapped him hard on the shoulder. "And just when I was hoping you weren't going to show up at all." He laughed hoarsely and looked around at everyone. He had a thin face, dark olive skin, a burly frame and a huge, thick mustache that bristled out in all directions from underneath his nose. Penny noticed with some interest that several gold, tarnished teeth flickered in his smile.

Noah gestured toward the man with the goggles. "This is Zayne, the captain of the dirigible and the main reason why it flies so fast," he said, a little edge to his voice. "A word of advice: don't leave loose articles lying about around him."

Zayne let out another wheezy laugh and climbed up the stairs into the dirigible. Noah frowned after him but went back to addressing Penny and the others. "Well, you've been given your instructions. Just deliver the sealed message to King Yulghrat and speak to the ambassadors about receiving his reply."

Penny felt a twinge of guilt at the confidence in the king's voice, wondering if this plan was for the best. She stared with uncertainty at Noah's trusting smile, anxiety bubbling within her chest. She was already regretting manipulating the king.

Simon waved a short goodbye to Gavin and Noah as he went up into the body of the airship. Noah shook hands with Hector.

"I commend your bravery, Mr. Arlington. You saved many lives at the ball. Thank you for everything—and if it's all right with you, I should very much like to talk with you at length upon your return. Would this be at all possible?" Noah questioned, and Hector nodded.

"Certainly, Your Majesty. I shall do my very best to answer your every query," Hector obliged, then bowed and followed Simon up the stairs.

Annette smiled at Noah and batted her long eyelashes. "Goodbye, Your Majesty. Until we meet again," she said, and he bent down to kiss her wrist. For the longest while it looked as if Gavin was not going to say goodbye to Annette, but as she stared at him with her most lugubrious gaze, he broke down and pulled her into a tight embrace. They said their final goodbye and Annette climbed up, sniffling and shooting long glances back. Penny turned to Gavin, her arm extended, but he pulled her into his arms.

"Please take care of Nettie for me—and don't you dare get hurt yourself. I'm already missing you, little Penny. Be careful out there," he whispered into her ear, then let go, his eyes ringed red with tears. Penny could do little else but nod and offer a reassuring smile. Noah stepped closer to her after she broke away from Gavin and took her hand in his.

"Penny, do take caution, won't you?" He studied her face, and Penny felt her heart flutter. She fought the urge to frown—something about him made her feel vulnerable. "I know—well, we hardly know one other…but I somehow feel as if I've met you before. Something is drawing me to you. I can't explain it." Gavin seemed to notice the tense atmosphere and stepped away, trying to look aloof. Noah leaned inward, unfazed by Penny's shyness.

"After you get back, I would be…thrilled at the chance to become better acquainted with you. Say you feel this way, as well," he said with impassioned zeal.

Penny cleared her throat of a disbelieving laugh, wondering how she could've possibly inspired the interest of a man like Noah. "Um, sure. Yeah, we could…hang out or something." The words sounded ridiculous even as she said them and Penny flushed.

Noah beamed at her regardless, leaning over once again to give her cheek a rough kiss. "Then I shall eagerly await your return," he proclaimed, stepping back to let Penny climb the stairs. "Good luck!"

Penny waved back at him as she began to ascend, her heart already climbing lofty heights without the need of any airship.

ANNETTE'S CONFESSION

Zayne peered down at them, a haughty smile spreading across his face. They stood in a chamber lined with churning gears and hissing pipes. The airship captain looked over each of them, laughing out loud when he saw Hector and winking at Annette.

"All right, ladies," he said, pulling the goggles down over his eyes. "This will not be a pleasure cruise, so I expect you to stay out of my way. First rule here is for you three—" he pointed at Simon, Penny and Hector, "Don't bother me or any of the crew down below. If any of us screws up, we all die." His eyes fell on Annette and his mustache twitched upward. "You, however, can bother me all you like, sweetness."

Annette was visibly affronted.

"Rule number two: if it's not in the cabin area, don't even think about touchin' it. Ever. Don't forget that, slick," he added, looking at Simon, who was already studying the twirling gears and steam-spitting pipes. "I'm sure there's something I'm forgetting, now..."he continued, his golden tooth gleaming. "Ah, consarn it. Just go by 'If you're not sure, don't friggin' do it.'" He snorted and led them through the archway at the end of the hall, up a spiral staircase and finally out a door with golden words emblazoned onto the front. Penny had to get her *pince-nez* glasses out to see it read *Cabin*. "Excuse me, but how will we be able to contact our maids and cooks?" Annette questioned. Zayne's face grew slightly purple and he gave another roaring laugh, and Annette cringed.

"You are somethun' else, princess," he choked out, his eyes watering underneath his goggles. "Get in there, all of you. We'll get to the goblin dung heap in about three days, so I'll see you then...toodle-oo, sugar lips."

Annette charged into the cabin, shaking with anger. "In all my years I have *never*—" she hissed, her face bright red with humiliation. Simon sidled up beside her and attempted to place a comforting arm around her shoulders, but Annette stalked away.

They entered into a room with a table, chairs, a few sofas, and a compact bar. The floors were made of fine dark wood and the walls lined with brass and gold. Penny noted with interest that all the furniture was bolted to the floor. The eastern wall was lined with large windows, each one draped in luxurious curtains. Leading out from the sitting room was a door with an ornate porthole.

Her heart pounding, Penny pressed her face against the window. The engines and their mechanics clanked to life beneath them, and she laughed with delight as the mammoth airship lurched forward and the propellers whirred faster, until they reached their maximum velocity. The ship picked up speed and the airship thundered toward the end of the runway. Penny almost lost her balance, and was thankful that Hector and Simon caught her by the arms as the nose of the dirigible made a dangerously sharp lift upward and shot straight into the cloudless Iverton sky.

Penny tried to catch her breath as the roads and steeples of the city shrunk away, hanging onto Hector and Simon's hands as she gaped at the view. From such a lofty height, the palace looked like a mere toy model and the traffic in the streets became miniscule dots, zooming along like busy insects. Penny could see the diamond-spotted Lake Olveria reflecting the sun and the coliseum where they had first seen Annette perform.

"Amazing! This is...*amazing!*" Penny cried, breaking away from Hector and Simon as she ran out onto the balcony to get a last look at the city as it rolled out of view. They joined her, looking a shade nervous as she leaned over the railing. Hector stepped up behind her, careful to keep his back pressed up against the wall, and attempted to catch Penny by the shoulders.

"That's enough, now. Let's go in before you go plummeting to your death, hmm?" he suggested, looking anywhere but over the railing.

"I'll be careful." Penny said, waving him off. Hector sighed and went back inside. Penny watched the leafy gardens, ivory sands, and tall pillars of the city fade over the horizon, breathless as joyous exhilaration swelled in her chest. A few small towns lay nestled between the grassy hills outside Iverton, but soon gave way to nothing but wild, untamed land that seemed to stretch on forever.

THE SUN SET over the hinterlands, smoldering orange and yellow clouds burning against the dusky purple of the evening sky. Soon, the golds and pinks of the sunset faded into the shade of night. The lanterns that lined the sides of the dirigible waxed into a dim glow as the stars began to blink in the distance

Penny climbed into bed beside a sleeping Annette. There was something comforting about the mechanical creaks and groans the ship produced. Penny thought of both the homes she'd left behind until her consciousness began to fade and she huddled closer to Annette. The twin moons gleamed in the gloomy sky like a pair of cat's eyes, casting a pale light into the room. Sleep took its time in coming, and as she was carried from one side of consciousness to the other, Penny knew where she was going and what she was going to see.

Her legs were covered with sharp flares of pain. For the longest time she could not see anything through the overwhelming darkness, but when her eyes opened, she realized that she had made it back home. She was sitting in her bed with the covers pulled up around her neck. The unrelenting pain that gnawed at her legs was too strong; it was as if someone was pinching her with sharp, long fingernails. She threw off the covers and her stomach clenched. Her bed was crawling with insects. She watched with deepening sickness, frozen as skittering spiders, crawling flies, and black beetles gnawed at her legs, which were now covered in angry red bite-marks.

Penny looked to her bedroom window.

If I jump it'll be all over, it'll end. It will be easy.

A piercing scream cut through the night, tearing Penny from her nightmare. She sat up, her body convulsing as she looked around for the source. A deathly pale Annette was sitting up beside her, clutching her chest as she tried to catch her breath.

"What's the matter?" Penny gasped, looking around for the source of Annette's fear while still shivering off the effects of her dream. Annette could not seem to speak, and a pounding knock at their door made both of them jump.

"Are you two okay? We heard a scream," Simon called.

"We're fine. False alarm, I'm sorry!" Annette sputtered, her voice shaking. They listened as Simon's footsteps padded down the hall. Penny looked over at Annette, confused when she threw off the covers and stood up, hugging herself.

"Why did you scream?" Penny asked, shaken. Annette looked at Penny, her eyes wide and her tousled hair illuminated by the moonlight.

"Something...very strange..." Annette said, sitting back down. "It was like— it was like I was somebody else for a moment. I was sitting in this bizarre room, lying in a bed...and my legs hurt a-and..."

"Were there a bunch of bugs in the bed? Were they biting you?" Penny asked, comprehension dawning. Annette winced and nodded her head.

"I get it—you saw my dream, I think. I suppose somehow... I'm also able to put memories or dreams of my own into other's heads just like I can take them," Penny mused, trying to work out how it had happened.

"*That* was a dream?" Annette acted violated. "But you said that dreams were wonderful! That was — that was—you have to go through that every night?" She seemed on the verge of tears, and Penny took her hand.

"They're not all like that. Well, maybe *before* they weren't all like that...I guess my dreams lately aren't all that nice. But usually they're great," Penny reassured her. "I'm sorry—I didn't know that would happen. I'll take care not to sleep too close anymore."

Annette still looked disturbed as she pondered this. "I wonder...could you show me what a nice dream is like? I don't think I could go to sleep again after that," she choked out.

Penny remembered the first time she had suffered a nightmare as a child, and was confident that the same fear must be coursing through Annette now. She struggled to think of a way to put a dream in her head.

"I don't think I can...I mean, up until a minute ago I didn't even know it was possible to...erm, *reverse the process* at all. It's much easier for me to show you your own memories. I could do that, if you like—it'll still feel like a dream," Penny offered. Annette put her finger to her lips and contemplated.

"Is it safe?" she asked, looking anxious.

"Completely," Penny assured her with the best smile she could muster. "Just think of a happy memory and grab my hand." She extended her hand, waiting until Annette decided on a memory and placed her hand on top of Penny's. Penny took a deep breath and cleared her mind, allowing the bright flash of light to coax Annette's chosen memory into her mind.

A small, chubby girl ran through her parents' home, holding ribbons in her hands as she burst into the dining room. Her flowing blonde locks were tied back in pigtails and she launched over to the chair and climbed her way up. The table was covered with a cloth and an expensive looking tea set was strewn about, amidst piles of cookies and cakes. Two other young girls, one tall and lithe who appeared to be several years older than the first, and the second barely old enough to talk, sat between an assortment of stuffed animals....

The memory dissolved away from Penny's eyes.

Annette looked exhilarated as she grasped the sides of her face. "My goodness! It's like...it's like living it over again!" she whispered, ecstatic. "It was as if I were really just there with Anita and Annabelle...I could hear their voices, feel the tablecloth..."

Penny contemplated what she had just seen "Those girls were your sisters...and you were...?" Penny inquired, remembering Valentine's cruel comments in the sewing shop. Annette flashed an almost frightened look at Penny.

"Oh, yes. That was me," she admitted, and fought past the sudden wave of gloom that had passed over her face. "Can I see one more? Please?" she requested. Penny nodded and took Annette's hand in hers, and another memory flowed into her mind...

...Annette, now just shy of sixteen, stood before her parents, sisters, Aunt Wendy and Uncle Theo. She smiled her brightest and took a deep breath, glancing back at Gavin sitting at the piano behind her. He had always been exceptionally lovely, even as a youth. Annette felt a fierce stab of jealousy at the sudden sight of his flawless face, but beamed over at him nonetheless. He gave her an encouraging wink and began to play the introduction to a song.

Annette sang out with all her heart, feeling her hands and body shake as she performed. She took care to hit all the notes, remembering where to breathe. Her voice was far from the astonishing instrument it would become in the future, but it was still nothing short of stunning. As the last note of the song rang, her family burst into applause, her mother running forward and taking Annette in her arms with a proud squeal. Annette felt humiliation when she hugged her mother's slender and bony frame in her soft one, but smiled without showing it.

"Beautiful, sweetheart. You'll do fantastic, no doubt," her father told her with glowing pride and a glinting smile.

"We'll all be cheering for you, my dear," Aunt Wendy announced, moving in also to get a hug from Annette.

"Thank you, thank you all," Annette said, feeling her confidence rise along with the nervousness in her chest. The auditions were tomorrow; there was no going back now. She looked back at Gavin and saw that his gaze was fixed on his father, appearing hopeful for a bit of acknowledgment. Uncle Theo was looking away, a strained look in his eyes. Annette felt her heart drop and slid away from her chattering parents and sisters to join Gavin on the piano bench.

"I thought you played marvelously," she told him, watching his expression change from somber to a bittersweet form of contentment…

…Annette's heart would not stop pounding. The adrenaline that snaked through her veins caused her voice to tremble and crack. Her eyes stung with tears but she kept them in, feeling the white-hot lights stream at her from every direction. The crowd was a black, hushed mass before her, their attention all fixed on her. But there was no need to see them to know who it had been. She knew who had called out that hurtful word, yet she continued to sing, feeling humiliated and disgusted with herself, predicting that the second she was off stage she would collapse into a puddle of tears. Annette was determined to keep going—or she had been until the laughter started.

It was one or two voices at first, coming from the same area as the stinging insult. More hideous statements about her body were being called out, each word digging into her like a knife.

It's her and her friends, her awful friends, *Annette thought as she tried to continue her song, feeling her voice dying in her throat as the derisive laughter grew louder and more grating on her ears.*

"Hey, dirigible, the airstation's down the street! Get off the stage!" It was a male voice this time, hoarse and broken by guffaws. Annette felt her knees shake and could do nothing but stand blinded by the hot stage lights. The laughter was echoed all across the audience now, mixed in with angry shouts, some directed at those who laughed, others calling out more cruel names. The accompanying music blared on as the first hot tears fell down her cheek. She felt teardrops, illuminated by the stage lights, fall from her face and splatter onto the stage. She could take it no longer.

Annette raced off the stage, covering her face with her hands, loud boos and harassing shouts trailing after her. She ran through the darkness of the backstage area, people trying to catch her and calling out her name as she violently pushed past them.

"Annette, wait! Stop!" She could hear Aldridge running behind her, his voice imploring. Another stab of sickness and guilt hit her; he had given her this chance and she had derailed the performance by running away. She escaped into the cold night, ignoring everything around her as she plunged herself into the deepest and most remote alleyway behind the theater. At the end of this dark and dingy place she collapsed to her knees in mortified vertigo. Undiluted wrath and dejected sickness washed over her in crashing waves. In a fit, Annette ripped the bows from her hair and threw them in the pile of garbage along with whatever bits of her costume she could manage to tear off. The urge to shrivel up and disappear to a place where no one could ever see her again filled her mind. She prayed to be invisible.

Her wails turned into anguished sobs and then were reduced to tiny sniffles. She was glad of the darkness; she could not see the way anything looked. She lifted her eyes skyward toward the stars, grieving at the loss of her dream. Annette was moments from another paroxysm of sorrow when a small voice got her attention.

"Hey," it said. The innocuous sound was enough to jolt Annette up from her misery and onto her feet. Her whole body trembled; this voice was unfamiliar.

"Is that you? The girl from...the play?" The voice was hesitant, male—but not unkind. Annette could see the man's vague form at the end of the alleyway.

"Who's there? What do you want? Come to torment me some more? Was laughing at how disgusting I am from the audience not good enough for you?" Annette yelled, feeling as much fear as she did anger. The stranger took several methodic steps forward.

"It's not safe here. People are looking for you—they're worried," he soothed, stepping over to Annette. She could barely make out a face in the darkness, let alone distinguish his features.

"You followed me here?" she sniffled.

"Yes, I was watching the play – it's awful what they did. It made me sick to watch..."

"No, I deserved it...I shouldn't be allowed to act or sing... I'm just a f—f—" Annette burst into tears again and the man put a comforting hand on her shoulder.

"Don't ever say that. You were fantastic."

The memory stopped as the present-day Annette threw herself back from Penny's grip, holding her stomach and moaning. Penny felt sickened by what she had just seen. She peered at Annette, who looked as if she might burst into tears once more. The girls stared at each other in uncomfortable silence, Penny feeling as if she had trespassed into forbidden territory.

"Annette, I didn't mean for—I can't believe that—I'm sorry..." Penny tried, but Annette shook her head, trying to keep her emotions together.

"No, no—it was my fault...I couldn't help but think of it and—oh, no...n-now I'm crying again," she whispered, wiping at her eyes. Penny inched forward and put an arm around her.

"It was Valentine, wasn't it?" Penny asked. Annette nodded, biting at her bottom lip as she scowled.

"She brought all her friends there that night—she planned it all in advance." Annette choked, anger sparking in her tear-flooded eyes. "I was only sixteen."

Penny hugged Annette as the actress caught her breath. "Why would she do a thing like that? Why does she hate you so much?" Annette wiped a final tear from her cheek and sighed. "Valentine was the most famous actress of her time... they called her *The Goddess of Iverton* once. My mother was a prop artist, and ever since I was old enough to talk she would take me to see the plays she worked on. That was where I first saw Valentine.

"She mesmerized me—she was *so* beautiful in her youth, so talented and full of life. I loved her, I wanted to *be* her...she was my hero. When I was young I watched every single one of her performances, desperate to be like her in every way. One of my first memories is when I begged my mother for singing and dancing lessons so that one day I could be as great as Valentine. When they discovered I had something of a natural talent, performing became my life. I did nothing but study music, dancing, and drama, and followed each so diligently I was removed from public school so I could train harder. It's because of this that Gavin and I became so close at an early age. We were both so deeply involved in the same activities.

"Finally, when I started to audition for some of the plays, I got noticed by Aldridge. He gave me a few chorus roles early on, but when I turned sixteen everything changed. That was the year I'd tried out for the lead...and I got it. I beat Valentine—the *Goddess of Iverton*. Of course it probably had something to do with the role being written for a teenager and Valentine was nearing her thirty-third birthday, but the fact remained...and she took it *personally*. I heard from Aldridge that she threw a fit and refused the supporting role he'd offered her. She couldn't accept that she got beaten out by someone that looked...how I looked back then...nor could she come to terms with the fact that she was growing old and that her career eventually had to change, so I became her scapegoat. Everywhere I went people were giving me dirty looks and saying the worst things, but I kept on practicing and going to rehearsals. My family was *so* proud of me—and I was proud, too. I'd never thought of myself as beautiful or special, but all of a sudden I *was*. My dreams were all coming true—that was until Valentine pulled her little stunt," Annette spat, referring to the memory Penny had just witnessed.

"She...she's pathetic," Penny whispered, feeling ill. "But she didn't beat you in the end. I mean, look at you. You're better than she ever was. How did you—?"

"Oh, it certainly didn't end there," Annette continued. "That night, I almost decided to give up on everything. I was completely ashamed of myself, but that man...the one who found me in the alleyway. He stayed with me until my friends and parents came and found me. He was so kind—he begged me not to give up—he said it would be a shame for true talent to go to waste and he made all these silly jokes and even gave me a present to try and cheer me up." Annette pointed at the green-glass earrings that she never removed.

"He said that in return for these earrings he wanted my promise that I would never give up—and for some reason that just stuck in my head. It was like he was some sort of messenger from Heaven, put there to keep me on the right track."

"What happened to him? Did you ever see him again?" Penny asked and Annette shook her head.

"I never caught his name, or even got a good look at his face. He slunk off as soon as my family showed up—but it was still because of him that I became who I am today. Though those next few months were hard, I was determined I wasn't going to let Valentine win. I spoke with Gavin about my... my...problem."

"He set me on this rigorous training program. We practiced together and he helped me get slim. Those years took a lot out of me, but I had set my mind on getting my revenge and taking my dream back while I was at it. I went to every audition without fail, but Aldridge couldn't accept me back after that fiasco. Still, I never gave up. Every year I got better with Gavin's help, but by the time I turned nineteen things still weren't looking up," Annette explained, her eyes starting to glimmer with excitement.

"When it seemed like all hope was lost, something…something extraordinary happened. I still can't explain how or why, but it did. I woke up one morning and it felt like my whole mouth was on fire. I tried to drink some water, but it wouldn't stop burning… when my parents asked me what was wrong, I remember I screamed something like *get away from me* and they did just *that*," Annette told Penny with deliberate meaning.

"That was when I discovered—well, what it is I can do." She shrugged, her eyes flickering with the danger of secrecy. "It was like a gift from Nestor, just like the miracles he once worked long ago. People would simply do what I told them to do. I eventually learned how to use it, erratically at first, but I got the hang of it. It was difficult, too, because every time I do it, it completely exhausts me—sometimes I can't get out of bed for days.

"Obviously I kept it a secret. I think my family might have had some inkling, but they're still confused. Not even Gavin knows everything. But it works every time…I can persuade anyone to do anything and they must obey. You saw how it worked on the king. You felt it when I did it to you…"

Penny nodded, the idea of this power scaring her a little. It surprised her that Annette had never used her ability for wicked purposes; any lesser person would have most likely abused it. But as Penny looked at Annette, she knew that the young actress understood the value of hard work.

"So…at the next set of auditions I asked Aldridge for a second chance…and he gave it to me…" Annette looked vulnerable. "Goodness, you must think so little of me."

Penny considered what Annette had done. "No. You deserved a second chance," she decided, leaving the rest of her reasoning unsaid. Annette seemed to like this remark, a devilish smile creeping across her face.

"Well, if you don't yet, you will now. During one particular production Aldridge cast Valentine and I together and she never allowed me a moment of peace. She made sure that every second I spent at rehearsal was torture, and it was evident that Valentine was going to try some other cruel trick to ensure that I had no future...so I decided that I would have to get there first..." Annette trailed off, as if relishing what she was about to reveal. "I reasoned that Valentine needed a hearty dose of her own medicine and after years of suffering her condescending remarks and schemes, I cooked up something special, just for her."

"What did you do?"

"I might've *mentioned* in passing how she should go on stage after shaving one side of her head, splattering her face with different paints and shrieking like she was completely insane. I politely asked if she would also holler out all the deepest secrets and private scandals of all the famous, well-to-do people who had trusted her during her career while she was on stage — and the funny thing was, she did exactly that." Annette fluttered her eyelashes, and though Penny had to admit to herself that it was a childish form of revenge, she could not stop a snort from escaping at the mental image of Valentine humiliating herself in front of hundreds of people.

"Needless to say, she has never worked again. But I was too careless. Ever since then she's been curious. She knows that I had something to do with her *episode* and I knew she would catch up to me eventually," Annette finished with a sigh. She took a deep breath and let it go with relief. "Ahh, somehow it feels so nice to get that all off my chest! I've never told anyone this before, you d—"

"Annette, don't you see?" Penny exclaimed as something dawned on her. Annette stopped talking and looked confused. "Deimos and Phobos! They were looking for a person with your specific ability and Valentine led them right to you. They weren't looking for something you *had*, they were looking for *you*. They want to use your ability to do something—something awful, no doubt," Penny choked out.

Annette sighed. "I know," she admitted, her shoulders slumping. "I knew it from the moment you told me what you'd seen in Deimos's head. I'm in deep trouble...But I couldn't have them hurting Gavin or Aunt Wendy if they came looking for me. I'm just glad, for now, that we're safe up here in the air."

ON THE SANDS
OF HULVER

Penny made it through the rest of the night without even a whisper of an unpleasant dream. Annette wished her a shy good morning, last night's conversation having left a somewhat awkward atmosphere between them. When they came into the cabin, Hector was already busying himself with making breakfast.

Annette readied them for their meeting with the Goblin ambassadors by explaining the correct mannerisms and methods of conduct. After some debate about their safety, Hector chose fake aliases to use for the meeting, and magically altered their badges. Penny found herself more than certain they were not the right people for this job.

The sea below them was dark cobalt blue, almost black in color, and frosted with white waves. There was something strange about the vast expanse of water without a single boat anywhere in sight. It was with a respectful fear that Penny watched the churning and heaving waves, her mind flooded with frightful images of the alien life that no doubt lurked beneath. She knew those murky waters were at the very least infested with the beasts the Elydrians called fomorians.

Penny took extra care not to sleep anywhere near Annette that night in case she had another disturbing nightmare. To her surprise, she made it through the night without dreaming at all. She awoke to the image of white-blue sky outside of her window, feeling refreshed and devoid of the usual exhaustion that had been weighing her down these past weeks. The weather was temperate, the sky bursting with enormous billowing clouds that dotted the skyline like lazy sheep grazing in a pasture. They opened several of the windows in the cabin and let the winds sweep in the perfumed sea air.

The day was lazy and carefree as they enjoyed the gentle rocking of the airship and amused themselves in the main cabin. As the sky changed from clear blue to dusty rose they ate dinner and settled down for the evening. Annette decided to turn in quite early and Penny hoped that Simon would follow her example so she could have a moment alone to talk to Hector. She didn't speak a word to him, hoping that the lack of stimulus would send him off to sleep. Her plan worked, and Simon's head rolled back and rested against the side of the couch, his eyes shut. Within minutes he was snoring, his top hat rolling on the cabin floor with the movement of the ship.

Penny rose from the couch and made her way out onto the balcony, knowing Hector would follow to ensure that she did not slip. Sure enough, he snapped his book shut with a sigh and stood from his seat. Penny smiled as she opened the door and a blast of brisk night air met her. Hector shut the door behind him, standing at a distance.

The night sky was speckled with stars and had become a luxurious shade of purple, a lovely backdrop for the two moons. The sea below captured the light of the shining satellites and glimmered back as if laughing. The voices of the wind and ocean collaborated to create a low moan, almost drowning out the clangs and sputters of the heaving airship and its ever-beating wings. Penny glanced over at Hector to gauge his mood. He stared out at the gossamer, lavender-colored clouds, seeming to not be paying too much attention to her. She took a deep lungful of briny air, and Hector's voice rang out above the roar of the wind and waves.

"It's about what happened the other night, isn't it?" he observed with a wry smile, still not looking at her.

Penny frowned, feeling shocked and just a tinge embarrassed. *Am I really so easy to read?*

"All right, let's hear it. I've been waiting."

She let out the breath she had been holding and decided to share what Annette had told her. He seemed to understand she was editing for Annette's privacy and didn't pursue the whole story, but rather listened, nodding his head every so often to show he was attentive.

"I had a feeling Annette was doing it herself...but there's still so much missing. I suppose Della will fix all that, though— once we find her, that is," Hector said at last. "I suppose our getting to Hulver means you and Simon should be able to return home in about a week's time. You must be excited." He peered over the edge of the railing.

Penny felt her heart sink but smiled, unsure why her emotions seemed so muddled of late.

"Yep, pretty excited," she said without enthusiasm, but Hector did not seem to notice. A question teased at the edges of her lips, but she held onto it, afraid of what the answer might be. The terse quiet between them seemed to grow to an unbearable tumult, and then Penny gave in to her curiosity.

"Erm—" she began, thrown off again when Hector looked toward her with mild curiosity. She turned away, finding it easier to speak when he was not in her direct line of sight.

"Well, I was wondering...when we—or I guess *if* we return to Earth," she corrected herself, knowing that she could not stop now and wishing that she had never started. "What will you do? That is, where will you stay?"

Hector turned his face to the clouds and for a moment the only sound besides the whipping wind and the airship was the steady pound of blood in Penny's ears. "I should think that a bright young lady such as yourself would have figured that out already," he mused. He turned toward her, his grin mixed with a sadness she could not interpret.

"Think about how our disappearance will look to the eyes of the Oregon police force. A young girl goes missing without a trace after her teacher was acting strangely. Don't forget, there was a room full of students who can confirm that. Later that night, the door to her house is beaten down, a burned mass of mangled human flesh is discovered at the scene along with forensic evidence of her teacher's presence at the home, and then they both go missing on the same night. What conclusions would you draw from that?"

"Oh…" Penny said, looking away again.

"I think it's safe to assume I'm leading Twin Rivers' most wanted list." He attempted to sound humorous, but Penny could not force a smile. Hector watched her from the corner of his eye. "It's not like there was much left for me on Earth. Besides, I feel—well, it might sound a bit foolish, but I almost feel as if I—ah…never mind," he left off.

"No, what were you going to say? I want to know," Penny urged, intent now.

Hector looked uncomfortable, but Penny didn't look away. "All right, all right. I was simply meaning to relate the fact that—I—" he stopped, sighing in defeat. "I don't know, it's strange. I've never really felt that I've belonged anywhere, not on Earth or on Nelvirna—or even *really* in Elydria…but on some days in this place…I feel like one day I could, perhaps." He glanced sideways at Penny. "It sounds ridiculous when I say it out loud, doesn't it?"

Penny looked at him with unusual serenity, thinking for a moment she might have caught a glimmer of that self he fought so hard to suppress, that sorrow he was determined to bear in complete solitude. She shook her head and returned his smile.

"No, not ridiculous at all. I—well, I know exactly what you mean," Penny murmured, thinking with distaste of her own awkward existence back on Earth and how life in Elydria seemed entirely different. She looked out at the horizon, feeling Hector's gaze on her.

"Well, if you understand…then how do you explain that dismal look?" he prodded. Penny's face flushed again, and she cursed herself for the second time that evening for letting her emotions show through.

"Now, now. If you get to pry, then it's only fair I should also be allowed at least one instance of shameless nosiness," Hector teased.

Penny hated to admit that his point was valid, and wondered for a moment if she should lie to him, but she could not find it in her heart to be dishonest after he had been so genuine with her. "Maybe I was—I was almost sort of hoping that possibly…" she scratched at her head and looked down at the churning waves below, feeling a little dizzy. "Well, I was hoping that when all this was over and done with…that we could still be friends…" her voice sounded small and pathetic in the wind, not at all how she wanted it to emerge, but even so Hector appeared touched. She grimaced, wishing she had lied.

"Penny…" he said with affection. Penny's heart leapt; it was the first time he had used her nickname. She turned to face him, noticing that he also looked quite flustered. Hector took a small breath and smiled, warmth showing behind his eyes. "You and I…we'll always be friends."

Not knowing quite how to reply to this, but feeling a warm sensation deep in her chest, Penny managed a pleased little laugh and ran a hand through her hair, stalling. The wind whistled by, filling the long hush between them. Hector clapped his hands together after a moment and turned away, reacquiring his usual formality.

"Well, if it is the same to you, I suggest that we go inside and get some sleep while we can. We should be arriving in Hulver within 3 or 4 hours—not to mention it is growing unbearably cold out here."

PENNY STOOD IN her living room. Only a feeble, dim light filled the room, and the carpet below her bare feet felt cold and flat, not at all like carpet should. Penny looked around, an innate sense telling her that something was wrong. This was her house, but something had been altered. She looked around, seeing the television, bright and flashing vague images; a plate holding the remains of a meal, the sofa, the bookshelf, and her mother's case of oddments. Her eyes fell on a tall lamp standing in the corner of the room.

"That wasn't here before…" Penny said aloud. She took a few steps toward the lamp. It was the only thing in the entire room that was giving off any light; it was the only thing keeping it away. She looked out of the window and saw rain splattering the panes, and a voice behind her whispered something. It was faraway and indistinct, but alarming. She tried to locate it, and with a shock saw the weak light from the lamp flicker. Turning back with a small yelp, she flipped the switch on and off, attempting to make it work. The light bulb fizzled and popped, and with a small electrical sound the light began to fade. Fear rising within her, Penny looked at the corner of the room, seeing a cluster of darkness gathering. A faint but familiar voice hissed from the growing spot.

"I come with the dark."

Blackness blotted out her vision, and Penny could see small shapes moving about in the gloom; they were unclear, sometimes in the shape of a grasping hand or a tattered cloak.

Penny raced away from the gathering dark toward the stairs, her bare feet slapping on the carpet that still felt too hard as the light dimmed. Penny gasped for air as a static electric sound itched and burned at her ears. She pounded up the stairs, hearing the voice again: an echo, calling to her, calling out her name. Her legs grew heavy as she chased the dying light at the end of the hall.

She was at the top of the stairs, battering away the invisible blockades as she reached the door to her room and threw it open with a shout. An arctic blast of air assaulted her as she pounded into the room. Wind licked at her hair and pierced straight to her bones, and something clamped down on her wrist.

It had caught up with her. Penny screamed and tried to yank her wrist away, but it held fast. Keeping her eyes away from the sanity-shattering sight of the masked entity, Penny made for the window. If it was going to kill her, she might as well take it down with her. She hurtled toward the open window, barely noticing as her clean room slowly decayed into grime, dead leaves and dry bones appearing before her eyes. She fought the masked entity, yanking it forward and feeling as though she was dragging an anchor along behind her. Her stomach hit the windowsill and turned, victorious, to face her assailant.

It was Annette.

"Annette?" Penny choked, her senses overloading as the nightmare melted away like a dispersing mirage. She looked around, fear welling up in her chest. The cold and the wind made sense now. Somehow she had made her way out onto the deck of the airship and now leaned precariously over the side railing.

Annette was grasping onto Penny's wrist with all her might. Weak and dizzy with confusion, Penny felt her foot slip on the smooth wood of the deck and her stomach drop out as she toppled backward over the railing of the airship. Annette lurched forward with her, now grasping Penny's wrist with both hands as Penny dangled over the side with nothing but hundreds of feet of empty air and freezing ocean below. The instant terror was so intense Penny could not make a sound.

"PENNY!!" Annette shrieked, her face red with strain as she tried her hardest to pull Penny back up over the railing. Penny kicked her legs through the air as she tried to catch something, anything, with her other hand. She felt Annette's strength failing, but the actress leaned forward with Penny instead of letting go. Penny felt sick, knowing exactly what was about to happen. Annette slid, but just as she was about to go over Hector appeared and grabbed her by the waist. Assessing the situation in an instant, he leaned forward and grasped Penny's loose hand and began to pull her up with Annette's help.

"Hold on! We've got you!" Hector called over the roar of the wind, his face pale. Just as Penny started to regain the ability to breathe and hope she would live to see another minute, Simon exploded onto the deck.

"I'm here! What's the ma-ma-maaaa—" He skidded to a halt just behind Hector, but did not stop in time. Simon slammed into Hector with a force that sent Hector and Annette toppling over the edge. He made a mad grab for Hector and caught his wrist, but the momentum of the fall pulled Simon down with him.

For one long, horrifying moment Penny could only stare up at the flailing bodies of her friends as she waited to die, and then a rush of air floated past her on all sides, slowing the freefall. A flare of light burst up and Penny felt a hand grab onto hers.

At first all Penny could see was a rushing river of stars in her eyes, but as they dissipated she could see that everyone hung around her in midair, all falling together with their hands haphazardly linked, but so slowly Penny thought she must be dreaming again. She realized then that the shooting stars were glowing runes emitting from Hector's hands. Penny took a great gasp of icy cold air and saw Simon had lost consciousness from the magic drain, and Annette was crying, her tears fluttering upwards in the wind.

"Look!" Hector cried. Out of the gloom and the ocean mist, Penny could see a dark mass of land with clusters of light glimmering in the distance. Below them loomed the black ocean and miles above was the Airship, still beating its huge wings and shooting off beams of light. Penny could not believe they were plunging from such a dizzying height. She braced herself for the inevitable as they neared the surface of the ocean.

The waves that had been mere spots of foam from the height of the airship were now thundering masses of water, crashing and exploding in eruptions of spray as they plunged into the sea, the churning surface feeling like a bed of blades on Penny's skin.

Penny was ripped away from the others as they were tossed by the merciless currents, the saltwater stinging her eyes and nostrils. She knew her only hope of survival was to get to Simon's wand. Breaking the surface, she fought her way through the waves and plucked the wand from Simon's limp body before he could sink. Not knowing what to do and feeling control of her motor functions slipping due to the cold, she willed with all her might that the puffy cloud that Simon had summoned before in the graveyard would appear before her eyes. As if the silver wand had been listening, the white cloud blossomed out from the tip and pushed Penny and Annette up from the churning waves.

Penny screamed as she saw Hector and Simon slipping away into the sea, knowing they had only minutes before their lives were claimed by the depths. Hector swam forward, spitting water, and heaved Simon's body toward them. Annette and Penny yanked him upward onto the cloud, and turned back for Hector. Penny's hand grabbed onto his slick one and Annette caught his wrist. Penny's chest tightened when Hector's hopeful expression turned into one of acute horror. Penny heard it before she saw it; an unnatural disturbance beneath the waves, accompanied by a venomous hissing.

From the dark depths of the ocean a creature's head burst from the water, its gaping orange eye glowing in the darkness. Its teeth were huge and long, like long swords of bone, and filthy green hair grew from the top of its scaled head.

In a lightning fast motion, the creature sank its long, crooked teeth into Hector's midsection and he let out a scream of utmost terror and pain. Overcoming her horror, Penny lurched forward and jabbed Simon's wand into the center of the creature's face. She felt the tip of it drive into the soft eyeball with a sickening puncturing sound, and the creature shrieked as blood flowed from its eye. It stopped gnawing on Hector's convulsing body long enough for Annette and Penny to pull him onto the cloud. Penny commanded the wand to bring the cloud higher and they shot into the air, the chill cutting into their damp skin. When they were a suitable length away from the surface of the restless waves, Penny allowed herself to breathe again. She commanded the cloud to travel toward the land mass only a few miles in the distance.

"P-Penny! Hector, he—!" Annette choked in hysterics, grasping at her chest as she hyperventilated. Dripping and shaking, Penny looked down at Hector in terror. Even in the darkness she could see he was drenched in his own blood and lay motionless. His chest was still rising, but only just.

"What are we going to do? He's going to *die!*" Annette sobbed.

"NO! He's not going to die!" Penny shouted back, trying her best to keep her mind clear as she steered them toward the shore with all the speed the little cloud could manage. The fog became thicker as they got closer, making it very difficult to see even a few feet in front of their faces. Penny was quite close to losing her mind from fear when she saw a gathering of lights.

Lights! Lights mean people! she thought, directing the cloud forward. In less than a minute the lights were just a few feet away and the water below had changed to sand. Penny urged the cloud to let them down, but instead of dropping them down softly, it disappeared and they crashed into the sand several feet below.

Penny got to her feet, aware she was caked in sand and blood and dripping with seawater. A fierce determination pulsed through her as she turned to find the lights she had seen from shore, but when she caught them in her sights crushing disappointment buried her like an avalanche. She dropped back down to her knees.

The lights were souls. The very same type of glowing entities Penny had seen flitting about between the gravestones in Lindenvale. There were at least ten or fifteen of them drifting above their heads. Penny was seconds from collapsing in hopelessness; they were stranded, and maybe miles away from any city.

Without immediate help Hector is going to die. If we stay in the cold in this condition for too long we are all going to die. And it is entirely my fault, Penny thought, sure that she would not be able to keep her tears back this time. As she buried her face in her hands and resigned herself to at least being close to Hector in the last moments of his life, a soft sound roused her and Annette from their despair.

A light came toward them, followed by the sound of someone's feet shifting through the sand.

"Hello..?" a voice called out from the haze. Annette gasped, her sobs shuddering to a stop. Penny was stricken with fright; the voice had not addressed them in Gobblish, but Andronian. Through the thick mists, the vague shape of a slouching human form advanced on them.

"Help us! Please! We're over here!" Annette cried.

From the veils of fog stepped a man, an eidolorbe in his hand.

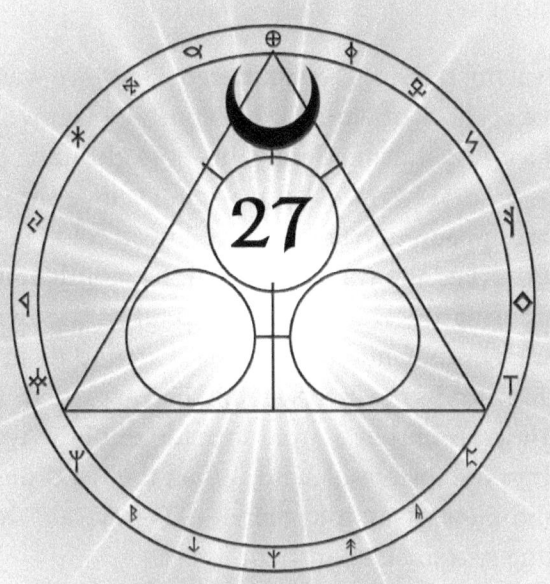

THE PUPPET MASTER

Penny's heart filled with dread at the sight of the approaching stranger. A black bandana obscured the lower half of the man's face and another wrapped around the top of his head. Wind-swept silver hair hung around his face and curious eyes peeked out from the space between the fabrics. The eidolorbe gripped in his bony hand was full of souls swimming and bouncing around inside their cage. The light emanating from the souls acted as a flashlight as the stranger brought it close to Annette's face and gave a strangled gasp. She was covered in Hector's blood.

"Our friend is hurt! We're stranded out here—please help us," Annette begged, hands clasped together.

The man pocketed the eidolorbe and rummaged around in the voluminous black jacket he wore before pulling out a tiny glass vial that appeared to have a few drops of water inside it. He shook it and sighed.

"I was saving this, too," he muttered. His voice was flat and held no note of shock or worry, which puzzled Penny. The man turned to face Annette and Penny, his eyes gleaming out from the shrouds around his face. With a small start, Penny noticed that his irises appeared to be bright yellow in color, just like an owl's. He uncorked the vial and turned the mouth of it toward the sand, pouring the water out in a spiral shape. Everything was still for an instant, and then the sand around them erupted as if something underneath the ground had exploded. The sand began swirling around in a rapid tornado until the world disappeared into the torrent of sand. When the wind died down and the sand blew away into oblivion, Penny saw they were now standing in a small apartment.

She goggled at their new surroundings. From the walls to the floor, strange, otherworldly objects and decorations were cluttered around. The ceiling was strung with small colored lights, paper lanterns, shimmering stones, and a dingy chandelier. In one corner of the room was a spiral staircase leading up to a loft and beside it a closed door. The walls were an explosion of paint splotches, scraps of wallpaper, posters, masks, and something that looked like a large collection of ticket stubs. It was as if a dingy, battered rainbow had crash-landed into the room many years ago and had been left to disassemble itself and collect dust.

The man with the bandanas crossed the room to where a kitchenette was crammed into the corner. Plucking up items from a massive pile of paraphernalia, he tossed a bull's horn, tambourine, musty blanket, and an old doll onto the floor, uncovering the same type of miniature Sophotri Penny had seen Gavin make calls with before they had left Iverton. Penny and Annette clutched each other as they saw him tap on it, call for the sanctuary, and speak with someone on the other end.

"Hey, Gorra, it's me. I need a surgeon and an alchemist here immediately. It's a life or death kind of thing," he said in heavily Andronian-accented Gobblish, showing he was originally from the Nation of Men. Annette raised an eyebrow at Penny, but she was too busy watching Hector's still form to acknowledge her. He was bleeding out all over the floor, his breath shallow. The silver-haired man joined them and looked over Hector, nudging the folds of his tattered shirt aside to inspect his wounds.

"Fomorian bite?" the man asked.

"Uh-huh," Annette burbled. The man glanced sideways at Annette once more, as if checking on something, and then quickly cast his gaze away, the skin behind his bandanna almost as pale as his hair. He reached into his pockets and pulled out two cross-shaped pieces of wood.

With a rattle and a shake two small objects, each about a foot tall, rose out of his deep pockets as if animated of their own accord. Controlled by the man's twitching fingers, they floated up into the air and over to Hector with blank eyes and frozen smiles. A chill ran up Penny's spine; they were grotesquely bizarre marionette puppets.

She dove to protect Hector, and the man shook his head.

"They won't hurt him," he said, and she edged away just enough that the puppets were able to grab Hector, one by his shoulders and the others by his ankles. Still controlled by their master, the puppets carried Hector upstairs and into the loft, his blood dripping as they moved. Penny shot a nervous glance at Annette as the man called the puppets back, set them down, and glanced at where Simon lay unconscious on the floor. His eyes were closed and his mouth hung open as he took rhythmic, rattling breaths.

"He okay?" the stranger questioned.

"He just fainted," Penny said in a thin voice. The man regarded them for a moment, then went off to search among his collection of things until he found a pillow and a few blankets. He helped lift Simon onto the makeshift bed and handed two more blankets to Penny and Annette, who wrapped themselves up.

Moments later a knock sounded at the door. Annette and Penny drew closer to each other as the door opened, revealing two female goblins. They were dressed in similar robes to the ones Armonie wore, except these colors were darker.

"Where is the patient?" one of them asked the man in Gobblish. He stood aside to let the goblesses inside and they followed the man up the staircase, glancing back at Penny and Annette with curiosity. Penny was bewildered as to why, and then remembered that they were both sopping wet, covered in blood and sand, and wearing their nightgowns.

Once the trio disappeared up the spiral staircase, Penny and Annette were left alone in a ringing silence. For a long while they stood, listening to the low murmur of voices and footsteps above their head. After it appeared the goblesses were not going to be back down for a while, the girls sat at a table with an assortment of old, mismatched chairs encircling it.

Penny sat in silence, the full weight of dread sinking in. She was sure that she was coming out of some form of shock, and that cold reality was preparing to tear her to pieces. The two puppets rested on the table beside them, eerie in their stillness. They each wore strange clothes that looked as if they had been sewn by hand, and their sculpted faces looked like something out of a half-formed nightmare. Each appeared to be humanoid, but more like twisted caricatures than accurate representations.

Losing what strength she had left, Penny covered her head with her hands, trying to work out what had happened, guessing that during the course of the vivid nightmare she had somehow started sleepwalking. This rationalization bothered her, because she had no history of being a sleepwalker. It was as if the masked entity had taken over her entire body.

The notion tormented her. She had chosen not to tell anyone about her dreams, chosen to ignore them, and because of this everything she cherished was now in jeopardy. Penny's miserable thoughts were broken by the sounds of footsteps.

The man was returning. He descended the staircase, feet now bare, and removed the bandana that previously hid his nose and mouth.

Penny had assumed from the color of his hair that the man was quite old, but seeing his face for the first time she was startled to realize he was in his mid-twenties. Beneath his startling yellow eyes Penny could see grayish purple discoloration—a sign that this was someone who lacked sleep. A golden earring was set in one earlobe, and gray trousers clung to bony legs. The large jacket seemed tent-like over his skinny frame. Despite his crooked, aquiline nose, his face looked as if it could be quite handsome if not for the lifeless, exhausted look to it. He studied the girls, crossing the room to join them at the table. His eyes strayed again to Annette, and after being stared at for too long, she grew agitated.

"What?" she spat. To Penny's surprise the man grinned, showing a single crooked tooth in an otherwise impeccable smile.

"It's really you," he murmured. "You're Annette Deveaux, aren't you?"

"You...know who I am?" The anger in her face disappeared and a wave of dull shock replaced it.

"*Everyone* knows you," he said with a lopsided grin.

Penny frowned, wondering how such trivialities could matter to them at a time like this. She cut into their conversation with domineering impatience. "Excuse me, sir, hate to interrupt, but is Hector okay?" Penny demanded, feeling her voice growing hoarse.

"So his name's Hector, is it?" the man wondered aloud, sounding somewhat interested before he shrugged. "I don't know yet. Looks like he got chewed up pretty good, but if anyone can save him, it's those two. Oh, and by the way, my name's Argent. No need for that 'sir' crap." He leaned back in his chair, observing Penny with interest. "What's your name?"

"Erm... it's Penny."

"And how is it that you know each other? Oh, and how is that you fell into the ocean? And why is it that you're all...in pajamas?" Argent inquired, not waiting for them to answer as he got up, shuffled over to the kitchenette and began rummaging through the cupboards. Penny and Annette shared a befuddled look, both lost for words. Argent leaned back to confirm they'd heard him, giving them both an imploring glance with his queer eyes as he set a dusty kettle on the wood-burning stove.

"It's a long story," Annette murmured in a voice that communicated she had no intention of telling him anything. Argent swept back to the table, his bare feet padding along the dusty floor of his apartment. He grabbed the control of the puppet, and with a careful twitch of his hand, it sprang to life and began moving around the kettle, gathering cups and sugar as Argent's hand commanded. Penny was transfixed by his skills as a puppeteer and watched, mesmerized, until Argent spoke again.

"Well, I'm not going anywhere anytime soon, and I assume you'd like to stick around until there's news about your friend," Argent shrugged, his hand still commanding the puppet with practiced ease.

Annette frowned again. "Well, what were *you* doing on the beach in the early hours of the morning?" she challenged, seeming to think a taste of his own medicine might cure him of his curiosity. Argent lowered his heavy eyelids, the ends of his mouth twitching up into the same lopsided grin.

"I was collecting souls. What were *yooou* doing?" he added, imitating her previous intonation.

"Collecting souls!? Whatever for?" Annette shot back, and Penny started to doubt the morality of their would-be savior. Argent made a small tutting noise with his tongue and shook his head.

"Now, now. You can't expect me to go rambling on when you're keeping all those secrets to yourself. First, tell me what you were doing in the ocean—other than trying to get your-selves killed, of course," Argent pried, his yellow eyes blazing behind his calm exterior.

"We fell from an airship and our friend Hector saved us by using a bit of magic to slow the fall, but we landed in the sea. We got away with using *his* wand—" Penny jerked her head in the direction of Simon who was snoring on the floor, "but Hector got attacked by the fomorian. Is that good enough for you?" She huffed and Argent's smile broadened. He looked down toward his pocket for a mere moment, and then back at her with something reminiscent of admiration.

"Indeed," he approved. "I was collecting souls so I can make some more of these." Argent laid his hand on the other puppet and it shuddered under his white fingers.

Penny shivered. "You...you put people's *souls* inside those things? How horrible!"

Argent shrugged. "I don't force them in. I only take the ones that want to come, the ones that aren't ready to leave yet. They're free to go any time they please, right Kasper?"

The doll shuddered again, and a hatch in the midsection opened of its own accord. A faintly purple wisp oozed out like incandescent mist and circled around Argent's shoulders before finding its way home, back inside the hollow body of the puppet.

"How do those things work? What do you use them for?" Penny asked, now enthralled. Argent looked pleased, which seemed to perturb Annette. She crossed her arms over her chest and her lips puckered into a pout.

"Why were you on an airship all the way out here with someone like her?" he asked Penny in response, honing in on the fact that he was not going to get any answers from Annette. Penny sighed.

"We were going to Hulver to see King Yulghrat on official business from Iverton," she offered. Argent raised an eyebrow as he glanced back down into his pocket.

"Now *that*…is an unusual bit of news," he said as the other puppet brought mugs of steaming tea to Annette, Penny, and himself. Argent took a quick sip of tea and made a face as it burned his tongue. Penny grabbed hers up, enjoying the cup's warmth that stung her frozen hands.

"Tell me everything," he requested and Penny scoffed.

"If we're playing by your idiotic rules, you should at least answer Penny's question first!" Annette argued, her anger evident.

Argent studied her until Annette's anger deflated and she fizzled back into an annoyed and embarrassed silence.

Argent looked away from them, propping his chin on his hand as he spoke. "The way I see it, you owe me quite a bit…I don't have to let you stay here. I didn't have to use the last bit of my Whirlwind Water, which was very expensive I might add, to transport us here, and honestly you are not entitled to my help in any way." He let his words resonate for a moment. "Disregarding that, I really do hate to see a person in trouble— that and I'm an avid fan of the theater," he added, pointing toward the wall where his patchwork of ticket stubs had been tacked up. "Now, if you're quite finished being obstinate, I'd like to hear the story, please."

"Why do you want to know so badly? It doesn't really concern you," Penny argued, trying to sound casual.

"Seeing as how you're all in my house with a dying friend and have little else than the clothes on your back, I would say that it rather *does* concern me. I'm not risking my neck if you're going to get me negative attention from the law. And by the way, lying isn't an option," he replied, taking something that looked like a coin out of his pocket and setting it down on the table in front of him.

Annette gasped, scandalized. "You are *not* supposed to have that! Those are for rangers *only*! How did you even get one?" she squawked. Argent laughed and leaned a bit closer to her.

"I *make* them for the rangers, Little Miss," he informed her, and Annette backed down again, huffing.

Wondering why they were getting into a tizzy over such a little object, Penny turned her attention to inspect it. It was round and flat like a disc, a crescent moon on one side. Noting her interest, Argent gestured for her to pick it up. Penny lifted it between her thumb and forefinger and studied it. She flipped it over to study three colored stars in a line, one green, one blue, and one red, each color looking murky against the black background.

"Say something to it," Argent prompted, seeming taken with Penny's curiosity. Annette remained incensed as Penny cleared her throat and spoke to the coin.

"Erm...my name is Penelope Fairfax," she stated, and the green star on the coin lit up. Argent smiled and took it back.

"It's a Lamia Lumen, but in layman's terms this is known as an Inquisitor's Eye. They were once used publicly, sold in the streets to anyone with yuebells enough—but apparently people couldn't deal with knowing the absolute truth all the time. Too many lives were lost and too many good things were destroyed over these. Because of all the fuss, many of the countries, including the Nations of Men and Goblins, outlawed them except for formal interrogation purposes. The nature of intelligent beings is a miserable thing, isn't it? Worlds such as ours cannot live without lies." Argent's smile was bitter as he looked at the coin.

"You see, the green star lights up when someone is telling the truth, the red for a lie, and the blue for a bit of both."

Penny nodded and leaned closer to Annette, getting an idea. Argent watched them.

"Can you—" Penny whispered, about to ask whether she could use her gift of persuasion to convince Argent to forget all about his interest in their story, but Annette was shaking her head.

"I'm just too exhausted. I don't think I could manage it, even if I really needed to," Annette whispered back. Penny chewed her lip and turned back to Argent for one last effort at trying to sway him.

"Come on...we've been through so much tonight, and we're too worried about Hector to focus. Anyway, aren't you tired? It's near dawn!"

Argent scoffed. "I'm always tired. I've got to open up the shop in a couple of hours—no point in falling asleep now." He shrugged and sighed. "Well, I guess if you're not interested in sharing, neither am I. I'll just tell the priestesses they're no longer needed and I'll show you all to the door. Good meeting you, Little Miss Annette. I've always been a huge fan." He grinned at her and Annette rose to her feet in a fury, slamming her hands down on the table.

"You're *awful!*" she cried, fresh tears swimming in her eyes. Argent chuckled, his expression portraying amusement, but Penny thought she detected the slightest hint of panic in his eyes.

"Look, I want to help you, but I know there's something strange here. Especially with you three." Argent pointed at Penny, then to Simon, and then up the staircase, obviously referring to Hector. "You three don't belong here. I can feel it."

Penny choked on her tea. "What...? How could you possibly—"

"Because he's a crafter, Penny," Annette answered for her, sounding rather bitter. Argent nodded with approval.

"Brilliant assessment, Little Miss." He smiled. "Perhaps I should give you more credit. Was it the comment about the Inquisitor's Eye?"

"I could tell from the second I saw you. Your hair, your eyes...I've never seen such *obvious* features," Annette said, a hard edge to her voice. Penny must have looked as lost as she felt because Annette turned back to explain.

"You can tell a crafter because of their hair and eyes—even their skin or teeth, maybe. They sometimes have an unusual color or quality to them, owing to the high amount of magic that's in their bodies." Annette turned back to Argent, her eyes narrowed. "Generally the more magic they're able to manipulate, the more distinct their features are."

Argent half-bowed from his sitting position.

"I still don't understand how he can..." Penny left off, not wanting to say anything concrete to confirm Argent's theory about the three of them not belonging in Elydria.

"It's because he can feel the magic around us. Crafters know where it is, how to use it, how they can change it...he can probably sense that you, Simon, and Hector are giving off a different magical field than the rest of us, isn't that right?" Annette looked at the crafter.

"Precisely," Argent agreed, looking impressed. "You know...I expected you to be obnoxious, but I never would have guessed that you would be smart, too," he teased Annette, and she glowered back with indignant rage.

"She's spot on, though—I can feel your buddy over there sucking up all the used up magic in this area as he sleeps." Argent looked over at Simon on the floor. Penny recalled Hector's theory about magic of Elydria becoming the raw material for dreams. "The magic's getting changed into something else — something like a different color, or a different shape. It's floating around you especially, Penelope. Did you know?" Argent raised his brow.

"Perhaps..." Penny hedged, shocked at the uncanny similarity between both Hector and Argent's grasp on how magic functioned.

"Now listen. I'm willing to make you a fantastic offer here...if you tell me your story and agree to help me with a few harmless experiments after your friend up there is in a more fit condition—if he survives—I'll let you stay here for free until you're ready to move on. I guarantee you won't find safer quarters in Hulver."

"Will you help us find the airstation and the palace while keeping me safely hidden here?" Annette bargained, her eyes narrowing in a fiery gaze.

"Certainly."

"And you won't breathe a word? Some very unsavory folks have it out for us—you should probably know that, too," Penny added, knowing that Annette would accidentally-on-purpose fail to warn him about the danger. Argent thought it over for a minute, then shrugged.

"I suppose I'm going to die at some point anyway—I might as well do something interesting on the way," he concluded.

"Then you've got yourself a deal." Penny reached out to shake his hand, a gesture he did not understand. She lowered her palm, feeling awkward.

"Now, let's hear this story before I have to get to work."

Annette and Penny looked at each other with tired eyes. Not seeing any way around it with Hector's condition, Penny started at the beginning.

AFTER HOURS OF Argent asking very detailed questions, policing them with the Inquisitor's Eye and snapping his fingers in their faces to keep them awake longer, they had fulfilled their end of the bargain. Argent seemed to be very interested in the magic they could perform, more so than the events that surrounded them.

"If this is true…I think… yes, that might work," he mumbled as he chewed on the ends of his stubby fingernails. He stood up and headed toward the door at the far end of the room, stopping just before going in to speak Penny and Annette.

"Make yourselves at home. Take whatever you need, just don't break anything. Also I would advise not going outside—

goblins won't take kindly to a pair of young girls covered in blood. Bathroom's upstairs. You'll be expected to compensate me for anything you eat or drink," he said and entered the other room. Penny caught a glimpse of another messy space before Argent shut the door.

Annette rose wearily from the table to look out at the light streaming in through the brilliant windows. All of the windows in Argent's house seemed to be made of collections of jewel-bright pieces of stained glass. Penny peered over Annette's shoulder.

Outside, Penny saw the front door of Argent's tiny home led directly to a flight of stairs, which stretched down to a shop-front of a most bedazzling variety. Beyond the storefront was a smoggy city with tightly wound streets, trafficked by goblins talking and pushing wheelbarrows.

"We're really here. We made it to Hulver," Annette breathed, gazing out with wonder at the small glimpse the view offered of the city. Penny stayed quiet for a moment as she stared out at the world beyond, her head fuzzy and her mind miles away from where she stood.

"What are we going to do Annette?" she asked in a small voice. Annette turned and sighed.

"We're really here. We made it to Hulver," Annette breathed, gazing out with wonder at the small glimpse Argent's stained glass window offered of the city. Penny stayed quiet for a moment as she stared out at the world beyond, her head fuzzy and her mind miles away from where she stood.

"What are we going to do Annette?" she asked in a small voice. Satisfied at last with their explanation, Argent had retreated into his workshop with the absentminded recommendation that they get some rest. Annette turned and sighed.

"I don't know," she whispered, looking as lost as Penny. "I thought this would be easy, you know? Gavin always makes everything look easy."

Penny lowered her head, expecting this would be the moment where Annette would start to blame her for what had happened. In a twisted way, she almost wanted Annette to blame her; the uncomfortable fact had gone unsaid for too long. Penny sank into a weak squat and covered her face with her hands, the emotions within her brimming over the surface. A small, miserable noise escaped and Annette knelt down beside her, running a comforting hand up and down her back.

"I'm sorry. I never meant for this to happen...if it weren't for me we'd all be fine. No one would be hurt and we'd be on our way to the castle without any trouble, but now we're stuck here with this...*creep.* I should've just—how could I let this happen to you? To Hector? What'll I do if he dies, Annette?" Penny half-sobbed, keeping her face covered. She bit down on her tongue hard to fend off the tears.

"It's not your fault, Penny. You didn't do it on purpose, and Hector's going to be fine. We all are. I don't know exactly how yet, but I know we're gonna get out of this." Annette peeled Penny's hands away from her face and tipped her chin up. She smiled, and that somehow alleviated Penny's misery more than any of her prior words had done. Annette helped her up and led Penny to the corner where Simon still lay sleeping.

"Come on, let's try and get some rest. I'm minutes away from passing out," Annette said. They produced a couple spare blankets and pillows from the mess of Argent's house and curled up on the floor beside Simon. Annette fell asleep right away, but Penny found she could not so much as close her eyes. She stared at the bizarre compilation of lights and lanterns Argent had turned his ceiling into, her mind unable to shut off while Hector's fate was uncertain.

Two hours after they had laid down, Argent emerged from the side room. Penny kept still and shut her eyes, hoping Argent would think she was asleep. He puttered around for a moment before leaving for the shop. Several minutes later

Penny could hear clangs and thumps below her as Argent opened for business.

Another half hour crawled by and Penny fell into a pseudo-sleep, but her momentary sense of calm was upset by the sound of footsteps on the stairs. Penny sprang to her feet, her entire body quivering. She watched two sets of goblin feet descend and waited at the bottom of the twisting stairs, her hands clutching her chest.

The first gobless, petite with shining white hair and milky eyes, halted when she noticed Penny. Penny's stomach twisted with fright and she found she could not muster the ability to speak.

"Can understand goblin?" the priestess asked in botched Andronian.

Penny licked her dry lips and commanded her lungs to breathe. "Yes. Please, can you tell me…" she begged in Gobblish, unable to finish the sentence.

The gobless leaned forward, her expression unreadable. "Ah, yes. Your friend…"

AT THE ATELIER

I t was quite a struggle," the gobless said as she strode down-stairs. "Argent called at the exact right time. If he'd waited any longer we would've lost him."

"He's okay?" Penny exhaled, feeling weak with relief. The first gobless nodded and gave a grin that would have looked terrifying at any other moment.

"He'll probably make it," the priestess said and patted Penny on the shoulder. She pulled a collection of flasks and bandages out from her bag and set them on the table. "Be certain that he drinks this medicine three times a day for at least a week, and avoid all types of exertion. By next week he should be back on his feet—as long as you don't move him. Do not hesitate to call us back if his condition declines. Oh yes, and this all comes to one amethyst and two emerald yuebells," the gobless reminded her and Penny experienced a twinge of panic. Hector's wallet was currently miles away onboard the Royal Dirigible.

"Erm, Argent has money, I think…" Penny stammered, knowing that though it was an awful thing to do, she had no choice.

"Ooh, he's not going to like that…well, let's go. Farewell."

Penny shot up the spiral staircase and into Argent's room. There was a desk piled with several well-loved books, assorted papers and a number of rather expensive and unusual objects. Penny saw a shimmering stone that looked to be made of brilliant green glass beside a box that was sealed shut by a lock. Next to them sat a jar of discolored jelly with something white and slimy suspended within, a pink glass mirror set with diamonds, and another puppet with a white face, tangled black hair, holes for eyes, and a dirty, smock-like dress the color of faded ink.

At the far end of the room, lying in Argent's bed under a green quilt was Hector. Penny tiptoed over to him and saw that he was sleeping, though there was a pained expression on his sallow face. His glasses were set on the bedside table, and Penny saw that in place of the shirt he wore a collection of blood-stained bandages. For half an hour Penny stayed beside Hector, monitoring his condition. When he did not stir once, she stumbled over to the washroom nearby, longing for a bath. It took a great deal of washing to scrub the bloodstains, sand, and sea salt away.

Wrapping herself in a towel, Penny peered through the colorful windows in Argent's bathroom to get another look at Hulver. Whereas Iverton had been orderly and clean, Hulver looked as if no amount of rhyme or reason had been bothered with in the design or construction of any structure in the entire city. The roads curved around off-kilter buildings and formed a veritable maze of pathways. Penny stepped down from the bathtub, looking at the bathroom walls. She ran her fingers over a painted moon and several images of galloping creatures and dragons winding around clouds and stars, figuring that Argent had painted them on the walls himself.

Back in the kitchen, deep exhaustion started to descend. In a daze Penny wobbled over to the deflated heap of blankets and collapsed beside Annette. Without the nagging sense of anxiety gnawing at her, she fell into a dreamless sleep.

PENNY EMERGED FROM blissful nothingness to a loud crashing sound and leapt up with a start. As her eyes adjusted she saw Argent standing before her, eyeing her spastic reaction with a grin. She groaned in vexation and Argent began to laugh.

"Good morning, little sis. Though it should be 'good evening' now, I suppose." On the kitchen table lay the source of the crash: her and Hector's travelling bags, Simon's collection of luggage and all of Annette's suitcases.

Argent stepped over to Penny, a crooked grin on his pale face. "I'm pretty sure this is the part where you say 'Thank you for carrying all our ridiculously heavy crap all the way from the Air Harbor, Argent! You're the best!'" he mimicked, and Penny looked at him, nonplussed.

"You went and—? But how did you—"

"It's not exactly hard to spot the Royal Dirigible of Iverton next to all the janky goblin airships. I just went aboard and told the captain that you all had found accommodations and would be out in the city for a while. He didn't seem to be too concerned about what was happening, so I just went and picked up this stuff. Though I shouldn't take all the credit, Hyde and Kasper did most of the work." He shrugged, and Penny saw that he held Hyde and Kasper's controls in either one of his hands. Argent's lips curled back again and he made the two puppets dance around the floor, creating a display that was both humorous and disturbing to Penny.

"Thank you, Argent. That was very thoughtful of you," she said, glad that she would have her clothes and possessions.

"Oh don't get me wrong, I really just wanted the money for the priestesses back. By the way, I took the liberty of taking that from your friend's wallet, along with a *modest* delivery charge. Hope you don't mind," Argent added and the warmth Penny had been feeling toward him vanished.

"Anyway, shop's closed now. I'm going to work in here," Argent said, and shuffled into the room on the other side of his living quarters without another word. Penny stared after him for a moment, and then turned to see Simon and Annette still fast asleep next to each other on the floor. Penny gathered clothes from her bag and went upstairs, taking the medicine for Hector in hand.

Upstairs Penny forced medicine into his parted lips, but Hector didn't wake. She fought with the idea of giving him the miraculous water she'd stolen from Warwick's Grotto to spare him the pain of recovery, but decided that it should be saved for a moment of mortal peril, if it were ever to arise.

Penny wandered back downstairs, feeling lost and hungry. Upon checking the icebox, she found nothing but a prehistoric hunk of bread, a large assortment of drinks, and a collection of the ruby-red potions that Penny suspected were the same as the ones Armonie mixed for them. It dawned on her how Argent could continue to work without needing sleep.

She helped herself to some water, but found this only made her hungrier, and went to consult Argent. Cautiously approaching the door, Penny listened to the sounds of sawing and banging that came from behind it before knocking, hoping that Argent would not be angry with her for interrupting.

"Yeah," his voice answered. She opened the door a crack and peeked inside, anxious what might lay behind it. Argent sat at a workbench covered in spare parts, wedges of wood, dowels, sheets of metal, springs, oddly shaped tools, and hunks of raw magic, all categorized by color and size. Sawdust lay all around, piled over the floor and gathered in heaps in the corners of the room. Along the shelves were rows of dried plants and mushrooms, doll parts and metal joints, deep hued jewels glinting, captive insects shuddering within their respective containers, and several thousand feet of thread. Sheaves of cloth material leaned up against the wall, and animal bones and bits of shining glass shards hung from the ceiling. A very bright light stood on the table, casting the rest of the room in bleak shadow. Argent wore a pair of eccentric glasses that had dozens of different lenses and knobs as he worked on something that looked like a flat silver disc with legs.

"What do you want?" he sounded perturbed as he used a type of onyx-colored sandpaper to smooth the sides of the disc. He picked up a metal pen with a red-hot glowing tip and started carving designs and letters around the rim of the disk as Penny watched.

"What is that thing?" Penny peered closer. Argent turned to glare at her before turning back to his work.

"Nothing that concerns you...just yet, anyway," he answered. Penny was surprised that such a disheveled person could express such an exactness and refined beauty in his work. "Your friend is still alive, right?"

"They said he would make it. What did you mean by 'just yet'?" she pressed.

"Good," Argent commented, starting on another flourish beside the one he had just finished. "Keep him alive until this is done and I'll tell you. Now get out, you're irritating me," he ordered, clicking a button on his glasses that caused a few of the lenses to spring back. Penny moved to leave and stopped, spotting a half-finished puppet lying on the workbench, its mechanical innards splayed.

"Why do you make those awful things?" Penny could not help but ask as she pointed to it.

Argent snorted in frustration and swiveled around on the stool, ripping off the outlandish glasses and setting them on the workbench beside him. "Because people pay a great deal of money for them and they make for wonderful help and companionship," he answered with little emotion.

"So basically you sell people's souls for money?" Penny challenged, crossing her arms.

"Pretty much. But like I said before, they're free to come and go as they please. The thing is, not many of them want to leave. They're afraid to pass on. So instead of having them wander aimlessly or maybe become a ghost, I give them a way to live on—and make a handsome profit along the way." He looked over at a huge safe in the corner with glowing affection.

"How come they're so valuable if souls are hanging around everywhere, then?" Penny countered.

"Frankly, because not too many crafters have the skill. It's astoundingly difficult to make one that functions at all, much less functions well. I think there is only one other crafter alive in the world who can make them as well as I can, and he was one of my mentors," Argent told her, and it was clear to Penny he wasn't bragging.

"So what are you, some type of crafting genius then?"

"Some people have said so. I was the youngest person in a millennium to get a license from the Guild—seven years old. I was called a prodigy a lot in my youth, but I didn't really do anything special—it just sort of comes naturally, you know?" Argent shrugged, looking a bit embarrassed.

"The Crafter's Guild? In Iverton? Why do you live in Hulver if you come from Iverton?" Penny questioned. Argent smiled his lopsided grin, looking at Penny with a distant curiosity as if she were a type of rare specimen.

"Well, I could think of a few good lies to answer that question, but the truth is because goblins—unlike humans—leave me the hell alone, and I value privacy," Argent declared. "And I never said I came from Iverton, I only studied there, but I can go back whenever I want. I've got an importer's pass, so I get to ride the airships for free. Now, would you kindly get out? I need to work." Argent stood and pushed Penny lightly out of the workshop by the small of her back.

SIMON WOKE VERY disoriented and jumpy, and it took Penny several minutes to calm him down. Annette, roused by his shouting, was eager to get back into her own clothes as soon as possible. As she bathed upstairs, Penny filled Simon in on what had happened while he was unconscious. He seemed wary of Argent and in no hurry to meet him, and also rather put out that he had passed out and been rescued by Penny.

"And it would've been such a good chance to impress Annette. The saving of lives is such an excellent inspiration for romance," he muttered, smoothing his mustache.

"Simon, you *do* recall that it was you who pushed us over the edge, right?" Penny asked, cocking her head.

"I knew you ladies would fall for me sooner or later," he replied with a half-smile and Penny laughed, glad to see he was already back to his normal self. Annette came downstairs looking fresh and lovely as if she had been through nothing more than just a run-of-the-mill bad day, and Simon went up to change as well. After discussing the fact that they were all ravenous, they came to the conclusion that it was time to find a meal.

Mustering up some courage, Penny led their small party out into Hulver, Hector's wallet grasped tightly in her hands. The moment they stepped outside and down the stairs, the buzz of the night hit them. Argent's shop perched on a small hill that overlooked the city. Using her enchanted glasses, Penny read the sign in front of his shop.

"Atelier Argent. Commissions welcome, inquire within," Penny read off the wooden sign that swung from an iron pole. The sides of the brilliant green shop were hand-painted with celestial images and metallic, golden carvings of stars and moons. Through the dark windows Penny could see glittering objects in glass cases.

They set off down the hill toward the labyrinthine city streets below. It was clear that Hulver was a city that never slept; cars running on steam and magic rattled by at a tireless rate through grimy streets. Penny had expected a number of anteloos crowding the lanes, but instead was shocked to see goblins riding creatures that looked like enormous pale centipedes with huge, ghostly green eyes. Far above their heads flowed a skyway of gargantuan moths, which looked to be the same species as the one Deimos had escaped on from the ball. Their huge wings blustered in the night air, the powder on their bodies creating an eerie luminescence in the sky. The twin moons of Elydria seemed closer to the world this evening and had taken on an orangey hue. Many goblins turned their heads to look at the humans who had come into their territory and Penny understood how the faeries must have felt when she had stared so shamelessly at them on her first day in Iverton.

Everything around them, from the alleyways to the buildings, looked dingy and battered. Yet out of all the surrounding gloom came fire-flashes of color from every window in the town. From what Penny could see, it was not normal to use clear glass for windows or lamps in Hulver, and in its stead jewel-colored stained glass shone out of every household and shop front. Scarlet, cobalt, and sea green paper lanterns hung from a number of shops, enticing street traffic to wander inside. Signs illuminated by magic blinked out from every corner at them, sputtering and hissing silent messages of discounts, advertisements for extravagant restaurants, and directions to risqué night-shows. Many of the vendors and eateries were open air or lacked walls dividing them from the street, and goblins came and went as they pleased, weaving in and out of shopping centers and jumping up on barstools next to compact kitchens churning out food of all kinds. If Penny squinted her eyes, it seemed as if a hundred broken shards of rainbow light were swimming in a rippling sea of black.

They stopped at an eatery that looked moderately safe. A short green curtain hung down from the low ceiling, separating it from the street traffic. Behind the curtain was a low counter with an entire kitchen on the other side, lit by crimson lanterns. Penny took a seat, feeling quite out of place as she watched the team of goblins cooking. At length a server approached and greeted them in Gobblish.

"What will I make for you, friends?" he asked.

"Erm, might you have any recommendations?" Simon suggested. Annette looked lost, most likely owing to the fact that she could not speak a word of Gobblish. The server thought for a moment, wiping sweat from his brow.

"Serpent stew—very popular. Three serpent stews, Ongkor," the goblin called back, turning away from them, not bothering to get approval.

"Serpent stew?" Annette repeated in a harassed tone after Penny translated for her. She groaned and put her head down on her folded arms. "I miss Auntie's cooking already... Oh!" She lifted her head up. "That reminds me! I haven't called Gavin." The server soon returned and slid three steaming bowls in front of them before demanding several ruby yuebells. They all stared at their dinner for a moment before Simon attempted the first taste. He chewed for a long time, then shrugged and nodded his head.

"Not bad," he concluded, and took another spoonful. Penny was hungry enough to try anything, but still tried not to look at what was floating around in the bowl. It had a salty, savory flavor. Penny ordered another bowl to take back to Hector, and once they had finished eating, the group left the steamy restaurant and headed back up the street.

Twenty minutes into wandering around the streets looking for the way back, Penny realized that they had lost their way. Not a single street in Hulver was straight or uncluttered, and it was no surprise that they had taken several wrong turns. Annette seemed on the verge of a panic attack when Penny spotted a goblin wearing a familiar type of coat, too similar to the ranger's uniform of Iverton to be ignored. He stopped when she tapped him on the shoulder, looking surprised to see a human.

"Please, sir. Can you help us? We've lost our way. We're trying to find a place called Atelier Argent, do you know it?" Penny inquired. The goblin ranger's eyes widened further at her perfect Gobblish.

"I think I know the place. I'll take you to it, if I can," he agreed and led them down a narrow alleyway canopied by an assortment of plumbing pipes and robes hanging on clotheslines.

"Erm, what's with all these decorations and posters? Is something going on?" Penny asked, and the Ranger looked back at Penny to see if she was being serious. He stifled something that sounded like a laugh.

"It's all for the Goblin Carnival. It starts next week—lasts for five nights. Happens every year. All the people celebrate before the winter is here, and at the end our king will make his speech," the ranger explained as he escorted them past a steam parts supply shop that looked somewhat familiar to Penny. "It's a great big party. You should stay around to see it, I think. Many from all over the world come to make merry the streets. Is this the place you are looking for?" He stopped at a small pathway that led to the stairs outside of Argent's shop.

"Yes, this is it! Thank you very much, sir!" Penny told him with a grin, which he returned. Penny cast her eyes aside and shivered, knowing that she would never get used to seeing goblins smile.

Hector was still fast asleep in Argent's bed, but looked as if his complexion had gained some color since she'd been away. After helping him drink some more of the thick green medicine, she attempted to wake him up. Although stubborn at first, he opened his eyes and looked around in confusion.

"Wh-where am I?" he croaked and tried to sit up, crying out in pain as a fresh spot of blood blossomed into the bandages that wrapped around his chest and midsection.

"Jeez, Hector, lie back!" Penny shouted, helping him downward onto the pillow as he winced in pain. "You just reopened your wounds!"

"*What happened?*" Hector's voice was high with uneasiness as he tried to orient himself. It took a moment to quiet him down before Penny could reiterate what happened. He turned a delicate shade of green as she described the fomorian attack. She tried to fill him in on what happened afterward, but could see that he was already drifting back off. Stopping her explanation, Penny helped him eat some stew before he fell back into the sanctity of sleep, overwhelmed by the pain.

Penny arrived downstairs to find Annette and Simon discussing their plans about what to do.

"Well, I don't see how we can trust him. I say we should get out of here while we still can." Simon shot a dark look at the door that Argent was barricaded behind.

"Hector could die if we move him, and I'm not going to wander around this godforsaken city while dangerous criminals are prowling around trying to abduct me. I say staying here is the safest bet we've got, even if Argent is a bit of a—*ruffian*," Annette disagreed, then turned to Penny. "What do you think we should do?"

"There's no two ways about it, we *need* to stay here," Penny conceded. "I'm not taking any chances with Hector's life. He should be back to normal in a week. Once he's feeling better, Simon, Hector, and I can visit the castle like Noah wanted, and then we'll be on our way to Mulgrith. Annette can decide then if she'll want to return to Iverton after that," Penny said, forcing herself to sound confident. Hector had always been the unofficial leader of the group and she was uncomfortable making decisions without consulting him, but Annette and Simon seemed willing to listen to her.

They all curled up on the floor in an attempt to get more sleep. Once Annette and Simon's breathing grew rhythmic, Penny tiptoed away from the blankets and opened up Argent's icebox in search of his stores of the ruby-red energy potion. She drained the bottle, coughing as the liquid burned her throat. She replaced the empty bottle in the icebox and went outside.

It was a few hours past midnight and the air had a nasty chill, but Penny coped. She was used to the cold after living in Oregon most of her life. A little ladder clung to the side of the building and led up to a space on the roof, and Penny climbed up it, at last getting a true look at the vastness of Hulver.

It was like a sea of glaring lights and signs, all winking back in pumpkin orange and Caspian blue amongst the gloom and smog of the city. The fluttering shapes of the large moths danced between the silhouettes of towers and lopsided structures. Penny did an about face and could see the foggy ocean several miles off. Further off to the south, a thick wall of trees trailed off into the distance until they became one with the black horizon line. She guessed this was Mulgrith and wondered how they were supposed to find a single person hiding in all of those trees.

Penny watched the stars in the sky fade away as the inky black changed to lavender and then to a weak shade of yellow. The morning began misty, and Penny shivered from head to toe in the moments before the orange-red sun rose again. As daylight swept through Hulver and smoke started to rise out of the chimneys, she heard the front door open up underneath her. Argent stepped into the early morning, blinking and scratching at the back of his head. As if he could sense someone watching him, he swiveled around, his silver hair fluttering, and looked straight up at Penny. He cocked his head to the side.

"What are you doing up there? That's my thinking spot," he called up to her. Penny tiptoed along the tiles of the roof and made for the ladder, climbing down onto the porch.

"I didn't know it was your spot, sorry. I was just killing time," she apologized, trying to ignore his curious stare. He watched her for a moment longer, then shrugged, seeming uninterested in prying so early in the morning.

"Are you going to open the shop now?"

"Yeah, wanna help? I don't have any employees, so it's always nice to have an extra pair of hands," Argent said.

Penny agreed, and he led the way to the shop at the foot of the painted stairs. She helped Argent open the front doors and carry a number of signs to the front of the shop, along with displays full of cheap magical trinkets, decorations, festival masks, and fireworks for the upcoming carnival. Argent took advantage of Penny's willingness to help and together they went about bedecking his entire store in carnival decorations.

By late morning the first groups of customers shuffled in and Argent asked Penny to help conduct sales. This was second nature to Penny, who had worked at her mother's shop since she was fifteen years old. By noon, the shop was swarming with customers. Argent turned on a good deal of charm as he stalked about the aisles and explained the functions and qualities of each of his products.

Annette and Simon got up around noon and smirked at Penny running up and down the stairs to do Argent's bidding. After noon Penny sent Simon to go and get lunch for everyone, and she stopped long enough to eat and give Hector his medicine. Annette tried to come down and visit them in the shop, but Penny had to remind her that it was not a good idea in case anyone recognized her, and the actress huffed back upstairs.

Business began to slow in the early evening, and soon there was no one left in the shop but Penny and Argent. The sunset's powerful light burned in and created fantastic reflections on the glass light fixtures and display cases. In the lull, Penny decided to inspect the different things Argent was selling.

"Did you make *all* of this stuff?" Penny asked, looking at a selection of miniature Sophotri Stones and crystal wands.

"Most of it. Some of the cheaper stuff is easier to buy in bulk from elsewhere, and some of the things are imported."

"What does this green powder do? And these necklaces?" Penny asked. Argent sighed in frustration and looked over at the sack of white-green powder she had asked about.

"That's Sleep Sand, it helps with insomnia. Knocks you out cold." He gestured to the sealed case of stone pendant necklaces, each displayed with a twin. "And those are Everstone pendants. They are extremely rare and valuable. If a single hunk of Everstone is cut into two or more pieces, the shards will never stop trying to find one another. Couples often buy these as marriage presents, because if one person is wearing one necklace, no matter how far away the other goes, they'll be bound to meet again one day."

"How romantic," Penny stuttered, looking at the Everstones with awe, then looking back at Argent. "Do they really work?"

Argent flashed his usual crooked grin. "They do," he assured her, and made his way back to the counter to resume counting his yuebells. Penny noticed he was still barefoot and suppressed a small giggle.

"The Atelier is really cool, I like it," Penny chirped, a sudden idea occurring to her.

"It likes you, too," he mumbled as he continued to scribble.

With a mischievous smile, Penny offered to help him out for the rest of the week in return for food, and Argent acquiesced after some consideration.

As the trio prepared for bed that night, Annette gave a loud screech as she lifted her blanket and an enormous black spider skittered out across the floor. Moments later she was still standing on top of the table while Simon hunted down the tiny creature in order to destroy it, as if it were a vicious wolverine. Argent poked his head out to see what all the commotion was about, and laughed himself hoarse at Annette. When he told her she should know his entire house was crawling with spiders, Annette went into a tearful rage, and fell asleep shivering and whimpering, jumping up and yelping every time she imagined she felt something skittering.

Penny drank the ruby-red potion again that night. She had come to the conclusion that if she never slept, she could never dream and would therefore not put herself or others in danger. If Argent could survive well enough without sleep, then, Penny figured, so could she.

AFTER FOUR DAYS, Hector's condition improved with every dose of the viscous green tonic. He was starting to look like the same Hector Penny remembered, but lacked his usual enthusiasm. The first time Argent spoke to Hector, it was apparent that the two were going to get along well. From the second they began to converse on the subject of magic, Penny's ears were flooded by a stream of technical jargon and she soon found that she was unable to follow along.

In the evenings after work and before he retreated into his workshop, Argent often climbed up onto the same rooftop that Penny haunted from the hours of late night until dawn and smoked a long silver pipe filled with something that perfumed the air with a sage-like fragrance. Annette and Penny joined him one night after dinner while Simon sat inside with Hector. As the trio on the roof looked out at the stars and the smoggy, shimmering city, Argent and Annette began to talk about theater at last and got into a passionate debate about classic plays versus newer releases, certain theatrical characters they liked or could not stand, and of course who was the most talented actor in Iverton. Penny noticed that Argent avoided talking about Annette or her prolific career in every way possible, even though Annette seemed intent on squeezing even the vaguest of opinions out of him.

One evening, after the conversation had wound down and Argent had scuttled into his workshop to begin work on his mysterious project, Penny helped Hector up to Argent's room. As he lay down, Hector looked at Penny with an embarrassed half-smile on his lips.

"Penny, thank you—I mean, for taking care of me and everything. This is all rather humiliating, so I think I'd like to apologize for making you go through this," he said, wincing somewhat and clutching his chest where the largest and deepest gash was still healing.

Penny looked at him with sympathy. "It's no big deal. I used to take care of my mom a lot, she was sick all the time when I was young. She was always frail, from the day she was born… and it rains so much back home." Penny felt her throat tighten a bit as she thought of the damp, leafy woods around her house. She kept talking to push the image from her mind.

"Anyway, I should be the one to apologize. If it weren't for me, none of this would've happened." A faint worry line appeared on Hector's brow.

"I've been meaning to ask, what happened exactly? Why did you try to jump off the side of the airship?" he asked, cautiousness in his voice.

Penny sighed again, beginning to feel even more muddled. "I—I was sleepwalking, I guess. It's a good thing Annette was there," she said, trying to make her words sound convincing, but knowing she had botched it. However, it appeared that Hector was in a state of such distress he did not bother to delve deeper into the truth. He winced as he tried to find a comfortable position.

"Does it hurt?"

"Immensely," he breathed.

Penny felt at a loss for words, knowing it would be hard for him to get any amount of peace or sleep in such condition. She thought of going to ask Argent for a sprinkle of the Sleep Sand he had mentioned a few days before when something occurred to her. A small bubble of eagerness swelled in her chest as she looked up at Hector.

"Here, give me your hand for a sec," she said, making a grab for it, but Hector pulled away. The sudden movement was too much for him and he gave a strangled yelp, groping at his chest in pain. Penny frowned and shook her head.

"Gosh, you're such a baby, come on—" Penny grasped his hand and he cried out again, this time in fright.

"Please! Penny, no! I don't want to see my memories, please—I—"

Penny gripped his hand anyway, feeling it tremble as she summoned the white flash of light. Instead of calling forth one of Hector's memories, she reversed the usual feeling, drawing instead on a memory from her own past...

Penny stared out at the still waters of the lake, one tiny hand clutching the front of her dress. The yellow world around them smelled of pine and wet earth. The lake was green and alive underneath the cold surface. Penny splashed through the water until her mother called her over. She ran, tripping over a root that protruded from the grass and falling forward onto her mother's lap, laughing all the while. It was warm on the blanket and the air was hazy. Paulina Fairfax picked her daughter up with a reassuring smile.

"Tell me again, Mom. I wanna hear again," Penny pleaded, closing her eyes as she pulled up blades of grass. She felt her mother's heavy hand on her back and heard her subdued laugh along with twittering birds and an orchestra of crickets.

"You've heard it about a thousand times, aren't you bored yet?" her mother wondered, running her fingers through Penny's hair. Penny shook her head, smiling to herself.

"Well, it happened quite some time ago in a place that's very, very far from here—halfway across the world as a matter of fact. Back then I was thin and beautiful – can you believe it?" Her mother laughed again, a comforting sound. Penny yawned, feeling the warmth and haziness envelop her. Her focus waned as sweet sleep swept over her eyes...

Penny withdrew from the memory with quiet control, her eyelashes fluttering as the real world materialized around her and a new feeling of serenity overtook her. Just as she had hoped, Hector had fallen into an untroubled sleep. She smiled to herself, proud to be gaining more control over her ability and marveling at the realistic quality of the vision. It was as if she had gone back to that carefree time when the world had been so small and simple.

Penny took care to place Hector's hand softly at his side, then sat on the ground beside the bed and let her head droop forward onto the mattress, her back resting on the wall. Her sleep-deprived body felt so heavy and stiff, and despite the awkward position she sat in, it was starting to seem comfortable. Before Penny could realize what was happening and fight it, she was asleep and free of worry.

THE BISHOP AND
THE KING

Tadaaahh!"

Argent slid out of the way to reveal the newly-completed contraption on his workbench. Penny moved closer, followed by Hector. Argent looked quite pleased with himself, despite his weary eyes. A strange sort of fishbowl held in place by ornate silver arms had been placed on top of the metal plate.

"What does it do?" Hector inquired.

Argent sprung to life as if he had been waiting for that very question. "Well, it may not do anything, I haven't been able to test it—mostly because it's useless without you two." Argent grabbed Penny by the shoulders and moved her closer to the machine. After placing Hector beside her, he took a moment to relish the image, and then clapped his hands together.

"Now, Hector, let me see if I understand this…you can take the magic that's floating around Penny and use it to perform enchantments, correct?"

Hector nodded his head.

"And can you control what happens to the by-product?" Argent prompted Hector again. Penny had never seen Argent so animated.

"Well, I suppose I could. Usually after I'm done with a spell the used up magic just sort of diffuses...but I suppose I could try. What is it that you want me to do?" Hector scratched at his head. In the last few days he had come to a complete recovery, and now seemed back to normal. He, Simon, and Penny were planning on visiting the castle that afternoon, but before they could make preparations to set out, Argent had wanted to unveil his project.

"All you need to do is waste magic," Argent announced, grinning. When Hector still appeared confused Argent attempted to explain again. "Basically, just use up all the magic you can, then try and push the *used* magic into this general area. Can you do that?"

Hector concentrated for a moment, and then realization dawned. "I see what you're trying to do! Brilliant!" he gasped, slamming his fist onto his palm. Argent nodded and gestured for Hector to proceed. Hector cleared his throat and closed his eyes.

Everything went still for a moment, and then the flashy glowing runes materialized around Hector's hands and wrists. Argent gave a victorious whoop. Within the fishbowl a ball of white hot light was forming, growing so large it threatened to overtake the glass.

"Stop, stop!" Argent cried, clapping Hector on the shoulder. Hector's hands dropped to his sides and he collapsed onto the bench beside a dizzy Penny. Not bothering to see how either of them was feeling, Argent scurried over to his machine and watched with rapt attention as the white light began to solidify into a hunk of trembling rock. Argent extricated the humming stone with the utmost care, holding the basketball-sized hunk in his palms as if it were a newborn child. His eyes were glassy and moist as he beheld it.

"You've—you've done it—I'm going to be the richest man—in all of Hulver. In the *world*," Argent sputtered, his chest heaving. His already pale face was illuminated by the faint glow of the ivory-white rock, making him look almost spectral. He looked at Penny and Hector with huge eyes.

"This is refined, raw magic in its *purest* form. Nothing like this has ever been seen by a living soul in the history of our world. This is more magic than the *king has!*" Argent leapt to his feet, screaming the last two words with elation. "You do realize this could solve the magic shortage? This is what we've all been waiting for. We're saved!"

Hector raised his eyebrows again. "Shouldn't that magic be just as much mine and Penny's as it is yours?" he reasoned.

Argent looked at Hector, wounded. "Y-yes, yes of course. But we can quibble about the details later! As long as you two are present we can make as much as we want!"

"How do you mean?" Penny inquired, curious how the process worked.

"Before I can explain how to use it, you've got to be able to think of magic in the correct sense. Imagine magic like—like water. Water can exist in the forms of ice, liquid, or vapor, but chemically, it's still water. Magic's the same way. Think of the magic from Elydria like ice—magic existing in solid form. This hunk of magic we made is what magic looks like, pure and distilled, but people like me have the ability to change it up a bit so others can use it. In essence we're like sculptors," Argent explained, looking at Penny to make sure that she was following.

"Now, imagine this ice gets superheated and it turns into vapor. This is basically what's going on when people use magical objects or use it as fuel. Once the magic does its job, there's a by-product. To people of Elydria this by-product is useless, so we disregard it when it just kind of floats away. This is where people from your world come in.

"The magic in its 'vapor' form travels through the Dawn Mirror, the intangible realm that connects our three planets, and ends up coming into your world, Penny. Now, according to what Hector's told me, that 'vapor' magic floats around until it finds a dreamer. When you dream, or I'm guessing when you use that special little power of yours, the magic begins to condense and hangs around you like an aura. Think of your dreaming as turning that vapor into liquid. Now, that 'water' will hang around you for a little while, but eventually it flows back into the Dawn Mirror again, then back into Hector's world, Nelvirna."

"So, this 'water' form of magic flows into Nelvirna. That's when people like Hector can use it to perform enchantments, or what have you. Essentially, when Hector performs a spell, the 'water' form of that magic will freeze and turn back into 'ice' as it travels through the Dawn Mirror. Finally, it shows up here in Elydria as this stuff—" Argent patted the huge hunk of raw magic on the table top. "It's kind of a weird analogy, but does that make more sense?"

"Yeah, I think I get it," Penny considered, "but I still don't get how we can just take it directly from one another…"

"Simple. We're just taking out the middleman, which in this case is the Dawn Mirror. All the Dawn Mirror does is move magic and souls along from world to world. When we do it this way, Hector just pulls the magic that's in your aura before it goes into the Dawn Mirror, and when he's done using it up, this machine gathers up the by-product. So instead of the magic being redistributed globally through the Dawn Mirror, we get it immediately right in this very spot."

"But you'll need at least one person from Earth and Nelvirna for it to do any good — and as you probably remember, I'm the last living person from Nelvirna," Hector told Argent, who nodded.

"Which is why I need to make use of your talents while you're still here," Argent pondered aloud, stroking his chin.

Penny jumped up off the workbench and swatted all the sawdust from her backside. "We've got to get to the palace, remember? We can decide what to do with the magic after we get back."

Argent gave them directions, and they collected up their royal badges and the message from King Noah. Hector collected Simon from the table in the front room of Argent's house, where he was busy trying to chat up Annette. The actress jumped up and followed them to the door.

Hector turned and gave her a hard look. "Where do you think you're going? I thought we agreed you were going to stay here." Annette frowned, giving her most pouty face.

"Hector, I can't stay here alone with *him!*" she whined, throwing a reproachful look back at Argent. "He's creepy..." she murmured so only Hector and Penny would hear.

"Sorry, Miss Annette, but it will be much safer for you here." Hector's decision was firm.

"We'll be back before you know it, Annette," Penny consoled her.

HULVER WAS ALIVE with activity and hordes of people crowding the streets. According to Argent, the Goblin Carnival was set to start the next day at dawn. Because of this the traffic in the city was staggering, making it hard to move and breathe. The three of them fought their way to the nearby Tunnels and took a stuffy Spider-Car to the center of the city. By the time they reached fresh air again it was nearing midday, but the sky was blanketed by a thick cloud cover that seemed to make the environment of Hulver, with its teeming crowds and halo of smog, all the more oppressive.

The palace itself was no challenge to locate. Its crooked black towers, ramparts and bastions spiraled up toward the sky at a dizzying height. The palace was built from ebony stone in a style that reminded Penny of the Gothic castles of Britain, only leagues more unstable. Many of the towers and halls appeared to have been piled on top of each other at random or added on as an afterthought years later.

Although they had the castle in their sights, the entrance proved difficult to find. The streets and alleyways were so twisted and cluttered with store displays it was almost impossible to find their way, even with Argent's directions. After squeezing through a narrow alleyway where pipes above their heads shot jets of steam out, the trio discovered a great balcony that led into the castle, set high above the ground at the end of a very long, wide street. It took a while before they realized in disappointment that it seemed to be a structure built only for members of the royal court to address the public.

At last Penny forced Simon and Hector to stop and ask for help. Several of the goblins pretended they were not being spoken to, but a kind young gobless with hair sweeping to her ankles showed them the way to the palace gates.

The entrance to the castle was tucked away from sight, and it was no surprise to Penny that they had missed it earlier. Two goblin soldiers stood sentinel to either side of the gate and gave the three of them dubious looks as they approached and showed their badges. One of the soldiers stepped into the castle and the group was told to wait.

Minutes later they were led through the gate. The inside of the castle was just as unwelcoming as the outer architecture. Stairwells, twisty corridors, and large obtuse doorways loomed out of every dusty corner. Candelabras caked with hundreds of years' worth of wax and cobwebs hung from the walls and ceilings of every room. The guard guided them through chamber after chamber, each one more imbalanced and off-kilter than the last, until they reached a massive antechamber within the heart of the castle.

"Wait here, honored guests," the goblin guard grumbled from underneath his horned helmet, and clanked off.

Penny looked around. At the very end of the cavernous hall stood three thrones, two made of dark wood and one in the center carved of a white stone that would've looked handsome, had it not been tarnished with so much grime. Aside from the thrones there was nothing else in the hall save six doors set off in odd, asymmetrical points throughout the hall. Something caught her attention in a quiet, stirring way; one of the doors on the far left was ajar. Behind it, shrouded in almost complete darkness, Penny was positive she caught a glimpse of something moving around. Before she could get any closer, another door at the opposite end of the chamber swung open and a tall goblin oozed out.

On average many goblins were around Penny's height or shorter, but this goblin was a jarring exception. He was a hair taller than Hector, who already stood at more than six feet. The goblin was emaciated and his thin skin had a gauzy texture. Penny could see the fragile bones working underneath it as he crossed the room to greet them. He had no hair to speak of, but wore a tall hat with the crest of the Angel Nestor embroidered into it. He smiled at them as he swept into the room, his many rich cloaks and robes fluttering about his feet.

"My friends, you have finally arrived. Word was sent from Iverton more than a week ago that we should be expecting a messenger party. We grew worried that you may have been, ah, *intercepted*…how glad we are to see that is not the case," the goblin said in a weak, breathy voice as he sidled up to them, wringing his delicate wrists.

"We ran into a spot of trouble. I apologize sincerely for our tardiness," Hector said with a regal politeness that seemed natural. He made a sweeping bow of humility before the skeletal figure.

The goblin nodded. "Please allow me to introduce myself. I am Bishop Flennig. Originally you were to meet with his majesty King Yulghrat, but unfortunately he is feeling unwell and will be unable to have an audience. I trust this will meet with the King of Men's approval?"

Hector replied that it would be no trouble at all.

"Eh, what did you say that your names were, friends?" the Bishop inquired with a certain shrewdness that rubbed Penny the wrong way.

Hector scratched at the back of his head before replying with the faux names they had determined ahead of time. "We didn't. I'm Professor Reginald Rasmussen of the Academy of Iverton and head of foreign language and relations department. This is my star pupil, Miss Miriam Winthrop, and my long-time friend and associate, Mr. Rex Snyder."

Looking unconvinced, the Bishop ushered them through one of the doors to a sitting room. Simon walked closer to Penny, whispering in English, "I thought Armonie said that only women were allowed to be members of the clergy in Elydria? Didn't the Angel guy, Nestor, make a decree about it or something?"

Penny shrugged, unable to look away from the open door. The black fissure of darkness beckoned to her. Something about it frightened her while also mesmerizing her in a way that she could not ignore. She caught another drifting movement in the darkness beyond and her curiosity flared up even stronger.

The door was swept from her view as they were ushered into a sitting room that was as comfortless as the rest of the palace. They were told to sit on a stone bench as the Bishop donned spectacles and unfurled the sealed envelope; his papery skin rubbing against the letter made an unpleasant sound. He finished reading the letter and looked up, his mouth agape.

"I must say, this news it most troubling," Bishop Flennig shuddered. "We of the Nation of Goblins are just as puzzled by the appearance of wraiths on Ciellos as you are. No official party of goblins attended the ball this year, and I assure you that we, as a Nation, are in no way associated with this tragedy. I must arrange for an official meeting with the human

ambassadors. I shall begin writing an official response immediately. Kindly wait here." The Bishop rose from his stone
chair and exited.

Hector turned to Penny and Simon, whispering in English, "Something's not right here. Why would a bishop
receive us and not the ambassadors themselves? And on top
of that, where is everyone? I haven't seen a single soul since
we entered the palace."

"You're right. It is weird, now that you mention it," Simon
muttered, glancing around in surprise.

Penny stood up and paced around the room. Something
was stirring within her, and she found herself humming
Row, Row, Row Your Boat, repeating the last line several times
under her breath. She could hear a low conversation on the
other side of the door where the Bishop had exited, but chose
to ignore it.

Life is but a dream, life is but a dream...

"Hector's right," she declared, her heart racing as she realized what she had been doing. "Maybe we should get out of
here, I feel like—"

"Shush!" Hector hissed, springing to his feet as his face
drained of all color. He pressed his ear up against the door listened for a moment. He spun and faced Penny and Simon with
an expression of frantic urgency.

"*Run!* We need to leave, now!" he commanded in a harsh
whisper, ushering them to the door from which they had
entered. He had just grasped the handle when the door behind
them swung open and a figure stepped inside. Penny's blood
ran cold. It was Deimos.

"Greetings, Professor Ras—Impossible. You're the girl from
the Ball—and *you*—!" the one-eyed man stopped mid-sentence,
his eye traveling from Penny's face to Simon's. Snarling, Deimos barreled over to the magician, who squealed like a frightened animal and cowered against the wall.

"*How did you*—?" Deimos roared, grabbing at Simon's shirt and yanking him forward as Simon's top hat toppled from his head. Without warning, Hector threw a solid punch that struck him square in the face.

Though Hector was not a man of great physical strength, the shock was enough to throw Deimos back for a moment. Simon snatched back his hat as the three of them scrambled out and slammed the door shut behind them. Hector shot back a sealing spell at the door, containing Deimos and the Bishop. They skidded across the wide hall, listening to the sounds of fumbling and angry voices behind the door. Penny ran in the direction she hoped led to the palace entrance.

"No! There are guards in front, we have to hide!" Hector cried and swiveled around to face the door that still hung open beside the thrones. Penny didn't have time to object and raced after Simon as he hurtled toward the door. Hector pushed the door at the end of the hall aside and slipped in, waiting for Simon and Penny to make it inside before returning it to its original almost-shut state.

It was as black as midnight in the room. Hector, Simon, and Penny huddled together as they listened to the sounds of pounding and wrathful yells from the hall beyond. Penny tried not to think of what could have been moving about in the darkness of the room they now cowered within. After several tense moments, a deafening crash was heard, followed by a clamor of loud footsteps.

"Where did they go?" Deimos's voice reverberated throughout the hall, sounding twice as intimidating as usual. There was a huffing accompanied with a fluttering of robes, and then the Bishop's voice shook through the halls between sharp breaths.

"They must've gone toward the exit. How could they have possibly known that we were going to—?"

"Silence, you old fool! Don't you realize who that *was*? It was that half-wit from the *other* world, *Adrielle's world*—I gave him a wand, remember? We told him to off that Fairfax girl that Lord Nestor wants dead, though he *obviously* doesn't have enough brains to assassinate a pofflin, much less someone like *her*. Besides, we only used him to get Adrielle's attention. The girl is already dead, we set some wraiths on her—but now he's here somehow and—" Deimos raged, but was interrupted.

"I don't understand, what do you mean?" the Bishop's voice wavered as he tried to catch his breath.

"There's no time to explain now, we've got to find him... and *not a word* to Lord Nestor. We'll be better off dead if he finds out that the Gaian human is in Elydria. Alert *every* ranger in Hulver to be on the lookout for a group of humans. Phobos and I will search the castle. Make sure it's on every Sophotri Stone in the city, even the private links. Go now!" Deimos and Bishop Flennig's footsteps rattled throughout the hall. Penny clung to Hector's arm as the footsteps drew near, but Deimos ran on, shouting for his brother. The clattering and banging faded.

"What do we do? We're trapped," Simon whimpered in the dark.

"Hector, you can teleport us away from here, can't you? To Argent's house?" Penny whispered, feeling like something had stuck in her throat and was blocking out most of her breath.

"The margin of failure is too high. We could end up separated, or somewhere awful. It's extremely dangerous."

"And getting skewered and served up to Deimos by a group of vicious goblin soldiers *isn't dangerous?*" Simon garbled.

"Look, just see if we can't find a way out first. If worst comes to worst, I can try. But I'm telling you it could cost us our lives," Hector spat, fumbling around in the darkness. There was a small rushing of magic and a little light popped up above their heads with a shower of shining runes from Hector's palm.

The chamber was circular and satiny purple draping hung from ceiling to floor around it. In the center of the room stood a low table with a very peculiar object on top of it. Penny took a step toward it, somehow enchanted through the alarm of panic that still rang in her chest. She drew nearer to see that the flat, disc-like object was displayed upon a golden stand. The edges of it were made of ornately carved gold, etched with images of angelic figures, staring eyes, and mysterious symbols. In the center of the frame was a smooth piece of clear crystal glass. Curious, Penny reached her quivering hand out, and a faint murmuring stirred somewhere in the room, as if an invisible audience of people had begun speaking in hushed voices all around her. Before her fingers could come in contact with the peculiar object, Hector grabbed her.

"Are you out of your mind, Penelope?" Hector chided, bringing her out of the light stupor. Penny joined in the search for another door, lifting back a few of the draperies, not really expecting to find anything. She had to placate Hector until he got up enough courage to teleport them away. An exasperated sigh came from across the room as Simon stamped his foot.

"There's nothing here, Hector! We've got to get out before they find us!" Simon pleaded, but Hector did not respond. Penny tossed a few cushions away from the wall and chanced a glimpse back at the gold and crystal disc that stood on the table.

Click.

Penny's head whipped around, searching for the source of the sound. She threw aside the purple curtain she had been digging around, shocked to see a small door in the wall behind it. With a subdued gasp she realized the small clicking noise had been her hand running across a silver doorknob.

"You guys, look!" called Penny as she threw the door open without a moment's hesitation and hurried through.

The first image that met her eyes was of a massive goblin dressed in a regal cape and tunic, sporting a magnificent platinum and diamond crown. There was no doubt in Penny's mind that this was, in fact, King Yulghrat, but something struck her as odd before she could even draw a sharp breath of surprise. The king was sitting propped up on a throne, lifeless.

He had made no movement or jerk of surprise when Penny had thrown open the door, and merely sat, still as a statue, his milky eyes staring at nothing.

Across the room, another figure slid out from behind another purple curtain. The figure floated, graceful and silent, feet barely touching the floor as he came into full view beside King Yulghrat's stiff form. The whole mass of his lithe and sculpted body gleamed with an ethereal light. Penny felt instant fear grip her, starting in the pit of her stomach and twisting slowly like a great whirlpool of acid.

"Deimos...? What is happening?" the man asked, his voice a musical lilt, more like the sound of wind or a bell's ring than a voice. Despite its wonderful quality, there was something dangerous and nauseating about it. Penny's neck prickled as the sound of it washed over her and felt her knees go weak. Two great white wings unfolded from the man's back as he turned his face toward the door, and Penny was overcome with the urge to weep in terror as she beheld the flawless visage of the man.

It was him. It was the man from the thunderstorm so many years ago. The beautiful, terrifying man who had haunted her nightmares since childhood; the man whose face had been burned into her memory by a flash of lightning.

No, not a man. An Angel.

The Angel gaped at her, his inhumanly beautiful face betraying shock. His long, flowing hair draped all around his face and body like curtains of white, diamond filament. A disc-like halo of heavy, spinning gold emblazoned with ancient glyphs floated behind his head. His wings flexed, showering the ground with shimmering feathers. Yet even wreathed by the radiance of his sublime beauty, his mannerisms spoke of a quiet malady. Something was weighing upon him—something hindered him.

Penny felt her legs losing strength. Hector yelled out behind her, his voice sounding miles away. She felt his hands grasp

her shoulders and Simon pressing against her back. In the last
second before the world was wiped away, the Angel's white-
blue eyes widened, the look of recognition in them impaling
her heart. Seconds later she was swept up from where she
stood and hurtled away through vast nothingness.

ALONG CAME A SPIDER

When Hector, Penny, and Simon materialized in Argent's house and crashed down with enough force to split the table in two, the entire room was instantly filled with wails of pain and confusion. Annette, who had been sipping tea, shrieked as the wood splintered out. Moments later frenzied footsteps were heard battering up the staircase, and Argent burst into the room and took one long look at the ruins that were once his furniture. He let out a stream of expletives so crude that Annette's jaw dropped in scandalized horror. Penny disentangled herself from the knot of limbs and pieces of broken wood.

"What—in—the—" seethed Argent, but Hector held up his hand to stop him.

"No time to explain! Everyone gather your things, we're leaving at once!" Hector ordered as he scurried to the corner, plucking his bag from the ground and tossing Penny's over to her. She caught it in midair and checked to make sure everything was still inside, her hands shaking.

"W-wait, what happened?!" Annette cried, looking from face to face.

"*My table!*" growled Argent, gesturing to the mess of wood that now littered his floor.

"Erm, as I just said—" Hector warned him, "you may want to gather up a few of your possessions in case they come by and—"

"*Who's* coming by?"

As if prompted, the Sophotri lit up from the other end of the room.

"Attention, citizens of Hulver! This is an emergency broadcast! Three dangerous humans, two male, one female, are loose in the city. If sighted, they are to be apprehended and turned in to the authorities. If you have any information about these three or their whereabouts, please contact the Bureau of Justice via Sophotri Stone. As a warning it shall be known that any residence or facility discovered to be harboring these humans will be immediately burned to the ground, and any citizen of Hulver, goblin or otherwise, who is found to be aiding these humans in any way shall be sentenced to life in prison. Thank you for your time, and keep on the alert," a stiff voice from the Sophotri Stone announced in Gobblish, then went on to repeat the message in Andronian and Therosian.

"What did you *do!?* What could you *possibly* have done?" Argent hissed, collapsing into a chair and holding his face in his hands for a moment before looking back up. "I need an explanation. Now!"

"We did everything we were supposed to, there was only one problem—Deimos was at the palace. He recognized Simon and now they're after us," Hector said, harried.

"That's not even the half of it," Simon added.

"What? What are we going to do?" Annette gasped, her face growing whiter by the moment. Argent stood up clutching his head and began to pace.

"Look, there's no way they could find out you're here, could they? I can't go to prison—not now—not when I'm this close to becoming the richest man in the world..." Argent pleaded.

"Argent, try to stay calm. Gather up anything that is of vital importance just in case something happens," Hector urged. Argent took a moment to process this, and then darted up the spiral staircase faster than Penny could blink.

"What's the plan, Hector?" Simon asked.

Hector shut his eyes for a long, worrying moment. "If we try to escape, someone in the streets will eventually spot us. If we hide out here, we'd be putting Argent at too great a risk. We have to get to Mulgrith somehow and try to find Della. The deep woods will be our best bet for slipping away and perhaps Della will help us get to safety for good. We just have to find some way of getting out to Hulver undetected," he pondered.

"Any chance of you being able to teleport again? You seemed to make it here all right," Penny guessed, and Hector shook his head.

"We were immensely lucky just now. I've never been to Mulgrith, which makes it exponentially more perilous. It would almost certainly exhaust both of you, and I'm not sure I'd be able to remain conscious long enough to complete the spell. I'm surprised you can still stand after the last one, Penelope," Hector nodded in her direction, looking skeptical.

The small silence was broken by another stream of strong curse words from upstairs. All eyes turned toward the spiral staircase as Argent, now wearing a pair of sandals, came charging down with his arms full with his three puppets, several hunks of raw magic, and a tiny green stone pinched between his index finger and thumb. He was snorting with rage as he stared down at them.

"Currently there are four goblin Rangers flying toward my Atelier on a moth. *WHY?*" Argent snarled.

Penny cringed. "Oh no. When we got lost last week...we asked that goblin Ranger for directions. He must've—"

Argent moaned, and Penny recognized the dread in his eyes. It was a specific brand of fright that she and her friends had recently grown to be so intimate with—the look of someone who was in jeopardy of losing every cherished thing in their world.

"Hide, you've got to hide! Maybe they'll go away—hurry, into the workshop." Argent pushed them all backward into his studio as he stuffed the last few objects in his hands into his wide pockets. He stepped in front of a dusty cupboard, threw open the doors with a clatter, and began tossing everything out in a fury. Clouds of dust billowed into the air as Argent stuffed Hector, Penny, Simon, and then Annette inside and slammed the doors shut again. There was barely enough room to squirm and Penny prayed that the dusty air would not cause her to sneeze. A tiny chink of light shone through the doors and they watched as Argent stuffed some of his belongings into a small side-bag.

The knock came at the door. Argent took a deep breath before striding forward on shaking legs. There was a click of the doorknob and the creak of hinges.

"Can I help you?" Argent could be heard saying in his badly-accented Gobblish. His voice was nonchalant, but even from far away Penny could easily detect the frantic undertone.

"Why, yes you can. May we come in?" a deep goblin voice inquired. Another creak followed by the telltale shutting of the door. The goblins were inside.

"What seems to be the problem? Does it have something to do with that announcement just now, because I can assure you—"

"Sir, would you mind telling us why this table is broken in half?" one of the goblins asked, interrupting Argent as if he had not heard a word.

"The t-table, yes. Um. Well, the truth is…I don't know. I was tending my shop just minutes ago when I heard a crash and I ran up here to find out what was going on. It's true, you

can ask the customers downstairs in the store—" Argent blath-
ered, but was cut off again.

"We've already spoken to the customers, thank you. The
reason we're here is because there have been reports from local
sources that three or more humans are presently staying at this
location, is this true?" a different goblin questioned and Argent
made a noise to show he was thinking.

"Oh, of course, in fact there *were* some humans here. Yes,
yes, my—my cousins were visiting a few days back. They were
interested in seeing the Carnival so I let them stay here for a
few nights. They've cleared out, though. Got a room at a hotel
closer to the castle, I think," Argent mumbled.

A goblin made a small noise in his throat, seeming unconvinced. "Well, you won't mind if we have a look around then,
will you? Safety precaution, you see. All human-owned property
in the area is being searched." Footsteps were heard climbing the
spiral staircase and moving about the main room. Penny's hands
clamped into tight fists as a goblin Ranger stepped into the workshop and began tossing Argent's prized possessions and delicate
tools aside like throw pillows. Argent appeared behind him, the
anxious look on his face betraying him. The goblin poked around
a bit more and turned back to face Argent.

"How is it that you came to own this shop, Mr.—"

"It's Argent Clemons. I inherited it from my teacher and
guardian when he died. He was a goblin, childless, who owned
this shop prior to my coming to Hulver," Argent explained, his
voice stronger now that he was telling the truth.

"And when was it you came to Hulver, exactly?"

"Umm—about sixteen years ago."

"And how old are you now?"

"Twenty-four," Argent breathed, and Penny could almost
hear his thoughts screaming that he was too young to be locked
away for life.

Another goblin thumped into the room. "Come on, Jurdie.
There's nothing here. We've got other houses to search," he

said. Penny felt the tension leave the room with the goblins. Annette let her head fall against the side of the cupboard wall, producing a low but unheard thump.

Penny was preparing to move out of the hot and stuffy cupboard as the goblins left their final words of advice with Argent when she saw it.

From the top of cupboard, perhaps roused by the small shockwave Annette had created, crawled eight quick legs, twitching and skittering as an overgrown spider scuttled down the side of the cupboard. Penny held her breath as she watched the black spider crawl into Annette's freshly styled blonde locks. In horror, Penny watched as Annette lifted her head up with a jerk when she felt the movement on her head. The quick motion caused the fat spider to fall from her hair down the back of her dress.

The moment she felt it, Annette gave the tiniest of squeaks. Even in the darkness, Penny could see she was struggling not to scream. Her hands clapped over her mouth and her eyes were wide as she tried to carefully bump up against the wall and smash the spider.

"Wait, what was that?"

"What was what?"

One of the goblin Rangers pounded back into the room. Annette's eyes went wide and she became very still, her eyes locked with Penny's in a look of utmost horror. The goblin poked through the room and just as he reached for the door of the cupboard, Simon leapt forth in a preemptive attack.

"Jurdie!" the goblin closest to them hollered as Simon jumped on him, pinning him to the ground. The rest of them tumbled out of the wardrobe, ready to fight. Two of the rangers bounded into the room, while the third leapt for Argent.

"Andro-trash! You'll rot in prison for what you've done!" A goblin pulled a pistol on Annette and everyone froze.

"Don't hurt her!" Argent broke free from his ranger, running forward. The silver-haired man grabbed at the controls of two of his puppets hanging out of his voluminous pockets. The puppet he called the Lady in Black and Hyde sprung to life and emerged from his pockets as Argent poised to strike.

"Goblins, *drop your weapons and get against the wall!*" Annette shrieked, her voice trembling with power.

The goblins followed her orders in perplexed chagrin, and Argent shot a surprised glance at Annette before pocketing his puppets.

"Get your things! Let's go!" Hector urged, gathering the group together and hurrying them out the door before the goblins could break free of Annette's orders. They sped down the stairs, hurtling down the hill.

Gently fluttering out in front of the shop sat the huge moth the four Rangers had used to get to Argent's house. Without bothering to wait for the others to catch up, Hector threw his leg over the moth's back. The creature made a strange purring sound and reached its antler-like feelers back to investigate Hector. Penny and Simon mounted the moth with clumsy movements, causing it to shudder in discomfort and make a louder, more agitated sound. Argent and Annette caught up with them just as one of the goblins burst through the front door, screaming at them to halt. For one horrorstricken moment they all sat on the moth, not knowing what to do.

"Argent, how do I make this thing move?" Hector yelled back at him.

"The antennae! Hurry!" Argent raged. Hector grabbed the feelers and with a shriek the moth began to flap its huge wings with powerful, sweeping motions. Penny gasped and latched onto Hector's back as the beast lifted off the ground and shot into the air.

They spiraled upward over Hulver, watching Argent's house get smaller and smaller as they sprang higher into the gray sky. Hector gave the moth another forceful tug, and it leveled out. Hector steered them in a circle, the moth straining under their combined weight. Penny looked down at their goblin assailants who, now hundreds of feet below, were mere dots.

"They'll be after us with a fleet of moths and dragonflies and every manner of flying machine in minutes. This poor thing can't hold more than four goblins, much less all of us. We need to land before she gives out," Argent shouted over the blustering wind.

"Understood. Mulgrith's only a few miles away, we can make it," Hector yelled, and urged the moth onward.

The dark trees of Mulgrith loomed closer. Now that the unwelcoming woods were at last staring her in the face, Penny felt that she might rather turn back around and take her chances with the goblin rangers. She kept craning her neck around to see if they were being followed, but so far the skies behind them were clear. After looking back for a fourth time, something strange caught her eye.

"Oh, God...look..." she pointed, squinting against the afternoon sun. From the edge of the city rose a trail of black smoke, reaching high into the sky. Argent stared at it, a stony look crossing his face as his entire body went limp. The arms that had been grasping Annette for safety flopped to his sides and his lips quivered. Among the vast rows of houses and shops in the distance, a bright blaze of flame became visible.

A particular building had become consumed in orange-red flames that licked upward to the sky, belching dirty black smoke from the windows and collapsing roof. Penny's heart sank and she looked back at Argent's devastated face. The puppet master's arms snaked around his own body, his eyes glassy and welling up before he shut them. An expression of acute pain swept over his face as he doubled forward, looking like he was collapsing in on himself.

"Argent..." Annette breathed, turning back and putting a hand on his hunched shoulder as he hung his head, his silver hair creating a curtain around his face.

"No… this can't happen—my shop…my magic…my *home*…" his voice was barely audible over the roar of the air. Penny turned her face away, not wanting to see anymore of Argent's pain. As the moth dipped closer to the treetops of Mulgrith woods, its body shaking with weakness, Argent threw his head back and screamed with such profound anguish that Penny felt a stab of grief in her own chest. He took a ragged breath, covering his face with his hands as the moth plunged under the canopy of the woods. The noise of his scream echoed in Penny's ears like a sick sort of broken record. For as long as she lived, Penny would never forget that sound.

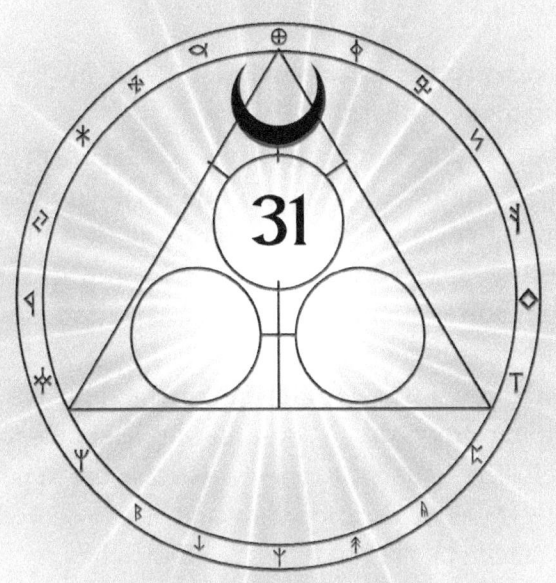

MULGRITH

A s soon as the moth touched down on the patch of tall grass, it shook the five of them off its back, and promptly fluttered up and away, leaving them lying on the forest floor. Penny got up with shaking legs, dusted herself off, and caught her breath. She squinted up through the treetops at the thick canopy of leaves almost blotting out the sun.

Penny helped the others to their feet, receiving a slight shock when she couldn't find Argent. It took her only a moment to locate him slunk off from the group and sitting with his back to a tree. Penny approached nervously, studying the destroyed look on his face.

"Argent...we should go, they're coming..." she said, extending a hand. He blinked and made no move to get up.

"Just leave me here," he requested, not meeting anyone's gaze.

"There's no time for this, we need to go. Goblins will be crawling all over these woods in a few hours. You said so yourself," Hector reminded him, shoving his glasses up his nose.

"I don't care if they catch me or not. Leave me be," Argent said, closing his eyes again.

Simon stepped forward, frowning. "Come on, man. It was just a shop…I know you lost a fortune in there, but money isn't everything. It's replaceable — your life isn't. And you can't really expect us to leave you behind," Simon urged, his eyes full of uncommon sympathy. Argent at last made a move in the form of a disgusted look.

"Maybe to you it was *just* money or *just* a shop, but to me it was everything — *everything!* You don't understand—it was all I had left, all that mattered to me—" his voice broke with emotion and everyone went silent. Penny and Hector shared a helpless look. Annette pushed past them and marched up to where Argent sat against the tree, his face slick with tears. She put her hands on her hips and looked down at him with disdain.

"That is *enough!*" she hissed, her eyes flashing. "You're an adult, aren't you? Start acting like one and not a sniveling little child!"

Argent stared up at her as if she had just slapped him. Seeing she had gotten a response, Annette puffed up even more, her voice becoming shrill.

"Don't be pathetic, Argent. If I've come to know you at all this past week, then I know that you're not just any pushover. You've got too much talent to give up living. *Every person standing here* knows how hard it is to lose everything that mattered to them. Penny and Simon were snatched away from their homes and brought to a completely different world without so much as a word of warning—everything and everyone that Hector ever loved was *destroyed*. But did they just crumple up and die? I remember wanting to give up when I'd lost all hope of my dream, but someone taught me differently. I won't accept this. I simply won't allow it. Now *get up*." She stamped her foot. Argent's face contorted into an enraged snarl and he jumped to his feet, facing Annette with a fearsome glare. For a moment

Penny was sure he was going to lash out at her, but instead he balled up his fists and bared his teeth.

"How...dare...you!" he gasped, his face red with anger and humiliation. There was fear in Annette's eyes but she held her ground without blinking. "Have you failed to realize that this is *entirely your fault?* The goblins were about to leave until *you* gave away your hiding place! Where do you get the *gall?*" Argent screamed at Annette, who remained steadfast.

"You're going to come with us...or I'm going to drag you," she growled back at him through gritted teeth.

Argent's chest heaved for a moment as he stared at Annette in fervid rage. With a noise of tormented frustration he turned and stalked away, retreating behind Hector and Simon while Annette watched him go with her arms crossed. Penny felt awkward as the flare of anger faded away from the atmosphere. She looked to Hector again, who seemed just as shocked. Her imploring gaze connected with him, urging him to say something fast.

"A-all right, then, everyone..." he began. "The deeper we go into the woods, the less chance they have of finding us. Let's try to be as quiet as possible, please. I know there's a lot we want to discuss, but let's wait until we find somewhere safer. Penny, erm, have you still got the camping supplies from Dewthorne?"

After checking her bag, she nodded and Hector gave her a tired smile. He gestured for everyone to follow him and they set off through the thick mass of trees, Argent dragging along slowly at the rear of the party, his face pointed downwards at the moss that carpeted the woods.

They moved along in their gloomy procession, now and then looking up at the black-barked trunks and fluttering leaves. Some of the roots and floral life that grew in the clearings were thorny and displayed shockingly bright colors that warned of poison.

It was inevitable that Penny's thoughts drifted to what had occurred at the palace. Everything had happened so fast, and now that there was nothing but an exhausting walk to distract her, the gravity of the events weighed down on her.

She still couldn't quite wrap her mind around it. She had come face-to-face with Nestor—the Angel, creator of Elydria, the deity Armonie, Elise, and Rhea worshipped. Penny shuddered to think Nestor had been the one that had ordered her death in the first place, and the one who appeared in her bedroom during the thunderstorm more than a decade ago.

But why? Penny thought with frustration. *Why is he doing all of this? Armonie painted him so differently...not anything like this monster that would make wraiths out of people—his children!*

Everything Penny had thought she understood was falling to pieces in her mind. She wanted to stop the world and go back to a time when none of this mattered. She was tired of trying to make sense of the twisting mass of questions that haunted her. Penny desperately wanted to lie down, to sleep and never dream again. *It would be easy to do*, she thought, *easier than going on.*

BY THE TIME the moons rose, every one of them had started to trip and stumble in the darkness. Hector announced that it was time to set up camp, and conjured a small ball of light while they arranged the campsite in the misty grayness it offered. They were deep in the trees now, and it felt as if the tall trunks were pressing in on them. The fire that Simon lit with a blast from his wand was meager and did almost nothing against the icy chill that ran in the breeze. After they set everything up and had heated a small tin of water over the fire, Penny, Simon and Hector spoke in hushed voices about the events from that afternoon, filling Argent and Annette in on what they had seen. Annette in particular did not want to believe that it had been Nestor they had seen in the castle.

"That's impossible. Lord Nestor loves us. He grants wishes to people in need and takes care of everyone in Elydria. He *created* this world," Annette insisted. Argent hung back from the group with a dark look in his eyes.

"It was him, Annette. I'm sure of it," Penny assured her with a serious gaze.

"If Lord Nestor is indeed our enemy, we might as well start saying our prayers," Hector voiced his worries.

"If this Nestor guy is so powerful, why didn't he just come find Penny himself? Or for that matter, why didn't he just destroy us when he had the chance? He's been sending his little cronies out to do his bidding—why couldn't he have just done it on his own?" Simon posed.

"Didn't you see him?" Penny said. "He looked—*sick* or something. Like he was weakened…I don't know."

"No, that's impossible," Argent cut through their conversation. "Angels can't feel pain or get tired. They don't need food, rest—anything. Their bodies are ageless and immortal. They get their energy from magic, which comes directly from the Dawn Mirror. They're essentially indestructible in every way. Surely even you must know that." Argent looked over at her, his eyes especially bright by the light of the fire.

"Earth doesn't exactly have an Angel like Elydria does or Nelvirna—"

"That's also impossible. Each of our three worlds was constructed in some way—by an Angel. Things couldn't be this way without them, you see—that Adrielle that you spoke of—she's definitely the one. She is to your world what Nestor is to ours." Argent sounded very sure of himself.

"Then why is she all secretive like? If people knew about Adrielle—well, it would save us a lot of trouble on Earth." Simon looked up, confused, and Argent shrugged.

"I haven't got the answer to that."

"How do you know so much about this, anyway?" Penny asked.

"My mother was a priestess," he replied. "Anyway, if you've got Nestor after you, Hector's right—you should all be pissing yourselves. Even if he is *sick,* as you say, Nestor couldn't be touched by the combined efforts of every army in Elydria. I don't have any idea what you've done to get on his bad side, but you'd better run and hide."

"Well, at any rate we're going to need to get some rest. We can talk about this more in the morning. Someone will need to stay awake and keep watch for a while, however," Hector looked from one face to another in hopes of seeing a volunteer.

"I suppose I can stay up a bit longer," Annette mumbled.

"Oh yeah, you'll be a *really* reliable lookout, especially if something dangerous like a spider comes along," scoffed Argent. "I'll do it, Hector."

Annette glared back at Argent. "Excuse me, but you can't just order me around. I already said I would do it, and that's precisely what I'm going to do."

Argent's laugh was demeaning at best. Penny decided to ignore their argument and get ready for bed. By the time she lay down, they had still not quit trading insults, and Hector suggested that they both stay up and watch for trouble together. Hector offered to take over after them and the matter was settled.

Penny tried in vain to sleep. Her body felt heavy, as if gravity had decided to double its load all of a sudden. She ached from head to toe as she rolled over onto her side, feeling the uneven ground under the blanket she slept on. Just as she started to drift off, voices disturbed her shallow slumber. Penny was about to sit up and look about for who was speaking when she picked up on the sound of Annette's voice and kept still.

"...not really what I was talking about, you see," Annette's voice was small. "What I meant was—well, I was a little too harsh earlier. I just had to say something to get you to move, is all...I never meant to—"

"Save it, I have no need of your sympathy. You were right whether you meant to be harsh or not."

"Well, just because it's true doesn't give me the right to be cruel about it. I'm—I'm sorry," Annette whispered. Argent sighed and there was a long silence in which only the spitting and popping of the logs in the fire could be heard.

"Don't worry about it," Argent said at last, still sounding as if he hadn't quite accepted her remorse.

"Argent, I'm being serious here..."

"Oh, hooray. I'm so proud of you. But it doesn't change the fact that I'm a homeless convict who's being chased down by a group of murderers and their almighty Angelic lord—but your earnestness just *warms* my heart, Little Miss." Argent sneered, and Penny could hear his misery lurking under the surface.

"It's not like I wanted this to happen, I was *scared*—I tried to keep quiet, I really did!" Annette sounded close to tears again. There was another long pause in which Penny could only hear Annette sniffling.

"Now who's sniveling like a little child, huh?" Argent's voice was cold. It was enough to push Annette over the edge.

"You...you are just plain *mean!* I'm sick with guilt over this, did that penetrate your thick skull?" Annette exclaimed, her voice going up a few octaves.

"Regardless of your feelings, I'm still screwed," Argent murmured. Penny could hear a rustling of fabric that meant Annette had risen to her feet.

"*Fine!* When we get out of here—"

"*If* we get out of here, you mean."

"All right, *if* we get out of here—if you come with us back to Iverton then...what if I buy you a brand new shop? An even bigger and better one, right in the middle of the Business District. Would you forgive me then?" Annette's voice trembled, her words ringing in the clearing even after silence fell. Penny half expected Argent to laugh off her proposal, but he did not. His voice started and then stopped, like something was caught in his throat.

"Little Miss, I—" Argent was befuddled, and thus unable to keep the emotion out of his voice. "That's—that's too generous. Are you actually being serious right now?"

"Absolutely. I already owe you my life, not to mention Penny's, Simon's, and Hector's. I have more than enough money—and if you really do blame me for what happened, I'd like to make it up to you. So just come with us and don't give up hope—I swear I'll help you get back what you lost," Annette promised. It was quite a while before Argent even made so much as a sound, but when he spoke his voice broke with feeling.

"And all this time you had me thinking you were just an obnoxious, spoiled, little—"

"*Hey!*" Annette did shout this time, but Argent's murmuring laugh quieted her. There was a sound of fluttering fabric once again as Annette sat back down.

"Don't get mad, I was only joking. Forgive me, it's been a while since—well, since anyone's been kind to me at all. Goblins are a solitary bunch, you know…I'd almost forgotten how to react." Argent sounded calm now, with newfound warmth in his tone. Annette snorted.

"A simple 'thank you very much, Annette. You're the most wonderful, gracious, and beautiful woman who has ever trod upon Elydrian soil' would suffice," she huffed. Both of them laughed quietly, easing the tension between them.

"So, it's a deal then?" Annette clarified.

"All right, Little Miss. A deal."

"SO, DOES ANYONE have any ideas of how we're supposed to find this Della person?" Hector dared to breach the topic the next morning.

"Haven't you figured out that glass ball yet? Adrielle promise it would lead us to Della—she said you'd know what to do with it," asked Simon as he looked to Penny.

"Well, she was mistaken. I have no idea what to do with the stupid thing, it might as well be a handful of dirt for all it's worth," Penny retorted around a mouthful of berries. She had slept without dreams, but awoken with a dry cough and stuffed nose and was not feeling very cooperative.

Argent raised a silvery eyebrow. "Mind if I have a look?" he requested.

Penny dug through her bag until she found the cherry pine box where she kept the orb and tossed it to Argent. He caught it in midair and examined it, turning the orb about in his pale fingers.

"I can tell you this much, it's not magic from this world. It's the same kind of magic that hangs around you, Penny," he said with deliberation.

"I could've told you that," Simon scoffed and made a face.

"Well, then, the question remains. How do we find her? We need to keep on the move to avoid any search parties hunting for us, but if we have any hope of finding her, we're going to need a plan," Hector reasoned. Annette poked her head up, looking as if she wanted to say something. All eyes went to her.

"Well, um—this Della is supposed to be a witch, yeah?" she tested and when everyone nodded to back her up, Annette continued, "Well, witches are kind of a folktale here. In legend, they can perform miracles like seeing the future or creating illusions. Allegedly they're said to live in places with a lot of magic—s-so…shouldn't we be looking for the place with the most magic?"

"That is precisely the type of thing I was hoping to hear, Miss Annette," Hector said and tipped his head in her direction before turning to Argent. "Do you think you could lead us in the direction of where the most magic is concentrated in the forest?"

EVEN IN THE light of day the woods were enough to exacerbate the growing sense of paranoia in Penny's head. Wherever they went, the leaves above their head formed an unbreakable seal from the sky, creating a dim and stuffy world beneath the branches. Now and then when Penny looked up during their arduous trek, she would see the fluttering, intricate patterns of moth wings as wide as quilts above the trees.

Near midday they came to a wide stretch of fiery-red, earthy brown, and gold leaves covering the ground, having left their skeletal hosts above as the chill of winter imposed upon the land. Many scrapes and bruises were suffered during this time, as it was difficult to see what lay underneath the cover of the autumnal leaves. When the blood-red light of a sunset filled the forgotten paths of Mulgrith they stopped for the night. After another dreary meal left them all feeling discontent and empty, they took turns puzzling over Penny's glass ball, giving outlandish suggestions of what to do with it, none of which worked.

That evening the mists came, floating in from the depths of the woods and snaking in white tendrils. Before going to bed that night Penny was shocked to hear strange, mournful music coming from a great distance from their camp. It was a thin, whining sound that came from a woody instrument. They all gathered together, collectively disturbed by the song.

Penny could not sleep that night. Though her body ached with exhaustion and her insides tormented her with hunger, she could not seem to relax. Her coughs broke the stillness and her sinuses filled with pressure. She lay sleepless until Simon shook her for guard duty. They sat back to back, looking out through the shrouds of fog.

A shock came when several of the massive centipedes trundled toward their camp, and Penny looked over at Simon wide eyes, unsure of what to do, but the centipedes snaked around them and went along their way. She received another shock as a storm of winged, humanoid creatures zoomed over their heads with enormous speed, each one a different colored fire-burst of light.

As dawn leaked anemic warmth across the forest, Penny wondered how she was going to continue on. There had been little food and even less rest during the last two days, and it was taking its toll on the group of weary travelers. Almost everyone suffered from a sore throat or stuffy nose of some degree.

Not long into the day's trek, the forest began to change, growing thicker, mistier, and greener with every step. The moss-engulfed trees twisted upward in malformed shapes. Annette almost screamed when a massive creature as tall and wide as a semi-truck crashed past, carving a small path of destruction as it went.

After a treacherous hike through the deep woods, the trees began to thin somewhat and the woods opened out onto a glade, where a waterfall poured into a clear pool. Argent explained that the water was rich in magic, and so they all took a drink from the icy spring. The water tasted of minerals, and it seemed to revitalize their tired bodies. Hector deemed it a nice place to spend the night, and Argent crafted a makeshift fishing rod from a tree branch.

Penny didn't realize how much she'd missed meat until she bit into the warm, crispy flesh of the grilled fish. It was full of nutrients and robust flavor from the enchanted pool. As darkness fell again, the improving mood was killed by the ominous sound of angry Gobblish voices in the distance.

Hector used magic to get rid of the campfire and they all scrambled to hide their belongings, throwing themselves into the underbrush behind a fallen log just as a group of goblins tromped into the glade.

"Ah…I smell smoke. They could be nearby! They've probably gone up ahead. Come on, let's go!" a goblin rumbled to his friend. A great rustling of plants was heard and the goblins charged onward, their voices growing quieter by the moment. Penny stood on unsure legs and helped Annette to her feet as Argent poked his head out from the trees.

"It was only a matter of time before they caught up with us," Argent sighed.

"We've got to move. We'll have to sleep somewhere with more cover—come along, no time to waste," Hector whispered. They took refuge in a soft depression in the forest floor that was snaked with thick roots and dewy moss, making beds in the soggy earth, and burrowing between the clefts of soil and ferns as they tried to no avail to get comfortable.

The group did not allow themselves a fire again, instead huddling in the blackness, shivering as the curling mists and dew condensed all around them. Through the endless shade of night Penny could hear large, powerful things moving about through the trees. She shut her eyes and tried not to think of what it was that was making such a disturbance. Twice she felt something crawling through her blankets and leapt up, slapping at her legs and arms, but when she looked closer at them, she found nothing.

In the deepest part of the night when even the chattering of insects and calling night birds had gone quiet, Penny could hear the whining of that same mournful flute off in the distance. She sat up and hugged her knees to her chest, watching as a haunted orange trail of lanterns drifted through the tall trees about half a mile away. Near daybreak Penny succumbed to her exhaustion and slept for an hour or two, and woke feeling absolutely hideous. Along with a searing headache and stiff joints, she was nauseated with dizziness and weak. If Annette hadn't helped her up from the mossy pit, she felt sure that she would have lain in the wet soil ringed with ferns and mushrooms until she died.

A LIGHT IN THE DARK

The leftover fish from the previous night stopped the violent shaking. Even through her daze, Penny noticed that everyone was giving her sidelong glances every so often. By the time they were ready to go Simon had worked up the courage to ask the question nagging at everyone's minds.

"Penny, that orb—perhaps you'd better look at it a bit more. We haven't got much time left and—"

"Didn't I say that I have no clue what to do with it?!" Penny snapped, regretting her fierce tone the moment Simon shrunk away from her. Fatigue and illness were starting to wear away at them all, and no matter how much they did not want to admit it, life-threatening problems were becoming a possibility.

"Are we growing nearer to the center of magical activity in this forest, Argent?" croaked Hector.

"Yeah, I can feel it. We should be there by nightfall if I'm not mistaken," Argent breathed, looking around with apprehension. "Let's just pray that Della does in fact live there—I don't know how much longer we can keep this up."

As they delved deeper into the trees, the forest indeed became more saturated with magic. The colors of the arbors, the moss, and even the flowers and mushrooms became more intense. Azure and molten gold veins ran through the leaves, and tall tree roots were becoming archways rather than traps for unwary feet.

Penny stared upward; the stretching limbs of the black wood trees looked to her like arms of the dead. The thought of this was enough to send a shiver up her spine. She pulled out the orb and looked it over, begging for it to tell her its secrets, but getting nothing in return. A slow fury was growing toward Adrielle for giving her such vague directions, and Penny could not shake the unsettling, unspoken feeling that her friends were beginning to blame her for not knowing how to use the glass ball.

As the trip wore on, huge glowing mushrooms started to appear all over the place, indigo butterflies perched atop their hoods. The group went down a hill and through a few more clearings, arriving at a flat section of the woods that seemed to stretch on forever. Everything was silent; no chattering animals or swooping birds played amongst the greenery, nor was any insect life visible. Argent's pace slowed after a while and he turned back to face the group.

"This is it. This is the most magic I've ever felt growing in the wilds. You can feel it too, can't you?" he whispered. The mist was so dense that it obscured most of the world from view, making it impossible to see more than ten feet in front of them.

"Yes, I think so," Annette answered in reverent apprehension. "It's a sort of humming or buzz..."

Penny felt uncomfortable as she stood between towering rows of ancient trees. A keen sense told her that they did not belong anywhere near this place, as if it had gone undis-

turbed for eons. They were trespassing here. She drew closer
to her friends.

"Look for anything out of the ordinary, but be careful.
With all this magic, there's probably something very dangerous living here." Argent took a careful step forward and the
group followed him in a tight knit cluster, not needing to be
told to stay close.

The flat land seemed to go on forever and without defin-
able landmarks. It looked as though the world had gone
through a green filter and Penny's eyes seemed to sting with
the onslaught of color. She felt a peculiar sensation, almost an
electrical buzz, whenever her fingers grazed the trunk of a tree.
Their soft, careful footsteps were like an ear-splitting racket in
the sacred silence of these woods. Something caught Penny's
eye in the distance and she stopped.

"Look!" she hissed, her voice cutting through the serenity
and causing everyone to jump. The unusual colors she had spied
became more obvious as she led them in a new direction.

They could now see a wide ring of mushrooms surrounding a field filled with delicate yellow and purple flowers that
smelled of honeysuckle, the scent hanging heady in the misty
air. The flowers grew around a deep green pool, with a surface
as smooth as a mirror. A willow tree draping its long leaves
over the surface was a stark contrast to the towering pines.
The weary travelers stepped into the ring of mushrooms, their
breathing apprehensive as they crossed over the threshold.

"Hey…" Simon spoke up, crossing the field of flowers and
bending down before the edge of the pool. Penny was beside
him in a moment. She looked where he pointed to and her
heart leapt.

Before them stood a stone, elliptical in shape, but not
extraordinary in any way except for what had been etched into
the surface. The words *Only Gods May Enter Here* were carved
in English lettering. Penny nearly sank to her knees in relief.

"This has got to be it! Hector, come see!" Penny whispered, beckoning Hector forward. A smile lit his face when he saw the stone and he seemed to grow younger. He clapped Simon on the shoulder in a silent gesture of approval.

Without wasting a moment, Penny took the orb out of her pack and with shaking hands pressed it to the front stone. Nothing happened. She dipped it into the water, to no result. Frustrated, Penny commanded the glass orb to tell her the way.

Nothing happened. Feeling foolish, she stuffed the orb back into her pocket.

ONE BY ONE they gave up searching for clues and went about setting up camp. After dusk, the only light that shone was from the ring of mushrooms that fenced them off from the rest of the woods. The night was too quiet and too devoid of life. They ate very little and talked even less. Penny could feel the expectant looks coming from everyone.

She decided to lie down early to save herself from the awkwardness of the situation, but kept herself wide awake nonetheless. Penny jolted awake as she felt the tickling of a dream beginning.

Her body was desperate for sleep, but she felt that she could not handle another nightmare, especially in this place of deep magic. She was sure that losing sleep for another night would be better than waking up to find she had tried to drown herself.

Hector remained awake long after the other had laid down to rest. Penny surreptitiously watched as he strode across the clearing through the flowers, his glasses alight with the reflection of the mushrooms' phosphorescence. He lay down beside Penny sometime near midnight and she closed her eyes to keep from being noticed. She listened to his breathing for a while, feeling the temperature around her dropping until even her bones seemed frozen.

There was not a moment before this that she could remember feeling so helpless, so small, and so alone. She lay there, struggling with her expended body and all its unrelenting pains, feeling the eyes of the forest on her back. Tears threatened to stream from her eyes and her heart sank even deeper with the notion that she was going to give in, after all the times she had stopped herself from weeping. Misery ate at her as she shook and whimpered in the frigid cold, until a small sound beside her stirred Penny from her misery.

"Penny?" Hector's voice was soft and cautious. She was sure he had been asleep. She said nothing, forcing her arms and legs to quit their shivering in an attempt to fool Hector into thinking she was asleep. "Are you all right?" Hector spoke again, ignoring Penny's poorly-concealed act.

"Y-yeah. I'm f-fine," she stammered through chattering teeth, angry with herself. She felt raw and exposed, and that was something she could not abide in Hector's presence. Hector propped himself up on one elbow and looked over at her with a searching glance, increasing Penny's feeling of defenselessness.

"You don't seem to be fine. In fact I could've sworn you were—"

"I was not crying!" Penny sat up with aggressive speed, and Hector leaned back. Penny hung her head, her shoulders resuming their shaking as she lay back down slowly and her voice cracked. "It's just so — so damn cold out here…"

"That's it?" Hector prodded.

On any other night, under any other condition, or even if Hector had spoken just a bit differently, Penny was certain she would have answered "Yes" and lit would have ended there, but Mulgrith had pushed her too far. Everything tumbled down before she could stop it, and hot tears burned her cheeks.

"I'm tired—tired beyond anything I thought tired could ever be. I haven't really slept for days and I feel like I'm dying, I'm scared senseless out here, everyone's blaming me for not being able to find Della, and I—I just want...I just want to go home..." Penny couldn't stop the tear flow and covered her face in shame. She hated everything about herself and this moment. Out of nowhere Hector's arms wrapped around her exhausted body and pulled her tight. She gasped, inhaling his signature cedar pine scent.

"Penny..." his voice effused comfort as he put his hand on Penny's back and held her, the warmth from his body soothing the cold in hers. Penny was rigid with shock for a few moments, but as she became aware of the safety and affection behind his gesture, she closed her eyes and leaned her head against his chest as her tears ebbed. With shaking hands she grasped Hector around his midsection and linked her hands together behind his back as she listened to his heart beat erratically in his chest.

"You're all right...Good Heavens, you are cold." Hector pulled her in tighter, then lay down beside her and used the blankets to cover them up. "Is that better?"

"Y-yes. Thanks," Penny stammered. She was starting to feel dizzy again.

"Why haven't you been sleeping?" Hector prompted from close beside her. Penny shut her eyes and took a deep breath before speaking.

"I—well, I haven't been completely honest up to this point. That night on the dirigible—I fell because I've been having this strange nightmare, always with this—I don't know, it's—it's like something from Hell. It wears a mask and a dark cloak. I saw it first on that night I almost died in Warwick's Grotto. It's like it's been following me since then, showing up every time I shut my eyes. It *made* me try and jump. I'm afraid I'll have another nightmare like before—and—" Penny couldn't finish the thought, and Hector frowned.

"I understand why you've been avoiding it, but for now I wish you'd go to sleep. You'll die without rest in a place like this. I'll stay awake all night long to ensure that nothing happens. You'll be safe, I promise," Hector assured her.

"B-but—"

"Don't worry…" Hector lifted his hand to try and perform the spell that sent Penny off to sleep, but she stopped him.

"No, not that, please…It feels too much like dying," Penny admitted, leaning forward until the tip of her forehead just touched his chest. Hector said something in a low murmur that Penny could not quite understand, but it was comforting regardless. The warmth from Annette and Hector on either side of her eased the ache and numbness in her bones, and Penny drifted to sleep.

"LET ME SEE it," Simon ordered, holding out his hand for the glass orb Argent was inspecting.

Argent pretended not to hear him. Simon made an irritable swipe for the orb, which Argent dodged. "Give it here!" Simon shouted, taking hold of Argent's wrist and tugging.

"Get away!" Argent yowled, batting at Simon's face.

"It doesn't belong to you!" Simon squawked, still fighting.

"It doesn't belong to you, *either*," Argent growled, stepping back as Simon lunged for the orb again. Hector, Annette, and Penny watched for a moment as the intensity of the scuffle increased. Penny rose to her feet and stalked across the clearing to break them up.

"Play nice, children," Penny snapped, pushing the two of them apart and holding her hand out to receive the orb. Argent tried to hand it over, but Simon made one final attempt to snatch the orb away, his fingers grazing the sides of the smooth glass. Penny watched it roll straight out of Argent's hand and plummet toward the ground.

She made a wild grab for it, but it was too late. The delicate glass landed on rock with a sickening crack, amidst a chorus of frantic yells. Frozen in horror, Penny watched in disbelief as the swirling sands that had been encased behind the thin layer of glass spun around in the air.

"*You idiot!* What've you done?" Argent snarled at Simon. Penny's eyes remained locked on the smashed sphere. The sparkling sand spiraled upwards, forming a gleaming trail in midair. Annette screamed as the sand streamed into Penny's eyes, nostrils, and mouth in a sudden rush.

Penny couldn't scream as the particles flowed into her, feeling nothing as the specs of white light blazed into her eyes. Once all the sand disappeared inside her eyes and mouth, Penny stood wobbling on the spot for a moment as all thought was wiped from her head like a wave pushing up onto the sand. She caught a final glimpse of her friends' expressions, stricken with stark horror, before she collapsed in a heap among the flowers.

THE WORLD
BETWEEN WORLDS

Water rushed past, frigid and green. It swept by until there was nothing but a dark tunnel that stretched on and then turned upwards, back into air. Darkness flew by, speckled with bright blue stars. The smell of limestone hung in the air.

Trees were all around now, some heavy with fruit. Everything came to a quiet stop in a clearing, pausing long enough for Penny to see a lone doorway. Then the world began to blur and fade, but a small star kept blinking, sparkling in quick flashes from the knothole of a willow tree, a willow tree just like the one...

"Just... like the one..." Penny mumbled as Argent lifted her from the ground. Her head lolled back.

"Penny, can you hear me? Are you okay?" Annette's voice was the first thing to draw Penny back into reality. Her eyes fluttered open to see the concerned faces of her friends peering down at her. Simon stood in the background, his hands still clamped over his mouth. Penny lurched out of Argent's grasp, almost falling on her face as she tried to recapture her footing.

"It—it was a dream," Penny said, her voice sounding as if it was underwater. It took a moment for her hearing and vision to regain normalcy.

"What did she say?" Simon questioned, still looking horrorstruck.

"A dream! Adrielle stored it inside the glass ball," Penny said with a breathless grin, unable to holster in her joy at having solved the mystery, however unorthodox the method had been. "I saw the way to go! It's in the pool, under the water."

"What?" Annette's bafflement was evident. Penny wobbled over to the side of the deep green pool and peered into the murky depths. Sure enough, she could make out a dark space near the bottom that she had not noticed earlier. Penny prepared to dive in.

Hector grabbed her shoulder. "Penny, what are you doing?"

"Please, just trust me, it's this way," she pleaded, and reluctantly Hector released her.

Penny took a deep breath and dove. She propelled herself down to the bottom, ears aching as the pressure increased. Off to the side of the pool was a long, dark tunnel. Fear flared up for a moment, but it was too late to turn back. Penny shot into the tunnel, swimming until all the light began to fade, and panic set in. The tunnel had seemed so much shorter in the dream. Penny kicked harder, her chest screaming with pain as she fought with all of her strength to move forward. It was much too late to go back now; if she tried to turn around, she'd drown before she got halfway.

To die in a place like this was unacceptable. Her head and chest pounded with pain until she thought they would explode, and Penny exhausted every last bit of energy she had to keep swimming. Just when the dark began to dissipate and a misty blueness shimmered above, Penny's lungs burst and she inhaled a mouthful of freezing water. She kicked upwards in desperation, hoping that she had not aimed wrong and was not about to meet a head full of hard stone and almost certain death.

Penny broke the surface, coughing up water as she tried to take a deep breath. She paddled forward until she found land and hacked up the last of the water. Collapsing on the stone beach, Penny cursed herself for being so thoughtless.

A moment later a sopping wet Hector broke the surface of the water, his glasses covered with clusters of droplets as he swam for shore, shivering. Clambering onto the beach, Hector dragged Penny to her feet and further onto dry land. Conjuring a blast of hot air from his hands, he proceeded to dry the two of them off. Penny looked around to see that they had surfaced in a shallow, subterranean cavern just tall enough for Hector to stand in. Electric blue mushrooms lined the sides of the cavern, and the pale blue stars from the dream now made sense. The smell and sounds of mineral-rich, rushing water echoed around them.

Simon, Annette, and Argent burst up from the water's surface, each of them clinging for dear life to the cottony cloud from Simon's wand as it pulled them onward, until they too became beached on the cavern floor. Once everyone had dried off, Penny led the way forward, following the only path they could see in the cavern.

The group made their way through the tunnel, crouching as the ceiling got lower and the sides began to press in. When a tiny spot of bright daylight shone warm and yellow into the cave, Penny pushed forward, her arms scraping the sharp stone that lined the cavern until she found a shaft that led back up to the surface. She strained to hoist herself up through the hole, bursting into warm sunlight that streamed from a cloudless blue sky. Scrambling out of the way, she helped Hector out next, and waited until everyone had climbed out of the hole to look around.

She didn't understand. The underwater tunnel and cavern had been long, but not long enough to have led them out of the vast woods of Mulgrith. They now stood on a dry and overgrown trail lined by pine trees. Bewildered, Penny took a few cautious steps forward, walking around the bend of the tree-lined path. It seemed the only obvious direction. The others followed.

A flurry of green needles and gold fruit whipped past their eyes, and right away the path opened up into a circular clearing with a peculiar doorway in the center.

The doors stood eight feet tall, made out of silver and bolted with black iron. Particles of dust danced in the warm falls of light, and the trees seemed to stretch even taller. Penny took a few steps through the sea of grass that spread out around the doors, circling the free-standing doorway. As the memory from her dream played out, Penny turned sideways and beheld the tall willow tree that grew at the edge of the clearing, feeling herself drawn to it.

Penny approached the tree, placed her fingertips on its gnarled trunk and searched for the knothole she had seen in her dream. Sure enough, it stared back at her from the face of age-worn bark. Penny poked her fingers into the grizzled knothole until she felt something metallic, and clenched her jaw as she worked her finger around the side of the object. With a mighty tug, she uprooted a platinum key that was no longer than her pointer finger. Penny rushed back across the tall grass to the doors.

Penny took a deep breath and allowed herself a moment to take in each of her friends' exhilarated expressions before inserting the key and turning it with a satisfying click. Feeling her heart fill to the brim with anticipation, Penny pushed the doors open. She almost staggered as a strange and wonderful new world opened before her eyes.

It was night on the other side of the doors, but the more disconcerting fact was that only one pearly moon stood fixed in the lavender sky, which blinked with almost too many stars.

In silent revere the group crept through the doors. The land beyond began with a gathering of white flowers that seemed to share the same color and glow as the moon above. The flowers grew in drifting waves beside cattails and long, untamed strands of grass. Water rippled underneath these plants and flowed out to create a shallow pond. In the distance, almost a mile away, Penny saw a white spire rising from the water like a brilliant tusk. In the face of the white stone was a lone arched window. It had to be where Della lived.

No one dared utter a word as they waded through the ankle-deep water that seemed to be too clean and clear to be real. The marsh of flowers and reeds gave way to a mosaic, and images of fish and octopi made from bits of colored stone rippled up at them. The surrealistic quality of this world bothered Penny more than the dark trees of Mulgrith.

"Penny, I don't like this place…" Annette whispered when they had almost gone the mile. The group could now see two other doorways leading nowhere at equal distances from the spire, forming a triangle around it and its ring of white flowers. Penny squeezed Annette's hand to comfort her.

"We've come too far to go back. Come on," Penny told her with a weak half-smile. The ground sloped upward as the ominous spire loomed high above their heads. A curved door made out of the same white stone faced them, sporting a round blue-glass window that flickered with the promise of candlelight behind it. Penny swallowed the last of her fear as she knocked, hoping that it would be enough to announce their arrival. After a short wait, Hector took a breath as if he were about to speak, but it ended in a feeble choke as the door swung inward and a woman appeared.

Wrinkles upon wrinkles covered her skin, showing an age more profound than anything Penny could fathom. Hair fell in long, healthy silver waves, all the way to wrinkled feet. Glassy, bulb-like eyes beamed out from under a sheer pink hood as a deeply-veined, age-spotted hand gripped the doorframe to calm as if to calm its shaking. Penny's heart lurched as tears welled up in the woman's eyes, her near-toothless jaw quivering when she tried to speak.

"Oh, how long I've waited for this day. You're here at last." Even the woman's voice trembled. She appeared unashamed to be crying, but her voice remained calm as she stepped backward and opened the door wide. No one made a move to enter.

"My dears, it's me—Della. I've been expecting you, come inside," she urged, curling her index finger inward. As if they stood on a moving floor, all five of them were pulled into the spire against their will, the door swinging shut behind them.

THE LITTLE WITCH beckoned their bodies upstairs, laughing at their frightened expressions. Penny felt as if she had become one of Argent's puppets and tried to fight against the magic pulling her, but it was no use. Della led them into a room above the entrance hall where a stone table with two long benches stood. The five of them were escorted over and made to sit, and Penny felt control flow back into her body again. Fear now incapacitated her.

Annette was the first to break the heavy silence. "E-excuse me...but what is this place?" she asked, looking at the window, seeming keen on avoiding Della's eyes. Della seemed to be taking in Annette's lovely face, and gave her an affectionate smile before answering the question.

"This is the World Between Worlds, my dear. It's a land of my own design—most everything that you see around you is an illusion. Each of those doors you see is a pathway to the three worlds. I've been hiding here for a little over four years now," Della explained.

Penny's breathing sharpened. Earth was just a doorway away.

"And why is that? Who are you exactly?" Argent asked, looking Della in the eye. The witch took a moment to gaze upon Argent also.

"I have known many names, many stories, and have lived through many ages...I was born in Greece, and my name then was Pythia." Della's eyes lit up at the look of recognition on Penny's face. She smiled an almost toothless grin. "But of course, you would know me."

"B-but that would mean—"

"Yes, I am from *your* world, Penelope." She shut her eyes for a moment and sighed. "I suppose it's only fitting that my story should be told just once more..."

"When I came into that world I was human, but I had a magnificent gift—something that not even the Angels of these three worlds could explain. I am cognizant of the possible and likely pathways that the future will take. I began my life out as each young spirit does, selfish and without sympathy for others. I escaped from the fate that was assigned to me and used my gifts for personal gain. Eventually, my innumerable indiscretions caught up with me and I had to answer to Adrielle. She had come to punish me, as I rightfully deserved punishment— but instead of giving me death, which would've been a simple solution for both of us, she did something very different.

"She was right to think that my talents could be useful to her and gave me the chance to be absolved of my sins. I became her eternal servant," Della lamented, looking miserable.

"What did she do to you?" Hector prodded. Della's eyes flashed upward at Hector and a wicked smile lit her face.

"The unspeakable—the abominable deed," she scoffed, which further proceeded to confuse Penny. "There is no way of attaining true immortality on this physical plane, not even the Angels are immortal...however, there is a way of slowing down the process. Only an Angel is capable of it—and it has only been done twice. But I must not say any more about that now, it would change too much of the future. My charge now is to impart, on you, knowledge of great importance, but you must not ask me to divulge anything more than what I will tell you freely. Do you understand this?"

"But we've come all this way and waited so long, can't you just—" Penny began in frustration, but stopped when Della gave her a dangerous look.

"Of course your curiosity is strong, little Penelope, and I understand how you must feel, but for the fate of our three worlds you *must* remain ignorant. I can only promise you that one day you will know everything," Della assured her and Penny nodded in quiet aggravation. Della took a deep breath and seemed to draw from something long awaited.

"As long as I have lived, I never thought that I would come to see the threat of the End Times. I speak not of the momentary death of a world, but of something much more profound. Worlds die and are reborn, as are Angels and all the living things of the land, sky, and sea. But certain things cannot be destroyed; things like energy, souls, and magic are eternal. At least, I had thought they were...but everything must have its antitheses," Della finished with a heavy gaze.

"What exactly does that mean?" Simon looked sick to his stomach.

"It means that when light came into being, shadow was left behind in its absence. Because there was a means of creation, there too must be a means of destruction. Angels are not responsible for creation, no, no... they are mere sculptors and shepherds of what was given to them. Creation is something entirely different, as is destruction. And that is exactly the threat that we face now."

A spike of fear entered Penny's heart. Hector's face was ashen. The reality of her words had yet to take full effect, and already unpleasant thoughts stirred in Penny's mind.

"What are you talking about? What does *any* of this have to do with us?" Simon bellowed, fear apparent on his face as he stared at a serene Della.

"It has *everything* to do with you—each one of you," she stated matter-of-factly, making Penny's stomach twist in vexation. "Be silent and I shall tell you how this all came to be."

"Seival, Adrielle, Nestor," Della repeated the names of the three Angels. "They are the lords of our worlds. They are siblings, just as their worlds are. But eternity weighs heavily, even on the divine. Four years ago Nestor turned with murderous intent against his own brother. It is an impossible feat to murder an Angel, but that did not stop Nestor from trying."

"He...he killed Seival?" Hector whimpered, looking devastated. Della shook her head.

"He *tried* to kill Seival. An Angel can only truly die by their own volition. Instead, he dismembered Seival and with the divine flame, scorched the remains and all of Nelvirna," Della said, as if the words were a bad taste in her mouth.

"You mean to say that it was that it was Nestor who destroyed my home?" Hector clarified, sounding anxious. Della nodded and he shut his eyes tight, enduring a wave of pain.

"Indeed. Nestor tore Seival and his world apart. The flesh of the Angel burned away and left nothing but his ruined stump of a body lying entombed deep within the ruins of Nelvirna, where it still exists to this day," Della continued, but Annette stopped her.

"But what happened to Seival then? If he's not dead, then—"

"He is shattered—and *that* is precisely why you are involved, my dear," Della answered. Annette looked terrified and bewildered. "Four years ago, when Seival was torn limb from limb, what happened to you?"

"Four years ago I—"

"You woke up *feeling like your mouth was on fire*?" Della finished for her, her white eyebrow raised, and she turned to face Hector. "And you? Four years ago, as Nelvirna collapsed around you, what happened?"

"I...pulled myself out of my world and onto Earth."

"Something only an Angel can do," Della added, watching as understanding lit his features. "Yes, *you* are what happened to Seival. His soul and his body lives on in you two, and that is why you are able to do such extraordinary things. Annette, my dear, the tongue of Seival is part of you —that is how you can persuade others to do your will—and Aín, you possess both of his hands."

Penny looked around to see whom she was speaking to and was shocked to see Hector looking down at his own hands in disbelief.

Aín? Why did she just call him Aín?

"And that's why I can travel between worlds? That was the reason I lived, and everyone else died? " Hector breathed, drawing his hands into fists.

"You were selected by Seival himself before his death. All of the souls that were to harbor his fragments were."

"Well, what about me? Why am I involved in this insanity?" Simon demanded and Della gave him a short look.

"Because you ran away all those years ago, Simon. Because of Oliver and Sam, and your dream to learn tricks, and because you said yes to Deimos. When you took the wand and went to find Penny, your fate was sealed. And as for you, Argent—" Della faced Argent and he looked up with a small start, "I think you know why you're here." Argent flinched and looked away, his yellow eyes shifting about.

"Well, why am *I* here? Why does Nestor want me dead? Why have I been having those dreams? Why do I produce so much magic, and *why* was my old life and everything in it taken from me? *Please…*" Penny begged, leaning closer to Della. The old witch laid her bony hand on top of Penny's clasped ones.

"Penelope, I cannot tell you. I am physically prohibited from sharing this knowledge…I swore an oath of deep magic, an oath which cannot be broken."

Penny felt her heart sink and crumble. She wanted to stand up and scream at the top of her lungs, to kick the vases and boxes that overflowed with flowers and break them into thousands of pieces, but instead she pointed her face away. Della let go of her hand and turned to face the others.

"Now is the time for you all to listen carefully. It is your duty, as the ones chosen by Seival, to reassemble his body. Nestor has already realized his mistake and has begun to collect the pieces of Seival to ensure Seival is kept in his shattered state. He already has Seival's head, legs, and spine," Della informed them.

"You must find those who remain alive and undiscovered before he does, then persuade them to join you. Two eyes, two wings, and his heart are still lost in Elydria. Find them and take back the other parts stolen by Nestor—then to Nelvirna you must flee. But be wary of Nestor, because although he is weak now, he can do everything that Aín and Annette can, and more. He can *see* the pieces that you hold within yourselves. Find the remains of Seival and resurrect him so that Nelvirna may also be reborn. Only then can you stop Nestor. Do you understand what I am telling you?"

"Yes." Hector stood up with a fire in his eyes. Annette also stood, facing Della with determination. Simon looked sideways at Della.

"Erm, suppose I just go home now and—"

"You will most likely die a horrific death should you decide to do this. Stay with them, Simon, it is your only hope of survival," Della insisted. Penny heard Simon grumble "Wonderful" before he hung his head and also stood. Penny studied Della, chagrined.

"And what about me? Will I also die if I choose to go home?" she growled, feeling a strange pain in her chest. Della faced her with a blank stare.

"Whatever you choose, Penelope, you will always be bound to your destiny. You will be just as safe at home as you will be in Elydria. Take that as you will," Della admitted, her answer surprising Penny. The anger and pain that had been building in Penny's chest drained away, leaving a raw emptiness that made her feel ill.

Della stepped back and clapped her hands together. As she drew her palms apart, a tiny case, like a miniature treasure chest with a golden latch, appeared floating in the air between her hands. The box zoomed from between Della's hands and stopped midair before Penny.

"Take it," Della instructed and Penny grabbed the chest, inspecting it. It had a golden lock on it keeping it from opening. "When this box opens, you will gain a tool that will help you awaken Adrielle. Keep it close and safe, Penelope, my dear. And now the time has come…soon I will have my long-awaited reward."

"Tonight will be an especially difficult one, you must act with caution. Always remember — the future is never certain, only *likely*. Destiny is as a current of water — difficult to struggle against, but possible to overcome. One slip and the fate of all three worlds could be changed forever. Gather around me, please." Della waved her arms and they obliged.

"I have one last piece of advice for each of you before we depart," Della told them, and looked to Annette, who wore an expression of blank resolve. "Annette, you are not helpless. You are not selfish. Remember that." Annette blinked with apparent surprise. Della glanced over to Simon, seeming to ponder her next words.

"Simon, the *left*-most corridor and up the stairs. Got it?" Della told him with unusual spunkiness. Simon opened his mouth as if to contest this strange set of directions, but thought better of it and nodded. Della gave him an assuring nod back and looked to Argent.

"Mr. Clemons. When you wake up you must go straight to the Air Harbor. Don't stop for anything and tell the captain to take off immediately. Fly to the castle," said Della with a wag of her finger. She approached Hector next and sized him up for a moment before speaking.

"Aín… I know this will be difficult for you, but…you must forgive yourself," Della said in singeing voice that seemed to pierce Hector to his core. Penny watched him out of the corner of her eye as he shifted in place. Before she could begin to ponder what Della had meant, it was her turn.

"Penelope Fairfax. You have no control over what you are afraid of, but you can control how you react to that fear. Trust others, but more importantly, trust yourself," Della advised. "Now it is finally time. Prepare yourselves. This may very well be the most important night of your lives."

THE GOBLIN CARNIVAL

The world around Penny began to melt away, looking like dripping paint. There was a moment where everything went black and quiet, and then a misty scene reformed. They had been spirited back to the edge of Mulgrith woods, the city of Hulver just visible in the distance.

Annette gasped. "How did we get here—where'd our things go? Penny—your bag, and all that stuff from the camp site!"

Penny looked down at her side and realized her bag was, in fact, missing. Della stepped forward, looking up at the yellow autumn sky with a sad smile.

"I sent them to the airship, everything will be waiting for you there." Della's voice had a bittersweet quality as she stared into the sky, seeming disinterested in them. The sun was sinking between two massive black hills, and Della stood transfixed by this, a quiet stillness in her body as the white-hot color reflected off her glassy eyes. "I had forgotten how beautiful it is, the sun. How warm it feels, even in autumn…"

Penny stepped up beside Della. The frustration and anger she had felt toward the witch softened somewhat as she saw Della's wrinkled face painted orange with the light of the sunset.

"I am glad to have met you," Della said to Penny with a light smile on her pale, cracked lips. "I am relieved...but I will miss the green woods and the wind and the sky. I leave everything to hope. Farewell. " She smiled again at Penny, and without hesitation turned around with her unearthly grace to face the last light of the blazing sun. She took walked out from the trees and into the meadow.

"What are you doing?" Hector called after her.

From out of the gathering dark, a human silhouette with a bristling ponytail trudged up the side of the hill with wariness in his gait, holding a rapier out at an angle. He was searching, prowling around the woods for something. As the figure drew closer, it spied Della standing on the dusky hillside and grew rigid. They regarded each other for one resonating moment. Della spoke to him, but her words were too quiet for Penny to hear. She pointed back toward where Penny and her friend stood together. The man lifted his rapier.

It happened all too quickly. Della made no movement to try and avoid the attack, standing with open arms as the man thrust his sword through her chest with lightning speed. A noise of shattering glass sounded and a brilliant, white-blue explosion of light erupted from Della's chest. Penny froze, helpless but to watch.

Did Della plan this?!

The man who kicked Della's body away as a shimmering soul escaped and rocketed toward the sky. Penny gagged in horror as she watched the assailant lift his rapier once more and glance in their direction. He strode away from Della's remains. As he stepped out of shadow and into the flame burst of orange light, Penny recognized him with a burst of jagged fear.

"It's Deimos! RUN!" Penny screamed back at her friends. Hector and Argent did not waste a second, racing away. Argent pulled his puppet's controls from his pockets as he followed them into the forest.

Why would she bring us right to where Deimos was? Penny thought as she turned to follow. She could hear Annette's panting and the rustling of petticoats behind her. Penny slowed so that they ran side by side, diving back into the trees of Mulgrith.

It seemed as if their escape might be successful when, with a heavy thud, Annette tripped and fell face first to the ground. Penny skidded to a halt and whisked around to see Annette's foot caught in an overgrown root, her leg bent at a strange angle as she winced. Penny rushed back to help.

"Come on, Annette! We need to move!" Penny grasped Annette's foot, trying to free her leg.

"It's stuck!" Annette screamed and her face contorted in pain. Penny looked back in the direction that Simon had fled. Her heart clenched; there was no sign of them. Penny yanked at the root, trying to force Annette's foot free. Penny had gotten it halfway out when angry shouts and the pounding of footsteps clamored in the distance. With a horrified gasp, Annette whipped in the direction of the sound like a deer noticing the presence of a hunter.

"I've almost got it, hang on!" Penny lied, strained. Annette looked at Penny, her eyes searching. Annette opened her mouth to speak, her bottom lip quivering with fright as she did.

"*Hide. Don't make a sound.*" Annette's voice shook with the force of the Angelic power within her.

Penny's heart sank. She wanted to scream at Annette and refuse outright, but her jaw had already clamped shut and the air in her lungs stuck. Her body moved of its own accord, throwing her unwillingly into the underbrush and curling up on the ground. Everything within Penny raged with anguish as she realized what Annette was doing, but she could not move a muscle.

Trapped within her frozen bones, Penny watched from a gap in the tall grass as a man burst into the clearing and threw himself upon Annette before she could even scream. He ripped her free from the root.

Penny felt tears burning in her eyes as she recognized the wild eyes and cruel smile of Phobos. The tall, burly man wrapped his thick hand around Annette's mouth as she squirmed and fought against him. Deimos caught up a moment later, panting as he beheld the restrained Annette in cold disbelief. Phobos clamped her against his chest and brushed Annette's corn-silk hair from her eyes, which were huge and streaming with tears.

"It's her! I can't believe it—it's actually her," Deimos gasped. He looked at Phobos with an intense stare. "We're saved."

Phobos smiled back with an uneven set of teeth. He seemed to be enjoying watching Annette thrash and squirm feebly in his vice-like grip. He indulged himself, mimicking her squeals of terror. "What are the chances? Now Little Miss Celebrity is *all* ours…" he proclaimed in a malicious tone and let out another harsh laugh. Penny's insides squirmed in disgust.

"Phobos, get your head clear. We need to get her back to the palace immediately. Lord Nestor needs her by nightfall—*in perfect condition.* She'll need to have her energy to help steal the names of all those filthy goblins at the speech tonight." Deimos paused, admiring Annette's beauty with an icy stare. "Patience. After tonight is over and her tongue has been removed—that's when we'll have our reward." His white lips curled up in a wicked grin as Annette regarded him with horror.

A throb of adrenaline rocked Penny's frozen body as Nestor's plan became clear to her at last. Deimos reached into his pocket and pulled out a handful of what looked like ground green quartz and nodded to Phobos, who removed his hand from Annette's jaw as Deimos tossed the powder in her face.

Annette went limp in Phobos's arms, and he threw her over his shoulder as Deimos rummaged around in his pockets again.

"What about those others she was with? They're still out there somewhere, eh?" Phobos leered out at the trees as Deimos fished a small vial out.

"Undoubtedly. We'll deal with them later—Lord Nestor needs her now or he'll have to attempt to do it himself." Deimos poured the vial out in a quick spiral around himself and his brother. Water rose up in a tornado of spray and mist, and when it receded, Deimos and Phobos had gone with it.

Penny lay immobilized, her mind racing since her body could not. A few minutes passed before control seemed to be returning, and she emerged from the shrubbery, shaking.

Why Annette? Why did you do it?

Penny stood in the clearing, holding herself and looking out into the trees. She wanted to call out for Hector, Simon, or Argent, but was terrified of being caught by the goblin rangers. Her entire body ached and shook as she tried to swallow tears and keep her mind off what was about to happen to Annette.

A blessed sound rang in her ears. Argent's voice was calling her name from the murky shadows of the trees, and her knees went weak with relief. Moments later Argent came leaping through the moss, Hector and Simon trailing him. He caught Penny by the shoulders.

"What happened? Where's Annette?" Argent demanded, panting and holding Penny steady as she shivered.

"They took her—Deimos and Phobos—they got Annette—" Penny sputtered, knowing she sounded pathetic as she sunk to the ground, Argent following as he tried to brace her.

"No…" he said in a hollow voice.

Hector was asking her over and over if she had been harmed. She did not have the strength to answer him. She sat on the forest floor as the light faded from the sky, feeling as if she had suddenly been emptied out and left as a miserable, empty shell. She'd let Annette be abducted. She had already let Della and Adrielle down.

Hector's fingers snapping in front of her face roused Penny out of her stupor. "Where did they say they were taking her?" he demanded. It took a moment for Penny's lips to cooperate and move.

"I think they were taking her to the castle. They're going to use her to steal the names of all the goblins at tonight's speech in Hulver—they said they would cut out her tongue." Penny shivered, her hands trembling as she leaned into Argent's strong grip. Argent blanched at Penny's words, but Simon was already on his feet.

"Then there's no time to lose! We've got to get her back, no matter the cost!" Simon flourished his wand and with a fiery flick the puffy white cloud materialized before them. "Let's go!"

Hector stared at Simon in defeat. "Simon, every guard in the city will be looking for us. It's the last day of the Carnival, there's no way we'll get there in time, and even if we did, how are we supposed to stop them?" Hector looked pained. Simon seemed close to a conniption.

"You've *got* to be kidding me! You're going to sit here while those *animals* mutilate our Nettie? I don't know what kind of friend you claim to be, but I'm certainly not going to let this happen. If I die, so be it. Annette needs us! " Simon bellowed, his face red with emotion. Argent leapt to his feet.

"I'm coming with you," he said, crossing the clearing to join Simon. Penny looked meekly up at the two of them. The crippling fear and helplessness she felt was almost enough to overwhelm her, but the sudden and vivid image of Deimos approaching Annette with a blade and sadistic smile was enough to get her to her feet.

"She'd go for me. I don't know if I can be of any help, but I can't sit back while someone I love is in danger." Penny wobbled over on unsure legs to where Argent and Simon stood facing Hector, who looked sick to his stomach.

"Do you not understand that this is *suicide*?" Hector implored. Penny, Simon, and Argent stared at him with tight lips and narrowed eyes. Hector hung his head.

"Oh, what am I saying? Of course I'll go—realistic chances of survival be damned."

THE CLOUD SOARED high in the skies above Hulver, dodging between moths and huge white dragonflies. Beneath them, the city was alight with its sequins of color, flares of light, and a chorus of noise. Shrieks of delight and excited chattering echoed through the streets as goblin children lit fireworks that detonated with snaps and booms. Paper lanterns, leering masks, and outlandish booths were propped up all around the city. The smell of grilling food filled the air. The streets were absolutely brimming with life, and crowds of people fought to move even inches from where they stood. A clock tower loomed up from the serpentine streets, its face a brilliant moon of green and orange. A combusting shower of fireworks rained down around the castle's jagged silhouette. Simon kept his gaze fixed on it as he commanded the cloud to sail onward.

"What will we do when we get to the palace?" Hector shouted over the roar of the wind.

"We'll need to sneak past the guards and find where they're keeping Annette. You can use your locating spell," Simon shouted back as they wove through the gathering of flying creatures and airborne machines in the skyway.

"How are we going to get past the guards?" Penny asked, still quivering with fright.

Argent smiled as he eyed the booths that lined the streets below. "I have an idea...Simon, fly low for a second," he ordered, grasping the control of Kasper and twitching his fingers until the puppet danced out of his pocket and floated beside him. Simon looked around for an opening and then plunged the cloud downward, just avoiding a collision with a string of paper lanterns. As they grazed the tops of the vendor's booths, Argent sent Kasper out. The puppet glided along and, at the exact right moment, grabbed at several carnival masks attached to the side of a booth. The goblin manning the booth shouted in rage as Kasper returned to the cloud holding the entire post from which the masks had hung. Argent thanked his puppet before stuffing it back into his pocket and distributing masks to Simon, Penny, and Hector.

"This should give us a smidgen more anonymity, I think," Argent grinned, donning a red mask with a long, beak-like nose. Penny pulled on an expressionless black and white mask while Simon guised himself behind an ostentatious feathered eyepiece. Hector's face was covered by his mask's pained grimace, and he struggled to fit his glasses behind it.

Raucous music poured out of restaurants and from street corners as the castle loomed closer. At long last, they floated up to the side of the gargantuan castle and its mismatched towers, which fit together like a lopsided collage. Simon dropped the cloud down into one of the alleyways nearby, and they darted into the street, blending into the surging crowd. As they struggled to get through the thrashing, humid cluster of goblins, a loud voice boomed over the mighty thrall. Many of the carnival goers stopped in their tracks to listen to the announcement, their masked faces turned toward the sky.

"Goblins and Goblesses, people of Hulver! The time draws near! At midnight tonight our majestic monarch, King Yulghrat, will be addressing the public at the castle with his annual speech. Please make your way to the castle by midnight!"

The carnival goers resumed their molasses-slow progress toward the castle. Argent led them to the spiked gates of the castle, but their hearts sank when they saw that it swarming with goblin soldiers.

"We'll never get around that many, and there's *no* way we can fight them. If we create a disturbance, our cover will be blown and they're sure to overtake us. What should we do?" Argent asked. Everyone was silent for a moment as they all looked around for inspiration. Penny found it hard to concentrate with the crackling of fireworks and screams of delight all around her. Then, without a word of warning, Hector lifted his hands, looked about to make sure no one was watching, and conjured an arcane circle the size of a car tire, which he proceeded to hurtle at the side of a nearby building. It collided with an explosion that outdid the rumbling of the fireworks. As the wall of the building began to disintegrate, everyone around them screamed, ducking to protect their faces.

The goblin rangers that had been protecting the castle gates went into a flurry and pushed their way out into the squabbling crowd, barking out questions and blowing whistles. Under the cover of confusion, Argent sprinted forward and led the others through the mob. Once they reached the castle gates, the four of them crouched, facing one another behind their masks.

"Okay, Simon and I will go in and find Annette. Argent and Penny, you two stay out here and keep watch for Nestor. Stop him if you can, but exercise extreme caution. Once we secure Annette we'll come find you—and if worse comes to worst, find your way back to the airship," Hector said in a hurried voice.

Argent shook his head. "We should really stay together—" he objected.

"Argent, no. I need you to go to the balcony where the king will make his speech. We will need eyes on the ground," Hector insisted, then discarded his and Simon's masks in the bushes. Before sprinting away, Hector grabbed Penny by the shoulders.

"Promise me you'll be safe," he pleaded.

Penny couldn't contain a pale smile. "I'll do what I can."

THE CAGED SONGBIRD

Annette's eyes sprang open at the sound of an all-too familiar voice, honey-sweet and laced with venom.

"Ahh, the princess awakens," the voice purred and Annette felt the touch of spiny fingernails against her face. Valentine Frost peered down at her with a satisfied smirk. Annette became aware of the feeling of cottony dryness in her mouth and a thick cord of fabric wrapped over her lips. The young actress lay supine on a soft, regal bed in the middle of a richly furnished room, her wrists bound behind her back. Valentine sauntered around the bed like a shark circling its prey.

"Poor Nettie. What have you gotten yourself into now, hmm?" Valentine jeered. "I *almost* feel sorry for you."

Annette struggled to roll over onto her side. Valentine put her fingers under Annette's chin and the younger woman froze. Valentine studied her face for a long moment before withdrawing her hand and bringing it back full force across Annette's face. Annette whimpered and cringed back, her eyes watering from the pain smarting in her cheek. Valentine's fiery green eyes reduced to slits and her voice changed, growing deeper and more menacing.

"And you thought you could get away with what you did. How droll," she hissed. "You *actually* thought that you could get away with making a fool out of *me*. Of course, I knew you were cheating from the beginning…I realized it from the moment you spoke to me that evening, when you twittered those *suggestions* like the brainless little bird you are and robbed me of my happiness. But I knew that if I waited long enough, you would get your comeuppance. This little songbird's been caged, and she's never to sing again. And my goodness, isn't that sweet?"

"Valentine," a commanding voice said from the corner of the room, and Annette jerked up with effort to see Deimos sidle into the room, his face livid. He had changed into a formal suit and a silk strip of fabric covered his bad eye. Valentine swooped around and faced Deimos.

"And what do *you* want?" she snapped.

"Stop this at once. It's disgraceful," Deimos growled, looking down his nose at Valentine. "Get to the balcony. Lord Nestor is waiting for you, and for Heaven's sake I hope you act a shade more distinguished in his presence."

Valentine sneered, taking a puff of her cigarette and blowing the scented smoke out her nostrils before leaving, her hips swinging as she shot one last twisted grin back at Annette.

Tears welled up in Annette's eyes as Deimos turned and looked her over, expressionless. He crossed the room and sat down beside her.

"Now, I'm not sure if you're entirely aware of what exactly we need you to do for us tonight, so I thought I'd make it clear beforehand. As I'm sure you've come to understand, it is the final night of the Goblin Carnival. Thousands of goblins are gathered to witness the king's annual speech, which will be occurring in about thirty minutes. Understand so far?"

Annette chose not to dignify him with a response.

"Now, your job will be simple. All you must do is put on the vocal magnifying ring here—" Deimos showed her a glittering ring, and Annette recognized it as the same type she used for her stage performances. The shadow of the life she had known and loved in the face of her awful demise was enough to send fresh tears spilling onto her face. Deimos continued, unaffected, "You will command everyone in the audience to tell us their full names. Lord Nestor would normally, of course, do this for himself—but he is conserving what little strength he has for the removal and reassignment of your tongue. Will you comply or will we have to use force? A simple shake or nod will do," Deimos assured, cocking his head to the side. "Please remember that your fate lies in our hands. A quick and easy death would be something you should begin to hope for—take my word for it, you do not want to test this."

Annette doubled over in choked sobs, trying to order her thoughts enough to decide what to do. The thought of trying to use her Angel's tongue for protection as soon as they removed the gag crossed her mind, but what chance did she have against Nestor? Her heart slowed to a defeated whisper.

Annette thought of herself as a good person, but she had always assumed that when given the choice to save others or help herself, she would unwaveringly choose the former. The shame and despair of being proved otherwise was almost more than she could bear.

She nodded her head, misery overwhelming her.

"Good girl," he whispered, and put a hand on her shoulder, making her skin break out in gooseflesh. Annette sat defenseless as Deimos's eye ran first over her face and then the rest of her body. His dark iris flashed back upward, connecting with her blue ones. "Even in such a wretched state your beauty shines through. No matter what Valentine might say, you really are a lovely creature…seems like such an awful waste to kill you." Deimos shrugged and stood, Annette watching him in sick bewilderment. He moved to the other side of the room and faced the wall as he spoke.

"Now we wait." He went silent then, and Annette stewed in the revulsion of what she was about to do. Something deep within her was screaming to stand up, to refuse and to go out fighting instead of playing part in the destruction of thousands of innocent lives, but Annette also couldn't bear the idea of being subjected to the unknown horrors of Phobos and Deimos's twisted desires.

A tortuous year seemed to be hidden within every minute spent in that room, the tension mounting between her and Deimos. It finally grew to its zenith when he turned back around, his bristled ponytail swinging as he gazed once more upon Annette. She regarded him with a wary stare. Deimos laughed with enjoyment, a sound which chilled Annette to the bone.

"You must be so frightened." He sauntered back over to her bedside and brushed the hair away from her eyes. "Perhaps Lord Nestor will take pity on you... he is kind to those who are loyal to him. He brought my brother back from the furthest reaches of madness in return for my help in creating Cyrus and all those wraiths." Deimos rubbed his chin, studying Annette in a way that made her stomach churn. His one dark eye traveled all about the room as if he were deliberating something.

"Truthfully, I may not be so opposed to helping you myself. It does pain me so to see such a lovely specimen destroyed. Beauty is a scarce commodity in dark times...I wonder — I could take it upon myself to persuade Lord Nestor to spare your life."

Annette made no movement as Deimos sat back down with a contemplative expression on his face.

"I wouldn't ask for much in return. All I would require in return would be your obedience. Can you promise me that?" Deimos prodded, and Annette knew he had misread her stillness as a hint at compliance. She stared into his eyes, Della's words echoing in her mind.

You are not helpless. You are not selfish.

Her expression remained impassive as everything came crashing down within her. The previous notion that she would comply with the sordid plot burned away and faded to naught. In an instant, Annette no longer cared what was to become of her life, or what she might be forced to endure as a result. Where there had only been crushing despair before now burned a flame of inexhaustible courage. She was ready.

She nodded to Deimos, feigning a look of innocent vulnerability. A smiled flowed over his lips and he reached to undo her gag. Her jaw clamped as she felt his fingers pry at the knots. Deimos let the cloth fall away from Annette's mouth, their gaze lasting less than a second before he lurched forward and pressed his lips hard against Annette's, not even giving her the chance to take a breath. Annette writhed in disgust as she felt Deimos grasp her head to stop her from breaking away. An icy shiver prickled at her spine as his other hand crawled up her stockings and under her skirts, gripping her naked thigh while a heady moan rumbled in his chest.

He held her steadfast as his lips moved across hers with greed, the hold on her leg growing painful. Annette made a small noise of aversion and tried to wriggle away, but this only seemed to excite him more. When she felt his lips part and his tongue slide into her mouth, she knew it was time to strike.

She felt his tongue cross her lips and bit down with all the force she could muster, tasting a rush of salty, hot blood. Deimos reared back, bawling in agony as a mouthful of blood dribbled through his teeth and down his face and hands.

Fighting the urge to retch, Annette sprung to her feet, spitting as she made a mad rush for the door. It was a trick to get it open with her hands bound behind her back but she managed, feeling a rush of victory.

Annette stumbled into the hall as fast as her shaking feet would move, Deimos's wails still ringing out behind her. Resolved now to her task, she hobbled down the dark hall, her ankle still stinging with pain from her fall in the woods. The castle corridor twisted, but Annette did not care where she was going. She only knew she had to put as much space between Deimos and herself as possible.

When a roar shook the hall from behind Annette, a rush of adrenaline crashed through her. Deimos appeared in the doorway, his front covered in blood as he drew the long blade from the sheath at his side. The image of him impaling Della became more vivid in Annette's mind than she cared for.

"*You will pay for that!*" Deimos's voice, thick with blood, erupted. She knew with her injured foot she was moving too slow to put any real distance between them. It was only a matter of time before he caught up. Deimos shot after her with his rapier lifted high, the blade whistling like a wasp in the darkness.

Annette took a deep breath and started to summon the Angelic power, but Deimos was too fast. She heard a rushing sound, and then a painful thump on the back of her head sent her tumbling to the ground. Deimos kicked her onto her back and reached down, clamping his sinewy hand across her throat, cutting off all her air. Deimos lifted her, choking the life out of Annette as he slammed her delicate frame against the wall. She could see his bloodstained grin through her watering eyes.

"Your suffering will be the makings of legend, Annette Deveaux," Deimos growled, blood still bubbling over his chin. Annette beheld him with feeble terror, confused when she saw a flicker of concern flash across his face. He looked at her chest and Annette peered downward to see a golden thread of light streaming from her body. Deimos's grip loosened.

"What...is this?" he sputtered. "What are you doing?"

Annette looked around, just as confused as Deimos, and spotted Hector and Simon speeding down the hall toward them. Empowered by the sight of her friends, Annette lashed out, her knee finding the pit of his stomach.

He howled and dropped Annette and she took a long, ragged gasp of air that stung her throat all the way down. Hector rushed forward and grabbed Annette as she wobbled in place. Simon hurtled himself at an incapacitated Deimos. They tangled while Hector pulled Annette out of the fray.

"Are you all right?" Hector gasped, waving his hand to make the golden thread disappear from Annette's chest. She nodded through quivering gasps, massaging her throat. She still couldn't speak.

Deimos leapt to his feet and shuffled around Simon, his raised his blade high like a scorpion aiming at its prey. Simon flicked his wand at Deimos and a shower of ice blustered out, but Deimos was ready. He pulled another sword with a wide, black blade from his belt, sweeping it through them, causing the icicles and hailstones to shatter in midair. As the fragments tinkled to the ground, Deimos sheathed the rapier and darted forward, ducking low to the ground and making a wide swipe at Simon, who leapt out of the way just in time to keep from getting his legs cut out from under him.

Hector spun his hand in a wide circle, an arcane circle blossoming from his fingers. Deimos stumbled for only a split second, but did not wait to see what Hector's spell was going to do. He roared with fury, hurtling himself toward Hector. With a graceful movement Hector laced his fingers into a bizarre hand sign and drove his interlocked hands through the golden circle, causing it to shatter into a hundred tiny shards of light.

The lights swarmed Deimos as he flew forward, and began crystallizing into a golden bubble around his body. As the fragments sealed themselves, everything went silent for a second, and then without so much as a confused blink, Deimos thrust his sword forward and pierced the golden bubble, ripping a wound in its shimmering side and causing white hot veins to course through the sphere.

"Seival protect us!" Hector yelped, leaping backward as Deimos tore out from the center of the bubble, heaving the full weight of the sword at Hector's head. Annette screamed as Deimos brought the razor edge of the blade down toward Hector's skull, but Hector crouched and tossed up his hands just in time, his palms sparkling with runes as he used the last of Simon's magic to arrest Deimos's movement in midair. Simon stumbled back, his face in his hands as he struggled to stay conscious. Deimos's expression of savage dominion changed to one of abject confusion.

Hector shoved his palms at Deimos, throwing him back into the wall where his head collided with stone. Deimos slumped down the wall, his blade clattering to the floor. Annette limped forward and landed a heavy kick to the side of Deimos's head, causing his good eye to roll back.

The three victors stood wheezing over Deimos's crumpled form, expecting him to shiver to life once again. Simon was the first to stumble backward and lean against the wall for support. His face was pinched, and he looked as if he were just holding onto consciousness after the large amount of magic Hector had taken from him. Hector stumbled over to Annette, untied her wrists, and looked her over for wounds as she trembled in shock.

"You're okay," Hector sighed.

Annette swallowed and nodded, hardly daring to believe that she had survived the encounter. She could not even begin to understand how Simon and Hector had found her, but it only took a few moments for the gratitude to come rushing out. She looked at both of them with a quivering lip and tried to form words without success. In a rush of emotion, she lunged forward with her arms spread wide to catch them both in an embrace. Hector whined as she caught him around the middle and squeezed hard.

"Look, we're very happy you're safe, but we need to get out of here—urgently," Hector reminded them, looking down the hall in the direction they had come in. "I'll just target Penelope and Argent with the spell and—"

"Hector, wait!" Simon shouted, his voice echoing as he pointed to the opposite end of the corridor, where a line of four doors could be seen. Hector seemed to not realize what he was supposed to be looking at and glanced back at Simon, nonplussed.

"Don't you remember what Della told me? 'The right-most corridor and up the stairs'! I think this is what she was talking about—"

"Oh, of all the idiotic—" Hector cried.

"No, no, no! I'm serious, I have a really good feeling about this. Come on, let's go!" Simon gestured for them to follow, but Annette stopped, putting her finger to her lips.

"Are you sure it was the right-most?" she wondered in a hoarse voice. "I could've sworn she—"

"No, I'm positive! Please, let's not waste time!" Simon did not wait for them to agree and galloped toward the door far-thest to the right. Hector sighed and they trailed Simon, plunging blindly into the darkness that lay ahead.

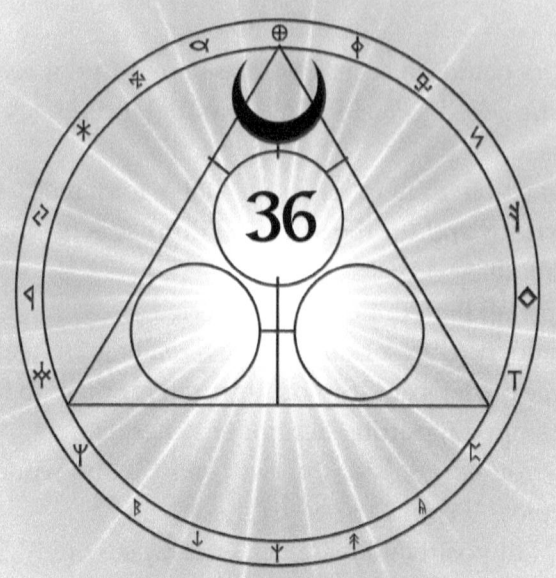

BENEATH THE BALCONY

"S tay close, Penny. You don't want to get lost in this," Argent warned as they stepped into the crowded street. The lane was hung with paper lanterns and gaudy decorations. Carnival booths lined either side of the street, and between them a heaving mass of bodies awaited the appearance of the king. The flashes of bright color from the fireworks and the menagerie of grinning masks were starting to send Penny into a state of frenetic anxiety. They burst through the thickness of the crowd and retreated into a deserted alleyway.

"We'll wait here until the speech is over," Argent panted, lifting his beaked mask to wipe the sweat from his brow. Penny saw unmistakable fear in his eyes; their chances of getting away unscathed were starting to seem slight.

"Argent...if they...if they don't come back after tonight, promise not to leave me, okay? I don't think I can—"

"I'll have none of that," Argent snapped, his sharp tone catching Penny off guard. "They'll be fine. And what do you take me for, anyway? I would never abandon a friend. Now shut up and see if you can spot anything out there." He pointed to the street. Penny smiled a bit behind her mask.

She poked her head out of the alleyway and peered into the crowd, feeling her heart almost stop beating as she came face-to-face with Phobos. He had been crossing through the group of people and squinting around when his eyes fell on Penny. She gasped and shrunk back into the shadows of the alleyway. Argent bristled at once, sensing something was wrong. Before Penny could explain, Phobos's shiny bald head bobbed into the grimy alleyway. His shoulders hunched over as he approached Penny and Argent.

"Hello, little brother, little sister. Why so sneaky-sneaky, eh? Shouldn't you be out watching for dear old King Yulgh-rat? You know it's dangerous for humans in Hulver right now," Phobos reminded them in his wavering voice as his eyes searched them. Argent grabbed Penny around the shoulders, and she let her breath escape when she realized that Phobos had not recognized her thanks to the mask.

"Just wanted a little privacy is all—if you catch my drift," Argent said, gripping Penny a little too tightly to be natural. Phobos looked down at Penny and then raised his eyes at Argent, a lecherous glint playing in them. Penny noticed with a shiver that Phobos's mitt-like fists were covered in bulging veins and flexing at his sides.

"Well, I'll leave you to it then. Might as well enjoy your-selves while there's still time…" He laughed his whining, high-pitched simper and turned to leave. The hulking man took a few steps forward, and then stopped as if a thought had occurred to him. "By the by, seen any other humans around, by any chance? I'm looking for some friends."

"No, sorry," Penny said at once. Phobos's forehead pinched in confusion at the sound of her voice and his eyes unfocused, like he was trying to remember something. He looked back at Penny and she felt Argent's grip on her shoulder become almost painful.

"Say that again," Phobos hissed.

"Wh-what?" Penny stammered. Phobos's wide eyes pierced through her, and then in a violent, jarring motion he ripped Penny's mask off and crushed it in his hand. Penny gasped as his eyes ran across her exposed face and understanding dawned.

"I knew it! You're that little grub from the Ball!" Phobos roared with a manic grin. Before he could move, Argent threw Penny backward and the Lady and Hyde came shooting out of his pockets, claws extended. Phobos intercepted them in midair, throwing both aside with one swoop of his bulky fist.

Penny retreated as the puppets soared forward again. The needle-sharp claws did not seem to faze Phobos even as they scratched scarlet lines into his bald head. He stalked forward with a dangerous smile on his lips and swung at Argent's midsection, throwing countless swaying punches, but Argent was too quick for him. Over and over he sent the puppets at the giant of a man, smashing them into Phobos's face and tearing at his hands, but Phobos did not even wince. Penny shivered behind him as he fought, looking for opportunities to help, but seeing none. Argent seemed to be growing more uneasy by the moment and Phobos picked up on this.

"So pale. Pale as a ghost. I'll catch you, Mr. Ghost, I'll catch you, I'll break your toys, and then I'll break you," Phobos taunted with a grunt as he jabbed forward, his fist grazing the very tip of Argent's crooked nose. The puppeteer bared his teeth and jumped back, using the Lady to help him make a high jump into the air and sail like an acrobat over Phobos's head. As he slipped behind him, Argent landed a quick kick to the back of Phobos's bald head.

"You can't hurt me, Mr. Ghost. You're only making it harder on yourself." Phobos reared back like a bull about to charge and Argent commanded Hyde forward to act as a shield, gripping the control with white knuckles as Phobos slammed into the enchanted marionette. Phobos was knocked back a few inches.

"Run, Penny, run now!" Argent cried. Penny tried to protest, but Argent reached back and pushed, forcing her into a run.

Phobos was too fast. "Not so fast, little grub!" he shouted with cruel delight, clamping so tight onto Penny's hand she was sure it would be broken once he released it. She shrieked as Phobos yanked her backward across the ground like a ragdoll. Argent galloped toward Phobos, now sending the Lady out, her claws extending into talon-like appendages as she aimed straight for Phobos's throat. The puppet hit her target with a sickening sound. Phobos made a small noise of alarm, and his grip relaxed enough for Penny to withdraw her hand, feeling as if it had been filled with broken glass. She stumbled to her feet and ran down the alley, reaching the end before she found she could not bear to leave Argent at the mercy of the murderous Phobos and turned back.

Phobos had ripped the Lady's claws out of his throat and brought his fingers firmly together around her tiny frame, using enough pressure to crush the life out of the puppet. Penny stopped, horrified. A bluish soul escaped into the air as the husk cracked and was crushed to pieces. Argent dropped the now useless control as Phobos tossed the puppet's limp remains to the ground and wiped the blood from his throat. As the puppet master fumbled to grasp Kasper's control, Phobos flew forward and threw his fist straight into Argent's face.

Argent's mask shattered on contact and Phobos's fist followed through the shards, hitting Argent with enough force to send him sailing into the alley wall. He collapsed in a silent heap beside the piles of garbage and filth.

"NO!" Penny screamed, unable to stop herself from running back in the direction of the crumpled mass that was Argent. Before she could even get halfway, Phobos turned to face her, his face splitting into a wild-eyed look of excitement. Penny slowed as he ran toward her. She tried to reverse direction and felt his body slam into her with the force of a locomotive, both of his giant hands catching her shoulders. She kicked at his shins, but it was no use. Phobos's shrieking laugh tore at her ears as he picked her up as if she were a mere child.

"Help! Somebody, *please!*" Penny gasped, screaming as loud as she could with the crushing force of Phobos's hands on either side of her body.

"No one can *heeear* you!" Phobos cackled, and threw Penny onto his shoulder as she kicked and beat at the sides of his face. Phobos stalked down the alley toward Argent's still body and Penny could see an angry red mark forming where Phobos had punched him. There was no sign of life from her friend as Phobos stepped over to Argent, still clutching Penny on his massive shoulder.

"Mr. Ghost should really start living up to his name, don't you think? Let's free him from his body so he can get some proper haunting done..." Phobos said with relish, releasing a peal of whining laughter.

Penny screamed Argent's name, willing him to wake as Phobos lifted his heavy leg and prepared to bring it smashing down on Argent's head. Frantic, she reached out and scratched at Phobos's eyes, feeling her fingernails scrape the soft whites. He howled, dropping Penny and grasping at his face in pain. She hit the ground with a thud, her chest seizing as she struggled for air. Phobos tripped backward and away from Argent, removing his hand from his face and looking at the spatter of blood that stained his sausage-like fingers in shock. Penny crawled along on her elbows toward Argent and felt a fierce kick to her side. She curled into a ball as lines of electric pain shook her body.

"You had to go and make me mad, didn't you? Bad move, bad girl. Bad, bad, bad..." Phobos loomed over her.

As Penny saw him towering above her, fear began to outshine the pain. Phobos leaned forward and put both his hands on either side of Penny's throat, not yet touching her, his fingers shivering as they threatened to clamp down at any moment. A tornado swirled in her mind as he brought his face closer and smiled, his lips twitching. A crescent shaped wound of scarlet floated in one of his eyes, making him look even more terrifying.

"I know my brother probably wanted to question you, but he'll have to get used to disappointment, won't he? It will just be too delicious to feel your neck snapping like a pofflin bone, I think," Phobos whispered, his voice wavering up and down. Penny was frozen with fright, unable to even think as his hands flexed, ready to squeeze the life out of her. Everything around her was too ugly, too ruthless, and too disturbing to process. She shut her eyes, waiting for the pain to come, to hear the fragile bones in her neck splinter and break apart under Phobos's iron-strong fingers.

It will all be over...everything will end and I won't have to be afraid anymore. I won't have to suffer the pain of losing Annette—of losing Hector, Simon, and Argent. I won't even have time to regret that I'll never see home again...I'll never see the sun again...

Death is easy.

Then, with a bell-like sound that cleared her mind of all discord, it was as if the solution had been injected into her head. Penny's fingers flew forward, grabbing at Phobos's hands before they could crush her throat. The white flash came even before Penny summoned it.

At a thousand bursts a second, images began to shoot out at her from Phobos's mind. It was not a single memory that Penny saw, but multitudes, flashing by in a rush. Feelings of crippling terror, oppressive paranoia, and anxiety barraged her. Images of Phobos confined in a dank room, chains binding his arms as he wandered around in circles in the dark, trapped—no way to escape from his head, tortured by a demon that inhabited his body. Things crawled deep within his skin; he was so small, too small. His words would never come out right even though they made so much sense inside his mind. The whispers exploded in his ears, coming and going in waves, lucid moments only made worse by the horror of knowing that the madness would come again, everyone's eyes looking on with fear and repulsed intrigue. The mind and the body belonged to something else now, the soul trapped, buried deep within.

As the images and sensations became more oppressive and violent, Penny willed to distance herself from the whirling memories out of sheer desperation. The urgency brought out a control over her power that she had never before experienced. She felt the memories barraging Phobos now, but she had separated her mind from his, though she still clung to his trembling fingers. Phobos was wailing now, the inhuman sounds escaping from his throat revealing his inner torment.

Phobos flung himself backward, ripping and tearing at his head as if trying to extricate the maelstrom of memories. With a final push of energy, Penny severed the bond between them, feeling control and clarity flow back into her with a powerful snap. She looked on in shock at Phobos writhing on the ground, clawing at his head and screaming. In a fit, he slammed his bleeding head on the ground over and over until he lay still, a thin trail of crimson flowing out into the tiny cracks between the stones.

Penny stood shivering, feeling her chest fill with a quivering, newfound empowerment. She took a deep breath and steadied herself, then tiptoed around the area where Phobos lay. Gathering what was left of her strength; Penny lifted Argent off the ground with an almighty heave and proceeded to drag his debilitated body down the alley, grateful the crafter was so skinny. With great effort, she tugged him into the street and the bustling crowd, where she laid Argent down beside a booth overflowing with toys and fireworks and sat with her head between her knees, gasping as the shivers died away. She figured she now knew what David must have felt like after felling Goliath.

In the distance the clock tower that hung above the city like a crooked obelisk began to sing. Penny's eyes snapped open again as the resounding voice of the bells echoed out over the city, loud enough to shake the ground where Penny sat. The crowd began to cheer and call out as the bells rang and a fanfare blasted out from goblin trumpeters. Penny watched as more fireworks shot up into the air from somewhere behind the palace, lighting the sky so it seemed as if daylight had returned early. Midnight had come.

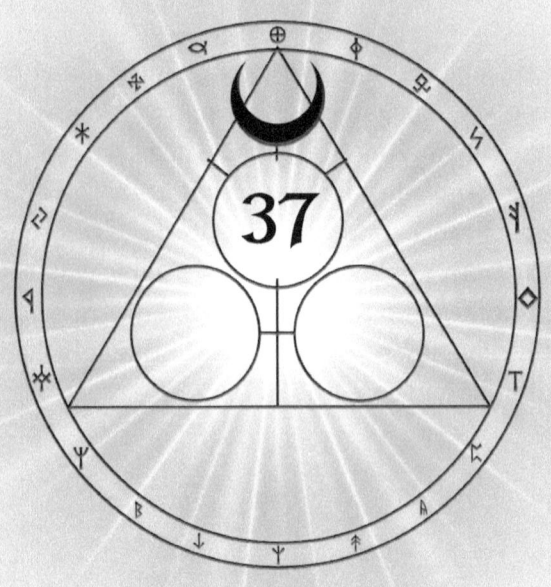

MIDNIGHT

Deep within the halls of the castle, Simon came to an abrupt halt, holding out his arms to stop Annette and Hector. A strange sound was resonating throughout the castle walls.

"What is that?" Simon murmured in alarm.

"Bells. It's bells," Hector hissed. "It must be midnight already—we need to get out of here." He took the lead. The darkness was unrelenting and the feeling that something might be waiting around every crooked turn tortured Hector. It wasn't until ornate candelabras still burning the stumps of candles began to appear that they all started to breathe easier. Rounding another corner, they came upon a flight of steep granite stairs leading to the palace towers. Beside the stairs on either side towered two large potted plants that appeared to be quite overgrown and unkempt, as if no one had pruned them in a long while. Simon shook with excitement, pointing ahead.

"Della talked about these stairs, too! We must be going in the right direction!" Simon headed up the stone steps at a swift pace, a hesitant Hector and Annette in tow. The stairs led to a room that was pitch black and empty, save for a small crack of light coming from the door standing ajar at the end of the chamber. A faint noise could be heard coming from behind it.

"People are cheering out there," Annette mumbled, her worried face caught in the sliver of color that severed the gloom. She pushed the door aside, letting a blast of blue-purple light flood into the room and illuminate the three of them in a mysterious glow. Flashes of white and gold flickered in as the sound of fireworks exploded above.

As soon as Hector caught sight of what was beyond the door, he knew that they had made a grave mistake. Perhaps a hundred feet away, the doorway opened out onto the balcony, decorated with purple draperies and a bone-colored throne, upon which sat the massive form of the Goblin King. Concealed behind in the shadows was Valentine, holding a control similar to the ones Argent used for his puppets, only quite a bit larger. As Valentine commanded the King's clumsy movements, she spoke into a silver bowl she held in her other hand. Her words boomed out from the body of King Yulghrat in a deep voice that spoke to the cheering crowd in Gobblish.

Beside Valentine stood Cyrus, his body stiff as a corpse, with the string of an eidolorbe wound around his one organic arm. The chain that ringed his neck dragged across the floor to the other side of the room, where it was held by the Angel Nestor himself, concealed from the balcony behind a purple curtain. His great white wings shuddered with agitation as he watched Valentine manipulate the dead king into making his speech. The Angel's long and terrifyingly beautiful face displayed only the most delicate hint of discontent, his eyes narrowed to slits. Annette caught sight of them and made a small choking noise, backing up into Simon. Nestor's head shimmered to the side, his white hair stained by the blue light from the balcony.

"It can't be—" Nestor's voice was musical, dangerous, and astonished. Valentine turned back to identify the interruption and stopped speaking at once, the silver bowl slipping from her hands and crashing to the floor.

"Seival's hands..." Nestor's eyes widened, looking like two moons in the shadowy room as he beheld Hector for a moment. All at once he rushed forward, his white arms outstretched.

Knowing he had no chance of teleporting them to safety with Simon's magic so depleted, Hector grabbed his companions by each of their shoulders and threw them out of the way. A confused murmur began going through the crowd outdoors as the king failed to resume his speech. Hector helped Annette and Simon to their feet as Nestor struggled to regain his footing. The Angel's movements were sluggish and his expression belabored.

"Get them!" Nestor commanded Valentine as his wings shook with rage, sending a shower of feathers through the air. "Don't let them be seen!"

Valentine leapt over the mess of the broken bowl and threw herself at Annette, her eyes blazing. She tackled Annette and the both of them went tumbling to the ground. Nestor gave a harsh tug to the chain at his feet and Cyrus shook into his unnatural movements and lunged for Simon. His ghastly white face and dead eye remained still, even as he caught Simon around the shoulders and held his metallic, clawed arm against Simon's throat, the sharp fingers drawing pinpoints of blood. Hector scrambled past and attempted to pull in what remained of Simon's magic, but the meager amount was not even enough to conjure up a spark. Before he could try anything more, Nestor was there, holding out his stony arm in an attempt to catch Hector by the front of his shirt. Seeing his last chance for survival, Hector made a mad dash for the balcony.

Annette and Valentine continued to struggle on the floor, spitting insults, pulling hair and scratching at each other's faces. Simon cheered for Annette as he struggled under Cyrus's metallic grip. Nestor tossed the chain aside and trailed after Hector.

"*Stop!*" the Angel commanded in a voice that held the same force as Annette's when she evoked her power of persuasion, but Hector found if he struggled with all his might, he could overrule its force. He sprinted past the purple curtains, hoping that Argent or Penny were still in the crowd somewhere. His mind focused on getting to Penny; if he could reach her, he would be able to perform magic once more and maybe save all of their lives.

Hector dove onto the balcony and a collective gasp rose from the crowd. He did not stop running until he was past the body of the king. He swiveled around just in time to see Nestor throwing back the purple curtains and stepping out onto the balcony behind Hector, his lips thin and his face the color of snow.

Screams of both confusion and joy began to erupt from people in the crowd as Nestor faced them. Some of the goblins below called out his name in shock. Hector backed up until he felt the stone railing and the leafy vines that clung to it against his back. He gripped it for support as Nestor advanced on him. The Angel caught Hector by the folds of his shirt and the crowd below burst into a cacophony of mixed sounds, crying out as Hector was lifted into the air.

"How dare you interfere, Nelvirnee scum? I thought I had eradicated the last of your people, but I suppose a few insects will always slip through the cracks," Nestor hissed as Hector kicked out in midair. Nestor let him drop to the ground without so much as flexing a muscle, and with a harsh jerk of his foot flipped Hector onto his back. He laid his foot on the center of Hector's heaving chest.

The Angel's hair and wings created a misty, ethereal glow around him in the night. Nestor's eyes remained fixed on Hector's hands as a calculating smile curled his lips.

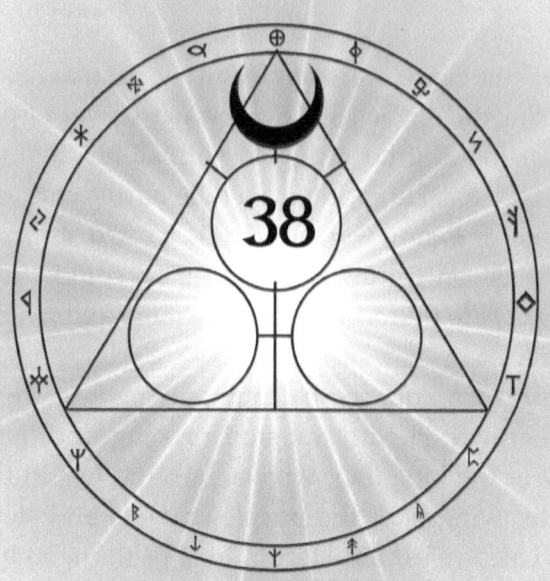

THE WEAVER RISING

The crowd below had gone into a fit. The rangers below tried to quell the disaster, but many of the goblins could not be controlled.

From only a few hundred feet away, Penny beheld the scene in stark, helpless horror, clutching herself around the shoulders. When Hector had burst out onto the balcony she had not dared to believe her eyes, but now that the shock had worn off and she saw Nestor threatening to crush the life out of him, something changed within her.

All reason drained from her mind, and a deep sense of instinct took over. Penny shot through the crowd, elbowing and shoving people out of the way, dipping and ducking when she could not bully her way through. Though her body felt heavy and wracked with pain, she would not stop. Emerging from the writhing mass of goblins, she caught sight of the vines that draped down from the balcony and over the street. Not bothering to look for a better solution, Penny scaled the fence below the vines, kicking back at the rangers who snatched at her ankles.

With a shaky spring upward, Penny leapt up and latched on to the low hanging vines. She held on for dear life, her crushed hand howling with pain. As soon as she gripped the plants she felt herself slipping, but it only took one look down at the spiked fence beneath her to get her climbing up with all her might. The rangers below her waved swords and spears in her direction as she threw one hand over the other in a desperate attempt to reach the top. A few of them tried to climb after her, but she fought them back with a few well-timed kicks. When her shivering hands touched the stone of the balcony, a second wind filled her shaking limbs and she dragged herself up and over the railing in one clumsy motion, tripping head over heels as she landed on the platform. Nestor looked up as Penny scrambled to her feet.

"D-don't—you—dare!" Penny screamed, pointing an accusatory finger at the Angel.

Nestor's eyes were glued to Penny as he took his foot off Hector's chest and stepped toward her. "You…it *is* you…" he hissed, his eyes wide with shock.

"Th-that's right!" Penny swallowed, taking a step backward. "It *is* me! You thought I was dead, didn't you? Guess you're not as smart as you think you are," she taunted, sounding leagues braver than she felt. Though her face displayed a defiant sneer, inwardly she was only moments away from fainting due to sheer terror.

"Penelope, *no*! Get to safety!" Hector yelled as he attempted to get back to his feet, but Nestor turned and swatted him away, his palm connecting with Hector's nose. His glasses were knocked askew and a stream of blood spurted from his nostrils as Hector fell back, wincing.

"*Don't… move*…." Nestor ordered, and Hector froze on the ground, his eyes staring in horror. Hector looked to be fighting against the command, but could not overcome it. Nestor turned back, facing Penny with a deep, seething anger that made her heart surge into a flurry of irregular beats.

A flash of color distracted both of them, and Penny turned to see Annette streaking out from the back room, her face sporting a nasty bruise and a few scrapes. She threw herself at the railing and took a deep breath, then bellowed at the crowd below, "RUN AWAY, ALL OF YOU!"

It took only a few seconds for the hordes below to stop their various movements, turn around, and stampede in the opposite direction.

Valentine burst out from the room beyond and ran forward, bellowing as she grabbed a thick handful of Annette's hair and attempted to throw her to the ground. Annette struggled, kneeing Valentine in the side of her ribs. Valentine stumbled back toward the railing, gasping for air and glaring at Annette with fearsome ire, one of her fingernails broken as blood dripped from the side of her face.

"You loathsome *brat!* You think you've won just by sending them away? You think it's over? You think that I'm just going to—wah—aggh!" Valentine's eyes grew wide with horror as her back hit the railing too fast and she toppled over.

Annette rushed forward and caught Valentine by her ankles. "Valentine! Hold on, I've got you!" Annette yelled, straining to hold her.

"Lord Nestor—please—help me!" Valentine begged as her ankles slipped from Annette's weak grip. Annette groaned as her strength gave out and Valentine fell from her grasp. Nestor looked on with vague interest, and Penny gasped in shock as Valentine's piercing scream cut through the night until it was silenced by a telltale crunch. Annette turned white and froze, unable to look over the railing.

Nestor, however, no longer seemed to be interested in Valentine's demise. He turned and advanced on Penny like a serpent preparing to strike. She rushed into the palace, Nestor following behind and gaining on her by the moment. As she plunged into the darkness of the room beyond, she was shocked to come face to face with Simon who, though restrained by Cyrus, was attempting to get his wand from out of his pocket. He looked up in surprise as Penny shot by, their eyes connecting for a split second. He yelled her name as she continued on through a door, but she did not stop.

Penny glanced back as she bolted through the door to see if Nestor was still behind her, failing to notice the staircase in the middle of the room. Her stomach did a flip as she went careening forward through the air and rolled down the flight of stairs, the granite rattling her bones until she came to a violent crash at the bottom. While she cringed and gritted her teeth through the unrelenting pulses of pain, the noise of wind on feathers whooshed above her head. With a flutter Nestor landed before her. Penny blinked her watering eyes to behold the irate Angel glaring down at her.

"It truly is you. Penelope Fairfax...I thought I might have been mistaken, that day you stumbled into my chamber. I was under the impression you were dead. But it appears you have somehow outsmarted me, and for that I applaud you—and I must admit, meeting you again after all these years is a touch exhilarating," Nestor said, sounding almost cheerful.

Penny panted, discovering she could not contend with the pain of trying to move. Nestor smiled and, to her great terror, took a seat on the step beside her. His huge wings folded behind his back as he continued to stare at Penny.

"I'm sure you've wondered—it *was* indeed me on that night so many years ago. I had found you after searching for so long and I would've succeeded in abducting you, as I had originally planned, if Adrielle hadn't been so keen on meddling in my affairs. It took years and years to figure out how to remove that seal she put on you—it was a genius bit of magic on her part, really...hiding you away so I could never find you." He reached out and cupped her face. She shuddered at the contact and took several deep gasps, her entire body aching with the strain of breathing.

"Why? Why are you doing this to me? To everyone? I thought you were supposed to be a…a *guardian* of life. Why would you—?" Penny breathed, but stopped when she saw the look of utter shock on Nestor's face. His lips parted as he looked at her with incredulity.

"You mean to say that…you don't know? Adrielle told you nothing?" Nestor's moon-like eyes shone into her. "You've no idea what this is about?" He barked out a hollow laugh without smiling, chilling Penny's bones.

"Oh, poor creature—you have been playing with things far beyond your comprehension. I must confess, I did not expect this at all. This changes things quite a bit," he said, more to himself. Penny stared at him in bewilderment.

"You must know that I never meant you harm personally, no. It was all because of my stubborn siblings…come now, I will heal your wounds." Nestor leaned forward and put his fingers to Penny's forehead. With a shudder and what seemed like a huge gust of wind, Penny felt the sharp pains leave her body. The bruises and cuts from her scrap with Phobos disappeared, along with the soreness from her fall. Though the pain had left, the heaviness and dizziness remained, weighing down on her more than ever. Penny stood up in disbelief, looking at her body to observe the miracle, and noticed the plants on either side of the stairs. Only moments ago they had been growing green and healthy, and now they had been reduced to a crusty brown pile of wilted leaves. Nestor gave an empty smile as he put a hand on her shoulder.

"Come and stop this foolishness now. I promise I will tell you everything as soon as I can. I'm sure you've been more than curious," Nestor told her, his face unfeeling. Penny was reminded of the wrought iron mask from her dream.

"You'll tell me…everything? Why?"

"Because you've done more for me tonight than any one of my followers has in months. You've brought me my brother's hands and tongue. Just what I expected of a—"

"What are you getting at?" Penny stepped back, breaking away from Nestor's hand. "I'd die before I let you hurt Annette or Hector," she snarled, balling her hands into fists.

Nestor's face fell into a frown. "Are you certain about that? I'll get to them anyway. Is standing between myself and the inevitable worth never learning the truth about who you *are*?" Nestor coaxed.

Penny faced him with unblinking tenacity. "Absolutely," she spat.

Disappointment shadowed Nestor's face and he sighed. "What foolish ends noble lives often meet," he said, shaking his head. With inhuman speed Nestor reached out and touched a finger to her chest, sending Penny shooting across the room into the wall. Nestor closed his eyes as if concentrating and appeared in front of Penny faster than her eyes could track. Once again he reached out with a single finger extended, and Penny only had a moment to jerk her head out of the way. As his fingertip connected with the wall that had been behind her only seconds before, the surface of it exploded into hundreds of tiny bits and showered the room with rubble. Penny jumped back again, almost falling victim to another explosive assault from Nestor's finger. He appeared to be getting more exhausted as he lurched forward to stop her, his face awash with apparent frustration. Penny stumbled as he rushed her again, backing her into the corner.

"Accept your fate, you can't escape. Be still and your death will be easy," Nestor commanded, his fingers trembling as they grasped for her.

*Death is easy…*Penny felt a thought stirring in the depth of her mind. She looked up at Nestor with wide eyes as she pressed herself into the crook of the corner. He was right, there was no escape—but perhaps fleeing was not the answer. Penny clenched her jaw, hoping that her insane idea had the slight-est chance of stalling the Angel long enough for her to get to Hector. Nestor's hand shot toward Penny's forehead and she ducked out of the way just in time for the wall to be obliter-ated again, creating a crater the size of a small pond. Instead of dodging away again, Penny reached forward and wrapped her hands around Nestor's stony forearm, catching a glimpse of his surprise before the white flash came.

Penny focused on thoughts of the masked entity that haunted her dreams in hopes that it would be enough to stun Nestor, yet as she summoned up memories of the nightmares that had plagued her for months, something very different emerged from the flash of white light.

She was stuck in the realm that separated reality from the dreams she tried to summon. She stood enveloped by the powerful, humming whiteness, watching as a face began to materialize before her. As the light streaming all around began to grow less intense, Penny recognized the mask from her dreams floating freely before her, without a cloak or body of any kind. Penny tried to breathe as she stared at its hol-low eyes, the sarcophagus mask smiling back with iron lips. Frozen with horror, it took her a moment to notice what was happening to her body.

When she looked down at herself, she saw with shock that three pulsing black veins were growing out of her chest, reach-ing toward the mask. They oozed with a light film of slime and a dark substance surged within them at rhythmic intervals. Penny could not even manage to scream as she watched them snake forward, wrapping around the mask like the roots of a tree burrowing into soil.

She felt her heartbeat getting more frenzied as even more of the root-like veins began to stem from her body. They sprouted from her neck and legs, all quivering and reaching out toward the mask. Her heart began to rage in her chest like a snare drum, intensifying until all she could hear and feel

was the frantic surge of blood. As her heartbeat grew to a panicked hum, Penny saw the cloak of the masked entity start to
flow out of the mask before her eyes as if it were ink spreading through water. Then with an abrupt silence, Penny's heart
stopped beating all at once.

Everything went deathly silent and still. Then with something that felt like a resonating snap in her chest, Penny's heart
started up again, this time beating at a normal rate. With a
final shock, the veins that had grown out from her body broke
off from her one at a time, each one feeling like a small sapling
being uprooted as it was drawn into the masked entity. From
within her, where the deep weariness and terror had been, there
now burned a light as bright as that of the sun. Across from
her, in the place where the black substance had been drawn
into, a sinister murmuring began to rise up, as if dry, cracked
lips were chanting and singing behind the mask.

"You are mine, and I am yours," the soundless voice that
she had come to know so intimately puffed into her ear. "I have
sought you before, and I will seek you again, and forevermore
until we burn together again."

The vision was ripped from Penny's eyes and the sight
of the goblin palace flowed back. Penny could now see that
where her hands had touched Nestor, two diseased-looking
black marks appeared to have been burned into his paper-
white flesh.

The Angel stumbled backward and wrenched his arm out
of Penny's feeble grasp, all the while gasping in horror at the
hand-shaped singe marks on his arm.

"What have you done to me, you horrible, wretched creature?! What is—how can you control the flow of Anti-Magic?"
Nestor demanded, his eyes widening as the deep, dark marks
started to flow up his arm, blemishing his flesh as they went.
He tore off the front of his cloak and shouted in repulsed panic
at the sooty discoloration snaking its way through the veins
in his neck, staining his face and eyes with poisonous black

spots. The Angel fell to his knees as Penny stepped back, goggling at Nestor as he gripped the sides of his head.

"NO! *THIS CANNOT BE! Silence! Silence, I will not hear your lies—begone, you—NO!*" Nestor howled, and his frenzied stare fixed in terror on an empty spot as if it were haunted by a specter that only he could see. The whites of his eyes were splotched with black lines that pulsed and bulged. Nestor roared, the sound one of utter belligerence and defeat. He spread his trembling wings to their full span and rocketed into the air without warning, tearing through the stone ceiling as if it were mere tissue paper and creating a shower of debris and rubble as he shot into the sky. Penny scrabbled forward and stared in shock through the gaping hole.

All she could see were the stars blinking back at her. She kept gazing upward through the puncture wound in the castle ceiling for several long minutes before realizing that all the heaviness and fatigue that had weighed down on her bones just minutes before had vanished. It had gone, and it had taken the Angel of Elydria with it.

A MOMENT OF QUIET

The walk back up the stairs was somehow just as tranquil as it was daunting. Though Penny did not know what to expect at the end of the balcony, a strange sense of quiet had come over her. The emotions that had been so uproarious minutes before had stilled. She pushed through the curtains and onto the balcony and heard Annette's distinctive scream.

"Penny! Thank Heaven you're all right!" Annette wailed, gripping Penny around her ribcage hard enough to restrict her breathing. "We thought you had—"

"Where's Nestor?" Simon yelled from beside her, fear still rampant in his gaze.

"I sort of—well, he's gone. It's hard to explain, I—"

"Are you hurt at all?" Hector hobbled forward, looking haggard. His nose had a slightly crumpled look and a splatter of dried blood smudged his face. There was disbelief in his eyes as he looked Penny over.

"No, I'm okay. Where's Cyrus? How did Simon get away?" Penny asked, looking around for some clue as to what had happened. Echoing shouts still rang out from below and several goblin stragglers continued to dash across the now almost-deserted square. It was only a matter of time before Annette's commands wore off and a group of angry goblin rangers stormed them.

"It was the Bishop. He flew up on a moth. Phobos and Deimos were with him, but they looked worse than dead. We tried to stop him, but he pulled out something that looked like a whistle and when he blew it, Cyrus came shooting out from the room and they—they got away," Hector sighed.

Annette, who simply refused to let go of Penny as if she were in danger of being swept away with the wind, gasped. "Where's Argent? Wasn't he with you?" she squawked, which set Hector and Simon off looking around them for any sign of the crafter.

Penny flushed with grim recollection. "I—I left him sitting in the street...you don't think when all those people ran off that he was—"

A loud groaning and creaking of hundreds of different mechanical parts sounded from above their head, interrupting Penny as a large shadow obscured the moonlight. The magnificent Royal Dirigible floated in an elephantine mass in the starry sky above. On the airship's deck they could just make out the outline of a silver-haired man waving energetically. Penny smiled, remembering Della's last piece of advice to Argent.

When you wake up you must go straight to the Air Harbor...

SAFELY ABOARD THE airship, Penny told them all, in great detail, of the confrontation between herself and Nestor and relived the vision of her final encounter with the masked entity.

"What could you have possibly done to make him react in such a way?" Hector wondered and Penny shook her head with a shrug.

"There's no way of knowing—I'm just grateful it *did* happen, otherwise I probably would've been reduced to a bloody smear," Penny said, then stopped as something occurred to her. "I do remember him saying something about Anti-Magic, though. Do any of you know what that is?"

Hector shrugged, but Argent's expression darkened a shade. Penny was sure Argent knew something as she studied the contemplative look in his eyes, but decided she would try to wheedle the truth out of him after they got back to Iverton.

Once all accounts had been told and theories had been discussed, the majority of the return journey was spent asleep or nursing their various wounds and recuperating. Every night Penny dreamt nothing but the harmless, nonsensical scenes that she had come to miss so dearly. The lightness she felt since Nestor had flown away remained.

When Iverton appeared as a tiny collection of miniatures outside of the Airship's windows, all five of them rushed out on to the railed balcony. Penny felt a sense of warmth and ease as she gazed upon the familiar sights of the castle and Grand Cathedral in the distance, feeling as if she were finally home for the first time since she had come to Elydria. As the huge dirigible bounced down on the runway and the golden staircase clanked out, Penny and Annette bounded down it, laughing in elation.

At the bottom of the stairs, a wonderful surprise awaited: Gavin, Wendy, and Humphrey. Annette gave a high pitched yell and leapt into Gavin's arms, then let go and threw herself on top of Wendy, all three of them making a riot of noise. Penny felt a great rush of emotion as Humphrey pranced up and down, whining as she skipped over to him. She threw her arms around his warm, furry neck as he licked her face. He pressed his cold, wet nose into her ear, sniffing it in the way that made her go silly with giggles. Humphrey gave Hector an energized sniff as he drew closer to the group, which Hector returned with a tentative pat on the anteloo's head. By the time Gavin swept her up into a bone-crushing hug, Penny had to turn her head away to wipe away the rogue tear that escaped.

"Oh, when we heard the news we nearly died of fright! Mother and I were in hysterics the whole night long until the captain sent word to the palace," Gavin cried, then looked up to the top of the flight of stairs where Zayne stood looking on the scene before him with revulsion. "Thank you, sir! It was really kind of you to let us know!" he shouted, waving up to Zayne. The Airship captain sneered down at him.

"Come now, there's not a moment to lose. The King and all the ambassadors and reporters are waiting at the castle. They're absolutely desperate for something other than the rumors that have been trickling in. Come, come," Gavin enthused, putting an arm around Penny and Annette.

The streets of Iverton were just as wondrous and alive as Penny remembered them, and she looked on with an even greater sense of sentimentality after the long absence. The clean, wide lanes busy with diverse life were far lovelier than the crooked, garbage-lined alleys of Hulver.

The moment the group arrived at the castle, chaos broke loose. Not a second after stepping out from the carriage, they found themselves swarmed by a crowd of people, all of whom were shouting. Some were demanding answers to wild questions, others lobbed insulting comments, and a few even broke into applause. One priestess burst into tears at the sight of them and commanded them to tell her what they had done with Lord Nestor. Penny was stunned at how much the public had discovered about that night, and if it were not for Hector and Gavin hurrying her along, she feared she might have been pulled into the mob.

Once they got beyond the castle gates, a few guards led by Captain Damari Baldera escorted them to the ivory towers.

They were taken to a chamber furnished with a long, polished table, and told to prepare for the King.

The young monarch burst into the room before they could even sit down, his cape fluttering behind him. "Do you people have any idea what you've put me through? First you disappear without a trace for weeks on end, and then when you finally *do* show up you bring this mess with you! I've been getting constant criticism for sending you instead of my most trusted ambassadors, and this honestly does not help that situation. I'd say that you lot have a great deal of explaining to do." Noah raised his eyebrows as he took a seat beside Penny and motioned for the others to sit down. He stole a shy glance at her, and Penny blushed furiously.

Annette first introduced Argent to explain his presence, then launched into a detailed explanation, barely taking time to breathe between sentences. Penny had to admit even to herself that the story sounded farfetched. Annette attempted to back up everything with all the evidence that she could, but took care not to go into too much detail about Della, saying only that they had met a kind witch in the woods who had helped them back to Hulver.

She wove a neat tale, and Penny noticed she was careful never to lie outright, but edited and omitted where she saw fit. Noah was stunned after she finished, sitting in silence for a full minute.

"It was *Nestor* who caused this? He's behind the appearance of the wraiths in our Nation? The Angelic Lord responsible for the death of King Yulghrat and countless others?"

"Exactly," Argent jumped into the conversation, laying his Inquisitor's Eye out on the table and sliding it toward Noah. "Use that if you don't believe us." Noah looked at the Inquisitor's Eye with a heavy stare, and then picked it up between his fingers.

"I would like to test each of your claims, if you don't mind. In the meantime, I'm sure you're all starved." Noah looked back at a guard and got his attention. "You, please tell Flynn to prepare something special." He turned back to the others and held up the Eye. "While we wait, would you mind...?"

Annette obliged, careful to word her answers for the Inquisitor's Eye. Noah looked astonished when the Eye continued to confirm her story.

Flynn arrived, looking as sour as he had at the ball, bringing the group heavy golden plates laden with a lavish, honey-roasted pofflin, baked herb potatoes, a crisp salad with wild nuts and berries, and oat bread still warm from the oven.

By the time the pofflin roast had been reduced to a few scattered bones and little else remained but a few scraps of salad leaves, Noah was at last satisfied with what he'd heard. He shook his head in stunned amazement.

"I'm sorry to have doubted you, my friends. I somehow knew deep down that sending you was indeed a good idea. I had a feeling that you were needed in Hulver—my advisors thought I was crazy, but I suppose a King's intuition is not to be questioned," Noah said with mild arrogance. The King looked off into the distance, a muddled expression on his face.

"I won't pretend that this doesn't make things much harder for me. This news is most disturbing—I don't want to believe Lord Nestor would do something like this, but I can't imagine how much worse it would've been if you hadn't stopped him. I was almost positive that I saw something....*special* about you all from the moment I laid eyes on you, and goodness knows Elydria needs heroes in these dark times. Please accept my most sincere thanks for your strength, your cunning, and your unfailing courage." Noah bowed his head to them, a gesture which seemed to resonate with Annette and Argent. When he looked back up, he seemed to be thinking again. "Well, I must be going. There's much to do...too much to do..."

"Does that mean we're allowed to go home now?" Gavin asked and Noah laughed.

"Heavens, no. I'll need you all here for at *least* a week. You and your mother needn't stay, Mr. Deveaux, if you don't wish to, but I'm going to need Miss Fairfax and her entourage," Noah said with a charming smile as Penny frowned. "You five need to meet with the ambassadors, my advisors, give your official statement to the rangers, talk to the heads of the other Nations, and we'll need to do thorough background checks..."

FOR THE FIRST few days Penny was relentlessly ushered back and forth from the private chambers in the castle to meetings and to introductions. She was talked at and talked about. What had happened in Hulver became well-known throughout all of Elydria in a matter of days, but Penny could still not get over the shock of seeing her name on the Sophotri Stones. Words like '*hero*' or '*scourge*' were constantly thrown about when describing Penny or her friends, and it unsettled her to say the least. Hector magicked up a series of documents that would support the fake identities they were assuming.

Annette leapt back into life at Iverton with a deftness Penny was not aware she possessed. As soon as she had time, she wrote an official apology to Aldridge and the Iverton Theater for her sudden absence and arranged meetings to be held at the castle with the heads of the entertainment departments to discuss future plans and the demise of Valentine Frost. Gavin seemed restless with Annette's new insistence on arranging her own affairs.

Argent, who had never been keen on speaking to anyone, much less news reporters or stuffy politicians, spent a great deal of time in his room. He and Annette had decided that she was to take in Hector, Penny, and Simon after their business at the castle was complete, and that Argent would stay with her until arrangements for his new shop could be made. One night at dinner Noah stopped eating and looked across at Argent for a long while. Argent tried to ignore his intimidating stare, but Noah broke the tension by speaking.

"Your surname, Clemons, sounds very familiar. Where have I heard that before?" Noah queried with brisk inquisitiveness.

Argent took a large swig of wine, grimacing as he put the cup down. "It's a very common name, Your Majesty," he sighed, looking away from the group with evident disdain. Noah shrugged and dropped the matter.

In the few days after the news had broken out, Simon had been made into an instant celebrity with the palace maids and female chefs. When he wasn't flirting with gaggles of girls in the palace halls, he could be found in the kitchens, where a number of cheerful young girls worked. Flynn, the head chef, would have none of Simon, and on at least three occasions was seen chasing Simon from his kitchen with a meat cleaver in hand. Flynn was often with Noah when he was not busy, and seemed to be in a perpetual bad mood, which only worsened when Penny came near.

As soon as things quieted down some, Penny attempted to reach Armonie at the Cathedral via Sophotri Stone. She wanted to keep her promise about letting Armonie know when they had returned and was shocked when the communications cut off after hearing Penny's name. After a few repeated attempts, each with the same reaction, Penny grew upset and decided to consult Gavin on the matter.

"Oh, Penny…think of what you've done to those people. Their entire organization lives to worship Nestor. They've been desperate for him to return for years now, and when he finally does, you go and drive him away all over again," Gavin said.

"But he was trying to—"

"No matter *what* he was trying to do, he's still their deity and leader. They'll have justified his actions by now, and you in particular will be named a pariah. I'd stay away from them, if I were you—but you needn't worry. We'll be sure to keep you safe!" Gavin promised with a smile.

A surprise came sometime around the end of the first week. One night after dinner Penny had retreated to her room when a small knock came at the door. Penny had expected perhaps Annette or Simon, but never Noah. She could feel herself clamming up as soon as he came into view. He smiled and bowed.

"I hope I'm not disturbing you, Penny. I know the hour is quite late, but I've only just finished working for today and I wondered if you might humor me for a bit," Noah said in a tone that made Penny's heart flutter and her voice come out all wrong.

"Erm, sure. Wh-what can I do for you?"

"Accompany me on a stroll in the gardens. I would be most obliged," Noah suggested, exuding confidence. The power in Penny's brain seemed to shut down for a moment and she stood in awe until it was able to reboot and form an answer.

"Erm—ok!"

Noah's face broke into an adoring smile and he took Penny by her arm, a small gesture that was just enough to send her head spinning again. He led her into the gardens that bordered the palace, speaking of the castle history as they walked.

Penny confided her first memory of the castle as they reached the front pathway. "I remember standing outside these gates for the first time and looking in, wishing I could come and see the gardens. That seems like a lifetime ago," she murmured and Noah gave her a curious look.

"And are you pleased? By the gardens, I mean," he asked, though Penny thought she saw something else in his eyes. She nodded to Noah with a shy smile and ran her fingers across the water of a bubbling fountain that shining with the reflection of the stars.

"Then I'm glad I could make one of your desires a reality, no matter how small." Noah drew closer to her side and grabbed Penny's hand, which was growing numb from the cold fountain water. Penny blinked, her fingers warming. She could think of nothing to say, so they continued strolling away

from the fountain through the solitude of lush leaves and topiaries. Noah seemed to pick up on Penny's speechless state, but
would not let go of her hand, holding it as if she were something fragile.

"I like this place at night much better than during the day.
It's almost like all the people have gone from the world and
I can finally be at peace..." He continued to talk, reminiscing
about the days when his stressed father took care of matters
of the state. Penny expected Noah to tell her that the old king
lost the will to live and died of some tragic illness some years
before, but the truth surprised her much more.

"It was a shock. Out of nowhere, my father woke me up
in the middle of the night and handed me the crown. He gave
me a bit of last minute advice and said he was off to Borbarro
Islands and he was never coming back. I suppose all the years
of listening to Damari reminisce about his home really made
an impression on Father. I suspect he's still there, living on a
beach somewhere." Noah gave a bittersweet sigh and looked
up into the sky.

Sensing his melancholy mood, Penny tried to cheer him up.
"Damari...actually talks?" she joked. To her great relief Noah
laughed out loud.

"Oh, yes. I can see how he might come off as unfriendly.
He's all business when he's on the job, but he can get quite
rowdy after hours. He and Flynn are my closest friends."
Noah explained how Damari had been captain of the guard
ever since Noah had been a young boy and he had practically
grown up under his care. The nature of Flynn's relationship to
him became clear as well. They had played together as small
children, Flynn being the son of the head chef at the time. They
grew into adulthood alongside each other, raised like siblings
instead of prince and servant.

Their stroll brought them back to the castle and Penny was
quite sorry when Noah bid her goodnight. He gave her hand a
gentle kiss before departing, promising he would see her again

soon. He kept his promise, and began popping up whenever he had free time. Their increased exposure to one another helped Penny to get over most of her nervousness, and she began to regard him as a true friend, but could not pretend that she did not notice his forward affections.

During the weeks after the return, Penny had seen very little of Hector. He was present during times when they were needed to speak with the foreign liaisons and barons, but otherwise his absence was notable. Whenever Penny came poking around his room, it was always to find it deserted. If she did chance to run into him, his thoughts seemed elsewhere. He refused to answer any questions about how he was spending his time, which perturbed Penny further. Her curiosity would not let her stand by for long, and she barged into his room late one night after a long day and found him leaning over his desk, which was almost swallowed by heaping piles of notes and dog-eared books. He jumped with surprise at her abrupt entrance.

"Good to see you're back to normal," Penny commented as he began grumbling about manners and knocking.

"I'm busy now, can't you come back later?" Hector requested, keeping his eyes focused on the book before him.

Penny scowled. "No. Where have you been lately? I—I almost sort of miss you," she stammered, yanking the book from his hand and scanning the pages. It looked complicated, so she closed it and set it aside. Hector groaned, obviously irked that she had lost his place. He sighed, leaning back in his chair and rubbing at his forehead.

"I've been working on something. I need some peace and quiet."

"What is it? What are you working on?" Penny tried to look at his notes, which he hastily covered.

"As it turns out, it's none of your business, though I expect I shall be finished by tomorrow evening, at which time I shall see fit to tell you." Hector picked up his stacks of paper, shuffled them and stored them in a folder on top of a high stack of books.

Penny frowned. "Why, of *course*, your grace. How rude of me to interrupt," she said with a mock curtsy.

"Off with you," Hector pointed to the door, but Penny remained firm.

"Sorry, but I don't take orders from Professor Arlington anymore. Or should I say... Aín?" she retorted and Hector's haughtiness deflated. He sighed and turned away with a melancholy smile that almost made Penny sorry she'd brought it up.

"So, you caught that, did you?" he murmured.

Penny began to feel rather guilty as she saw the sorrow that he attempted to hide with a quivering smile. "Well, yeah...I mean—why'd Della call you that?" she asked in a more delicate manner and Hector cast his gaze to the window on the far side of the room.

"She called me that because it's my name, or at least it was in Nelvirna. I wasn't born as Hector Arlington. I picked that name for myself shortly after I came to Earth," Hector explained with an element of fragility in his tone.

"I see, that makes sense... but why'd you go with Hector?" Penny asked him and he perked up a bit.

"Well, when I was familiarizing myself with the classic pieces of literature from Earth, I came across *The Iliad*," Hector explained, looking a little pleased under the veil of his sadness. "I don't know if you know the story or not, but Hector's courage was enormous, especially when compared to the cowardice of Paris. It—It made an impression on me. After reading it I decided that I would never allow my courage to fail as Paris's had...that I would become like Hector. It's stupid, I know..." Hector stammered, avoiding Penny's eyes. She looked at him with sympathy, then stepped forward and put a hand on his shoulder as he continued to look away.

"You've more than lived up to it..." she told him with affection. Hector glanced up at Penny with a mixture of surprise and poignant emotion. Their gazes connected and Penny felt her heart leap and flutter in a way that was almost painful. She tried to look away, but found that she had lost the ability to as she studied the flecks of green and brown in Hector's eyes. For a brief moment she caught a glimpse of something like guilt in his stare, but she didn't have time to inspect it much longer as a voice from behind interrupted them.

"Ahh, I thought I heard something *steamy* going on in here..." Simon's voice sang into the room.

Penny swung around to face Simon, wrenching her hand away from Hector's shoulder before the magician could make any more unnecessary comments.

"What do you want?" Penny asked, her voice a tad nervous. Simon stepped into the room, raising an eyebrow at the mountain of books on Hector's desk before he launched into what was on his mind.

"I thought it was time we all had a little parley. It's only a matter of time before we're sent away from the palace and back to Annette's house...we need to be certain of our plans for the future," Simon conjectured, taking a seat on Hector's bed and grabbing a purple fruit from the bowl on the desk.

Questions arose about the night of the confrontation in Hulver and what exactly had happened. None of them seemed to think that Nestor was gone for good, and they puzzled over the tiny treasure chest that Della had given Penny, wondering when it would open and what would be inside when it did. It seemed to be an unspoken truth that they would all stay together and follow Della's orders as well as they could—that they had to go on and try to find the remaining pieces of Seival that were still lost somewhere across Elydria.

"The eyes, the wings, the heart. That's five pieces all together..." Simon muttered out loud, stroking his thin mustache as he thought.

"It could be as little as three people, as many as five," Hector said, thinking aloud. "I suppose our best bet would be to look for people with extraordinary talents, something that sets them apart from others—like Annette."

"Or they could just be gloomy recluses who stay inside reading all day, like you!" Penny added with a roguish smile. Simon stared off in speculation, ignoring Hector and Penny.

"The heart of Seival—perhaps a person with the capacity to love in a way that humanity has never known! How intriguing." Simon's eyes looked unfocused, and Penny could tell his imagination had already begun to elaborate on this possibility.

"Leave it to Simon to fantasize about the dismembered heart of an Angel," Penny smirked.

Hector laughed and stood up. "I suppose even with the most extensive planning, our efforts would be worth nothing. If I've learned one thing from living in Elydria, it's that trouble has a way of finding us whether we want it to or not," he said with a finality that seemed to end the conversation.

THE NEXT MORNING Penny got the news that they were going to be released from the palace in two days' time. From that moment on, everyone rushed to get last minute arrangements in order before their departure. The day was long and arduous and by the time Penny had gotten everything done, night had fallen.

Penny wandered through the castle that night after everyone had gone to bed, saying silent goodbyes. By chance she stumbled into the ballroom. It seemed extraordinarily empty as Penny tiptoed through it in the shade of night, each footstep giving a resounding echo as she crept to the same balcony where she and Noah had talked the night they met. The view of Iverton was as astonishing as ever and it captivated her for a long while. Enjoying the lights that blinked throughout the sprawling city, Penny knew that this calm in the storm would only last for so long, though the idea did not frighten her as much as it would have in the past. Rather, it made her appreciate the serenity of the lull and let her relish the moment of quiet that life allotted to her.

"Penny?" a voice called and she turned to see Hector stepping out onto the balcony. She greeted him with a wide grin, surprised to see him out and about. "Whatever are you doing out here? It's cold—I expect it'll begin to snow soon."

"Just getting one last look before we go. What's wrong—you look like—"

"I've got something I need to tell you," he stammered, looking down at his feet. She tensed, wondering what it was that Hector had sought her out to say. Hector looked up at Penny with a misty smile.

"I've finished what I've been working on…" he started off, looking at her with equal parts joy and rue. She waited with an expectant gaze for him to continue. "I've finally figured out how to do it—I can take you home now."

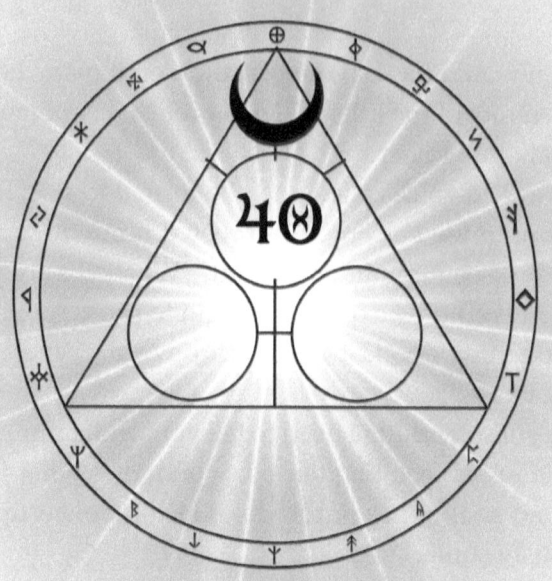

PENNY'S CHOICE

I t took almost half a minute for Hector's words to sink in.
"You mean...you're saying that..."

"I mean that whenever you wish to return to Earth, you can.
It took me this long to figure out how to do it—but somehow,
ever since Della told me I could...I just sort of *knew* how to do
it. After I mastered that, it took even longer to work out how to
appear at the exact right location, but I think I've got it down
fairly well. Just say the word and I'll take you there. I'll take you
home," Hector said with a small smile as Penny beamed.

"Well, what are we waiting for? Let's go! I can't wait!"
Penny cried, overjoyed at the idea that she might be back in
her cozy little house and jumping into her mother's arm in
just a few moments.

Hector looked astonished. "Don't you—don't you at least
want to say your farewells to everyone? I know Annette will be
heartbroken when she finds out you left without saying goodbye, and I'm sure His Majesty would—"

Penny shot him a dangerous look and he stopped. She considered the goodbyes waiting to be said, and it was at that precise moment that the grief hit her. Could she look into Annette's face, the girl who had come to be her closest friend, the person with whom she had defied death time and time again, and tell her that they were going to have to part ways? Was it going to be possible to try and explain to Simon why she was leaving them? She did not want to look at Gavin's confused and hurt expression when he heard the news, or see tears gather in his gray eyes, or have to endure Argent pretending he would not miss her in the slightest. Least of all, she didn't want to lie to Noah when she told him where she would be going.

"I don't know if I can, Hector," she murmured, looking down at her shoes as the excitement of the moment ebbed away as quick as it had come. She could not bear to look at Hector's bewildered expression.

"But don't you want to take a last look around? Don't you want to see Humphrey just once more? I know he's going to be—"

"Look—I'm not that strong, okay?" Penny fought back tears as she thought of Humphrey sitting in the stable waiting for her return, unaware she wouldn't ever be back. "I can't sit there and watch as I hurt everyone...I don't want to live with those memories. I'd much rather remember everyone as they were the last time I was with them—happy, carefree, and together, not when they..." Penny could not bring herself to finish the sentence.

Hector shrugged, a forlorn expression on his face. "Suit yourself. Let's go get your things," he said, walking off in the direction of the hall.

Penny trailed after him, forcibly turning her thoughts to consider the fact that she would be stepping through her front door in a matter of moments, where her bed would be waiting, and her mother might have banana muffins sitting on the kitchen counter.

They walked back to her room, where it only took a few moments to gather up the rest of Penny's things and put them into her bag. Penny handed the miniature treasure chest that Della had given her to Hector.

"You guys are going to need it way more than I will back home," she explained, and Hector nodded before stowing it in his pocket. Penny sighed and looked around her room for a final time. She made a feeble attempt to smile at Hector. "Ok...I think I'm ready."

"Are you absolutely sure about this? Because if you left anything incomplete or unsaid, you may never get another chance to fix it. I—I probably won't be coming back to bother you," Hector reminded her with a stony expression that made Penny's heart sink even deeper.

"You won't? Oh. I guess that...makes sense." Penny hung her head, trying to swallow the sadness that kept threatening to bubble over. Before she could let her emotions get the better of her, she shook her head and gritted her teeth. "Yes. I'm sure, let's go."

"All right...remember, hold on tight. I don't know what'll happen if you accidently let go and I'm not sure I want to find out, either," Hector said, opening his arms for Penny. The whirlpool of emotions within her calmed somewhat as Hector laid his hand over her back and gripped Penny tightly to his chest. She could smell that light, alluring scent of cedar pine as she felt him reach out with his other hand.

The world seemed to rip apart at the seams and they were plunged into the raging torrent of soundlessness that Penny remembered in vivid detail from the first time she had travelled between worlds. This time, however, as she passed through the intangible wall between Earth and Elydria, she felt not fear, but sorrow.

A tranquil scene snapped into Hector and Penny's view, along with the feeling of being spit out of a tube. Penny gasped and stumbled away from Hector, feeling dizzy as her eyes attempted to refocus. It took a moment for her eyes to decide to work, and all the breath left her body as Penny beheld her home. She stood still, taking in the image of the house that for so long had seemed like a memory from a faraway dream. Her eyes fell on the spot where she had sat on her last morning here and she could not suppress an emotional, bubbling laugh. Unable to contain herself, Penny raced toward the front door and Hector followed, unlocking it with a wave of his hand and a sparkle of golden runes.

Penny flew inside as the smell of home filled her nose. Though it was wonderfully nostalgic, it seemed different somehow, as if something vital had been altered.

"*Mom! It's me!*" Penny hollered at the top of her voice as she ran deeper into her house, her eyes seeking the familiar and comforting sights. The squishy couch, the TV, and her mother's kitschy figurines in their glass casings all stood illuminated in the pale, shivering lights that dotted the ceiling. There was no answer from the second story or anywhere around her, so Penny ran into the kitchen.

"Muffins! Oh, my mom's muffins! Hector, come here, you've gotta try these!" Penny cried, swiping a chocolate one from the counter and shoving it into Hector's face as he stepped into the kitchen. He removed it from his mouth and gave Penny an amused look.

"Best thing you've ever tasted in your entire life, right?" Penny laughed, not waiting for him to answer as she grabbed a muffin for herself, turned a sharp corner and put her foot up on the stairs. Hector called her name, halting her ascent. She halted mid-run, a heavy pressure weighing down on her heart as she turned to face him. One look at his expression and Penny knew what he was going to say, and discovered that she adamantly did not want him to go.

"Penelope…" he said softly, stepping across the room and grasping her arms, "I think it's time."

Penny tried to hide the fact that her heart felt as if it were splitting in two and smiled at him. She began speaking very fast and with jarring pauses, feeling that the more she spoke, the more it would fight off the sense of loss threatening to tear her apart. "You're leaving already? You've got to at least stay to help me explain to Mom where I've been. Without your magic as proof, she'll think I'm cr—" Penny stopped herself as she listened to what she was saying. "That's a complete lie, of course she'll believe me, but I still thin—"

"Penny, you and I both know that wouldn't be a very good idea," Hector interrupted.

Penny's eyes stung. "B-but…you can't leave. I—what am I going to do without you?" she murmured, looking away to hide the sudden onslaught of tears. Hector laughed and stroked her hair, a sweet and unexpected gesture. Penny wanted to throw herself into his arms and beg him not to leave, but she could not make her body obey.

"You'll be fine, I know it—goodness knows you're brave enough," Hector said and laughed again, but it was an empty sound.

"You—you're not going to forget about me, are you?" she asked, meaning to sound humorous, and knowing she ended up sounding pathetic.

Hector frowned. "I don't think it's possible for someone to forget their dearest friend—and owing to the look of brazen disbelief in your eyes I feel compelled to add that I truly mean that." He raised his eyebrows, taking his hands off Penny and stepping back a few paces.

She turned back toward the stairs, squeezing her eyes shut as she began the climb. "Just go—I don't want to watch you disappear," she called back with finality. Not waiting to see if he would speak to her again, Penny climbed up the stairs louder than necessary, making sure her footsteps blocked out any sort of sound Hector might make as he vanished forever.

Penny meandered through the dark halls of her house, fighting back tears all the way and thinking of the nightmare that had visited her time and again. She stepped in front of the door to her room, half expecting to see it full of filth and dead insects, but when it swung open, Penny saw all of her possessions almost as she had left them. She walked inside with trepidation, surprised to find she felt frightened. Moving past her bed covered in stuffed animals, Penny picked up *Murder at Woodrow Manor* with a dry laugh. The bookmark was still inside, like her mother had known that someday Penny would return and want to pick up reading from where she left off.

Penny stepped over to her desk and looked over her mismatched oddments and computer, unable to bridle the intense feeling of eeriness weighing down on her. It was as if this room that had once been her sanctuary from the world was now sterile and unwelcoming, like she had no business being here any longer. She almost began to feel nauseated with bittersweet emotion as she looked at the photos of her and Madeline stacked on the table beside her college books. She backed away from it all, wishing that there had been bugs and dead leaves instead of this unsettling sensation.

What's wrong with me? I should be overjoyed...I've been wanting to come home for months now, I—

It hit her like a punch to the gut. Penny felt the color drain away from her face as she swayed in the center of her room, surrounded by the ghosts of her past. It did not take long before the sense of urgency overtook her and she was down the stairs in a heartbeat.

"Hector, Hector! Wait, please! Don't go!" she screamed at the top of her lungs, her heart crashing away in her chest. She had not felt this desperate for anything before, not when she was being assaulted by the merciless vententula plant in the woods outside of Dewthorne, not in the cemetery beside the wraith, nor when she had stolen Deimos's memories, or even stood up against Nestor on the palace balcony in Hulver.

"Hector! *PLEASE!*" Penny shouted, feeling the hot tears pour down her face as she landed downstairs and found nobody there.

"Please, please don't be gone... *HECTOR!*" Penny howled, stampeding through the living room and out the front door. The tears were coming fast and with stinging pain now. She could see nothing outside but the blurry, meager glow of twilight on her driveway. There was no sign of anyone. Pure anguish hit as Penny fell to her knees, covering her face with her hands as she sobbed. She had made the worst mistake of her life, and realized it moments too late.

Hector's not coming back...I'll never see Annette, or Simon, or anyone ever again. I'll go back to my empty life and be forced to continue on as if nothing ever happened, thought Penny through her coughs and sputters, feeling that no amount of willpower could make her return to her dead-end college or resign herself to a mundane future. She was close to a complete collapse when a strained voice called out from behind her, coming from the front door of her house.

"Penny?" the voice cried, accompanied by hurried footsteps on gravel. At first she was sure it was her mother and was confused as to how her voice had altered so much in the months that she had been gone, but when she looked up through her watering eyes to see Hector racing toward her, Penny almost passed out with relief.

"Hector! I thought you left! I thought you'd gone..." she gasped, getting up and wiping the tears away from her eyes as surging happiness swept through her. "Hang on, why didn't you leave? What were you doing in there?"

A look of shyness crossed Hector's face. "Well, it's a bit embarrassing, but those muffins—I wanted to take a few back with me, I...I didn't think you'd mind," he stammered, his face turning pink. Penny laughed out loud and wiped the last of her tears away.

"Leave it to you to be thinking of sweets at a time like this," she laughed in relief and Hector became more flustered.

"N-never mind that! What's wrong, why were you screaming?" Hector asked, looking worried.

Penny looked at her feet and sighed. It was not going to be easy to make him understand. "Let's go back inside. I'll make some tea for you and you can have a muffin or two while I explain."

SHE COULDN'T HELP but feel redeemed as she put the kettle on the blue flame of the stove and sat down in front of Hector with her hands folded. "I think I may have made a mistake. I…I want to go back with you and stay in Elydria."

Hector's jaw dropped. "What?! All you've wanted since we ended up there was to get home, and now that you're here you want to go *back* to Elydria? Are you feeling quite well?" Hector stretched out a hand to test her forehead's temperature, and she batted it away with a frown.

"Look, it's hard to explain but…well, in Elydria I kept having a dream that I would come back to my room and it would be filled with all this weird stuff…things like dead leaves and bugs, bones and dirt, you know?" Penny told him, and Hector gave a shallow nod, looking as if he could not understand how the two were connected. Penny cleared her throat and went over to the counter as they teapot began to hiss.

"Well, I couldn't understand what it meant before, but I do now. When I said I wanted to come home all those times before, I was confused. I didn't just want to *be* home…I wanted to go back to the time before. I wanted the simplicity of not having to live with danger around every turn and the responsibility of carrying out Adrielle's orders. I wanted to go back to being the person that I was before this happened, not to this place," Penny elaborated, shutting off the stove just as the teapot began to whistle and pouring the steaming water into two cups.

"But I can't do that no matter how much I want to. My old life has been erased...this place, this home—I don't fit into it anymore. Not when I've been to Iverton and flown on the back of a giant moth or had conversations with dragons. This life, no matter how nice it was then, doesn't have a place for me in it anymore. Do you understand what I'm saying?"

"I think so," Hector said as she handed him a mug of steaming tea. Penny sipped her drink and looked around at the green kitchen and its collection of houseplants that no longer belonged to her.

"The person that I was—she's as good as dead now. I must've left her sitting on that curb that morning. I've still got more to do in Elydria. So, that's why I have to go back. I want to help you look for the missing parts of Seival, and I want to learn all the answers to the questions that will be sure to drive me crazy in the meantime," Penny explained with a small smile, feeling her heart fluttering.

Hector smiled back with genuine emotion. "I'm...well, I'm glad, though I'm still not *quite* sure about your reasoning." He lifted his eyebrows again, taking a bite of the muffin and savoring the taste.

Penny blinked. "Y-you're glad?"

"Of course I am! I was certainly not looking forward to telling Annette that you weren't going to be back," Hector confessed, taking a long drink of tea and watching Penny with calculating eyes, as if to gauge her reaction. She shook her head and got up to locate a pen and a piece of paper, then sat down at the table and began to write, taking a break every few seconds to take a sip of tea or a bite of muffin.

"What are you doing?" Hector asked, trying to make out what she was writing.

"Writing a note to my mom. I don't want her to think I'm dead or something like that," she explained, nibbling on the end of the pen as she thought of what to put down next. Hector looked astounded for perhaps the hundredth time that night.

"You're not going to wait for her to return?"

Penny frowned. "She'll never let me go, and don't think I want to see her crying and begging me not to leave, even if I do miss her more than anything else in this world. I—" Penny found it hard to go on as terrible sadness welled up within her. She cleared her throat.

"I'd love to see her again, but I know it's for the best that I don't—not right now. I can't let anything change my mind. I know we'll see each other again, and when we do it'll be at the exact right time. You can meet her then, too," Penny looked at Hector with a grin, and then went back to writing.

Hector shook his head and sighed. "I simply will never understand you."

When Penny's note was done, she crept upstairs to her mother's room and opened the door. It was dark inside and seemed foreign in a way it never had before. On her mother's pillow she laid the note, which explained that Penny was doing fine, that she would be back one day and for her not to worry. Penny could not help but shed a tear or two when she thought of her mother reading the letter. It fell short of what Paulina deserved, and she knew it. Penny removed the rune pendant from around her neck and laid it on top of the note, knowing that her mother would understand its meaning and realize that it was indeed her daughter who had come by that night. She stood by her mother's bed for a long moment, running her fingers across the covers and smelling Paulina's familiar lavender fragrance. With a final glance around, Penny stepped into the hall and closed the door.

Hector was waiting for her in the center of the living room with his arms crossed. She sighed and looked about her old home, so much tinier than she remembered. Hector waited with the utmost patience as Penny gave her final, unspoken goodbyes to the house that was once hers. When she looked up at him with confidence, they both knew it was time.

Penny closed her eyes as Hector wrapped his lean arms around her and prepared to make the jump to Elydria again. The thought of what was waiting for her on the other side of the darkness made a bubble of hope expand in Penny's chest. A world of infinite wonder that beckoned and called with its siren song: a world that had broken Penny apart and rebuilt her to be stronger than she ever could have imagined. She breathed in the faint scent that surrounded Hector and dwelled on the faces of her friends and the unbreakable bonds that had transformed her forever. She felt Hector reach out and pull the two of them into the gap between realities, and Penny let the vestige of her old self slip away like a gossamer shawl falling from her shoulders.

As the silence and speed overtook her body, Penny could not stop herself from smiling as she dreamed of all the wondrous things to come.

ABOUT THE AUTHOR

Award-winning author, unabashed nerd, and knight-errant A.R. Meyering is the creator of the steampunk-fantasy series The Dawn Mirror Chronicles. When she is not lost in the world of writing, she dabbles in reality from time to time, having worked as a website content writer in her native Southern California. Her dark fantasy novel, *Unreal City*, was the winner in the horror category of the Literary Classics International Book Awards, was named quarterfinalist in the Amazon Breakthrough Novel Award, semifinalist in the Kindle Book Awards, and garnered positive reviews from *Publishers Weekly* and Readers' Favorite. She has had a lifelong love affair with history, food, travel, and reading. She is rarely seen without her pugs, Zuul and Vinz Clortho and lives in Kumamoto Prefecture, Japan with her husband.

www.ingramcontent.com/pod-product-compliance
Lightning Source LLC
Chambersburg PA
CBHW022238020726
47496CB00004B/968